JM

CAPTIVE OF HIS KISS

The bedroom door crashed against the wall. Startled, Micaela clutched her gown to her chest and wheeled to see who had intruded . . . and found herself staring at the very last man she expected to see.

"You!" she choked out, trying to cover herself.

"You?" He had turned the city upside down to find this woman and here she was, standing in the middle of his bedroom.

"Kindly take yourself off, captain," Micaela said, drawing herself up to face him. "You are invading my privacy." When he didn't budge, she glared at him. "Get out of my room—*now!*"

When he still refused to move, Micaela scampered across the room, intent on escaping. She nearly leaped out of her chemise when a velvet-clad arm shot past her shoulder to block her intended escape route.

"Running away—*again?*" he asked.

Micaela backed away from the powerful threat of his muscular body. "Please remove your hand from the door and let me pass," she ordered.

But before she could retreat another step, Lucien slipped his arm around her waist and drew her to him. She could tell by the way his gaze fastened on her lips that he intended to kiss her. "Don't you dare, damn you!" she sputtered, trying to turn her head away.

"Oh, but I do dare," Lucien assured her. He framed her face and brought her petal-soft lips to his. . . .

OTHER BOOKS BY CAROL FINCH

ONCE UPON A MIDNIGHT MOON

Carol Finch

Zebra Books
Kensington Publishing Corp.

http://www.zebrabooks.com

ZEBRA BOOKS are published by

Kensington Publishing Corp.
850 Third Avenue
New York, NY 10022

First Printing: September, 1997
10 9 8 7 6 5 4 3 2 1

Printed in the United States of America

One

"No, I won't do it!" Micaela Rouchard erupted in defiant protest.

Arnaud Rouchard's slate-gray eyes narrowed into angry slits. "Micaela, remember your place."

Mon Dieu, how many times in the past eighteen years had she been told to remember her place? Too many to count! Her *place,* according to her father, was within the restrictive confines that Arnaud decreed for her, acting the submissive role of daughter.

Arnaud believed a woman was to be seen on the outskirts of activity and conversation—like scenery on a stage. A woman wasn't allowed to voice her opinion, most especially if it conflicted with a man's. A woman was to be a man's silent shadow, the extension of his will. There were other commandments in the gospel according to Arnaud, but Micaela was too outraged at that moment to remember them.

Many a time, Micaela had heard Arnaud mutter that God had cursed him by saddling him with this unruly child he referred to as his daughter. Micaela had always wondered what her father implied. It always sounded strange the way he phrased it, especially when he spat the words in a bitter tone.

"Micaela, you must apologize to your father for that disrespectful outburst," Marguerite Rouchard murmured to her daughter.

Micaela's gaze shifted from her father's stormy glare to her mother's downcast face. Arnaud had browbeaten Marguerite into submission so long ago that she now buried all emotion deep inside her and trod lightly around Rouchard Plantation, attempting to avoid Arnaud's fiery temper. In Micaela's opinion, living such a restrained existence was like a life sentence in hell. The status of wife and daughter in this domineering French aristocrat's home was barely a notch above slavery.

"You *will* marry Carlos Morales," Arnaud decreed, as only Arnaud could. "These are my wishes and you will carry them out."

Arnaud clasped his hands behind him and paced the bedroom. "Since you have taken it upon yourself to keep abreast of politics, and other matters which should not concern a woman, you realize we face difficult times in New Orleans. We are forced to form alliances with ruling Spanish officials if we are to prosper."

Micaela knew of the turn of events that left Louisiana in Spanish hands. After France lost the Seven Years' War, King Louis XV secretly deeded the North American colony to his Bourbon cousin, Charles III of Spain, so the British couldn't get their greedy hands on it.

Two years ago, Commissioner de Ulloa had arrived in New Orleans, swaggering through the streets with his arrogant Superior Council at his heels. French citizens were outraged to learn that Louis XV had handed them over to Spain without informing them. Discontented citizens balked at the new regime, and mass meetings were being held around the city, secretly planning a revolt.

"I don't agree with my fellow countrymen that revolution is the solution," Arnaud was saying when Micaela got around to listening. "I prefer to form alliances with the Spanish." He stared pointedly at Micaela. "I have dealt with *rebellion* in my own home so often that I have developed a loathing for it."

Was she being blamed for Arnaud's refusal to side with disgruntled Frenchmen who wanted to oust the Spanish commissioner? Why not this, too? she asked herself. She got blamed for just about everything that went wrong at the plantation.

"Carlos Morales is downstairs waiting to escort you to the Spanish ball," Arnaud went on to say. "He has offered for your hand and I have given permission." His gaze narrowed in response to Micaela's furious expression. "My will *shall* be done, Micaela. Do not doubt it."

Another of Arnaud's lofty commandments.

"You will become the liaison between our family and the ruling government. If you were not so selfish and rebellious by nature, you would realize this is the perfect means of securing your brother's future and ensuring his prosperity."

"And what of mine?" she dared to ask, drawing her mother's alarmed gasp. "Is my future happiness of no consequence? Do you plan to marry me off to a man I dislike, just so my brother Henri will have the necessary Spanish connection?"

"Micaela, hold your tongue!" Arnaud ordered, his face turning a shade of purple. "I make the decisions here and you will do as you are told."

Erupting temper catapulted Micaela off the edge of her bed, but her mother clutched her arm and pulled her down. "Don't provoke him," Marguerite cautioned.

"You have defied me once too often," Arnaud snapped. "Is it not humiliating enough that you coaxed and prodded the Gray Sisters, and even the padre, at Ursuline Convent to teach you more than a woman should know? I sent you there to learn to cook, sew, and practice proper manners. Instead, you hounded the padre into teaching you Latin, geometry, astronomy, and only God knows what else!"

Arnaud would be beside himself if he realized Micaela had become as well educated as her older brother. She decided not to point that out while her father was in one of his towering rages.

"And you know perfectly well how I felt when I discovered

you had secretly taught my slaves—men, women and children alike—to read and write. It simply is not done! They are slaves, not scholars.''

Arnaud wheeled to pace in the opposite direction, trying to bring his flammable temper under control. ''And don't think I don't know that you have disguised yourself as a boy to attend those conspiracy meetings against the Spanish. For that reason alone, I intend for this marriage to take place immediately. If rebellion comes to New Orleans, the Rouchard name will not be linked to it.'' He rounded abruptly on his daughter. ''You will not become a part of this rebellion. Do you hear me, Micaela!''

Of course, she heard him. His booming voice was bouncing off the bedroom walls.

''You have fifteen minutes to dress and accept this betrothal to Carlos. I will escort you downstairs to sign the wedding contract I've drawn up. The announcement will be made at the Spanish ball this evening. And you *will* attend it, behaving like a proper lady—for once!''

When Arnaud spun around and stormed away, Marguerite took her daughter's hand, giving it a sympathetic squeeze. ''Don't push him, Micaela,'' she whispered. ''I assure you that you'll find his alternative plan no more appealing. If this marriage does not take place, Arnaud will whisk you off to Natchez to live with his widowed cousin.''

According to the custom of the times, young ladies unsuited for marriage were foisted off on widows and spinsters. Micaela cringed at the thought of keeping house for Cousin Catherine, who was mentally imbalanced.

It was unmistakably clear that Micaela would be sent away from Rouchard Plantation—into marriage or seclusion.

''Carlos seems taken with you, and he is a member of the Superior Council,'' Marguerite murmured as she laid out a blue silk gown. ''Make the most of what life has to offer, but don't fight the inevitable.'' She glanced briefly at her daughter, and then at the door, as if expecting to be overheard. ''Rebelling will only bring heartache. I ought to know,'' she whispered confidentially before she exited from the room.

Micaela cursed her predicament. Long ago, she had given up trying to please her father, to earn his affection. Arnaud doted over his son and avoided association with his daughter. In Arnaud's book, Micaela counted for nothing. She was a chattel to be bartered and traded for personal benefit and financial gain.

While Micaela was shunted aside and expected to submit and obey like a dutiful slave, Henri was allowed to entertain friends, and parties were held in his honor. *Henri* was pampered like a prince. At age fourteen *Henri* moved into his private wing and took a slave girl as his mistress. At sixteen, *Henri* sailed to France for formal schooling—after years of studying with his private tutor and a dance master who taught social etiquette and protocol. As a graduation gift, *Henri* was deeded a house in the French Quarter and a young courtesan was placed at his beck and call.

Micaela felt slighted, but she didn't resent her older brother. What she resented was the lopsided customs favoring men over women.

Knowing her father also kept a mistress in the French Quarter was yet another wedge that drove them apart. Micaela had vowed never to enter a marriage where fidelity was a one-sided venture. What her mother humbly accepted, Micaela could not. Perhaps there was no such thing as love, but she wasn't about to settle for human bondage!

Still fuming, Micaela wrestled with the whalebone stays on the back of her gown. She stared at her reflection in the mirror, knowing she could not be true to herself if she accepted her fate and knuckled under to Arnaud's dominance the way her mother had. She had to make a life for herself somewhere else—anywhere else! She was sick to death of being denied choices. No man was going to dictate to her as her father had. No man was going to break her spirit as her mother's had been broken!

Resolved to make her break for freedom, Micaela made preparations to see her through the night. She would pretend to accept her fate and accompany her unwanted betrothed to the soirée, but she would not be returning home where she had never truly been welcome—or wanted.

Glancing at the mantel clock, Micaela scooped up a few belongings and stashed them in a satchel. She darted across the breezeway that led into her brother's private quarters. Reaching the darkened stairway, Micaela tiptoed down the steps to attach her satchel to the underside of Carlos's carriage. She hurried back to her room, arriving only a minute before her father appeared to escort her downstairs.

"I see you have come to your senses," Arnaud said as he offered Micaela his arm in a mocking parody of politeness. "Since your betrothed is one of Don Antonio de Ulloa's trusted advisors, you will be in a position to ask favors for me and your brother. You will also enjoy all the luxuries a wife could possibly want."

"And what of the luxury of love?" Micaela countered before she could bite back the bitter words.

Arnaud halted on the staircase and glared at Micaela. "Do not sass me again. Especially not in front of Carlos. If you behave yourself you can earn his respect and devotion."

"And shall I expect him to keep a mistress in the French Quarter, just as you do?" she dared to ask right there on the steps.

Arnaud's face exploded with color, as did his temper. "How dare you!"

"And how dare you speak to me of respect and devotion." Fiery green eyes clashed with stony gray. "A man cannot claim to respect a wife if he keeps another woman at his beck and call. I cannot understand why Mother tolerates your disgusting habit."

For a moment Micaela believed her father was going to strike her. It would not have been the first time. But to his credit, he didn't leave his mark on her before presenting her to Carlos. Instead, he slashed her with words that nearly took her legs out from under her.

"You have been my cross to bear for almost two decades," Arnaud hissed between clenched teeth. "Do you wish to know why? It is because you behave like my brother. In fact, you *are* his child, plagued with all his failing graces. Every time I look at you I see Jean, and I remember the betrayal of my brother and my wife!''

Micaela staggered beneath the harsh declaration. If Arnaud hadn't yanked her upright, she would have cartwheeled down the steps and landed in a heap.

Scowling due to his impulsive outburst, Arnaud towed Micaela down the steps. ''If not for the scandal that would have arisen from vicious gossip I would have cursed my brother and my wife in public and refused to let either of them in my home. But I value my reputation and my pride. As for your mother, she is paying her penance daily.''

Micaela was stunned to the bone. Now she understood why Arnaud avoided her, why he treated her like an outcast. No wonder Marguerite was meek and subservient. Arnaud never allowed her to forget what she had done.

Shocked into silence, Micaela didn't react when Carlos sauntered across the parlor to press a kiss to one side of her face and then the other. Benumbed, she listened to his effusive flattery. He went on—and on—about her bewitching beauty and the honor of becoming her betrothed.

Learning that she was being sold into marriage for favors from the Spanish officials, and that she was illegitimate, brought Micaela close to tears, but she vowed not to break down until she had escaped. She simply signed Arnaud's contract and moved mechanically beside Carlos as he led her to his waiting carriage.

During the ride to Tchoupitoulas Gate, where the ball was being held, Micaela stared out the window, totally immersed in thought. Carlos didn't seem to notice her preoccupation. Teeming with self-importance, the Spaniard delighted in hearing himself talk—mostly about himself. Micaela only had to nod her head now and again to pacify him.

Arnaud's biting comments had triggered dozens of half forgotten memories from childhood. Now Micaela understood why her mother was noticeably absent whenever Jean arrived for a rare visit. No doubt Arnaud would not allow Marguerite to be in Jean's company. She understood Arnaud's hostility toward his brother, toward her, understood the snide comments about Micaela being so much like Jean.

Each comment had been a jab of reprimand—a condemnation. Arnaud had reinforced Marguerite's guilt and used her indiscretion to his advantage—as he did all else. All that kept him from spreading the truth was his fear of besmirching the family name. Marguerite would be reminded of her betrayal until the day she died.

Micaela also understood why she knew nothing about love. It was nonexistent in her home. Her grandparents had contracted Marguerite's marriage to Arnaud, just as Arnaud contracted Micaela's. That was the way French aristocratic marriages had been arranged for centuries. Arnaud was nothing if not entrenched in family honor and tradition. He ruled the plantation like a kingdom—with an iron hand. His royal-blooded mentality demanded that he protect his pride and family name. . . .

Micaela found herself engulfed in a skinny pair of arms and soundly kissed the instant the carriage rolled to a halt. Her very first kiss was delivered by thin, demanding lips that mashed her mouth against her teeth. Revulsion spurted through her. It was disgusting! If Carlos's embrace was a foretaste of passionate technique Micaela wanted nothing to do with him—or it!

"Ah, *querida,* I have waited far too long for that," Carlos rasped when he came up for air.

Micaela hadn't waited nearly long enough. Kissing, she discovered, was not the least bit pleasant.

When Carlos bore down on her again, she pressed her palms to his chest to keep those frog-like lips and bristly black mustache at bay. "We mustn't keep Don Antonio de Ulloa waiting."

"*Si,* of course." Reluctantly, Carlos eased into his own space and reached for the door latch. He looked at Micaela covetously before he climbed from the carriage. Later, he promised himself, he would appease his lusty appetite for this blond beauty.

There was not another woman in this bustling seaport of twelve thousand inhabitants who could match Micaela's extraordinary appearance. Since the first day that Arnaud presented himself, and his family, at Tchoupitoulas Gate for formal introduction, every eligible Spanish bachelor had been mesmerized by Micaela. Soon, Carlos would claim the woman his associates dreamed about. And since Arnaud had handed over his daughter tonight without the usual chaperone, Carlos intended to take advantage before he returned his betrothed home.

Since Arnaud was so anxious to gain privileges with the Superior Council, ensuring his crops reached the most profitable markets, Carlos had offered a tempting arrangement. When Carlos married Micaela, he would exempt Arnaud from the tariffs that French and Americans were ordered to pay on imports and exports.

Arnaud *thought* he had received preferential treatment, but he was only one of many that Carlos had negotiated with for his own financial and personal gain. In addition to his salary as a Superior Councilman, he was secretly collecting a fortune in under-the-table bribes. And very soon, he would also reap the pleasurable benefits of this wedding arrangement.

As Carlos lifted Micaela from the carriage, she caught sight of the lights blazing from the windows of the tavern beside the wharf. The meeting to organize the revolt was already in progress. Ah, how she wished she could don her disguise and attend the rally.

The idea of independence—personal and political—held great appeal for Micaela. But she couldn't declare *her* independence, until she suffered through the stuffy soirée with Carlos as her companion.

Micaela asked herself why she hadn't walked away from this miserable existence years earlier. It wasn't as if she were leaving precious memories behind. All these years she had been like a lost child pressing her face against a window pane, never allowed to join the family circle. Only the Gray Sisters at Ursuline Convent, and padre, offered Micaela love and kindness. Micaela would have considered taking refuge at the convent, but she suspected that was the first place Arnaud would search for her. She would have to find somewhere else to hide so she couldn't be dragged off to marry this spindly-legged dandy!

Biding her time, Micaela rubbed shoulders with the haughty Spanish Councilmen and the French concubines who, like her father, would do anything to assure receiving special privileges from the new regime.

The very thought of surrendering her body for favors turned Micaela's stomach. She had never met a man who tempted her to experiment with the passion that men clumsily forced upon women. Honestly, Micaela doubted she could feel anything except resentment toward the men of this world. Her only fond memories were of Uncle Jean. *Her natural father,* she reminded herself. Jean had taught her the meaning of affection. He accepted her as she was, encouraged her lively spirit and quick wit. It was Arnaud who tried to smother the life and soul from her.

While Carlos twirled Micaela around the dance floor, she made a mental note to send a message to Jean in St. Louis, informing him that she had escaped from the prison she had called home. Jean had established a lucrative fur trading business after Arnaud inherited the family plantation on the Mississippi River. Jean would understand Micaela's need for freedom. He would also assist her if she became desperate. But, she reminded herself, that was another of the places Arnaud would look for her. She didn't dare involve Jean further.

When Carlos delivered Micaela into another set of male arms, then swaggered off to consult with Don Antonio, Micaela stared at the cocky commissioner who ruled New Orleans with an inconsiderate hand. The commissioner knew no more about government management than he did about endearing himself to French citizens who had been handed to him by the stroke of Louis XV's pen. Don Antonio was an astronomer—of all things. He dealt better with celestial constellations than dyed-in-the-wool Frenchman who balked at his highhanded regulations.

Like a king calling order in court, Don Antonio rose from the elevated dais. The orchestra fell silent as the flamboyantly-dressed commissioner strutted down the steps.

''It has come to my attention that one of my distinguished officers will soon be married.'' Don Antonio gestured toward

Carlos whose white teeth beamed in his dark face. "Señorita Micaela Rouchard has accepted Carlos's proposal."

Micaela had accepted nothing of the kind, but she kept her mouth shut while the commissioner raised his goblet of Madeira wine in toast.

"May this union bring peace and good will to New Orleans."

Setting the goblet aside, the commissioner swaggered toward Micaela. Signaling the orchestra, Don Antonio whirled Micaela around the dance floor. Don Antonio, who usually had his head in the stars, danced as poorly as he ruled the city. When he bent to kiss Micaela full on the mouth, she nearly gagged for the second time that night.

To her dismay, Don Antonio's slobbery kiss became one of many. Micaela was passed around the Superior Council like a tray of hors d'oeuvres. First chance she got, Micaela turned aside to wipe her face.

Kissing was definitely overrated. And why a woman would succumb to more intimate acts Micaela couldn't imagine. She never intended to!

While Carlos chatted with his associates, Micaela inched toward the terrace door, hoping to make a discreet departure. She got as far as the south end of the portico before Carlos came to fetch her.

Without preamble, he captured her in his arms to claim another kiss. When his hand slid between them to cup her breast, Micaela left her fingerprints on his leathery cheek.

And then, Micaela witnessed the dark, vicious side of his nature. Snarling curses, he backhanded her. Micaela stumbled against the four-foot stucco wall that surrounded the portico.

"Never lay a hand on me again," Carlos spat at her. "You are mine now, body and soul. I will take what I want wherever and whenever I wish. If you will not let me treat you as my wife, then you will be treated like a *puta.*"

"I will be neither to you or any man," Micaela replied in defiance.

"You will be both," he growled as he pounced.

Micaela's uplifted knee robbed Carlos of breath and drove him to his knees. His panted curses serenaded her as she scaled the wall and disappeared into the darkness. Hurrying toward the carriage, Micaela retrieved her satchel.

She set her sights on the lighted tavern on the wharf. There and then, she vowed that no man would touch her or dictate to her again. She would find a place on this earth where she could control her own life, make her own decisions. Never, she vowed, as she took off across the dock at a dead run, would she find herself at the mercy of another man!

Pulse pounding, Micaela ducked behind the stack of crates outside the tavern. Hurriedly, she doffed her gown and donned her disguise of homespun clothes and felt cap. Before she could fasten the last button on her baggy shirt and tuck it into her breeches, a roar erupted from the tavern.

Pulling the cap low on her forehead, Micaela scurried around the corner to see the armed mob marching toward Tchoupitoulas Gate. Led by Joseph Villeré, four hundred men stormed the Spanish garrison where the party was being held. Micaela joined the mob that approached the fort, watching the alarmed guards scramble for their lives.

Micaela considered it a stroke of luck that her escape was followed by such a distracting event. Don Antonio de Ulloa, and his cocky council—one Carlos Morales in particular— were about to be ousted from office.

With supreme satisfaction, Micaela watched the commissioner and councilmen scuttle along the pier, rushing toward their Spanish galleon, before the mob overtook them. Flares and torches lit up the wharf as the French flag was hauled up at Place d'Armes, proclaiming victory. Shouts of independence, demands for free trade and the return of human rights rang through the damp night air.

Micaela found herself caught up in the chant of *Liberté!* . . . Until Carlos Morales wheeled on the gangplank to see her spotlighted by the torch that blazed beside her. A satanic sneer puckered his pitted face as he brandished his fist at her.

"I'll see you pay for this," he shouted at her before a volley of pebbles rained down on him. Swearing colorfully, Carlos dashed across the deck to take cover.

While the commissioner and councilmen scurried below deck like rats, the leaders of the French revolt freed the galleon from its mooring. Shouts of victory accompanied the Spaniards, who were left to drift down the river to the Gulf of Mexico.

Micaela's fate had been sealed when Carlos spotted her. She could not remain in New Orleans for fear the Spanish would return to reclaim power. Carlos would hunt her down and punish her for the part he presumed she had played in the revolt. She had to leave the city posthaste.

With her satchel slung over her shoulder and her head downcast, Micaela zigzagged through the cluster of American sailors who had gathered on the pier to watch the Spanish galleon drift away. While the crewmen were preoccupied, Micaela slipped unnoticed across the gangplank and hopped onto the deck of the American ship. Not a living soul was on hand to question her presence. She wandered around the schooner, acquainting herself with the various cabins and storage compartments.

She gasped in astonishment when she opened the portal to the captain's elegant cabin. Never in her life had she seen such expensive furnishings aboard a ship. King Louis himself couldn't have designed a more regal chamber to rest his royal bones!

Red velvet drapes covered the bay window that overlooked the stern. Golden tassels formed a valance that stretched from port to starboard. An oversize royal blue velvet upholstered chair graced one corner of the cabin that was lined with bookcases. In another corner sat a polished oak table that gleamed in the lanternlight. In the far corner, a hand-carved double bed, complete with satin sheets, waited invitingly for the captain's return.

No expense had been spared by the American captain, Micaela noted. The man had surrounded himself with every convenience and luxury. The Great Cabin was a home in itself, taking up as much space as three normal-size rooms. Micaela couldn't imagine what might have been missing from this floating mansion. The owner of this palatial cabin clearly had expensive tastes and insisted upon resplendent comfort.

Too bad Micaela couldn't enjoy the luxury of this cabin during her journey to—wherever. Instead, she would have to stow away in the gloomy hold, wedged between crates and sacks, living like the rats which scuttled through the lower decks in search of food and shelter.

Yet, living in cramped spaces and dark niches was better than returning to Rouchard Plantation to face her father's wrath. Her *uncle's* wrath, she quickly amended. As it turned out, her father was her uncle and her uncle was her father. . . .

Micaela refused to acknowledge the turmoil roiling inside her. All she wanted was the freedom to make a life for herself, away from Arnaud's domination and smoldering resentment.

A woman's giggling laughter, mingling with a man's baritone voice, jostled Micaela from her silent reverie. The sound of approaching footsteps threw Micaela into instant panic. Her alarmed gaze darted around the room when she heard the door latch rattle. *Mon Dieu,* she was about to be caught in the captain's private chamber. She shuddered to think what the penalty was for that!

If she were captured and thrashed, her feminine identity might be discovered. Micaela well remembered how it felt to be passed around the Superior Council and slobbered over. She shuddered to imagine the degradation she would face if she were passed around this colonial crew.

If these Americans were anything like the rowdy Kentuckian keelboatmen, Micaela wanted nothing to do with them. Their wenching and drinking were well known in New Orleans. Most decent folks gave a wide berth to the uncivilized backwoodsmen who sold their goods, then celebrated wildly in the city. These American mariners might be as raucous as those Kentuckians— maybe worse.

Micaela dived under the bed the instant before the door creaked open. She lay on her back, staring up at the rope frame that held the mattress aloft. How, she wondered, was she going to escape from this latest predicament in the midst of a night fraught with emotional upheaval?

* * *

"Would you care for another drink, *cherié?*" Lucien Saffire questioned his buxom companion.

The woman giggled giddily. *"Oui, capitaine."*

Micaela lay as still as a corpse beneath the bed while the tipsy female plunked onto the satin sheets. When articles of clothing drifted to the floor, Micaela inwardly groaned. She had the unshakable feeling she was about to receive a second-hand lesson in passion.

"Bring that drink and that magnificent body of yours over here, *ami*," the woman purred like a besotted cat.

Micaela was in no position to determine if *"ami"* had a magnificent body or not. All she could see was his black Hessian boots. The man's deep, resonant voice appealed to feminine ears. The man spoke English with a distinct, seductive drawl.

Micaela's English was excellent, as were her Spanish, French and Latin. In any language this captain had the kind of voice that sent unexpected tingles down a woman's spine.

Lucien Saffire eased down on the edge of his bed to offer the paramour another drink. "We never agreed on a price. Don't you think we should?"

The woman tittered. The mattress suddenly shifted. Micaela scooted sideways, her face flushing beet-red in embarrassment—for herself and the shameless harlot who was selling her wares to the American captain. No matter how desperate Micaela became, she would never resort to such a belittling profession. She'd starve to death first!

"I'll leave the price up to you, *capitaine*," the doxy cooed. "The more pleasure you receive, the higher the price . . . *oui?*"

Micaela inched toward the wall when the mattress swung on its rope support. The moans, gasps and groans above her indicated the poor woman was being tortured within an inch of her life! The bed swayed to and fro, brushing against the tip of Micaela's nose. She forced herself not to think about what was happening above her. She counted to ten in Spanish and English, then recited the months of the year in Latin—

anything to distract her from thinking about this appalling situation!

Thank God, the crude sexual ritual wasn't long-lasting. Apparently, though, it was unpleasant for the doxy. She was still whimpering and shrieking and squirming for freedom. The captain, Micaela concluded, was quick and brutal about appeasing his lusty appetite.

When the captain's bare feet hit the floor, Micaela turned her head away. Face flaming, she listened to the whiskey bottle clank against the glass, heard the rattle of coins being fished from the pocket of breeches. The coins landed with a dull thud on the sheets.

"My, you do work fast, *capitaine,*" the wench said as she sat up on the edge of the bed.

"I'm a very busy man."

Micaela frowned at the utter lack of emotion in the captain's voice. Minutes earlier he had used that seductive tone of voice to coerce this harlot. Now he was dismissing the woman with bored indifference. God, how impersonal he sounded after being so intimately involved a moment ago!

Micaela didn't like what she was learning about the male species in general, and this American captain in particular. It was glaringly apparent that courtesy and consideration extended no farther than the bedside manner required to initiate passion. Either this man had no heart or all men became cool and detached after sating their animalistic appetites. That must be the case, she decided. Carlos Morales had certainly turned brutal and cruel after being rejected for groping at her.

"If you want me to stay a while longer—"

"There's no time," Lucien cut in. "We'll be casting off in a few minutes. I suggest you fasten yourself into your clothes and be on your way, unless you plan to set up business along the coast of Carolina."

With an unladylike snort, the wench scooped her clothes off the floor and dressed on her way to the door. "You're a hard man, *capitaine,*" she muttered.

"You have been generously compensated for tolerating my hard ways," he said before the door slammed shut.

Micaela wondered if the expression on the captain's face was as impassive as his tone of voice. Blackbeard the Pirate had nothing on this man, she decided. He used women, left them gasping in pain, and then discarded them. Micaela vowed to steer clear of this heartless, insensitive cad—once she managed to sneak out from under his bed!

Lucien plopped into the wing-backed chair and propped his feet on the matching ottoman. "Ah, Cecilia, you have driven me to this dreary existence. . . ."

The tormented sound of the captain's voice surprised Micaela. Moments earlier the man had been the personification of cool indifference. Now his voice rang with something akin to anguish. Micaela wondered what Cecilia had done to provoke this man to turn to anything in skirts to appease himself. Had Cecilia jilted this American captain? Was this hasty tryst, and others like it, a misdirected attempt to rout the love of his life from his mind? Or perhaps Cecilia had turned her affection elsewhere to punish the captain for something he had done. Probably, Micaela decided.

This is none of your business, Micaela chided herself. She had problems aplenty. This hot-blooded captain, who had tortured the harlot in the name of passion, was to be avoided at all cost.

The rap at the door jolted Micaela from her pensive musings. The door whined open to admit another pair of shiny black boots.

Two

Lucien Saffire glanced up when his longtime friend ambled into the Great Cabin. "Are all the men back on board?" he asked before he sipped his drink.

Vance Cavendish nodded his blond head as he strode over to help himself to Lucien's fine stock of brandy. "Aye, but there was plenty of disturbance on the wharf during your absence, none of which you will be pleased to hear about."

"Don't tell me that Spanish weasel has gone back on his word," Lucien grumbled.

"Actually the weasel has no word left to back out on. While you were in the French Quarter, a mob of Frenchmen descended on Tchoupitoulas Gate and sent the Spanish officials scattering from their *soirée* and fleeing for their lives. At present, their galleon is drifting down the river."

"What!" Lucien choked on his drink, his eyes bulging. "Do you mean we bribed that slimy rascal for naught? We could have sold our cargo without paying the tariff?"

"So it seems." Vance let the smooth brandy glide down his throat, then smiled in appreciation. "There is talk of establishing a new republic. The French are hoping their hated Spanish rulers won't be back."

"I wouldn't want to wager on that," Lucien murmured.

"I wouldn't either," Vance agreed. "I expect those Spaniards will find a way to have their revenge."

"I can well imagine the consequences the French will face. The deal we struck with Carlos Morales may still be to our advantage, should he return."

Carlos Morales? Micaela thought, wild-eyed. These Americans were in cahoots with Carlos who took bribes so cargo could be unloaded without tariffs? What were these Americans anyway? Freebooting pirates sailing under a colonial flag? They obviously had no loyalty to England, because they were defying British Navigation Acts.

No doubt, these Americans also slipped into West Indian ports, owned by France, Portugal, Spain and Holland. Micaela had heard it said that the tropical islands were teeming with merchants who bought and sold anything to anybody if there was money to be made.

If Carlos Morales accepted bribes to better himself financially, Micaela wondered if Arnaud Rouchard had offered her as a form of bribe to lessen the taxes he paid to the Spanish regime. She wouldn't put it past Arnaud.

Vance scooped up Lucien's discarded shirt and tossed it to him. "If we're going to catch a favorable breeze in the Gulf at dawn, we should cast off. I don't want to be around if the Spanish Superior Council decides to return."

"And I don't want to take sides in this revolt until I see where the chips fall," Lucien replied.

Shrugging on his shirt, Lucien ambled toward the door. When he realized he was still barefoot, he pivoted to retrieve his boots—one of which lay half under the bed.

Micaela's breath froze when a lean, tanned hand swooped across the plush carpet, missing her elbow by scant inches. *Mon Dieu*, that was a little too close for comfort!

"I hope your tête-à-tête improved your black mood." Vance smiled wryly as he watched Lucien sink down on the edge of the bed to stuff his feet into his stockings.

"There is nothing wrong with my mood."

"No? I swore your afternoon dealings with Morales had soured your disposition."

"My grandfather is the one who put me out of sorts," Lucien grumbled as he shoved the second boot into place." Rising, he dug into his pocket to retrieve the letter he had received before sailing from Charles Town harbor the previous week. "I am being lambasted with threats of disinheritance."

Vance blinked owlishly as he reached back to close the Great Cabin door behind them. "Disinheritance? You mean the old codger has abandoned his begging and pleading and has resorted to drastic measures?"

"My grandfather is nothing if not persistent," Lucien muttered as he strode up the steps. "But then, so am I."

"I think you and Adrian should sit down and discuss what happened. All you have left is each other. Adrian is an old man. You haven't spoken to your only living relative face-to-face since—"

"I have no intention of speaking to him again—*ever*," Lucien cut in quickly. "I cannot forgive him, and I cannot, and will not, call a truce and pretend nothing happened."

"And so, to punish Adrian, you have marched a string of less than respectable females through your cabin, and around Charles Town, just to defy his wishes." Vance shook his head morosely. "You do not approve of your own wild behavior. I can see it every time you tote some wench on board for a quick tumble. You also delight in letting word reach Adrian that you swagger off to the social clubs to drink and gamble. You are purposely ruining your reputation because you know it irritates your grandfather. I think—"

"Vance," Lucien's rumbling voice indicated the subject was closed to discussion.

"Well, it's true," Vance forged ahead. "You were blind where Cecilia was concerned and you are stubborn where Adrian is concerned."

"Enough!" Lucien rounded on his well-meaning friend, his eyes burning like hot blue flames. "I was in love and my grandfather destroyed my happiness. He will not be allowed to forget, and I'll be damned if I make it easier for him!"

"Even at the cost of losing your rightful inheritance."
Undaunted, Vance grinned at Lucien's thunderous frown. "Tell
me, good friend, are you punishing him or yourself?"

Without responding, Lucien continued across the quarter-
deck. Vance stared after him. There was a time when Lucien
Saffire, had been amusing and delightful company. His dry
sense of humor, his zest for life, had been infectious. Nowadays,
Lucien neither provided nor sought amusement. He had become
a man without a home, save the elegant Great Cabin.

Adrian Saffire had tried every method imaginable to rebuild
the broken bridge between himself and his bitter grandson, but
Lucien defied every attempt at reconciliation. For five years
and two months, Vance had delivered messages from Adrian
to Lucien. Vance had even read a few of them—when no one
was looking. Adrian had beseeched, apologized, and finally
threatened Lucien, hoping for some type of communication—
something to end this extended silence. But Lucien had drawn
so far into himself after tragedy struck that it seemed no one
was capable of touching his emotions.

In pure, premeditated defiance, Lucien had nurtured a reputation as a womanizing hellion. Tormenting guilt and festering
resentment drove him, colored his every thought. He lived
to irritate his grandfather, to make Adrian suffer as Lucien
suffered.

Ah, Vance would give most anything to have his old friend
back. Playful amusement and vibrant laughter had once been
Lucien's most endearing traits. Now he was just a shell of a
man who existed without enjoying life.

Taking his position beside Lucien, Vance pondered ways of
returning his friend to the vital, lighthearted man he had once
been. But one look at Lucien's unsmiling face indicated that
it was going to take nothing short of a miracle to turn this
tormented man's life around.

During the days that followed Micaela's escape from New
Orleans, she forced herself to come to terms with the events
that had drastically changed her life. She had gotten past the

tears, the dejection, and she had accepted her illegitimacy. If it was true that difficulty developed strong character, then she was building strength daily. By sheer will and determination, she vowed to make a life of her own, to put her past behind her. Once she set her feet on solid ground, she would find a place to make a new beginning. Until then, she meant to survive as best she could in the hold of the schooner.

In the dark hull, day and night were pretty much the same. Micaela slept during the afternoons, then prowled the companionway and main deck at midnight without risking detection.

Her only discomfort came in weathering the fast-moving storm that caused the schooner to pitch and roll. Her stomach roiled with each rising crest and dipped with the troughs of the waves, but Micaela had curled up in the corner and fought down her seasickness.

Anxious for her nightly breath of fresh air, Micaela tiptoed across the deck to absorb the beauty of stars twinkling above the silvery sea. On two previous occasions she had seen the captain at a distance as he strolled the moon-drenched deck like a restless spirit. Micaela had never viewed the captain in full light—above the calves of his bare legs, that is. She didn't care to know his name, not after the embarrassing incident she had overheard the first night on board ship. She knew all she needed to know about this captain who had no scruples where women were concerned. Therefore, she refused to approach him, requesting assistance. She had served her time under Arnaud's stern rule, and she vowed to avoid any situation that would grant a man control over her life. She vowed to depend solely upon herself, to survive by her wits. She was going out of this world owing no man.

Micaela's thoughts trailed off when she heard footfalls echoing across the moon-dappled deck. A familiar voice wafted in the breeze, and Micaela peeked around the corner of her hiding place to watch the captain move toward the helm with panther-like strides.

"I'll take the last two hours of your night watch, Beecham," Lucien volunteered.

"Thanks, cap'n," the coxswain murmured as he headed toward the steps.

When Louis Beecham disappeared into the companionway, Micaela inched toward the bow, then backed up so she could appraise the towering figure of the man who stood at the helm. To her dismay, she had to agree with the doxy who claimed this captain had a magnificent body.

By the light of the midnight moon and the glowing lantern, Micaela appraised the muscular specimen above her. The captain's linen shirt gaped open to the waist, revealing washboard muscles and a thick matting of chest hair. Black breeches molded to the powerful columns of his legs and hugged the private part of his anatomy—where she should not have been staring! Damn, what betraying eyes she had! She didn't even like this man!

Forcing her gaze upward, Micaela noted the windblown raven black hair. The captain's tanned face boasted strikingly roguish features. His eyes glimmered like mercury in the light from the lantern that swung on the beam beside him. His full lips were pursed in meditation as he stared at the silvery caps that danced like mythical elves on the sea.

Micaela guessed the American to be thirty or thereabouts. From where she stood, he appeared to be ten feet tall—though an inch or two over six feet was probably nearer the mark. He was a sinewy package of masculine strength—and Micaela would hate to find herself on the receiving end of any blow he delivered. Carlos Morales had bruised her cheek when he backhanded her, but one wallop from this brawny captain would send her rolling across the deck like a wooden keg.

Although Micaela wouldn't say this captain was handsome, because there was nothing refined about him, he had a rugged, earthy quality that drew her gaze. He reminded her of a sleek lion perched on a mountain, commanding the world around him. She suspected he was like Arnaud—domineering, demanding, and unconcerned about the needs and feelings of others.

She knew for a fact that his passion ran hot, then cold.

Though she didn't approve of him, she felt a certain unwanted fascination while she studied him in the moonlight. . . .

"You there!"

The deep, baritone voice exploded like thunder. Startled, Micaela stepped back a pace—and tripped over the coiled hawscr rope. She landed with a thud and lay there like a trembling sinner in the ominous presence of the Lord.

"Who the devil are you?" Lucien stared down at the scrawny ragamuffin who was dressed in shoddy brown breeches, wrinkled shirt and oversize hat. He didn't recall signing on a new recruit for this voyage. This waif had obviously stowed away for a free ride.

When the urchin bounded up and darted into the shadows, Lucien scowled. He couldn't give chase without leaving the wheel and drifting off course. "Come back here, boy!" His command was flagrantly ignored. "I said . . . report to me at once!"

Although God Himself couldn't have sounded more intimidating, Micaela defied the order. She had become proficient at disobeying commands. Defying her father had prepared her for this moment. After eighteen years, Micaela had to thank Arnaud for teaching her *something*.

Like a shot, she raced down the companionway. She didn't dare let the captain know his stowaway was a woman, for fear she would be dragged off to his bed to endure the humiliating kind of torture men forced on women.

The captain's booming voice rolled like a thunderclap, but Micaela was out of shouting distance in the blink of an eye. She scurried into the hold, tucked herself into a corner, and thanked her lucky stars the captain couldn't leave the helm to give chase.

Lucien muttered under his breath as he stared into the dark companionway. He was going to teach that little brown mouse of an urchin a lesson he would not soon forget. How that scrawny squirt had slipped past this gimlet-eyed crew, Lucien couldn't imagine. But for sure and certain, the brat would be dragged from his niche and put to work to earn his keep.

When Vance Cavendish came on deck to take a shift at the wheel, Lucien stepped away. "We have a stowaway on board," he reported.

Vance blinked in surprise. "We do?"

"Either that, or an oversize brown rat that moves like streak lightening is scampering around this ship," he said with a snort.

"He must have sneaked aboard while we were watching the rebels drive the Spaniards out of the city," Vance mused aloud. "Do you plan to track the scamp down and put him to work or feed him to the sharks?"

"Have you a preference in the matter?" Lucien questioned as he crossed his arms across his chest and leaned against the railing.

"If I were presently aboard my own ship, I would see that the lad was well fed and then put him to work, rather than make shark bait of him." Vance cast Lucien a pointed glance. "There was a time when I could accurately predict that you would do the same, but no longer, I'm afraid."

Lucien regarded his best friend from beneath jutting brows. "What the hell is that supposed to mean?"

"It means I don't know you as well as I used to, now that you've forgotten how to laugh, smile and take life in stride."

Lucien sniffed disdainfully. "I find little to laugh and smile about these days."

"Too true, you've made your life a prison sentence." Vance glanced solemnly at Lucien. "Go talk to your grandfather when we dock. End this feud before your embittered silence eats you up like poison."

"I'll let you know when I need advice," Lucien muttered.

"You need it now," Vance insisted. "Your grandfather is an old man, Lucien. If you think you have trouble living with memories of the past now, consider how you will cope if Adrian departs from this world before you make amends. Can you live with that more easily than the troubles that haunt you now?"

Lucien pushed away from the railing, then tossed his meddling friend a stern glance. "I would appreciate it if you would find someone else to bestow all this profound advice on."

"Sorry, but you're stuck with me."

"Then I am indeed in dire straits," Lucien said with a snort.

"Indeed you are. Lucky for you that I have enough gumption to offer constructive criticism."

"Why should I listen to a man whose life is not a smidgen better than mine? We both share the sea as our mistress. We sail from port to port to deliver cargo, and that is all there is to life."

"God, Lucien, you're depressing me. I'm doomed to become as gloomy and brooding as you are."

Lucien ignored the jibe and walked away. "If you need me, I'll be chasing down that urchin who is hitching a ride with us."

Leaving the ship in Vance's capable hands, Lucien made his way through the nooks and crannies on the lower decks. At irregular intervals he halted to listen for sounds that might alert him to the urchin's presence. No sound betrayed the little culprit.

Lucien checked every storeroom for signs of occupancy— and turned up nothing for his efforts. After two hours, he returned to his cabin. He stopped in his tracks when he noticed the empty spaces on his bookshelves. Until this moment, he hadn't realized several items were missing.

Unless he missed his guess, the waif had sneaked into the Great Cabin to gather reading material. Copies of Addison's *Cato,* Thomson's *Seasons,* and Young's *Night Thoughts* had disappeared. Lucien wondered what else had been stolen from his private quarters. Quickly, he checked the contents of his liquor cabinet, finding nothing out of place. A hasty search of his desk revealed that several candles and a tinderbox had been confiscated. Lucien suspected the little squirt had also sneaked into the galley to swipe sea biscuits and hard tack to provide nourishment while he hid out.

Lucien decided to let the urchin stew in his own juice for the rest of the night. Tomorrow, he would track down the little beggar. If the boy had approached him directly, requesting passage, Lucien might have taken pity and let the lad work off the price of a passenger ticket. But Lucien had no tolerance for sneaky cowards. That stowaway would catch an earful when Lucien got his hands on him.

Lucien poured himself a glass of brandy as he mulled over Vance's words of advice. If he could find it in his heart to forgive Adrian, he knew he should make peace with the old man. But forgiveness didn't come easily, because Lucien couldn't forget what his grandfather had done. Even threats of disinheritance couldn't force Lucien to break the five-year silence.

And yet, disinheritance could cause problems in the Saffire shipping line, Lucien reminded himself. Although he had control of the shipping business, Adrian still owned two of the four ships in the fleet. As things stood now, Lucien was in charge of all four merchantmen that traded far and wide, despite England's hampering Navigation Acts. For years, sea merchants like Lucien had thumbed their noses at England's restrictive regulations that forbade trade with foreign markets. Three years earlier, King George III had imposed another unfair tax on colonists to pay the debt incurred by the French and Indian Wars. Americans, had made a stink about the Stamp Act. Thankfully, the tax had been repealed, but Parliament had tightened the laws regarding foreign trade.

Lucien wondered how long it would be before the colonists on the eastern seaboard revolted as the French had done in New Orleans. The situation with England was becoming progressively worse.

If Adrian sold his two ships to an outside investor, Lucien ran the risk of doing business with a man who might side with English policy. The last thing Lucien wanted or needed was a partner, especially if the co-owner opposed his political views or decided to replace the captains and crew with some of his own men.

Vance Cavendish captained one of Adrian's ships—one that had been dry-docked in Charles Town for repairs caused by a tropical storm. Vance had volunteered to accompany Lucien to New Orleans rather than remain idle for two weeks. If a new owner took control of Adrian's two ships, Vance might find himself demoted to first mate. Lucien refused to let that happen. Vance might have been a bit free with his advice, but he was a master of the sea. So were the other two captains who sailed in the Saffire fleet.

Perhaps he should make amends with the old coot before Adrian did something rash, Lucien mused. If he and Adrian came to speaking terms, perhaps the old man would be appeased.

Well, Lucien would consider it. If he didn't, Vance would probably pester him to death now that he was on board. In fact, Lucien had the sneaking suspicion that was one of the reasons Vance had come along for the ride—to persuade Lucien to consider a reconciliation.

Tossing down the remainder of his brandy, Lucien eased into bed. He closed his eyes against the wash of painful memories triggered by thoughts of his grandfather. Damn it, Lucien had come so close to discovering happiness—only to have it snatched away. After losing Cecilia, he had refused to let himself become involved with another woman, even the ones Vance had discreetly hand-picked for him. Lucien didn't want to endure the anguish of loving and losing again. He had buried himself beneath a heap of resentment and bitterness—all of which he directed toward his grandfather.

But for Vance's sake, for the sake of the shipping company, Lucien might be forced to confront his grandfather. After five years, he still wasn't sure he was ready to retrace the footsteps where he and Cecilia had walked arm in arm, making plans for a bright, promising future.

Maybe he wouldn't see her standing there, staring up at him with that seductive smile. Maybe he wouldn't hear her provocative voice calling to him in the wind. . . .

Lucien thrashed in bed, trying to stifle the tormenting sensations the flood of memories evoked. Adrian had shattered a young man's dream. Those days of carefree laughter and pleasure were gone, thanks to Adrian. Damn him!

And then again, Lucien thought as he tossed and turned in

bed, maybe five years of separation and silence wasn't enough. Maybe he should let that old coot sit there and rot!

Methodically, Lucien worked his way through the schooner to locate the elusive waif. After a thorough check of the top three decks, he made his way deep into the hull to search the stacks of cargo bound for Savannah and Charles Town. Although it was high noon, and the October sun splashed across the quarter-deck, the hold was pitch black.

Carrying a small lantern, Lucien stepped around the sacks of grain that were piled from floor to rafter. There, tucked between a pyramid of wooden barrels and grain sacks, Lucien found the lad sound asleep, his head resting on a sack. The missing books and candles were within arm's reach.

Curious, Lucien studied the smudged face beneath the felt cap. He guessed the lad to be no more than fourteen. The boy lay sprawled in utter tranquillity, as if he hadn't a care in the world. Ah, it had been years—five of them, to be exact—since Lucien had enjoyed such serene slumber. How he wished he could curl up in this dark, cozy place and forget what troubled him.

When Lucien inched closer, the planked floor creaked. When long thick lashes fluttered up, Lucien found himself staring into the most startling pair of green eyes he'd ever beheld. While he stood there appraising the pint-sized urchin in tattered clothes, the boy squawked in alarm and bolted to his feet.

Since the boy had tucked himself into a corner, Lucien was confident the stowaway couldn't escape, not without going over the top of Lucien . . . or so he thought. To his astonishment, the lad scrambled up the pyramid of barrels like a kitten climbing a tree. Lucien was so busy admiring the waif's amazing speed and agility that he couldn't react quickly enough when tumbling kegs fell in an avalanche on him.

"Argh!" Lucien winced when the first barrel cracked against his shin, followed by the second, third and fourth. He stumbled back, frantically twisting to hang the lantern on the nearby hook before he tripped over the grain sacks behind him. He hit the floor with a thud and flung up both arms to protect his head from the rolling kegs. Growling, he shoved a barrel off his chest to glare at the urchin who now was scrabbling over a stack of crates.

To his rising irritation, he watched the urchin swivel around on his wooden throne and grin mischievously. "A mite clumsy, ain't ya, cap'n?"

Lucien bristled at the taunting, uncultured accent that reminded him of a Kentucky keelboatman.

"You little brat!" While Lucien tried to gain his feet, the boy propped himself on his hands and outstretched a foot, poised to give the second pyramid of barrels a kick. "You're testing my temper, squirt, and you're doing it at your own risk. When I get my hands on you, you'll be stacking up this fallen cargo all by yourself!"

"*If* you can catch me. You haven't done it yet, and I doubt you ever will."

Micaela snickered at the captain's murderous glower. She had let herself be intimidated the night she saw this brawny American standing on the quarter-deck, looking as invincible as God Almighty Himself. But now she had the captain right where she wanted him. One swift kick of her boot heel and he would be buried beneath a casket of kegs. He wouldn't be able to dig his way free before she climbed down the back side of the pyramid and scampered out the door.

Lucien Saffire was not accustomed to being sassed by anyone—with the exception of Vance Cavendish. Being mocked and challenged by a skinny urchin with devilish green eyes put Lucien's temper at high tide. Snarling, he bounded to his feet, intent on scaling the pyramid and yanking that ornery squirt off his lofty perch.

Quick though Lucien was, he moved much too slowly. The grinning waif shoved his heel against the barrels, starting another avalanche. Lucien bellowed in outrage when a bouncing keg struck his shoulder, knocking him off balance. In the time it took to blink, Lucien found himself at the bottom of a stack of upended barrels.

Craning his neck, Lucien glowered up at the spot where the

urchin had been sitting an instant earlier. Lucien's colorful oaths were followed by the sounds of taunting laughter.

"It's been nice visitin' with ya, cap'n. Guess I won round one, now didn't I?"

Muttering, Lucien squirmed free, then hurried around the strewn barrels in hot pursuit. It was infuriating to have that pint-size ragamuffin make a fool of him. And such insolence! Lucien fumed while he dashed off to check every door and storage closet he passed. That brat was going to learn to respect his elders. He would be saluting and rapping out "yes, sir" and "no, sir" before Lucien was finished with him. Tolerating the presence of a stowaway was one thing, but putting up with a smart-mouthed squirt was ten times worse!

After several minutes of futile searching, Lucien stormed back to his cabin to pour a drink that would cool his temper—he hoped. Reaching for the nearest bottle, he guzzled his drink and then spit it out in a showering spray. To his disbelief, someone—as if he couldn't guess who!—had spiked his expensive whiskey with whale oil. Lucien was fortunate he wasn't standing near an open flame. He would have gone up in smoke!

Scowling mightily, Lucien stalked toward the door. He plowed into Vance who carried a heaping tray of food. Dishes went flying. Lucien and Vance ended up in a tangle of arms and legs. Food was slopped on their shirts and dribbled down the wall of the companionway.

If Lucien hadn't been growling like a wounded tiger, he would have heard the impish snicker wafting from under his bed. He had missed his chance to catch his mischievous stowaway who had been hiding right under his nose.

"What in the hell—" Vance croaked as he plucked globs of potatoes off his shirt.

"That ornery little guttersnipe poured whale oil in my whiskey!" Lucien erupted. "That was immediately after he left me buried under a pile of barrels. When I get my hands on that scrawny squirt, I'll tear him limb from limb and hang him from the yardarm!"

It had been five years since Vance had seen Lucien display so much emotion. It was highly amusing to see this self-contained man thrashing his way to his feet and storming into his cabin while he wore his lunch on his shirt. Vance was greatly relieved to discover Lucien was still capable of expressing emotion—even if it was roiling anger.

"And do you know what else that little scamp had the nerve to do?" Lucien muttered as he wiped off his soiled shirt.

Vance bit back a grin while he watched Lucien scowl and pace the carpet. "What did the little scamp do?"

Lucien spun around to stalk in the opposite direction. "That snippy squirt sat atop that pyramid of barrels and grinned at me like a smug prince! Who the hell does he think he is? Why, he dared me to chase him up that wooden mountain, then he sent another tumble of kegs crashing down on me."

Vance strangled a chuckle when Lucien wheeled around, his arms flailing like a duck preparing for flight.

"That little beggar took off and had the nerve to laugh at me, damn it," Lucien bugled in outrage.

"Oh-ho, now there's a crime punishable by death," Vance managed to say with a straight face. "I say we hang him, soon as we lay hands on him."

Lucien frowned darkly when he realized Vance was teasing him. "We'll see how amusing you think this is when you try to track him down." He made a stabbing gesture at Vance. "I'm putting you in charge of capturing that brat."

"Do you mind if I take my meal first?" Vance questioned as he ambled back into the companionway to gather the scattered dishes.

"I'd like to make a feast of that brat's boiled heart for lunch," Lucien muttered as he reached for a fresh bottle of brandy. Cautiously, he tested the contents before gulping a drink.

"You'll have to settle for ham and potatoes," Vance said, coming to his feet with tray in hand. "I'll be in my cabin with a fresh tray of food, if you care to join me."

When Vance made his exit—his broad shoulders shaking in silent laughter—Lucien hissed a few more curses to the taunting image of lively green eyes embedded in a smudged face. That waif might now be hiding, laughing himself silly, but his triumph would be short-lived. Lucien vowed to have his revenge. It would be a full day before the ship docked at Savannah to sell cargo, then another day's voyage to Charles Town. That urchin wasn't going to jump ship in Georgia without Lucien knowing about it, even if he had to stand as posted lookout the whole blessed time. That brat was going to get his just desserts, so help him he was!

Three

While Lucien stamped off to take his noon meal in Vance's quarters, Micaela wormed out from under his bed, then confiscated a few more candles and books to occupy her time. Tormenting the magnificent monster—as she chose to call the nameless captain—was becoming an amusing pastime. In her opinion, the captain deserved to be tormented after the awful way he'd treated his whore. He had left her moaning, groaning and gasping in agony.

For spite, Micaela short-sheeted the captain's bed and loosened the rope frame with the bed wrench. The snarling captain would be in for one whale of a surprise when he plopped down on his satin sheets. He would sink all the way to the floor! Too bad he couldn't sink all the way to the bottom of the sea.

When the coast was clear, Micaela skulked from the Great Cabin to make a new nest in the hold. Knowing the captain was sending his friend on a search-and-find mission put an impish grin on her face. There would be booby traps galore to greet her new pursuer. Micaela was anxious to know how amusing the captain's friend would find her once *he* became the brunt of her jokes.

* * *

Lucien lounged in his chair, relaxing after his shift at the bridge. An unidentified thump in the companionway caught his attention. He glanced up from the book he was reading to see Vance burst into the Great Cabin. Or at least Lucien presumed it was Vance. It was difficult to tell, considering his friend's appearance.

It had been years since Lucien had burst into uproarious laughter, but the sight before him was downright hilarious. Molasses clung to Vance's blond hair and streamed down his shoulders and chest in gooey rivers. Axle grease smeared both sleeves of his shirt, as well as the placket of his breeches. The grimy garments clung to Vance's body like second skin. A small-size crate encased one foot and the metal hoop of a keg dangled around Vance's neck.

"So . . . how goes the search, oh great hunter?" Lucien questioned between snickers.

"I have never been so humiliated or incensed!" Vance burst out. "I stumbled into three consecutive booby traps and landed on my back. That's when I saw that little brown mouse with devilish green eyes grinning down at me from atop the pyramid. I didn't have time to clamber to my feet before he sent a few more barrels crashing down on me."

Fuming, Vance thumped across Lucien's cabin. Then he realized Lucien's blue eyes were sparkling with laughter. If that pesky little devil's pranks could incite Lucien's amusement—even at Vance's expense—it was worth the price. It was good to hear Lucien's laughter again. Maybe this escapade with the scrappy prankster could take Lucien's mind off his troubled past. If that were possible, Vance didn't mind being made to look the fool.

"Do you know what that ornery younker had the nerve to say to me while I lay in a pool of grease and molasses?" Vance asked.

Lucien burst into another round of snickers when a clump of molasses dropped off Vance's forehead and stuck on the tip of his nose like a wart. "No, what did the brat say?"

"He said: Tell cap'n to send me a worthy challenger. I'm havin' a field day with you two clowns," Vance quoted verbatim.

Lucien jerked upright in his chair. "Clowns? The squirt called us *clowns?*"

Vance gestured for Lucien to toss him a towel to wipe the grime from his face. "Maybe we should pit the brat against Timothy Toggle. He's the Goliath on this ship."

"True, the man is as big as an ox, and just as strong," Lucien replied. "But he is too slow-witted to outsmart that little fox."

"Jeremy Ives is as quick as a cat. He could give the brat a good chase."

Lucien gave his dark head a shake. "Jeremy is a mite hard of hearing. That squirt would be all over him like a rash before Jeremy knew what hit him."

"We could post guards at the door and let the lad rot in the hold for a few days," Vance suggested.

"And spoil the squirt's fun? I prefer to match wits with him. Sending an army after him would indicate we admitted defeat."

"And if we should lose?" Vance asked. "What then?"

"Then perhaps we should sign him on. That kind of inventive ingenuity would be welcome around here. In fact, that rascal might make a fine sailor, once he learns his place."

"Learns his place?' Vance scoffed at the absurdity. "That lad defies authority. He's already tangled with the two superior officers on board, for the pure sport of it. That says a lot for the brat's gumption. I have the unshakable feeling that squirt wouldn't bat an eyelash at challenging God Himself."

Lucien cocked a thick brow. "Does that mean you're ready to raise the flag of surrender and give the lad free rein of this ship?"

"It might be safer," Vance mumbled, glancing down his gooey torso.

Lucien came to his feet and ambled over to retrieve the ledgers from the top drawer of his deck. To his disbelief, the drawer dropped to the floor with a crash, smashing his toes.

Chuckling, Vance strode over to gather the items that had scattered across the floor. "That brat is really asking for it.

Maybe we should round him up by whatever means possible and tar and feather him.''

"Maybe we should at that," Lucien mumbled as he repaired the drawer.

"Before we fight the next skirmish, I'd like to take a bath and get a few hours of sleep."

When Vance clomped out, Lucien sank down at his desk to study his ledgers. The cargo he intended to sell in Savannah was stashed in a separate compartment in the hold—hopefully, it was untouched by that waif. Lucien had purchased kegs of nails, plowshares, and fine silks in the West Indies, all of which would bring a high price in Savannah.

Closing the ledger, Lucien peeled off his clothes and flounced on the bed. He squawked when the bed gave way and he dropped to the floor. When he levered upright, he noted that the hem of the sheet was hooked on his feet. That rascal had short-sheeted the damned bed, too!

He scowled momentarily, then broke into a reluctant smile. That boy was issuing a challenge. He kept leaving mischievous reminders that he was alive and well and stalking around Lucien's ship.

Very soon, Lucien promised himself, the ornery scamp would make a careless mistake. Lucien would have him by his scrawny neck. Then Lucien would be the one snickering in devilish delight!

Micaela smiled to herself, remembering each prank she had pulled on the captain and his friend. She had both men going around in circles trying to capture her—without success. Setting traps had become an amusing way to pass the time before she sneaked ashore to begin her new life.

Although Micaela had her heart set on hating the captain, she found herself intrigued by him. She was curious about his relationship with the woman named Cecilia.

Ah well, she reminded herself. It didn't really matter. Once she left the ship, she would never see the captain again. But he would definitely remember the stowaway who had given him fits.

An unfamiliar tingle skittered down her spine, as she remembered his resounding laughter. The captain had been amused when his friend returned, covered with goo. Micaela wondered if he had laughed after he stretched out in bed . . . and hit the floor. She doubted it.

She was going to miss outwitting the captain, she realized. Going to miss staring up at him beneath the light of the midnight moon from her hiding place in the shadows.

Plucking up her satchel, Micaela made her way toward the upper deck. She had no intention of being spotted when the file of sailors trooped down to the hold to unload cargo. Tucking herself in the storeroom, Micaela waited for the first wave of sailors to pass, then followed at a safe distance. She managed to crouch between two water barrels before the second wave of crewmen filed past.

The click of boot heels against the planks alerted Micaela to someone's approach. Heart thumping, she inched around the wall to find another place to hide. Her gaze darted to and fro, as she tried to plan her means of escape. Whoever had approached from starboard had blocked her path so she couldn't scamper across the gangplank and disappear into the crowd milling on the wharf.

Impatient, Micaela poked her head around the corner. The captain was leaning negligently against the railing, his arms and legs crossed in front of him. Micaela swallowed apprehensively when he stared straight at her. Micaela shrank back, poised to cut and run the instant the captain approached.

To her surprise, he made no move to pounce. Frowning, she craned her neck around the corner to see twinkling blue eyes staring back at her.

"Thinking of going somewhere, squirt? Think again. This schooner is bound for Charles Town. You are going to see this ornery game of yours through to the end, so don't think I'm going to let you slip past me."

"You gonna hang me from the yardarm if ya catch me, cap'n?" she questioned in an uneducated drawl.

"Would you like that, squirt?" Lucien tossed back.

"Nope, can't say that I would. I've grown fond of my neck." Despite her attempt to keep her mind on a purely intellectual plane, Micaela found her betraying gaze drifting down the captain's sinewy torso, admiring his striking physique. She was beginning to realize why the strumpet had allowed herself to be lured into his chamber, even if he had tortured the poor woman in bed. Despite his wicked ways, this was a most attractive devil.

"Sizing me up for the kill?" Lucien chuckled.

Micaela fought down a blush. "Why else?" Then she grinned impishly. "Did ya sleep well last night, cap'n?"

"As a matter of fact I did, after I repaired the sag in my bed and lengthened the sheets you shortened for me."

Lucien was amazed that he was actually enjoying the challenge presented by this scrawny squirt. His mundane life had altered because this brat gave him something else to think about.

"Captain, could you come here a moment?"

Lucien glanced over his shoulder when Louis Beecham summoned him. Then he glanced back into those enormous green eyes that carefully monitored his every move.

"Scamper back to your nest, little mouse," Lucien taunted. "Savannah isn't ready for the likes of you." A wry smile pursed his lips as he turned away. "From now on, we'll be playing this game by my rules."

"Meanin' what, cap'n?"

Lucien halted to glance back. "Afraid to find out, squirt?"

"I ain't afraid of nothin'. I just wanna make sure you ain't got no perverted ideas in mind."

When Lucien realized what the sooty-face urchin implied, he erupted in a bark of laughter. "Good Lord, no, brat!"

"Then I accept your challenge from here to Charles Town."

To Lucien's amazement, the scamp stepped into full view and swaggered toward the companionway.

"I just hope you ain't a sore loser. If it'll make ya feel better, I'll go easier on you in our next round."

Lucien held his ground while the urchin tossed him a mocking salute, then sauntered down the steps with a cocky spring in his walk. My, that scamp was incredibly sure of himself, wasn't he? How did he know Lucien wouldn't pounce the moment he turned his back?

A slight frown beetled his brows when he realized the squirt had just shown him an act of good faith and trust. Lucien didn't understand why he was pleased with the unique rapport between him and that intelligent brat . . . But he was.

Enjoying a sense of security, Micaela threaded around the dwindling supply of cargo to make her new nest in the further-most corner of the hold. While the crew was on the wharf, enjoying a few hours on solid ground, she scooted the barrels across the floor to form a tunnel she could crawl through—in case she found herself cornered again. The new route led to the back wall, then to the door, assuring her safe passage if the captain tried to apprehend her again.

Since her days had become nights, Micaela nestled in between the crates to munch on the food she had swiped from the galley while the cook was in the scullery scrubbing dishes. Her appetite appeased, she scrunched down on a discarded gunny sack to catch forty winks.

In her mind's eye, she could see herself standing on the wharf of Charles Town, waving triumphantly to the captain. She would escape this schooner without the captain realizing she was a woman. God have mercy on her if the captain accidentally discovered that the squirt—as he was fond of calling her—was a female! She doubted his sense of fair play would still apply.

Micaela drifted off to sleep, sure that the captain would never know he had matched wits with a woman.

The feel of a steely hand clamping across her shoulder and pressing into her chest brought Micaela awake with a start. She shrieked indignantly when a masculine hand fastened on her breast.

"What the hell—?" Lucien quickly snatched his hand away and stared incredulously at the urchin he had sneaked up on.

Lucien had anticipated the squirt would return to the hold for a nap, giving him the chance to enter the dark niche unnoticed. He had intended to scoop up the ragamuffin before the lad could send kegs crashing on him. Never in Lucien's wildest dreams had he expected to latch onto a woman garbed in men's clothes. But there was no mistaking those firm mounds of feminine flesh he had inadvertently touched.

Lord above! This was a *female!*

While Lucien was hunkered over, coming to grips with the startling realization, Micaela bit savagely at his hand. Yelping, Lucien shrank back, hoping he still had five fingers. Micaela bounded up, then rammed Lucien with her lowered shoulder. Caught off balance, he landed with a thump. His breath came out in a whoosh when Micaela used his belly as a springboard to bound over the top of him. She dived between the row of crates near the back wall and disappeared from sight before Lucien could scramble to his feet.

Muttering, Lucien rolled onto hands and knees, trying to squeeze through the narrow tunnel of kegs and crates, but his shoulders were too broad. Bolting up, he circled toward the door, hurtling the objects in his path. The instant he saw the brown felt cap poke from the end of the improvised tunnel, Lucien pounced. To his dismay, he came away with only a handful of hat. The head beneath it shrank back like a turtle seeking the protection of its shell.

Inside the wooden shaft, Micaela was reciting her repertoire of curse words that she had heard on the docks of New Orleans. Like an arrogant imbecile, she had slept the afternoon away, certain the captain was too occupied with his duties on the wharf to track her down. That assumption had been costly.

Now here she was, trapped like a rat. And even worse, the captain knew she was a woman. The thought of his hand and arm pressed familiarly against her breast reminded her of the unpleasant encounter with Carlos Morales. God help her, she was not going to wind up in the captain's bed being tortured!

Frantic, Micaela backed deeper into the tunnel. While Lucien bounded off to stand guard at the opposite end, she took the weight of a keg on her back and lifted it out of her way. Setting the keg on end, she stepped onto the pyramid of crates on the back wall. Reaching on tiptoe she extended herself just enough to grab the oak beam that ran horizontally across the length of the hold. Pulling herself up, she curled her body on the beam and crouched upon it. There was only enough crawl space between the ceiling and the thick timber to inch forward like a caterpillar.

From her bird's eye view she spotted the captain the same moment he clapped eyes on her. She watched his owl-eyed gaze flood over the tangle of silver-blond hair that cascaded over her shoulders like a matted cape. His gaze drifted over her derrière and outstretched legs. No doubt, he was seeing her in an entirely new light, visually undressing her while she lay on the beam. Damn that rake!

Dumbstruck, Lucien stared at the silky blond tresses that glowed like sunbeams in the lanternlight. Dozens of baffling questions assailed him as he peered at this daring female who had the most fascinating knack of walking up walls and hanging on ceilings.

Who the devil was the woman? Why had she stowed away on his ship?

Now that Lucien thought about it, he realized those enormous green eyes, fanned with thick lashes, better suited a female. Her oval face was marked with delicate features—covered with soot though they were. Lucien shook his head in astonishment.

While Lucien stood there, asking himself questions that had no answers, and re-adjusting all his perspectives, Micaela inched toward the tower of barrels five feet in front of her. If she guarded her step, she could race down the pyramid of barrels before the captain could dash to the door to intercept her. Casting him one last glance, she swung both legs off the beam and dropped to the kegs. The pyramid tumbled, forming a barricade that would protect her while she scrabbled toward the door.

Micaela was only a few feet from the door when a hand shot out to grab her by the ankle. Yelping, she toppled off balance.

While the captain yanked on her leg, she dug in her nails, trying to pull herself from his grasp.

It was no use. He dragged her toward him, then flipped her onto her back before she could squirm free. Grinning victoriously, he plunked down on her belly.

"Now, young lady, suppose you tell me what this little charade is all about."

"S'pose I don't," she sassed, wriggling in vain to free herself.

Lucien stared into the smudged face and belligerent green eyes, amazed at the woman's defiance in the face of defeat. This spirited female possessed more than her fair share of spunk.

"You cruel despoiler of women!" Micaela shrieked. "Do you plan to abuse me, just as you tortured your doxy? If you touch me, I swear I'll make you sorry!"

Lucien blinked, baffled by the comments. Abused a woman? He hadn't abused a female—ever. And how did this imp know about his encounter with the harlot from New Orleans unless she had been. . . .

Lucien's breath lodged in his throat and his eyes bulged. Good Lord, had this woman been hiding in his room during that tryst?

Micaela knew the instant the captain realized how she had come by that intimate information. His blue eyes nearly popped from their sockets. He was gaping at her in disbelief, mixed with another emotion she couldn't quite decipher. Surely he didn't find that amusing. It wasn't funny—not to Micaela. She knew how a man tormented a woman in bed, because she had been there to hear it all.

Another shocking realization exploded in Lucien's mind while he pinned Micaela to the floor. If this imp thought he had tortured the strumpet, then she didn't know the slightest thing about passion.

Lucien could just imagine what this untried female thought she had heard taking place while she was hiding under his bed. She expected him to "torture" her, because she was convinced that was what men did to women. Thanks to him, this naive beauty had a distorted view of intimacy.

For five years, Lucien had gone about the business of spoiling his own reputation to spite his grandfather. Until now, he hadn't given a flying fig what anybody thought, because he didn't care about much of anything. He had been hurting too much inside for anyone's opinion to matter. Now, he would have preferred this female think the best about him, not the worst.

While Lucien sat there, wondering how he could explain, how he could set things right without further distorting this woman's misconceptions, she jerked her hand from his grasp. Before he realized what was happening, he saw a wooden crate coming at him with amazing speed. Two quick blows caught him between the eyes. Pain exploded through his skull. With a dull groan, he collapsed, unable to keep a restraining grip on his captive.

Before the captain's bulky weight pinned her down, Micaela flung herself sideways. With a heave-ho, she pushed the captain's lifeless body aside, then scrambled to her feet. Grabbing her cap to conceal her mop of hair, she scampered toward one of the storerooms.

Damn, that was close! Micaela thought with a gulp. She had escaped without being tortured and she had retrieved her cap. Now it was imperative that she flee this ship without being captured again. Micaela cringed to think what would happen to her if she was!

"Are you all right?"

Lucien groaned when he was jostled back to consciousness. Groggily, he opened his eyes to see Vance's fuzzy image swimming above him. Propping himself on a wobbly elbow, Lucien gingerly inspected the knot on his forehead.

Vance smiled knowingly. "You must have had another encounter with the squirt."

"The lad isn't a *he*," Lucien mumbled. *"She's a she."*

Amber eyes blinked in astonishment. "Are you certain?"

Lucien wasn't about to explain how he knew. He suspected

his blundering attempt to capture the stowaway had confirmed her low opinion of men in general—and of him in particular. How the hell was he to know the "lad" had breasts until he grabbed hold?

"Take my word for it," he said as he staggered to his feet. "I've never known a woman with that much keen wit, not to mention the speed and agility of a chimpanzee. Are you absolutely sure about this?"

Avoiding Vance's persistent question, Lucien braced himself against the wall. "We have to find her," he insisted.

"We should call in the crew," Vance advised. "Together we can—"

"No," Lucien cut in.

"Why not?"

"Because that would be against the rules."

Vance gaped at him as if he'd sprouted antlers. "Against the rules?" he repeated. "There are rules in this game of hide and seek?"

Lucien absolutely refused to call in the crew. If he did, he would lose what little respect that spirited female had for him— and it obviously wasn't much, considering the incident she'd overheard while hiding under his bed! Lucien wasn't going to surround her like a hunted animal after she had bested him several times. Neither was he going to concede. He wanted to set things right—somehow.

Every time Lucien thought about that imp lying beneath his bed while he—Hell and damnation, the incident didn't bear thinking about!

"I want to search every nook and cranny," Lucien said as he wobbled off, bracing his arm against the wall for additional support. "I intend to check in, under, around and above every room."

An hour later, Lucien was muttering under his breath, frustrated by his inability to locate the elusive female. Damn it, how could she vanish into thin air?

Well, she had to be around here somewhere, he assured himself. Climbing topside, he jackknifed his body over the railing—at stem, stern, starboard and port—wondering if that human fly was clinging to the outer shell of the schooner or dangling over the bowsprit. He suspected Vance and the crew thought he'd gone mad, but he did not intend to rest until he located that wily female.

While Lucien was leaving no stone unturned, Micaela was sprawled at ease in the hull, concealed by stacks of crates and kegs. She had overheard the captain's conversation with his second in command. She had let the captain think she had fled from the hold, then she had doubled back to bury herself in the cargo. Sure enough, the captain hadn't searched around the kegs before he tore off to inspect every niche of the ship.

Sooner or later it would occur to him that she had outsmarted him. But when he came to search the hull, she would seek refuge in a place he had already checked.

Although Micaela didn't have much use for men, she did admire the captain's sense of fair play. He could have called in his crew to flush her out like a fox trailed by hounds. To her surprise, he had refused to do that. Maybe he was a beast in bed, but he had played this game of cat-and-mouse by gentleman's rules. Why? Micaela had no idea. But she silently thanked him for giving her a sporting chance to escape the ship.

The following morning, when the ship docked in Charles Town, Micaela had already conjured up her means of escape. It was quite simple, actually. It was ingenious, too, if she did say so herself. Grinning at her own cleverness, Micaela jotted the note she intended to leave for the captain, thanking him for the free passage and the amusing challenge. She wished she could be around to see the look on his face when he realized she had slipped away unnoticed, but that was a risk only a fool would take. Micaela had no intention of being foolish enough to get caught!

Four

Adrian Saffire lounged on the plush seat of his private coach. He removed his wire-rimmed spectacles, absently cleaning them with his monogrammed handkerchief while he peeked around the curtain that covered the window.

The previous week had exhausted him. He'd made three trips back and forth between the plantation on the Cooper River and the elegant townhouse in Charles Town. He had spent every waking hour wondering if his latest ploy to break the silence between him and his grandson would work. Over the lonely years, Adrian had thought up dozens of schemes to bridge this gap, but Lucien Saffire had become a stubborn, begrudging man who turned a deaf ear to pleas and threats.

Adrian did not have time on his side. He was in his seventy-fourth year, and he was no closer to reconciliation than he'd been the day Lucien walked away without looking back.

To say that Adrian was desperate to mend the split in the family, and ensure the propagation of the Saffire name, was an understatement. He would like nothing better than to witness the marriage of his grandson, followed shortly thereafter by the birth of a great-grandchild. Unfortunately, that rapscallion perpetuated an infamous reputation in every port. All this, to humiliate and punish Adrian for interfering in Lucien's personal affairs and unintentionally wreaking disaster.

At first, Adrian had begged for forgiveness—not that it had done any good. Then he had issued requests, followed by stern decrees. Yet, nothing brought Lucien back to Adrian's doorstep. The belligerent rascal had refused to set foot in the townhouse or on the plantation. Lucien had made his schooner his home.

In absolute frustration, Adrian had struck his final blow— the threat of disinheritance. Lucien had sailed off to New Orleans with his load of West Indian cargo without responding to the message. Adrian had no choice but to take the threat a step further, in a desperate attempt to bring Lucien back— infuriated or otherwise.

Adrian had conducted interviews at his townhouse, searching for the perfect beneficiary to inherit his vast fortune. He had spoken to scads of applicants who were eager to fill the position of his companion. Of course, Adrian didn't reveal his true reason for wanting to hire a particular type of companion, though he suspected Lucien would figure it out the moment news reached his ears.

This companion had to meet very specific qualifications and possess the right characteristics. Thus far, Adrian had been hugely disappointed with the prospective companions who landed on his doorstep. He was looking for a young, intelligent woman who showed signs of proper breeding, a woman who had enough spirit to withstand Lucien's black temper and enough beauty to turn his head.

Once Adrian located a woman he deemed a capable, suitable match for his rebellious grandson, the trap would be set. And considering Adrian's advanced age, he didn't have time enough to devise many traps. Blast it, this last-ditch effort had damned well better work! And it would—if Adrian could locate the perfect female.

He had interviewed a score of women who were long on beauty, but sadly short on brains. He met passably attractive women who possessed adequate wit, but they were lacking gumption and lively spirit. If wishing would have made it so, Adrian would have plucked out the characteristics he had observed in those few dozen women he'd met and rolled them into one perfect package. So much for wishful thinking. He was no closer to locating a suitable beneficiary and challenging mate for his grandson than he had been the day he began conducting these confounded interviews!

Inching open the curtain, Adrian stared at the sleek schooner that was being maneuvered into its berth at the pier. Tapping his cane on the ceiling of the carriage, Adrian signaled his groom, Hiram Puckett, to deliver the most recent message to Lucien. Very soon, Adrian would know how Lucien reacted to phase two of this disinheritance scheme.

This silent feud was going to end—one way or another—Adrian promised himself. If Lucien didn't agree to Adrian's terms, then that stubborn boy could watch his inheritance land in someone else's hands.

Adrian watched from the window as Hiram Puckett stood stoically on the wharf, waiting for the gangplank to be set in place. Surely this latest message would draw a reaction from Lucien. How could it not? Adrian was pulling the rug out from under his grandson. Surely this decree would make that rascal furious enough to speak.

The prospect of losing half the Saffire fleet to a total stranger would get a rise out of Lucien. After all, Lucien had made the shipping business his life, except for all that wild carousing and those skirt-chasing escapades that irritated Adrian to no end.

Lucien would come, and Adrian would select the perfect companion and beneficiary to make this threat stick. Lucien would recognize the seriousness of the situation and would remain in Charles Town long enough to deal with it—and long enough for Adrian to make amends. But confound it, he was running out of time!

Micaela scrunched down inside a barrel, then carefully replaced the lid. Smiling triumphantly, she waited for the crew to carry the cargo ashore. She was going to be delivered to the

pier without detection. The captain would never know how she
had managed to sneak past him.

"Bloody hell!" Timothy Toggle grunted as he heaved the
keg onto his buffalo-size shoulders. "What's in these barrels?"

"Nails, I reckon," Jeremy Ives said, flashing his bulky companion a teasing grin that displayed a few missing teeth. "Too
heavy for you, Timmy?"

Timothy—who held the undisputed title of biggest, stoutest
member of the crew—picked up the gauntlet and balanced the
keg on his shoulder. "I can carry my load, just fine."

When Timothy staggered around the strewn crates, Jeremy
snickered in amusement. "If you ask me, you're getting a mite
flabby around the middle."

"Quit yammering and grab some crates," Timothy muttered.
"The sooner we unload this cargo, the sooner we can find some
willing wenches to ease our needs. And by damned, I've never
heard any of my women complain that I'm getting soft!"

"What wench would dare insult you?" Jeremy said as he
hoisted up a second crate. "You would sprawl atop her and
squish her flat as a shadow."

"Shut your trap," Timothy grumbled. "I can handle the
ladies and carry my own weight around here better than you."

"Oh yeah? Well, my little tarts don't have any complaints
about me."

"A measly little shrimp like you would say something like
that," Timothy smirked as he struggled up the steps.

"I'm no shrimp, you big baboon."

"No? Try telling that to the tart we shared in New Orleans."

While Timothy and Jeremy were exchanging their usual
insults, Micaela was soaking up their conversation from inside
her barrel. For the life of her, she couldn't understand this
obsession men had with sex. What was there about the males
of the species that made them think their prowess in bed was
more important that their intellect? Men were indeed strange
and curious creatures.

More and more, Micaela was realizing that marriage—or
any close encounter with a man—was to be avoided. Men had
no regard for a woman's needs or feelings. Suffering through

Carlos's demanding kiss had been distasteful. Listening to the captain take pleasure in torturing his harlot had been disconcerting. Overhearing these sailors had been revolting. Micaela decided that if she never had to endure another repulsive kiss or clumsy grope it would be dandy fine with her.

When Timothy swung the barrel off his shoulder and dropped it none too gently on the wharf, Micaela's head slammed against the keg, jarring her teeth. Despite her discomfort, she experienced an exhilarating sense of satisfaction. She had cleverly eluded the captain and his second in command. No doubt, the captain would swear she could appear and disappear like a disembodied spirit.

Micaela would have liked to rise from the unloaded cargo like a genie floating from a bottle to taunt the captain, but she decided it was wiser to gloat in private. She couldn't risk having the captain give chase again. Besides, she had more important matters on her mind. The time had come to focus her thoughts and energy on beginning her new life.

She had enough coins to provide her with food and lodging for a week, while she sought employment. Her wardrobe was definitely going to be a problem, because she had only one gown left to her name. She needed to find a means to support herself immediately. But no matter what, she was not going to resort to marriage as a means of financial support. There had to be another way for a woman to survive, and Micaela intended to find it!

While Micaela was huddled in her keg, Lucien was frantically searching the schooner. He had awakened this morning to find the note that had been slipped under his door—a note that tauntingly declared the end of a challenge. Being bested by a mere wisp of a woman was aggravating, but Lucien cringed at the thought of being unable to correct the chit's notion that he abused women for his lusty pleasure.

Lucien scowled to himself, wondering how that innocent female was going to survive in society when she had such distorted views about men. He had a certain responsibility to

that misfit of a female and he damned well knew it. She was
far too attractive and fascinating to cut herself off from men.
Whether she knew it or not, she needed a good talking to!

When the storage closet swung open, Lucien glanced anxiously at Vance. "Have you found her?"

"I'm afraid not. I even checked the riggings and sails to see
if she had climbed to the crow's nest. But the lass is nowhere
to be found."

Lucien racked his brain, trying to put himself in that clever
sprite's shoes, wondering where he would have hidden. . . .

"Hell and damnation," Lucien erupted. With fiend-ridden
haste, Lucien charged down the companionway.

Falling into step, Vance followed Lucien as he dodged the
sailors who filed up from the hull. When Vance reached the
hold, he watched Lucien shove barrels aside like a dog digging
up a bone. "You think she doubled back to the hull?"

"I'm beginning to think she never left it," Lucien replied.
"She did the exact opposite of what I predicted, damn her
sneaky hide."

Vance chuckled while Lucien plowed his way to the back
corner, rummaging through the remaining crates. "Amazing.
Absolutely amazing. She outfoxed us fair and square."

Stamping forward, Lucien brandished a candle and two volumes of Shakespeare in Vance's grinning face. "Blast it, this
is all I have left of her. She's gone!"

"How could she possibly slip past a flood of men toting
cargo from the hold?" Vance mused aloud.

Before Lucien could solve that exasperating riddle, Hiram
Puckett arrived on the scene. Bowing, Hiram handed Lucien
the letter.

"From your grandfather," Hiram announced. "This time he
insists that I await your response."

Lucien's curse shook the rafters. He was well and truly
frustrated that he couldn't track down the mysterious woman.
That, compounded with Adrian's decree that he had deeded
his worldly possessions to a new beneficiary, had Lucien swearing two blue streaks.

"Now what?" Vance wanted to know. When Lucien thrust

the letter at him, Vance blinked in disbelief. "Good gad, the old man can't be serious about this. He cut you off because you refused to communicate with him?"

"I assure you that Master Saffire is quite serious," Hiram confirmed. "He has drawn up the contract denouncing Lucien's right to inherit his estates and the two schooners he has purchased and equipped. When he names his beneficiary, the legal documents will be registered in the Assembly." He stared somberly at Lucien. "Unless you agree to meet your grandfather, the arrangements will be finalized."

Hiram lifted a graying brow. "What shall I tell your grandfather?"

"You can tell that conniving old—"

"Lucien, guard your tongue," Vance cut in. "We are discussing your legacy, you know. You cannot stand aside and allow the ships and homes to be signed over to a total stranger."

"He won't do it," Lucien said with a snort. "Adrian has tried to twist my arm a dozen different ways already. This is just another attempt to bring me to heel. When this scheme fails, he will come at me with another."

"Do not underestimate Adrian," Hiram warned. "He has vowed to see this matter settled—for better or worse, once and for all. Do not think for even a minute that you can ignore him. Your grandfather is as determined as I have ever seen him."

"He is also quite mad," Lucien muttered. "We shall see how his document holds up before the Council and House of Commons when I insist that my grandfather has lost touch with reality."

"You would have your grandfather declared insane?" Hiram gasped, appalled.

"Lucien, just go talk to him," Vance implored. "It's time you and Adrian buried the hatchet somewhere besides in each other's backs. If you don't discuss this matter, you could be cutting your own throat. You can't let a stranger squander the fortune that you and your father and your grandfather have amassed. For God's sake, be sensible."

Lucien stared pensively at the candle and books clutched tightly in his fist. First off, he had been outsmarted by a pint-sized female. Now his domineering grandfather was trying to shove his back against the wall, forcing him to break the five-year feud or lose his inheritance.

"Consider what Vance and I have said," Hiram counseled. "Is refusing a meeting with Adrian worth the loss of your rightful legacy?"

A fond smile hovered on Hiram's lips as he stared at Lucien. "Since I helped raise you, I'm aware that stubborn is your middle name. Indeed, you inherited your obstinacy from Adrian. It is no wonder the two of you constantly butt heads, but the time has come for reconciliation."

Lucien considered Hiram's words. Even if he lost the legacy, he could make his own fortune. It was on principle alone that Lucien decided to confront the old buzzard. If Adrian would give away a legacy, just to force Lucien to break the silence, then Adrian must truly be getting desperate to mend the rift.

A wry smile pursed Lucien's lips as he peered at the candle and books. Perhaps he could find a way to outsmart Adrian, just as that blond-haired female had outsmarted him. Lucien had learned a great respect for games that matched wits this past week. Perhaps he should practice a few of them on Adrian.

"Well, Lucien, what shall I tell your grandfather?" Hiram persisted.

While Vance and Hiram waited anxiously, Lucien brushed his fingertip over the candle, remembering a smudged face, flowing silver-blond hair and luminous green eyes. He missed matching wits with that lively sprite. He wondered how his grandfather would have fared against that wily creature. She probably could have devised a way to counter Adrian's latest threat.

Finally, Lucien glanced at Hiram. "Ask Adrian what he plans to serve for supper on Thursday."

"Thursday?" Hiram's thick shoulders sagged in relief, but concern still etched his leathery features. "Thursday is five days away."

"If Adrian has waited five years to drag me to his doorstep, what difference will five days make?"

"I shudder to guess," Hiram grumbled uneasily.

"Shudder all you wish, Hiram, but I have business to conduct on the docks. I will be there Thursday. Adrian can take it or leave it."

Lucien had an elusive female to track down before he dealt with his grandfather. That woman definitely had not seen the last of him. She was not going through life with the wrong impression of intimacy, even if Lucien had to sit her down, tie her in the chair and force her to listen.

Better yet, he would like to show her how wrong she had been about passion, he thought with a scampish grin.

"Couldn't we schedule this peace-treaty meal for Monday?" Hiram questioned.

"Thursday," Lucien insisted. "Tell Adrian it will be Thursday night or no night at all. And he better not serve crab soup and scalloped oysters. He knows I hate fish smothered in rich sauces."

Hiram broke into a grin. "Anything else?"

"Yes, Vance will be joining us for dinner. He doesn't like scalloped oysters, either."

Nodding slightly, Hiram marched off to convey the message to Adrian.

"Captain? What the devil are we hauling in this cargo?"

Lucien turned to see Timothy Toggle standing behind him. "The usual. Potatoes, nails, silk, Flanders lace, molasses, pig iron and casks of rum." He frowned at the odd question. "Why do you ask?"

Timothy plucked up another crate, then turned toward the door. "The keg I carried ashore on my first trip felt more like a hundred pounds instead of the usual fifty. Not that I'm complaining, but I was curious—"

Lucien's stunned gaze darted to Vance. "So that's how she pulled it off." He shot off like a rocket, zigzagging around the crew that filed up the steps. "Come on, Vance, we've got to find her before she slips away!"

Micaela peeked over the rim of her keg, hoping for a break in the activity around the unloaded cargo. The minute she saw the captain and his friend dashing across the deck, Micaela bounded from the barrel and took off at a dead run. She raced along the crowded wharf until she spied an abandoned carriage pulled by two gleaming black horses. Unaware that an old man was propped in the corner of the carriage, Micaela clambered onto the perch. She snapped the reins, sending the horses lunging into a gallop, putting even more distance between herself and the captain.

She hunkered over on the seat so that no one behind the wobbling phaeton could tell who was driving. The vehicle skidded sideways when Micaela cut a sharp corner to veer down the congested streets of Charles Town. She swerved right, then left, zigging and zagging down Broad Street. Although she heard the bells of St. Michael's chiming the hour, she didn't have time to enjoy the magnificent view of the cathedral spires or admire the impressive stone buildings of the Exchange. Micaela only had time for a fast getaway.

When a young lad, chasing his barking puppy, darted in front of her, Micaela stamped on the brake, very nearly catapulting herself off her perch. Although the young lad and his pup escaped unscathed, Micaela heard a thud and groan from inside the coach.

Mon Dieu, was there someone inside the coach? Micaela grimaced at the thought of the wild ride she had unintentionally given her passenger—and the trouble she would face for swiping the carriage.

Apprehensively, she climbed down, then peeked through the window. When she spied the elegantly dressed man lying face down on the floor, she opened the door. Micaela stared at the elderly man whose powdered Ramillies wig sat cockeyed on his bald head. His wire-rimmed spectacles were bent out of shape—just like his temper, she suspected. And worse, one lens of his spectacles had cracked.

"I'm so sorry, sir! I had no idea you were seated in here." Micaela climbed onto the step to hoist the old man onto the seat. Noticing the lack of color in his wrinkled features, she removed her cap to fan him. "Are you all right, sir?"

Adrian slumped on the seat, staring at the feminine face and cascade of blond hair. Attentive green eyes, embedded in a smudged face, peered anxiously at him. His blurred gaze drifted over the tattered men's clothes, and he shook his head, trying to make sense of what he *thought* he saw.

When Adrian opened his mouth, and nothing came out, Micaela pressed her hands to his shoulders, urging him into a reclining position. She loosened his cravat and adjusted his lopsided wig, then fanned his wrinkled face more vigorously.

"You didn't hit your head, did you? Or bite your tongue?"

Adrian stared at Micaela in dazed astonishment, struggling to catch his breath so that he could speak. As of yet, his vocal apparatus wasn't functioning properly.

"I'm really sorry about this," Micaela apologized as she fanned his face. "I thought the carriage was empty. Someone was chasing me and I was desperate to escape. If I had known you were in here, I would never have put you through such a terrifying ordeal, even if I took the risk of being captured. I am not what you think. I'm ... I was in dire straits, but the worst is over." She smiled tentatively. "I hope the worst is over for you, too."

Micaela leaned closer to see if the poor man—whose brains she had clearly scrambled with her wild shenanigan—was still breathing. "Can you hear me, sir? Can you see me?" She clutched his limp hand and squeezed. "If you understand what I'm saying, move your fingers."

After several apprehensive moments, Micaela felt the gnarled fingers wiggle against her hand. "That's a relief," she said with a gusty sigh. "I was afraid I'd killed you." She flicked a piece of grass from the shoulder of his expensive jacket and brushed the dust from his sleeve. "I will replace your broken glasses, even if I have to pay for them in installments. I'm a little short on funds, but purchasing new spectacles is the least I can do after the fright I gave you."

Micaela didn't realize she was chattering like a magpie until she finally paused to take a breath. Concerned, she appraised the old man, watching with relief when a smile twitched his lips and the color returned to his face.

"My dear lady, are you always this rambunctious?" Adrian croaked, struggling to sit up.

"I'm afraid so," she admitted. "Does that shock you, sir?"

"I am neither shocked nor surprised by much of anything these days," he said as he appraised her dowdy clothes. "Are you in the habit of dressing like a man or is this the disguise that aided in your escape from an evil pursuer?"

Micaela broke into a grin. The old man was being an exceptionally good sport. How she wished her father—her *uncle*— had been as tolerant. Arnaud would have thrown a conniption if he had been upended and unintentionally abducted in his own coach.

"There are times when a lady must resort to ingenuity if she is to survive," she replied.

"And this was one of those times," Adrian presumed as he took inventory of his injuries. Other than cracked spectacles, a queasy stomach, a knot on his head and scrapes on his knuckles he was in reasonably good shape.

"Truly, sir, I never intended for you or anyone to get caught up in my difficulties. I can take care of myself," she felt compelled to tell him.

"Obviously." Adrian looked her up and down. "I doubt that whoever was chasing you stood much of a chance. You seem quite capable of handling difficulty. In fact, I would guess you prefer to handle it yourself. Is that a fair assessment of your philosophy, young lady?"

Micaela chuckled and nodded her head. "Yes, sir, I suppose that would be a fair assessment."

Adrian took the dingy cap from her hand and fanned his face. He appraised this vivacious female, a woman of startling wit and obvious beauty. Having spent a week interviewing a raft of young women to fulfill the position as his companion, Adrian could spot a woman worth her salt in a matter of minutes. This was the kind of woman he had in mind. She teemed with undaunted spirit and intellect. In addition, she would clean up quite nicely, he predicted.

There was no need for Adrian to continue his search. This feisty female met all the necessary qualifications. Her sincere nature, her obvious concern for his welfare were commendable credentials. She was no shrinking violet, that was for certain. She showed all the signs of irrepressible spirit, staunch independence and free thinking. She looked Adrian in the eye and replied to his questions without the usual coy batting of lash that so annoyed him.

"If you're up to traveling, I will see you home," Micaela volunteered. "If you point me in the right direction, I'll have you on your doorstep posthaste."

When Micaela stepped back to shut the door, Adrian latched onto her arm. "Since you need refuge, you are welcome to take it at my home."

"I couldn't impose," Micaela insisted. "I've already injured and inconvenienced you. My problems aren't your concern. And anyway, I should be safe now. I am the one who is indebted to you."

"Then I am calling in the debt," Adrian declared. "You will be my house guest. I insist on it. You have been more stimulating company than I have enjoyed in years."

"More stimulating than is healthy," Micaela added wryly.

"I am a lonely man who could use a bit of stimulation."

Micaela eyed him warily, wondering what he implied. "I don't believe in making many concessions, especially when it comes to men."

Adrian burst out laughing, then grimaced when a sharp pain stabbed him in the ribs. "You misunderstand, lass. I am a lonely man, but I'm also an *old* man. I did not imply that I wanted improper privileges. I am offering you a job as my companion—in the most honorable and respectable sense of the word."

Micaela blinked, stunned. "You want to hire me to be your friend?"

"Yes, my dear. I have learned that nothing in life comes without a price."

"Things like friendship should," she insisted.

His graying brows furrowed as he studied her astutely. "Have I offended your idealism, lass?"

"Yes," she said honestly. "I would like to think that at least friendship can be given without expecting something in return."

Adrian liked this young woman immensely. She was assertive, caring and honest, and she was going to suit his purpose very well indeed.

"You are on salary as of this moment," Adrian declared. "Now take me home. You can tell me why you're garbed like a ragamuffin, chasing up and down these streets, while we share a cup of tea. I do love lively tales!"

Micaela peered at the elderly gentleman who appeared to possess his own brand of incorrigible spirit. She liked his style, his sharp mind. Fate had tossed the old gentleman in her path and provided her with food and shelter. The captain would never find her while she was tucked safely in the home of this elderly aristocrat.

"I accept," Micaela said with a smile. "I promise that the next leg of your journey won't be as harried as the first."

When the door eased shut, Adrian broke into a wide grin. His new companion was going to work out splendidly. Now, if only he could get his muleheaded grandson to agree to a meeting! If Lucien still refused reconciliation, Adrian was going to proceed with part two of his plan of naming a new beneficiary. This delightful young lady would be a credit to the family name. Let Lucien pit himself against this quick-witted female, instead of those empty-headed chits he cavorted with these days.

For the first time in five years, Adrian felt confident that he had devised a way to break Lucien's silence. That stubborn rascal was going to come to heel this time, because Adrian had conjured up a surefire method, complete with his lovely new companion as bait. Ah, he couldn't wait to see the look on Lucien's face when he realized he not only had to speak to Adrian again, but he would have to do his bidding as well! The feud was finally going to end!

Lucien kicked over the empty keg on the wharf and muttered several ripe oaths. If Hiram hadn't detained him, Lucien might have caught that cunning female before she lost herself in the crowd. But by damn, Lucien wasn't giving up the chase. He would find her, only to prove to her that he could. He would turn this town upside down if that's what it took!

Lurching around, Lucien summoned four trustworthy members of his crew. "I want you to inquire at every inn and hotel in town to locate a young lady with silver-blond hair and sparkling green eyes." The order drew four toothy grins. "It is not what you're thinking so wipe those smiles off your faces and pay attention. The lady stands about five foot three inches tall and weights a little more than a hundred pounds. When you locate her, do not underestimate her, whatever you do. She can be as slippery as an eel, so don't let her out of your sight for even a second. When you find her, three of you keep an eye on her while the fourth man conveys the message to me. Do *not,*" he repeated emphatically, "take that female for granted!"

When the men trooped off on their unusual mission, Vance tapped Lucien on the shoulder. "You're carrying this game too far. She bested us, so let her be."

"No," Lucien objected. "She has not seen the last of me."

Vance studied Lucien for a pensive moment. "Is something going on here that I don't know about?"

"No," Lucien hedged. "Trust me, Vance, I know what I'm doing."

"You haven't known what the hell you were doing for five years," Vance smirked. "Why should now be any different?"

"Well, it is, damn it!"

"Why?" Vance wanted to know.

"Just because," Lucien muttered before he wheeled around and stalked toward the gangplank.

"Ah, just what I like," Vance said with a snicker. "A reasonable, definite answer."

Five

Micaela stepped down from the carriage to appraise the sprawling three-story brick townhouse. She could not believe her good fortune. Adrian Saffire, her new employer, was obviously a member of the Carolina gentry.

After Adrian showed her around the spacious rooms downstairs, he sent her up to one of the bedrooms to freshen up. The housekeeper—Gretta was her name—showed Micaela into an elegant two-room suite with a four poster bed, Chippendale highboy, Hepplewhite chest-on-chest and dozens of expensive keepsakes that looked as if they had been gathered from around the world.

When the brass tub had been filled by a string of servants carrying buckets of water, Micaela shucked her grimy garb and sank into the water. She luxuriated in the simple pleasure she had done without during her voyage. This was far better than nightly spit baths!

With cloth in hand, she scrubbed her face, then washed her hair. When she climbed from the tub, she stared at the soiled garments, then frowned. The satin gown she had worn to the Spanish ball was too dressy for tea, but it was that or the men's clothes.

Wrapping the fluffy towel around her, Micaela padded to the wardrobe closet, hoping she could borrow something appropriate. Costly tailored waistcoats and breeches filled the closet. Crisp linen shirts were stacked in the drawers. This was definitely a man's room.

Gretta rapped on the door and breezed into the room. To Micaela's astonishment, the plump housekeeper was laden down with packages. "Gifts from Master Saffire, mum," she announced as she spread a fashionable gown on the bed for Micaela's inspection.

"I can't accept this," Micaela said, wide eyed.

"Of course you can." Gretta grinned pleasantly." The master sent one of the servants to fetch everything you need, right down to the unmentionables. This gown might not be a perfect fit, but I'm a fine hand with a needle. Your other gowns will be tailored to fit. He plans to take you to the seamstress bright and early in the morning."

Micaela was overwhelmed by Adrian's generosity. Her supposed father had never been this kind to her, yet a stranger had taken her under his wing. Life, she decided, was full of puzzling ironies.

"Where is Adrian? I need to speak with him. I cannot possibly let him buy all these things for me."

When Micaela sailed toward the door, Gretta's giggle erupted behind her. "If you wish to speak with Master Saffire, I suggest you dress, mum. Adrian warned me that you were a wee bit unconventional, but clothes are still all the rage in Charles Town."

Micaela blushed up to the roots of her hair. She had been so intent on speaking with Adrian that she had nearly bolted from the room wearing nothing but a towel.

While Gretta fastened her into the pale green day dress, Micaela wound her damp tendrils of hair into a bun and pinned the curly mass atop her head. Within a few minutes she was whizzing down the steps to find Adrian lounging in his study.

When Micaela sailed into the room like a rush of spring breeze, Adrian nearly spilled his glass of mint julep. He suspected this young lass would be attractive—once she washed off the sooty smudges and shed those baggy clothes—but the transformation was breathtaking! This lovely butterfly had emerged from her dingy brown cocoon and Adrian could do nothing but gape in astonishment. Her voluptuous figure was a perfect match for her enchanting face. Adrian silently congratulated himself for stumbling onto a rare treasure.

"Master Saffire," she began, drawing herself up in front of him.

"Adrian," he corrected. "And your name, young lady? I forgot to ask while I was in my rattled condition."

"Micaela Rouchard," she formally introduced herself. "I do appreciate these lovely clothes, but it isn't necessary—"

Adrian flung up a hand to forestall her. His admiring gaze wandered from the top of her head to the toes of her new shoes. "I insist, my dear Micaela. You cannot accompany me around town, attending theaters and balls in baggy breeches. Consider your new wardrobe your uniform."

"You are entirely too generous. I'm sure there is someone in town who could serve as your companion without your having to spend a fortune outfitting them. Perhaps I should be on my way—"

"Nonsense," Adrian interrupted. "There is no reason for you to decline this job." He frowned thoughtfully. "Unless of course you do not like bossy old men."

"You are not bossy," she insisted. "Persistent, yes, but then so am I."

Adrian smiled wryly. "Then you must have an aversion to eating three square meals a day, wearing the finest garments money can buy, and suffering through the enjoyment of plays, musicals and balls."

"I have no complaints about any of those things—"

"Good, then it is settled," Adrian declared.

"But—"

Adrian chuckled. "My dear Micaela, this arrangement will be to our mutual benefit. Simply accept my offer of employment and the gowns I intend to provide for you and let's get on to the pot of tea, shall we?"

Micaela stared at the old gentleman who was incredibly

generous and kind. He was right, of course. His offer was a godsend and she would be a fool to refuse it.

"Very well, Adrian, I will take this job, but I intend to pay for my clothes."

"You will do nothing of the kind."

Her chin tilted to a determined angle. "Then I will work for nothing."

"You most certainly will not!"

Micaela stared down the elderly patriarch who looked at her through cracked spectacles. Although Adrian was a persistent man, she did enjoy his company. He already seemed more of a father to her than Arnaud had been. Indeed, Adrian seemed to enjoy her spirit rather than condemn it. Although he was being a bit stubborn about letting her pay for her garments, Micaela knew there were ways of getting around that. She would take money from her weekly salary and pay him in installments. If Adrian refused to be reimbursed she would shower him with gifts.

"I do like the gown," she murmured as she accepted the tea he handed to her.

"Good, then you won't complain when I cart you off to be fitted for ball gowns and riding habits."

"Adrian . . ." she said warningly. "Even generosity should have certain limits."

"Just humor an old man, lass." He plucked up a copy of the *South Carolina Gazette* to catch up on the news. "Supper is served here at promptly eight o'clock. I should like to take a drive through town shortly thereafter. But not—" he grinned at her from over the edge of his newspaper, "—at high speeds. We will leave the driving to Hiram Puckett. . . . Good God, I almost forgot!"

Bemused, Micaela watched Adrian scuttle off. She didn't have the faintest idea what was wrong. Shrugging off his abrupt departure, Micaela sipped her tea and savored the feel of solid ground beneath her feet. When Adrian didn't return within a few minutes, she took her cup of tea and went upstairs. Whatever Adrian had forgotten reminded her that she had forgotten to send off a letter to her natural father, informing him of her whereabouts. Jean Rouchard was the only one who needed to know where she had relocated. In fact, he was probably the only man alive who cared.

Adrian's shoulders sagged in relief when he saw Hiram drive up in a rented phaeton. He couldn't believe he had forgotten about his trusted servant!

"What the devil happened, Adrian?" Hiram asked as he climbed down.

"Not to worry, Hiram, everything is fine. I simply had another matter to attend to." He glanced curiously at Hiram. "Did you speak to Lucien?"

"Yes, sir. Your wish has been granted. He has agreed to come to supper on Thursday."

Adrian would have jumped for joy if he thought his old bones would have withstood the exertion.

Before Hiram could question him about his unexpected departure from the wharf, Adrian sent him off to summon the lawyer. Now that his plans had been put in motion, he wanted the legal documents in proper order. When Lucien arrived, he would realize that his grandfather meant business this time. That young rake's days of gallivanting hither and yon, besmirching the family's good name, were over. Lucien would have to marry the lass Adrian had selected for him.

Adrian smiled to himself as he watched Hiram's coach speed on its way. Everything had fallen into place—after years of turmoil and frustration. Adrian had found a delightfully entertaining companion who brought joy and laughter to these quiet halls. He had also managed to maneuver his grandson into agreeing to a conference. This was turning out to be the best day Adrian had had in years!

Lucien slopped brandy into his glass and downed the drink in one swallow, but the whiskey didn't cool his irritation. After five days of searching for the mysterious female, he had come up empty-handed. How in the hell had that woman vanished like a puff of smoke? And *why* had she become such an obsession to him?

For the life of him, Lucien couldn't figure out how and when that woman had gained such a phenomenal hold over him. It wasn't as if they had shared the slightest romantic involvement. His interest couldn't be accurately labeled as physical attraction, because he had only touched her once—and that had been by accident.

It was *mental* fascination, he realized with a start. And that was absurd!

Mentally attracted to a woman? Lucien swallowed his brandy and shook his head in exasperation. If he confided such nonsense to his closest friend, Vance would probably laugh himself sick. Even Lucien was astonished by the thought!

Yet, for whatever reason, the woman had an unprecedented impact on him and he couldn't get her off his mind. And he had damned well better, because he was due at Adrian's townhouse in less than an hour. With any luck, Lucien could persuade Adrian to tear up that ridiculous document that named a new benefactor and then he could get back to business as usual.

Lucien donned a clean shirt, tied his black cravat, and grabbed his waistcoat. When Vance arrived a few minutes later, Lucien inhaled a bracing breath and surged through the door of the Great Cabin.

"Nervous?" Vance chuckled at the grimly determined expression on Lucien's face.

"Apprehensive is nearer the mark," Lucien clarified. "I'm not sure how I'm going to react when I see Adrian again."

Vance noted the bitter scowl that settled into Lucien's bronzed features. "I thought it was unfair to condemn Adrian for the unexpected actions of another," he murmured as he fell into step beside Lucien. "It was Cecilia who made that critical decision, after all. Not Adrian."

"My grandfather drove her to it," Lucien muttered. "She would still be here, if not for his meddling."

"The problem is that you are a very intense individual," Vance dared to point out. "When you get something into your head, it drives you, compels you. Take that episode with the stowaway. You've had search parties picking this town apart to locate her. And why? Because you can't leave it alone, can't accept the fact that the clever chit slipped through your fingertips.''

"There were things left unsaid between us that needed to be said,'' Lucien replied. He hopped into the rented coach and stared straight ahead.

"What things?'' Vance wanted to know.

"It's private.''

Vance rolled his eyes skyward. Lucien had the infuriating habit of closing up like a damned clam. No amount of prying could force him to share his innermost thoughts.

"I wonder what Adrian is serving for supper,'' Vance said, for lack of much else to say.

"Crow, I suspect. Since I swore five years ago that I would never be back, he will undoubtedly take this opportunity to throw the broken vow in my face.''

"Oh, for God's sake! If you're going to be irascible the whole blessed night, I'd rather be the honored guest at my own hanging. Why are you dragging me along with you anyway?''

Pearly white teeth flashed in the lamplight that illuminated the street. "You're along to prevent me from strangling the old buzzard. After all, you know what an intense individual I am. And thanks so much for pointing out my shortcomings. Is there anything else about me that you would like to criticize while you're at it?''

"You can be sarcastic and spiteful when you feel like it,'' Vance threw in.

"Thank you for yet another insult.''

"Don't mention it. What are friends for?''

Finally, Lucien slumped back on the seat to expel the breath he felt as if he'd been holding for five days. "Lord, I'll be glad when this night is over.''

Vance patted Lucien's rigid shoulder. "I know, but this reconciliation has been too long in coming. If you and Adrian will each give a little, maybe the two of you can make a fresh start.''

Lucien wasn't prepared to be that optimistic. A civil conversation shared over a meal was the best he was hoping for.

When Adrian heard the abrupt knock at the door, he hoisted himself from his chair. He glanced anxiously at Hiram who waited like a posted lookout.

"He's right on time," Hiram noted, checking his timepiece.

"He was always punctual to a fault," Adrian remembered.

Drawing himself up, Adrian stared at the door through his new spectacles. He was a bundle of nervous anticipation. This evening was a crucial milestone in his relationship with Lucien. This scheme was destined to produce results. It would either drive Lucien away for good or bring him to heel. This cold war would finally be over—one way or another.

The past few days had confirmed Adrian's belief that he had made a wise choice in hiring Micaela Rouchard. She was everything he hoped for. Her delightful wit and zest for living had done wonders for his morale. She teased him, pampered him, and she entertained and amused him. Now, if only Lucien could get over being indignant long enough to realize what a great favor Adrian had done for him, things would work out splendidly.

When Hiram opened the door, Adrian pasted on a cordial smile and extended his hand. "Lucien, I'm glad you could come."

Lucien stood rooted to the spot. There were five paces separating him from his grandfather's peace-treaty handshake—one step for each year they had been at odds. The first step, Lucien realized, was the most difficult. It was a symbol of his concession.

Both men sized each other up for a long moment. Lucien let his gaze wander over his grandfather, noting the changes in the old man's appearance. Although Adrian's shoulders sagged more than Lucien remembered, and new wrinkles etched his face, there was an inner sparkle in those chocolate brown eyes.

Adrian studied Lucien just as thoroughly. Time and experience had matured this young man. Even though Lucien had always been strikingly handsome, there was a new maturity in his features. Lucien possessed the Saffire family traits—chiseled mouth, olive complexion, and dark wavy hair. He would be a tribute to the family, to the tradition of his ancestors—*if* he chose to honor and preserve it.

Determined to bridge the gap, Adrian took the first step toward reconciliation. To his relief, Lucien matched him step for step, until they finally clasped hands.

The world screeched to a halt. Servants came out of the woodwork to welcome Lucien home. The sentimental members of the household shed a few tears, while the rest of the staff smiled in long-awaited satisfaction.

"It is a grand day," Hiram declared. With an expansive sweep of his arm, he gestured toward the dining room where the fine silver and china had been set out in honor of this monumental occasion. "I suggest we open a bottle of wine to toast this reunion."

No one dared to disturb the peace by opening sensitive topics of conversation that might instigate an angry outburst. Lucien and Adrian discussed the weather, the plantation on Cooper River and the shipping business.

When Adrian felt he could procrastinate no longer, he mentally formulated his thoughts and dived into the heart of the matter. It had to be done, he told himself. Micaela would be summoned downstairs in a few minutes. All hell would break loose if Adrian didn't explain the situation. Lucien was going to need time to adjust to the idea—before he laid eyes on his intended bride.

"Now, about the documents . . ." Adrian cleared his throat, then tugged at the cravat that constricted his neck like a hangman's noose.

One thick black brow arched and penetrating blue eyes homed in on Adrian. "Yes? What about them? They have been tossed into the hearth and burned, I hope."

Adrian swallowed a gulp of wine and glanced away. "Not exactly."

Lucien's faint smile vanished as quickly as it had appeared.

"Not exactly, Grandfather? Either they exist or they do not. Which is it?"

Well damn, Lucien was pushing hard, refusing to let Adrian progress through this explanation one part at a time. Now, there was naught else to do but blurt out the announcement, allow Lucien to explode in outrage, then let him have a look at the new heir to the Saffire fortune.

"I have signed all the necessary papers and I have named a new beneficiary, just as I said I would," Adrian announced.

"You what!" Lucien bounded from his chair so quickly that he banged his knee. The silver candelabra and imported English china rattled on the table. Blazing blue eyes burned down on Adrian. "If the deed is done, what the sweet loving hell is this reconciliation all about?"

"The documents are strictly business," Adrian clarified quickly. "This is a social gathering. Did you agree to come here tonight only to secure your fortune?"

Lucien braced his hands on the lacy tablecloth and glowered at his grandfather. "I'm not sure why I'm here," he admitted between clenched teeth. "But since I am, I want to know who you bequeathed the Saffire fortune to."

"My beneficiary is a very intelligent and capable individual who has already proved an ability to carry out the managerial duties of this house. In fact, things have not run this smoothly in five years."

Indeed, they hadn't. Micaela had turned out to be a whiz at mathematics and organizational efficiency. Three days earlier, while Adrian was poring over the ledgers and household accounts—squinting through his cracked spectacles—Micaela had offered to make calculations for him. To his amazement, she had tallied the numbers accurately in her head while Adrian was trying to figure them on paper. She had balanced the budget within a few hours and devised all sorts of ways to cut unnecessary expenses.

After he discovered how keenly gifted the lass was, Adrian had given her free rein of the townhouse and put her in charge of accounting. The house was running like a well-oiled machine and servants scurried enthusiastically to do her bidding. The transformation was amazing!

Micaela's bubbly personality had injected new life into everyone. She had personally consulted each groom and servant, requesting suggestions that would make their duties easier and more enjoyable. Micaela had set aside specific times during the day for refreshments and socializing. The servants were twice as productive, knowing they would take a well-earned break in the kitchen, feasting on snacks and punch before returning to their chores. Even Lucien would be impressed— if he wasn't so busy being furious.

"And where," Lucien hissed, struggling to control his temper—and doing a lousy job of it, "—is this phenomenal individual? In hiding, I suppose. He's afraid he'll be torn limb from limb for preying on an old man whose only living relative refuses to be coerced and manipulated!"

"Hardly hiding," Adrian corrected. "My beneficiary has taken over your room and is preparing to join us in a few minutes. But he is not a—"

Before Adrian could explain that he was a she, Lucien cut him off with a snarl. Spinning around, Lucien stalked into the foyer, intent on tracking down the conniving bastard who had played up to Adrian in order to steal Lucien's fortune.

It was obvious that Adrian had become senile. Some devious scoundrel had made himself at home in Lucien's bedroom. Just wait until he got his hands on that weasel! He'd see to it that the scoundrel wished he had never been born!

Micaela shook her head in dismay when she saw the elegant gown Gretta had laid out for her. One of Adrian's new purchases, no doubt. It was going to take her months to repay Adrian for his extravagance.

Well, she didn't have time to fret about that now. Adrian had announced they would have guests for dinner. Micaela had seen to the last minute preparations before bounding upstairs to bathe and change. Wiggling into her chemise, she smiled at the thought of the dear old man who treated her like family.

Adrian had been an answered prayer, and she already loved him dearly. He had escorted her to the theater on Queen Street to enjoy the comedy performance of *The Recruiting Officer,* and they had attended the orchestral concert the previous night. In addition to that, Adrian had placed her in charge of his financial ledgers and management of the household. Micaela was thrilled and humbled by his trust in her, his faith in her abilities.

When she had suggested changes to improve conditions at Rouchard Plantation, Arnaud had not been the least receptive. The man would suffer a seizure if he knew Micaela had been given duties in Charles Town that were supposedly above a woman's capabilities.

At long last, Micaela felt useful, wanted. She was allowed to put her ideas into action without being ridiculed and stifled. She had cast off that oppressive yoke Arnaud had strapped to her—

Her thoughts came to an abrupt halt when the bedroom door crashed against the wall. Startled, Micaela clutched her gown to her chest and wheeled to see who had intruded. Her legs nearly folded up beneath her when she found herself staring at the very last man she expected to see.

Probing blue eyes raked over her exposed flesh, missing not the smallest detail—not even the tulip-shaped birthmark on her inner thigh!

"*You?*" Micaela choked out, trying to cover herself as best she could.

"*You?*" Lucien chirped.

Astonished did not capture the extent of Lucien's surprise. The woman he had turned the city upside down to find was standing right smack dab in the middle of his bedroom. And furthermore, he was stunned to realize this elusive female was even lovelier than he dreamed possible. She reminded him of an enchanting goddess with her peaches and cream complexion, her lusciously formed figure, and her firm, shapely legs. Her silver-blond hair cascaded over her shoulders and framed her flawless face.

Her lacy chemise did more to entice than to conceal her

alluring curves and swells, leaving too much to his active imagination. After nurturing a reputation as a connoisseur of women for the past five years, Lucien could recognize rare beauty at a glance. This woman was one of Mother Nature's greatest handiworks. Damn, who would have thought *she* was the person he had come upstairs to strangle!

While Lucien stood there gaping, Micaela was doing some assessing of her own. She had been unwillingly fascinated by this ruggedly handsome devil while she was aboard his ship. Now, here he was, garbed in the fanciest trappings money could buy, looking debonair, dignified and one hundred percent devastating male. If she hadn't known this rake lured women into his lair to torture them, she might have found herself hopelessly attracted to him.

Might have, Micaela quickly reminded herself. This captain was a rogue of the worst sort. Even if she was vividly aware of his masculine appeal, she knew he was a woman's nightmare. He dealt in humiliation and pain, and Micaela vowed to have no part of it. . . .

Giving herself a mental shake, she drew herself up to face him. "Kindly take yourself off, captain. I don't know what you are doing here, but you are most definitely invading my privacy."

"Just as you invaded mine that fateful night in New Orleans?" he countered with a mocking smile. "I'd say we are even, squirt."

Micaela's face flamed as she turned her back on him. "I was desperate to take refuge on your ship. Had I known I had entered a torture chamber, I assure you that I would have hidden elsewhere."

She turned to face him. "I asked you to leave, captain," Micaela insisted. When he didn't budge from the spot, she glared at him. "Get out of my room—now!"

To her dismay, Lucien defied her command. He kicked the door shut with his boot heel and strode toward her. "This is *my* room," he informed her. "I was born here, in fact."

Micaela stared at him, slack-jawed, her arms sagging. Remembering her state of undress, she jerked the gown beneath her chin, but not before Lucien feasted his hungry eyes on her bosom.

"*Your* room?" she parroted, bewildered.

Lucien opened the wardrobe closet. Tossing aside his jacket, he shrugged on the royal blue waistcoat that had been a birthday gift from his grandfather—a gift Lucien had refused to accept.

"My clothes," he confirmed as he flicked a piece of lint from the sleeve. "This garment was designed by a tailor named James Phelps. The old Englishman owns a shop on Broad Street."

"I don't care if the tailor has a shop on the moon," Micaela snapped. "I don't care who *you* are, either. I simply want you out of here so I can dress!"

Ignoring the command, Lucien dropped into a mocking bow. "Lucien Saffire, my lady, whether you care who I am or not."

"Saffire?" Micaela squeaked, eyes rounded. "You are—?"

"Adrian's grandson."

"He never mentioned that he had one," she said, studying him suspiciously. She sank down on the edge of the bed—his bed. Stung by that disturbing revelation, she bolted back to her feet. "Are you the guest who is coming to dinner?"

Lucien was caught off guard by her questions. Did she truly know nothing about him? What game was Adrian playing here? Had that old goat simply become so bewitched by this unique female that he had signed the inheritance over to her without her knowledge?

Surely not. Lucien knew how shrewd this woman could be. She had outsmarted him a dozen times already. She must be playing this charade for his benefit.

When Lucien advanced on her, Micaela retreated into the sitting room. Ironic, he thought. In living memory no other woman had avoided him. He wasn't sure how to react or proceed with this misfit of a female.

Micaela scampered across the sitting room, intent on escaping through the door. Her mind was buzzing in confusion. Why hadn't Adrian mentioned a grandson? Probably because Lucien was the black sheep who embarrassed the family. Who would want to admit kinship to this devilish philanderer?

Micaela nearly leaped out of her chemise when a velvet-clad arm shot past her shoulder to block her intended escape route. "Mr. Saffire, I—"

"Lucien," he corrected at close range.

Micaela marshaled her courage and pivoted to confront the muscular man who towered over her. "Please remove your hand from the door and let me pass."

"Running away again, squirt?" he challenged.

"That depends."

"On what?"

"On your intentions, of course. I have no desire to find myself mauled like the poor woman in New Orleans."

Lucien inwardly winced. True, his intentions weren't all that noble at the moment. This lively beauty stirred his blood, no question about that. She had the most kissable mouth ever etched on a woman's face and eyes that intrigued and beguiled. To see her was to want her, though he knew she wanted nothing to do with him—she, with her distorted impressions of passion.

When Lucien didn't respond, or remove his hand from the door, Micaela eyed him warily. "Are you here to antagonize me because of that fiasco on your ship?"

"Possibly."

Micaela backed away from the powerful threat of his muscular body, the arousing scent that was disturbing her ability to think clearly. "Please leave or allow me to do so," she ordered brusquely.

Before she could retreat another step, Lucien slipped his arm around her waist and drew her to him, pinning her between the door and his masculine length. The feel of his virile body molded familiarly to hers threw Micaela into instant panic. She gouged him in the midsection with her fist and tried to fling herself from his arms.

Lucien grunted in discomfort, but he recovered in time to haul Micaela back to him. He was damned tired of chasing this female. Since the moment he had walked into his bedroom, he'd had the impulsive urge to taste those sensuous lips. If nothing else, he was going to enjoy a kiss for consolation.

True, Lucien knew he was scaring her witless, but if ever a

woman needed to be kissed properly it was this woman. She needed to know that his was not the kiss of death or the touch of torture. Damn it, this was for her own good as well as his.

When Lucien curled his hand beneath her chin, tipping her face to his, Micaela's heart slammed against her ribs. She could tell by the way his gaze fastened on her lips that he intended to punish her with a kiss. Not that again! Carlos Morales's kisses had been punishment enough.

"Don't you dare, damn you," she sputtered, trying to turn her head away.

"Oh, but I do dare," Lucien assured her. "It's time you learned that kissing is nothing like taking a dose of poison."

Before his lips could claim hers, though, the door of the adjoining bedroom creaked open. Lucien scowled at the untimely interruption. It seemed Micaela's first lesson in passion was going to have to be postponed. Damn. . . .

Six

"Lucien? Micaela? Where are you?"

Adrian walked toward the door that joined the boudoir to the sitting room. "Lucien?"

Reluctantly, Lucien dropped his hands and pivoted toward his grandfather. He smiled tightly as he emerged from the shadows, leaving Micaela to half collapse against the door.

"My, my, aren't you full of surprises, Grandfather."

Adrian grinned smugly. "I wanted this to be a memorable occasion." He glanced around Lucien's broad shoulders. "I assume you met Micaela Rouchard. Where did she go?"

Micaela hurriedly stuffed herself into her gown, then sailed past Lucien to latch onto Adrian's arm. She flung Lucien a glower that assured him that he had come as close to her as he was ever going to get.

"I hope my grandson didn't startle you," Adrian cooed, patting the dainty hand that was curled around his elbow. "He can be such a beast at times."

Lucien winced at Adrian's choice of words. Micaela was taking Adrian's comment to heart.

"Now that you have made each other's acquaintance, shall we dine?" He glanced at Lucien and smiled craftily. "I asked

Micaela to plan dinner. What did you say was on tonight's menu, my dear? Scalloped oysters and crab soup? Ah, my favorite!''

Oh great, thought Lucien. Scalloped oysters on top of all else.

As Adrian strode away, Lucien frowned ponderously. He wished he knew what game his grandfather and this cunning female were playing with him. But only God and Adrian knew what the devil was going on around here.

Lucien had the unshakable feeling he was going to find out after supper.

Vance nearly dropped his wine goblet when Adrian appeared in the dining room with a young woman on his arm. It took only one glance for Vance to recognize this stunning beauty. How had she gotten here? Lucien had hunted high and low, and here she was, right in Adrian's home. Unbelievable!

"Micaela Rouchard, I would like you to meet Vance Caven-dish. He is the captain of one of the ships in the Saffire fleet, as well as an old friend of the family," Adrian introduced. "His parents own a plantation on the Ashley River, and his grandfather was one of my dearest friends."

Micaela bit back a grin when the man she had turned into a human jar of molasses bowed politely. Since he pretended this was their first meeting, she followed his lead. Awkward though it was, Micaela managed to maintain a dignified air when Adrian seated her between Vance and Lucien.

She suspected both men were as uncomfortable as she was, since they shoved their scalloped oysters around with their forks without eating them. She had never been partial to oysters, but since they were Adrian's favorite she had placed them on tonight's menu.

Throughout the meal, Lucien's arm brushed against hers, constantly reminding her of his disturbing presence—as if there was a chance she could forget! She felt like a skittish colt being gentled and tamed. For what purpose? She definitely had her suspicions about this devilish rakehell.

Earlier, when Micaela had found herself trapped in Lucien's arms, she had been hounded by conflicting emotions. Her naive body tingled at the feel of his muscular torso pressed to hers, but her mind screamed warnings. Physically appealing though he was, she didn't trust this blue-eyed devil.

"Micaela, would you like to take a stroll this evening?" Adrian inquired while Hiram cleared the table.

Would she ever! Lucien was suffocating her with his presence. The masculine scent was clogging her senses. "Yes, I am in need of fresh air," she enthused.

"Vance and Hiram can accompany you. Lucien and I need to speak privately." He grinned at his grandson. "I believe there are a few things Lucien would like to discuss with me. Are there not, my boy?"

Lucien smiled as politely as he knew how. "Mmm, yes, now that you mention it, there are one or two points I think we need to clear up."

"I rather thought so."

Employing gallant manners, Lucien rose to assist Micaela from her chair. He pressed a kiss to her wrist, though she tried to pull away for fear of having her fingers bit off at the knuckles. "It has been a pleasure, Micaela," he murmured before he turned and strode toward the study.

Adrian followed his grandson into the room and closed the door. With a careless ease that revealed none of his frustration, Lucien took a seat across the table from Adrian who stared pensively at the chess board in front of him.

"Shall we begin?" Lucien prompted.

"Begin what? This game of chess? Or are you waiting to hear another apology that you never accept?"

Lucien's face closed up. "I want to know what game you're playing with me. Then I will determine how, when and *if* I want to play along."

Reaching out with a gnarled hand, Adrian moved the ivory pawn to another square on the chess board. "I have signed away your inheritance. Does that disturb you, Lucien?"

Lucien considered his strategy before he repositioned the ebony pawn. "I have my own fortune and you know it."

"Then you care nothing for the family legacy?" he asked as he moved his rook.

"That depends on the strings you have attached to it." Lucien sent his queen's bishop for a walk.

For several moments both men studied the chess board in profound concentration. In a daring move, Adrian left his queen vulnerable to attack. Or was it merely a baited trap? Lucien wondered suspiciously.

"The strings I have attached are these," Adrian said eventually. "Micaela doesn't know that she has inherited my fortune. I have not mentioned anything about my family to her. She never knew of you until you arrived tonight. And in turn, I have respected her wish for privacy about her previous life. I hired her as my companion and she accepted, after much persistence on my part. She fusses at me for showering her with gifts and garments which she insists she doesn't need and intends to pay for. She has taken over management of my home and delights in the responsibility.

"For her, there are no strings attached to my generosity. She has no demands to meet." Adrian smiled craftily. "If you want to reclaim the fortune she now commands, then you must court her in order to win it back. But don't think for one minute that I won't tell her that I have given her the fortune that once belonged to you."

Lucien sank back in his chair, staring at Adrian in disbelief. Adrian had stacked the deck against Lucien in a daring challenge. The old buzzard was trying to keep Lucien off the seas, and in Charles Town, to court his rightful inheritance. That sneaky old goat!

Adrian also claimed that he would inform Micaela that the fortune belonged to Lucien. In essence, Adrian would leave Micaela thinking that Lucien was only courting her for the money she controlled. Hell and damnation! How many nights had Adrian stayed up to conjure this scheme?

Lucien might just as well spread invisible wings and fly to the moon. Considering how leery Micaela was of men—of Lucien in particular—she wouldn't be receptive to pretentious flirtation. The only conceivable way to reach that kind of woman was through deep, abiding love and constant reassurance that his intentions were pure.

Lucien had no intention of doing any such thing! He had vowed never to love again. He knew all too well the anguish and grief that came from loving and losing. He refused to put himself through that kind of hurt again, not even for his own legacy!

Besides that, Lucien was scheduled to sail to the West Indies in two days. He didn't have time for Adrian's exasperating games.

"It would have been simpler if you had played the matchmaker by signing our lives away like a royal prince and princess," Lucien muttered irritably.

"Ah, wouldn't it?" Adrian eyed his grandson with devilish delight. "It is true that Micaela is the one I have chosen for you, for there isn't another woman like her in the colony. She is witty, wise beyond her years, and yet charmingly innocent."

Adrian didn't know the half of it! Micaela was a man-hater whose weird notions about passion were a hurdle a saint might not be able to overcome. Lucien, self-admittedly, was no saint.

"If I decide to accept this outrageous challenge to win her affection, she will assume I am romancing my lost fortune. It might take years to gain her trust and devotion."

"Exactly." Adrian didn't bother denying it. "Micaela is bound to hear about your infamous reputation with the ladies. You will have to bend over backwards if you hope to redeem yourself in her eyes. You will also have to stay home where you belong, instead of sailing from sea to shining sea." He moved his queen across the chess board and grinned wryly. "Admit it, boy, this is one challenge you are going to have to accept or risk losing half your fleet to my beneficiary."

Muttering, Lucien's arm swept across the table, scattering kings, rooks and pawns everywhere. "You never learn do you, Grandfather? Tampering with my life once wasn't enough for you, was it? Well, it was enough for me. You can give Micaela all the fortune, because I have no need of it. But ask yourself this, old man—" Lucien leaned forward. "What if the woman is promised to another? Maybe that's what lies in her previous life. Or maybe she is playing you for a fool. Perhaps the truth is that you set a trap for yourself and will find yourself penniless when you reveal that she is in control of everything you own."

Adrian slumped back in his chair, forced to consider what Lucien said. But it only took a moment for Adrian to reject the accusations. Micaela was anything but manipulative or pretentious. Furthermore, he refused to believe she might be married. She possessed a kind of naive innocence that was impossible to mistake. That was evident each time she glanced at Vance and Lucien during the meal. Adrian was a fair judge of character, and he relied on well-honed instincts. No, he assured himself, Micaela had never been intimate with a man.

"Of the three of us, I believe Micaela to be the purest of heart and spirit," Adrian said in her defense. "She is enthusiastic, sincere, and assertive. If you had been here this week to see her in action, you wouldn't doubt her for even a second. The servants dote over her. They rush to assist her. My ledgers and accounts are balanced for the first time in years. And because she is so vibrant and alive, I feel reborn. She is good for my soul."

Lucien almost laughed aloud when Adrian got carried away defending the chit's honor and integrity. "If she is personally responsible for the dramatic change in you, then perhaps you should marry her."

"She doesn't need an old man," Adrian snorted. "Surely you agree that she is witty, attractive and desirable."

"That is beside the point."

"You wouldn't consider her for a wife, even if I had not set such a difficult challenge before you?"

"I vowed never to marry after—" Lucien slammed his mouth shut and glared at his grandfather.

"People can change their minds," Adrian said softly.

"But some people never change," Lucien countered. "You are still the meddling old rascal you always were."

"And you are still the bullheaded billy goat of a man that you always were," Adrian retaliated.

Their eyes locked in a visual duel, like exploding pistols at twenty paces.

"Fine then," Adrian said between his teeth, "if you aren't man enough to win the heart of a true lady, go back to your meaningless encounters with your harlots, sail the seven seas in your private cabin. I have found a trustworthy substitute for my prodigal grandson. And when I take Micaela to the plantation, I'm going to sit back and watch her manage my properties better than I can. You will be the one whose life bears no pleasure or meaningful purpose, not me.

"I have begged and pleaded with you to put the past behind us. I told you I deeply regret my part in the tragedy, but I did what I thought was right, and you continue to punish me because of it. Perhaps it is high time I punished you for believing Cecilia was worthy of your love. But you were too blind to see, too stubborn to listen—"

"Don't speak her name, damn you," Lucien hissed. His fist slammed against the table like a pounding gavel. "I loved her. No matter how you choose to rationalize and twist the truth, I cared for her and you killed her."

"I did no such thing!" Adrian protested hotly. "She did that all by herself and you damned well know it!"

Lucien raged on, determined to speak his piece once and for all. "Now you have the unmitigated gall to dangle my inheritance in my face like a carrot before a mule, challenging me to court the woman *you* have decided I should marry. And worse, you will let her believe the worst about me from the very onset of this ridiculous courtship—"

Realizing his voice had risen to a shout, Lucien forced himself to sit back in his chair and haul in the reins on his temper. "What if Micaela decides to deed my wealth to me, because she is so *honest* and *pure of heart* that she knows it is my right to have it? Then you have lost at your clever game. If you signed the fortune over to her, then it is hers to keep or dispense as she sees fit."

Adrian shook his head. "I have already considered that loophole. The contract states that Micaela cannot give my properties away. Since I have faith in her judgment, I expect that if she does marry, she will chose a man worthy of controlling the

Saffire fortune, just as she is worthy of being the granddaughter I never had.''

The silence in the study was as thick as hasty pudding. Both men held firm in their stand, refusing to budge an inch. It seemed the legendary trait had passed through every generation of Saffires.

Finally, Adrian asked, ''Do you accept or decline this challenge, Lucien? I want to know here and now.''

''I decline,'' Lucien replied, his chin uplifted in defiance.

''Why? Because Micaela is too much woman for you to handle?'' he goaded his grandson.

''No, I decline because you served me scalloped oysters for supper and you know I hate them.''

On the wings of that ridiculous excuse, Lucien rose to his feet and strode out the door. By damn, he was going to defeat Adrian at his own game. He wasn't going to waste months courting his inheritance like a proper gentleman. He didn't have the time or the inclination. Instead, he was going to *steal* it back like a damned pirate!

Micaela returned to the townhouse to learn that Lucien had left. Though she was relieved, she was curious to know what had transpired between Adrian and his grandson. She had pumped Hiram and Vance for information, but neither man would explain. All they divulged was that Lucien and Adrian had not seen each other in five years.

When Micaela sought out Adrian, he wasn't in a talkative mood. He sat in the parlor, staring at his wife's portrait, sipping the customary glass of syllabub he drank each night before retiring to bed.

Obviously, Adrian's confrontation with Lucien weighed heavily on his mind. Micaela could sympathize with the old man. Thoughts of Lucien Saffire had certainly kept her off balance—especially after that near brush with disaster in the boudoir!

Bidding Adrian a quiet good-night, Micaela mounted the steps to her room. The moment she stepped into her bedroom a shadow leaped at her. A kerchief covered the lower portion of her face, smothering her shout of protest. Although Micaela fought like a wildcat, she found herself bound, gagged and rolled up in the bedspread like a mummy.

There was no question as to who had pounced on her. She would recognize that man's scent and touch anywhere. She also had a pretty good idea where Lucien was taking her: to his ship for his brand of torture. The beast! she thought as she bucked and squirmed in outrage.

Smiling devilishly, Lucien tossed the wriggling bundle over one shoulder and patted her on the fanny. "Calm down, squirt," he murmured.

Calm down? How could she calm down when she knew what awaited her at this man's cruel hands?

Lucien strode out the terrace door and descended the steps, pausing at irregular intervals to readjust the wriggling bundle that kept shifting on his shoulder. Too bad Adrian wouldn't have the slightest idea what had become of the bait for his trap until it was too late, Lucien mused as he headed toward the waiting carriage.

Vance frowned warily when Lucien placed the squirming bundle on the floor of the carriage. "What the devil have you done? If that is who I think it is—"

"It is," Lucien confirmed as he grabbed the reins and urged the horse into a trot.

"Are you mad?" Vance crowed. "What do you expect to accomplish with this outlandish prank?"

"You should be asking what Adrian did to drive me to desperation," Lucien calmly suggested.

"What did he do?" Vance muttered, clearly disapproving of this underhanded plot.

Lucien smiled wryly as he urged the horse into a faster gate. "I'll explain later."

When Lucien reached the wharf, he hopped down to scoop up his captive. With Vance following in his wake, Lucien marched across the gangplank and descended to the Great Cabin. When he had dumped Micaela on the bed, he reversed direction, tugging Vance with him into the companionway.

"Now are you going to tell me what is going on?" Vance asked impatiently.

Towing Vance far enough away from the locked room, so as not to be overheard, Lucien hurriedly explained. "My grandfather has decided he wants me to marry Micaela in order to control my own inheritance. The old rascal signed everything over to her."

Vance did a double take. "She doesn't know about this scheme?"

"Not yet, and she won't until I decide to tell her." Lucien grinned scampishly. "It was Adrian's intention for me to court her and win her over—properly, of course."

"If she suspects you want to marry her just so you can regain control of your inheritance, it could take months to convince her of your honorable intentions." Vance stared pointedly at Lucien. "And damn it, that is *only if* your intentions *are* honorable—which I doubt they are."

"That is exactly the way Adrian has it figured," Lucien agreed. "He doesn't think I'll have time to cavort all over town, further besmirching the Saffire name, if I am properly courting the woman who controls my inheritance. That old goat wants me to give up my ship and come home to manage the plantation. He thinks he has devised the perfect plan to ground me."

Vance threw back his blond head and laughed. "I have to give the old rascal credit, Lucien. He may be old, but he still has a mind like a steel trap."

"Doesn't he though." Lucien glanced back at the locked door. "Unfortunately for him, I plan to sail to the Indies with a load of cargo in two days. I don't have time for extended courtships and wily games, so I've decided not to play by his rules."

Vance stared suspiciously at his friend. "What in Hades are you going to do?"

"It isn't what *I'm* going to do," he corrected. "It's what *you* are going to do."

"Me?" Vance bleated. "You leave me out of this, Lucien."

"As captain, you have the legal authority to perform marriage ceremonies. That is exactly what you're going to do—tonight. I will concede just far enough to make Micaela my wife, but that is the extent to which I plan to be manipulated by that old buzzard.''

"Lucien, you can't be serious," Vance muttered. "We are not discussing a playful counterprank here. We are discussing wedlock. *Lock,* Lucien, as in now and forevermore.''

"I have never been more serious in my life," Lucien assured him. "Tomorrow I will deliver my new bride back to Adrian, and I will retain control of my inheritance. But I will not sacrifice returning to the sea, just because my grandfather wants to landlock me.''

"You realize, of course, that Micaela may object to this.''

May object? Lucien had no doubt that Micaela would oppose the marriage, so he hadn't bothered to ask her. She was bound to think the worst about him, especially after Adrian filled her in on all the sneaky little details. Lucien had no choice but to do what had to be done. He would deal with his hostile bride when the time came.

"Micaela will be allowed all the freedom she desires once the vows are spoken. After all, this is nothing more than a marriage of convenience.''

"It is a marriage of madness," Vance snorted. "And furthermore, my legal jurisdiction only pertains to the times when I'm at sea—which you will notice that we are *not* at the moment.''

Lucien grinned mischievously. "We will be directly, because I plan to weigh anchor.''

Vance wagged a lean finger in Lucien's smiling face. "If you follow through with this crazed countertactic, you may well be rousing a sleeping tigress who'll come at you with claws bared. Micaela Rouchard doesn't strike me as the kind of woman who takes kindly to decrees. She is extremely independent. Why else would she have stowed away on this ship, then set off to find her own place in the world.

"If I were guessing, I would say that someone else along the way tried to force her to do something she didn't want to do, so she flitted away. She may try the same tactic after you force her into marriage.''

Lucien shrugged, unconcerned. "She is free to do as she wishes once the vows are spoken. This arrangement should suit her perfectly."

"I wouldn't presume to assume what she will think," Vance warned. "She is as much her own woman as you are your own man. This is a drastic mistake."

Lucien didn't have time to stand around arguing the point with his well-meaning friend. The sooner the deed was done the better. Micaela could throw a ring-tailed tantrum if she wanted, but she was going to become his wife. That was the concession he had decided to make to get his grandfather off his back.

Determined of purpose, Lucien strode back to the cabin to prepare for his wedding—or all-out war, as the case turned out to be. Micaela came up fighting the instant Lucien unrolled her from the bedspread.

"How dare you!" Micaela seethed. "Release me at once or I shall have your grandfather—"

Lucien waved off her threat with the flick of his wrist. "It is Adrian's desire that we wed, and so we shall," he said matter-of-factly.

She reacted as he expected—speechless astonishment, followed by vocal objection. "I will not have any man lording over me," she spewed, green eyes flashing, "especially not an abusive monster like you!"

Biting back a smile, Lucien watched her full breasts heave with every breath.

"I do not want or need a husband, now or ever!"

Lucien swaggered forward, watching Micaela plaster herself against the wall to avoid physical contact. "You wouldn't even consider taking a husband who has no intention of *lording* over you, as you choose to put it? Nothing will change except your name," he told her calmly. "You'll have unlimited freedom and adequate funds at your disposal. In fact, our marriage will protect you from men who might have designs on you."

Micaela eyed him suspiciously. "What are you getting from this ridiculous bargain?"

"A lovely bride." He uplifted his hand to trace the belligerent line of her jaw, but she slapped his arm away as if he were a pesky mosquito. "I'm giving you your way in all matters, except for the marriage itself. I think I'm being extremely generous."

"And *I* think you're quite mad," she said with great certainty.

"We are both pawns in my grandfather's scheme," he insisted. "But once the ceremony is concluded we can get on with our separate lives."

The rap at the door indicated the makeshift preacher had arrived. Vance stalked inside, looking none too pleased with the situation. "Shall we get on with this farce?" he grumbled, shooting Lucien a reproachful glare.

When Micaela darted for the door that Vance had neglected to lock, Lucien hauled her to his side. She kicked his shins to splinters, and Lucien was forced to twist her arm so far up her back to restrain her that she shrieked in pain. Lucien knew he was confirming her belief that he was a beast when it came to women, but damn it, the little spitfire wouldn't stand still!

While Vance hurriedly rattled off the first and second paragraph of the wedding vows, Micaela glared meat cleavers at her soon-to-be husband. She noted that Vance skipped over the part about loving, honoring and obeying since she'd made it clear that love, honor and obedience wouldn't be a part of this exasperating bargain.

"Lucien, do you take this—" Vance glanced at Micaela's outraged expression and smiled in spite of himself, "—this furious, unwilling woman to be your lawfully wedded wife?"

"I do," Lucien declared.

"And Micaela, do you take this madman—who is going to regret his actions when he comes to his senses—as your lawfully wedded husband?"

When she refused to respond, Lucien gave her arm a persuasive twist. "Ouch! Damn you!"

"We'll take that as a yes," Lucien insisted.

He retrieved the ring he had intended to give to Cecilia, then slipped it on Micaela's finger. The gold band was a few sizes too big, but Lucien decided it was appropriate. The ring was as loose as the ties that bound husband and wife in this unholy state of matrimony.

"Then by the powers vested in me—and I sorely wish they weren't—I pronounce you madman and wife," Vance concluded. "You may kiss the bride . . . at your own risk."

Vance slammed the book shut and stalked toward the door. "I also officiate funerals at sea, should one of you fail to survive the wedding night." This remark he directed at Lucien, who was having one helluva time restraining his captive bride. "Congratulations, Lucien, I expect your wedding night is going to be everything you *deserve* it to be."

When the door clanked shut, Lucien promptly locked it. Before he could wheel around to reclaim his grasp on Micaela, volumes of books sailed across the room like hurled grenades, pelting him on the head and shoulders. Agile as he was, he couldn't dodge all the oncoming missiles.

"Stop that!" Lucien barked.

"Curse you, Lucien Saffire," she raged at him. "I swear you'll regret this. I plan to be your bride from hell!"

Lord, Lucien had no idea this misfit female had such a temper! She stood there, in the height of fury, expressing her outrage. He was pretty sure she was devising the most painful way to murder him—first chance she got. And if he didn't exert some control over her, she was going to leave his elegant cabin in shambles.

Determined of purpose, Lucien strode across the room to put a stop to his new bride's furious tantrum. Micaela shrieked when he snaked out a hand to shackle her wrist. When she raised her arm to smack him on the cheek, he caught her flying elbow. Deftly, he knocked her feet out from under her, sending her off balance.

When she collapsed on the floor, he followed her down— and noted the terror in her eyes. He imagined she was reminded of that night when she heard Lucien "torturing" the strumpet in New Orleans. Lucien cursed under his breath. Micaela was forcing him to turn into the beast she believed he was, and he could do nothing to change her low opinion of him while she battled him tooth and nail—literally biting and clawing at him in an attempt to escape. After several anxious moments, Lucien plopped down on her belly and held her arms above her head.

"You bastard," Micaela seethed. "I will hate you forever for this!"

"I promise to climb off the instant you calm down," he tried to bargain with her.

"I refuse to calm down until you climb off!"

Lucien muttered in frustration. If he climbed off, he suspected she would tear him to shreds. And damn it, he had no desire to make Micaela more of a man-hater than she already was. He didn't want to hurt her, but this marriage wouldn't be legal and binding unless they were man and wife in every sense of the word. If it wasn't consummated, Adrian would find a way to drag out this whole mess.

It wasn't that Lucien wasn't eager to do his husbandly duty, for he'd been intrigued by this lively female since the moment he realized the clever waif was a woman—a very desirable and alluring woman. But Lucien had never once forced himself on a woman—despite Micaela's ill-conceived notions. He wasn't about to start abusing women now.

So how the hell was he to tame and reassure this wild-hearted woman that he wasn't a monster? Dear old Shakespeare would have said: Love her, simply love her. Lucien figured his best bet was resorting to seduction—if only Micaela would cooperate— which she wouldn't!

In all his thirty years Lucien had faced no greater challenge. Outsmarting Adrian was mere child's play compared to taming this blond-haired misfit. Lucien cringed at the thought of tying her to the bedposts, for that would confirm her loathing opinion of him. So what was he to do?

Well, damn, he could think of no other solution except restraint. Lucien muttered as he reached for the discarded rope. Micaela had already consigned him to the farthest reaches of hell. He might as well get this over with.

Within a few minutes Lucien had Micaela's arms secured to the headboard, her feet lashed to the footboard. He expected her to burst into tears and beg for mercy, but apparently she was too furious to cry. By the minute Lucien became more aware that his new bride was like no woman he'd known. She didn't use tears as a weapon, and she didn't concede a battle, even if the face of defeat.

This was definitely going to be the kind of wedding night that wouldn't be easily forgotten!

Seven

Rising from the edge of the bed, Lucien strode to the liquor cabinet to pour two drinks. When he sank down beside Micaela, she flashed a glower hot enough to melt the iron off a skillet. He chose to ignore it.

"Here, drink this," he ordered, holding the glass to her lips.

Reluctantly, Micaela sipped the peach brandy and studied him with wary caution.

"Without your knowledge, Adrian drew up a document, naming you as his beneficiary, giving you complete control over the Saffire fortune," he explained.

"But I've asked for nothing," Micaela assured him without a moment's hesitation. "I would have deeded it all to you if I had known."

"That is precisely why Adrian stipulated in the contract that you can't give the inheritance to anyone except your husband or your child. You have become his bait to bring me under his thumb."

He paused to offer Micaela another sip. She reflexively drank. "Adrian is a very determined man," he went on. "He wants to see me wed and settled down to manage the shipping business from port. Adrian is obsessed with handing down the legacy to the next generations, but I haven't been cooperative. Since I haven't taken a wife, my grandfather decided to chose one for me. You, Micaela, are the pick of his crop.''

"Adrian has been nothing but kind and generous to me. I refuse to believe he would be so devious as to force us into wedlock."

Lucien smiled faintly. "You actually like that old buzzard, don't you? Even now, you refuse to admit that he's the root of this problem."

Micaela frowned darkly. "I seem to like him a good deal more than his own grandson does. What caused this feud between you?"

Lucien refused to discuss the incident that still tormented him. "That is between Adrian and me. You and I have to concern ourselves with the arrangements of this marriage that neither of us wants. Adrian has been partially pacified, but you and I will make this marriage suit our individual purposes. You can rule the roost at the townhouse and plantation, if that is your desire. I will continue to ship cargo, just as I've done the past eight years."

"And I won't be forced onto this torture rack but once?" she asked with blunt candor.

Lucien sighed audibly. They were back to that misconception again. "The intimacy between a man and his wife is anything but torturous, Micaela."

"For the man, perhaps," she countered in a resentful tone.

His index finger curled beneath her chin when she refused to look at him. Bringing her luminous green eyes back to his, Lucien smiled engagingly. "What if you discover that lying in my arms brings more pleasure than pain?"

"Knowing what I know, I don't think that's going to happen. Rather, I will cheerfully lie and claim this marriage has been consummated, should anyone ask."

Perhaps Micaela could be satisfied with the lie, but Lucien couldn't. He wanted Micaela. She made his blood run hot. She challenged him, made him want to dispel her ill-conceived notions. Since that moment when he'd come within a hairbreadth of kissing her, he'd been craving a taste of those velvety lips.

"I'm going to kiss you, Micaela," he forewarned as his head moved deliberately toward hers.

Micaela was a bundle of nerves encased in twitching skin. She stared at Lucien as if he were about to thrust a dagger into her heart. "I'd rather you didn't."

Lucien hopelessly shook his head. "I would dearly love to know who left you with such an aversion to kissing."

Her head snapped up, and she stared bitterly at him. "It was my former fiancé, if you must know. I was contracted in marriage against my wishes to Carlos Morales. I was nothing more than the gambit in the bargain. Does the name, and the situation, sound familiar, Lucien? I have traded one disaster for another."

Lucien winced. He didn't appreciate being compared to that cocky Spaniard. He also understood why Micaela was so determined to retain her freedom of choice. Thus far, she had been used for other men's purposes—Carlos's, Adrian's, and now his own.

A wave of tenderness swept over Lucien as he stared at his reluctant bride. He had intended to remain emotionally detached while seeing this wedding done, determined to put Adrian's connivance behind him. Yet, Lucien felt the need to compensate for the torment he had unintentionally inflicted on Micaela. She was the innocent victim who deserved his kindness and consideration.

Furthermore, Lucien felt the overwhelming need to erase the taste of another man's bruising kiss, to convince Micaela that he wanted to give and share passion, not ruthlessly abuse her.

Ever so slowly, he leaned toward her, until his lips were a fraction away from her sweet mouth. Displaying gentle patience, he brushed the lightest breath of a kiss over her petal-soft lips. Although he wanted to drink his fill from her lips, right down to the last succulent drop, he realized this was no longer about what *he* wanted. He needed to assure her that he offered pleasure, not pain. He wanted to dissolve Micaela's misconceptions and inhibitions one by one.

Dedicated to that purpose, he kissed her creamy cheeks, her

eyelids, and the pert tip of her nose. Easing away, he studied her reaction to slow, sensual lovemaking. He smiled to himself when he noted the stunned expression in those enormous green eyes. He rather thought he had taken this mistrusting beauty by surprise.

Lucien's masculine scent hovered over Micaela, fogging her confused senses. She had just realized the difference between Carlos's repulsive kisses and Lucien's brand of seduction. The touch of his sensuous lips left Micaela with the odd sensation that her skin didn't quite fit, as if it were expanding and swelling out of proportion. Muscles and nerves that had been rigid with fearful apprehension melted as he traced the curve of her lip with his forefinger. When his moist lips drifted over her mouth a second time, Micaela found herself responding like a river flowing with its current. And still, Lucien made no attempt to physically overwhelm her. He took only what she offered without pouncing on her.

When he bent to kiss her again, his mouth was like liquid heat on hers—a warm, compelling caress. Rippling sensations coursed through her. Enthralled, Micaela imitated his masterful techniques, marveling at the unexpected pleasure she experienced.

When his fingertips skimmed her neck to swirl over the fabric of her bodice, hot splinters of desire pierced her. She gasped when Lucien spread a path of featherlight kisses over her collarbone. When his warm breath whispered over the swell of her breast, Micaela felt herself straining against the confining ropes. When he tugged away her lacy chemise to expose the dusky crests to his hungry gaze and flicking tongue, Micaela felt a flood of unexplainable need spread through her.

"Exquisite torture," Lucien murmured against her quivering flesh. "There's a difference. One brings pain, the other pleasure. It was never my intent to hurt you, but rather to pleasure you, Micaela."

The newness of a man's hands and lips on her body taught her shocking discoveries about intimacy and erased her notions of endured torment. A moan tumbled from her lips when he teased her taut nipples, plucking gently until she arched toward him. Fire sizzled through her blood when he bent to suckle one aching peak, and then the other.

His hands were never still a moment, and Micaela could no longer keep track of where they wandered while her mind was stumbling down the darkened corridors of desire. She was amazed at the raw hunger gnawing at her. Lucien's tender kisses and light caresses called forth an answering response. She longed for the freedom to explore every muscular inch of him, to return the pleasure that multiplied with each accelerated heartbeat.

When his hand dipped beneath the hem of her gown to skim across her thigh, Micaela gulped for air. White-hot sensations stole through her. His hand glided slowly up to her waist, pushing her pantaloons out of his way. When his fingertip teased the ultrasenstive flesh between her thighs, her groan of sweet torment died beneath his kiss. He cupped her tenderly, stroked her. His fingertip delved into her most secret places, imitating the thrusting motion of his tongue.

Indescribable pleasure sent her senses reeling. His thumb brushed over her aroused flesh as he teased her with his fingertip. The hot rain of desire burned through her, making her shiver uncontrollably. When he lifted his hand to trace her lips, she tasted her own hunger for him, and the thought sent wild pulsations rushing through her. His mouth slanted over hers, sharing the taste of her response, and Micaela began to ache with such profound need that she swore she would scream if he didn't satisfy the burgeoning ache he had aroused.

"Lucien, please," she gasped, uncertain what she wanted and needed from him. "Do . . . something. . . . Make the ache go away. . . ."

Lucien inwardly groaned as he dipped his fingertip into her silky heat and felt her burning around him like liquid fire. He was burning *with* her, sharing her answering response, he realized. In her innocence, he discovered a new dimension of passion—one so pure and sweet and spontaneous that it took his breath away.

When he raised his head he saw the spark of passion flaming in her eyes. Unfulfilled need buffeted him like a tidal wave.

He knew he had aroused her beyond her wildest expectations and could satisfy his own raging hunger without a battle. But something about this woman compelled him to do more than fulfill this marriage contract. It was no longer a question of legality. This proud, willful female had touched emotions that he thought long dead and buried. He wanted to give her a night of inexpressible pleasure, to teach her that not all men took from women without giving in return.

Lucien caressed her intimately, feeling her wild spasms of pleasure quivering against his fingertip. He slipped two fingers into her honeyed heat, spreading her slowly, gently, filling her completely, tugging at her and then holding her suspended in rapturous sensations while her feminine essence secretly caressed him.

"Lucien? What is happening? I swear I'm burning up inside. . . ."

"And you'll swear you're dying," he murmured before his hot tongue encircled the coral tips of her breasts. "That is the magic of desire, Caela. It offers the sweetest, most gratifying kind of death—the kind that brings you back to life again and again."

Micaela didn't understand what he meant, but she was certain her heart was going to beat her to death before she could solve Lucien's puzzling riddle. Her senses were so saturated with the taste, scent and feel of his powerful body that she felt as if she were sinking into a steamy fog. Shock waves riveted her when his fingertips and flicking thumb tormented her to the limits of sanity. Feverish pulsations pelted her like bullets, converging into a long, nerve-shattering convulsion of pleasure.

Vaguely, she felt the ropes fall away from her wrists. Impulsively, she glided her arms over his shoulders, feeling the whipcord muscles of his back flex and contract beneath her untutored touch. When she would have clung to him as though he were her anchor in a storm-tossed sea, he withdrew to untie her ankles. Her face flushed with embarrassment when he removed the last of her garments, leaving her naked to his all-consuming gaze.

When Micaela tried to cover herself and turn her head away,

Lucien framed her face in his hands. "There's no shame in this," he whispered. "You're absolutely exquisite. I've never known anything so pure or lovely." Reverently, he kissed her. "I need your touch. Soothe the ache of wanting you beyond bearing. Touch me the way you want to be touched, so I can learn all the ways to pleasure you."

Micaela reached up to skim her hand over his bronzed chest, following the thick matting of hair that descended down his waist to disappear into the band of his breeches. When she pressed her lips to his flesh, Lucien's heart slammed into his ribs—and stuck there. He had never set such a slow, sweet cadence when he took a woman to his bed. And never had he been so aware of each kiss and caress. Neither had he been so conscientiously patient with a woman. But the price demanded to be part of Micaela's first experiment with passion was that he give all the tenderness in his power to give.

And still this exquisite moment seemed to demand more. More, Lucien was afraid, than he knew how to give. He had just begun to earn this wide-eyed innocent's trust. His instruction in intimate pleasure was far from over. Lucien wasn't sure he possessed the kind of self-control needed. Holding himself in check was torture. He felt as if *he* were on the rack—pulled and stretched in all directions by passion that reached phenomenal proportions. He wanted her like hell blazing, but his torment came in knowing he couldn't rush her from innocence to womanhood without frightening her again.

The first hurdle to overcome was dealing with the shock of seeing a naked man, Lucien realized. In the past, he'd never given much thought to shedding his clothes and easing into bed. He was giving it considerable thought now.

Almost hesitantly, he unfastened his breeches and tossed them aside. Sure enough, Micaela shrank away, staring at him goggle-eyed. He reached out to fold her clenched fist in his hand, leading her fingertips to the velvet pulse of his manhood. When she would have recoiled in profuse embarrassment, Lucien held her hand against his aching flesh, then leaned down to kiss her.

"We are at each other's mercy," he whispered. "You have

the power to give pleasure or pain, just as I do. I ache for your touch, Caela.''

While she held him tentatively in her hand, Micaela heard him groan. She remembered the ragged gasps and moans that had escaped her when Lucien brought her to dizzying plateaus of pleasure. Suddenly, she realized what she had heard when she had been *under* Lucien's bed, rather than *in* it. His skillful seduction had dragged the sounds of rapture from her lips, and she wanted to draw those same sounds from him. But she had only begun to explore him when he eased her to her back.

"I can wait no longer," he panted. "I need you beyond bearing."

When he guided her thighs apart with his knees, Micaela clutched him to her, prepared to give herself up to the passion she saw glittering in his eyes. But when Lucien surged toward her, taking masculine possession, pain exploded like a lightning bolt. Micaela shoved at him, trying to twist away.

Lucien felt as if he had taken a bullet through the heart when he saw the look in her eyes. He felt as if he had broken the trust she had placed in him, as if he had betrayed the faith she put in him not to hurt her. He would give anything to spare her this pain, to erase that look of wounded betrayal.

"I'm sorry," he murmured. "It can't be helped, no matter how gentle I try to be. But I swear I will compensate for your pain. Just relax, love." His lips fluttered over hers as he moved slowly within her. "If I could bear this initial pain for you I would. Believe that, for it is the truth."

He took her lips beneath his as he pressed deeply inside her, breaking the last barrier of her innocence. Micaela bit back a cry, so tense and terrified that she couldn't make herself relax. For a moment, Lucien stilled, giving her time to adjust to the intimate invasion. She swore he was absorbing her very being, stealing her strength, her will, her very identity.

His whispered assurances began to ease the apprehension roiling through her. Finally, she began to relax, to adjust to the newness of passion. He withdrew, then gently guided his hips to hers, setting a slow pace that summoned that aching need that had consumed her before she experienced the stab of pain.

His gentleness and consideration touched her deeply. Micaela realized that beneath Lucien's veneer of cool detachment beat the heart of a tender, thoughtful man, not a lusty beast. He was attentive to her needs, aware of her discomfort.

Lured by the knowledge she had gained about this ruggedly handsome American who was now her husband, Micaela gave herself up to the ribbons of pleasure channeling through her. Her body began to move in rhythm with his, meeting his penetrating thrusts. She felt a sense of wonder as desire claimed every fiber of her being.

Suddenly, she was swamped by sensations that left her hot, breathless and disoriented. Her muffled cry broke the silence as Lucien drove urgently into her, appeasing that frantic burst of need that exploded inside her. Micaela never expected the incredible sensations that left her spinning out of control. When Lucien clutched her to him, she felt the shuddering pulsations vibrate through his masculine body and whisper into hers.

In the aftermath of passion, Micaela smiled, thinking how utterly foolish she must have sounded when she spouted off about torture chambers and moans of pained torment. Sweet mercy, how Lucien must have laughed at her naiveté. Micaela bit back an embarrassed giggle. As it turned out, she hadn't known what she was talking about.

"Did I do something amusing?" Lucien asked huskily.

"I was marveling at my own ignorance," she confessed. "Next time I find myself *under* a bed, I will understand what is going on *in* it—"

Her voice evaporated when the reality of Lucien's previous tryst slapped her in the face. The thought of Lucien's sharing such delicious intimacy with dozens of somebody elses stung her pride. She had no right to be jealous, she knew that. Lucien hadn't offered love and devotion in this bargain. She had surrendered her innocence to a man of vast experience. Essentially, he had seduced her into becoming another conquest. She had become such a romantic fool that she had forgotten that Lucien was only securing the fortune Adrian had placed in her name.

"Caela?" He tilted her face up, forcing her to meet his questioning gaze. "What's wrong?"

"Only everything," she burst out in frustration. "Is this when I'm supposed to thank you kindly for the lesson that cured my severe case of ignorance?"

Micaela chastised herself for getting caught up in the mystical spell Lucien spun around her. She may have had a lapse of good sense, but she could not let herself forget what this wedding night was all about—sealing contracts and men manipulating her for their own purposes. Nothing had changed and nothing ever would, she thought bitterly. She might have learned the difference between torture and exquisite torment, but she was still the pawn men used to play their exasperating games. Micaela quickly retracted every kind thought she'd had about Lucien when he was spinning a web of hazy passion around her.

She would not let herself make more of the moment than what it was. Yes, Lucien was skillful enough to make her feel special, unique—as if these sensations they shared never existed until they were in each other's arms. But for him, this was just another night when he appeased his needs. Damn him!

"How many other innocents have you tutored, Lucien?" she asked bitterly. "And how many more have—?"

"Don't spoil this unique moment," he interrupted.

"Unique? My eye," she sniffed. "I imagine you have lost count of the unique moments in your life. I count them as one. What can be memorable about this night for you, except that it happens to be your wedding night. What did you save, and save for me alone?"

Humiliation was beating her pride black and blue. She felt the childish need to lash out at *him*, because *she* hadn't put up a fight. That made no sense, but blast it, he *was* responsible, she reminded herself.

Lucien cursed under his breath when he noticed the trickle of tears Micaela tried to conceal from him. This lovely siren made him wish he'd come to her as pure and innocent as she had come to him. Of course, she wouldn't believe that he had saved something special for her. She wasn't experienced enough to know how little a man could give a woman when he sought only to appease his basic needs.

For the first time in years, Lucien had no desire to get up and leave. He wanted to hold Micaela, to reassure her, even when he knew Adrian's scheme, and this hasty marriage, had erected obstacles between them.

"I did save something special for you," he whispered as she turned her back on him. "One day, maybe you will see it for what it is. But no matter what, you're my wife and nothing is going to change that."

Muffling a sniff, Micaela scrunched up on her side of the bed. She might have become a woman in Lucien's arms, but she was not going to become an utter fool. "Then the bargain is complete," she declared. "Come morning, I expect the right to lead my life while you sail off to lead yours."

"Caela—"

"Those were your terms," she broke in. "Learn to live with them, Lucien. You took what no other man has taken from me and you have no right to ask for more. You have had all of me that you are going to get!"

Lucien sank back on his pillow and stared up at the ceiling. Silently, he cursed his grandfather for this scheme, scolded himself for making matters worse. But it was done, and he was free to come and go as he pleased.

So why did he have this unshakable feeling that leaving Micaela behind when he sailed away wasn't going to be as easy as he thought? Lucien had the remainder of the night to ponder that question, because Micaela rolled up the extra quilt and placed it in the middle of the bed. She made it clear that she was conceding only as much as the bargain required.

Shoulders slumped, hands clasped behind his back, Adrian Saffire paced the confines of his office, pausing at irregular intervals to sip his morning glass of mint-sling. He stared apprehensively out the window, then went back to his pacing.

Since Gretta had arrived an hour earlier to inform Adrian that Micaela couldn't join him for breakfast—because she was nowhere to be found—Adrian had been wearing out the floorboards. He put the entire staff on alert and sent out a search

party, but he had a pretty good idea what had become of
Micaela. Damn that rapscallion, Adrian fumed. He should have
known Lucien was up to something when he stalked off the
previous night.

Adrian muttered a half dozen oaths when he saw the carriage
halt in front of the townhouse. Eyes narrowed in irritation, he
watched his grandson hop to the ground, then turn to lift Micaela
down. Sure enough, that rascal was up to something.

Hissing and sputtering, Adrian scuttled into the foyer and
whipped open the door. "What is going on?" he demanded.
He glanced at Micaela in concern, looking for bruises and
abrasions. "If you harmed this lass in any way, I swear you
will pay dearly for it!"

"I'm only returning my bride before I set sail for the Indies,"
Lucien took supreme satisfaction in saying.

The word *bride* hit Adrian like a doubled fist in the midsection. "What?" he said, jaw sagging.

Lucien grinned. "Your ears do not deceive you, old man. I
said *my bride*. We were married last night at sea. Vance officiated at the ceremony."

Adrian could have cheerfully shot Lucien. His stunned gaze
shifted to Micaela. The radiant smile he had come to anticipate
each morning had vanished. She simply stood there staring at
him as if he were a stranger.

Damn that Lucien. He had cleverly sidestepped all the proper
customs of courtship and forced Micaela to marry him. Nothing
had worked as Adrian had planned.

When Adrian scowled, Lucien burst into laughter. "I was
certain the news of my marriage to the bride of your choice
would please you, Grandfather. I can't tell you how it disturbs
me to see you upset."

Disturbed? Lucien? He was nothing of the kind. He was
grinning in spiteful glee and Adrian wanted to strangle him.
"You think you've outsmarted me, do you? Well, we shall see
about that."

"Another game, Grandfather? I can't wait to hear what challenge you have in mind for me next time."

While Adrian stood there seething, Lucien drew Micaela into

his arms and made a spectacular display of kissing her farewell. Adrian astutely noted that his grandson suddenly became tender and attentive toward his bride. What looked at first like a mocking parody of affection became a sentimentally sincere kiss—if Adrian was any judge of kisses. He was. He had seventy-four years of experience to his credit, after all.

Watching the gentle embrace provoked Adrian's wry smile. Perhaps not all had been lost in this whirlwind wedding. Unless Adrian missed his guess, and he wasn't prepared to admit he had, Lucien felt a certain attachment toward his quickly-acquired and hastily-abandoned wife. Although Lucien delighted in showing his disrespect to Adrian, the young buck was offering respect to Micaela in the way he held her. And *that,* Adrian decided, would bring this cunning rakehell to his knees one fine day. Adrian hoped the hell he lived long enough to see it come to pass!

"If I must concede that you defeated me, then I insist on announcing your wedding by introducing my granddaughter-in-law into society. You will, at the very least, agree to attend your own reception at the plantation, won't you, Lucien?"

Lucien was having too much trouble prying his lips away from sweet temptation to second-guess his grandfather's motive. "I suppose I could find time to put in an appearance at my own reception," he murmured, his gaze, his thoughts, still glued to those entrancing green eyes that could smolder with passion, twinkle with mischief, and blaze with temper—as they were now. "Unless a tropical storm tosses us off course, I'll be there."

"Good, we will hold the party in two weeks. That should allow ample time for you to return to Charles Town." Adrian purposely drew Micaela away from Lucien who was still stroking her arm in a lingering caress.

Adrian shoveled Micaela through the door and closed it behind her. Then he rounded on his smug-looking grandson. "Don't think for one minute that I don't have the foggiest notion what you did to that sweet, innocent lass," Adrian ground out between clenched teeth. "It was bad enough that you stole that girl out from under my nose to marry her without courting her properly first. But if you dared to treat her like those strumpets you parade through your Great Cabin, just to infuriate me, I swear by all that is pure and good in this world that I'll make you regret it. You may have reclaimed your inheritance, but I will make sure Micaela understands what it means to be cherished by a man.''

Lucien's brows flattened over his narrowed blue eyes. ''What the hell is that supposed to mean?''

''Exactly what you think it means,'' Adrian said, and smirked. ''If a woman marries a man who purposely nurtures his notorious reputation, then it's only fair that she pick and choose her lovers during her husband's absence. In fact, while Micaela is in my care, I will see that she never lacks for masculine attention.''

Although Lucien recoiled at the threat, he vowed not to give his grandfather one smidgen of satisfaction. ''Do you think I care?'' he said with a reckless shrug.

''I really don't give a damn what you think, Lucien,'' Adrian said sharply. ''When you return, you might have the distinction of being married to the most sought-after beauty in the colony. We shall see if your male pride can tolerate the idea of having several young men taking your place—in every sense of the word—beside your bride.''

Having delivered that parting shot, Adrian slammed the door in Lucien's face. There, let that scamp chew on that possibility while he was at sea and see how much he liked it! This feud wasn't over, Adrian mused, not by a long shot. Adrian wasn't going to be satisfied until he brought that ornery grandson of his to heel and made him sit like a trained dog!

Scowling, Lucien lurched around and stalked to the carriage. Well, what did he care if Micaela gallivanted around town? He had accomplished his objective, hadn't he? He had married his inheritance without falling into Adrian's trap. Lucien had wedded and bedded his bride. The marriage was legal and binding, just like Adrian's damned document.

Adrian had gotten what he wanted—to see his wanderlust

grandson wed. Lucien had what *he* wanted—unlimited freedom. This marriage would work to his convenience, as well as Micaela's. In fact, all things considered, the three of them had reached a compromise—sort of. Life would go on as usual for Lucien. Adrian would have an enchanting companion to amuse him, and Micaela would have security, protection and wealth. A fair bargain for one and all.

Lucien snapped the reins, sending the steed into a trot. Two blocks later he was muttering under his breath. Although Micaela was out of sight, she wasn't out of mind. Try as he might, Lucien couldn't forget that incredible night in Micaela's arms. She had left him feeling vulnerable and out of control for the first time in his life. Each time that blond-haired beauty's image flitted through his mind, he felt the coil of desire unraveling.

The poignant memory would fade soon enough, Lucien convinced himself. Soon, his bride would be another insignificant interlude in a long line of shallow affairs. Lucien had vowed five years ago that he wouldn't let his emotions become involved. Loving and losing Cecilia had been pure hell, and he wasn't going to let himself care that deeply for a woman again. Love could tear out a man's heart and crush it. Love was not going to be part of this bargain, he assured himself. The only lady Lucien craved to obsession these days was the mistress of the sea. She could be gentle, untamed, and challenging, but she never ripped a man's heart to shreds.

Lucien had done what he had to do to counter Adrian's scheme. He would return to his wedding reception, playing the role of a gentleman for the duration of the night. Then he would set sail again. His life would be back on its even keel, and he would be satisfied.

On that confident thought, Lucien returned to the wharf to load the cargo bound for the Indies.

Eight

Micaela knew Adrian felt guilty about his part in this whirl-wind marriage the instant she turned her wounded, accusing gaze on him. He dropped his head like a scolded puppy.

"I trusted you, Adrian," Micaela whispered. "I thought you were my friend."

"I'm sorry, Micaela."

He clutched her hand and frowned at the golden band. Micaela knew without asking that the ring must have been meant for Cecilia. The ring was probably meant to be a disturbing reminder to Adrian. Obviously, Lucien's subtle jab had struck its intended mark.

Micaela stared down at the gnarled fingers that squeezed her hand, then peered into Adrian's solemn brown eyes. "Friendship is meaningless without honesty." Her gaze pierced him, making him squirm in his skin. "To your grandson, I was a means to an end. Is that all I am to you? Do my feelings, my hopes and dreams count for nothing?"

"If it were physically possible to get down on my knees and beg forgiveness, I would do it, but I'm afraid these rusty joints would lock up," Adrian said quietly. "I truly am sorry, lass.

I was so fiercely determined and desperate to have my grandson back that I considered little else.''

''Now that I've been caught in the middle of this ongoing feud, and used as a pawn by you both, I think I have a right to know what started this cold war,'' she said.

Adrian nodded, then ushered Micaela into the parlor. ''You're right, lass. You deserve to know what can make two grown men behave like selfish ogres.''

Finally, finally! Micaela was going to get to the bottom of this mystery. Her curiosity was killing her.

Adrian dropped down on the sofa and organized his thoughts. ''This feud erupted five years ago when Lucien fancied himself in love with a saucy young woman named Cecilia Dellano.''

Micaela remembered the first night in Lucien's Great Cabin. He had whispered the woman's name with agonized reverence.

''Cecilia's family was struggling to make ends meet on their small upriver farm. I believe she was envious of the prosperity the Saffires enjoyed,'' he continued. ''Cecilia was a pretty lass who could easily turn men's heads, and she was never at a loss for beaux. But Cecilia set her cap for Lucien, because he could provide all the luxuries her family was doing without. She was one of those women to whom social prestige and material possession meant everything. She used her good looks to acquire what she wanted, but she was sorely lacking in the qualities of honesty and sincerity.''

Micaela knew the type, but she reserved judgment on Cecilia, because she suspected Adrian was a mite prejudiced. He obviously had disapproved of the girl. Apparently Lucien held opposing views. Micaela reminded herself there were at least three sides to every story.

''Cecilia began making herself available to Lucien shortly after my son and his wife died in a storm at sea. They were en route to Savannah to make trade arrangements with local merchants. Lucien was devastated by his loss. He wanted something, or someone, to fill the empty space in his life.''

Adrian leaned his head back, staring unseeingly at the wall. ''It was a difficult time for Lucien and me. I didn't believe Cecilia was as sincere and devoted to Lucien as she pretended to be. I tried to advise Lucien that he represented wealth and prestige to Cecilia, and that she was holding onto other options, in case her play for Lucien fell through.''

A muddled frown knitted Micaela's brow. "Exactly what are you trying to say, Adrian?''

"I'm trying to say, as delicately as I know how, that Cecilia was seeing several men while Lucien was at sea. He was trying to reorganize the shipping business after his parents died.''

"How did you know about Cecilia's ... activities?" she prodded.

Adrian squirmed uneasily in his seat, refusing to meet Micaela's unblinking gaze. "Because I hired one of the young swains at the plantation to follow her. It seems Cecilia enjoyed flaunting her beauty and wielding the power she held over men—the more the better, from what I could ascertain. I don't believe Cecilia would have been true to Lucien, even if she had managed to marry him.''

Adrian wasn't painting a complimentary picture of Cecilia Dellano. Micaela wondered if Adrian considered Cecilia unacceptable marriage material for an aristocrat. Perhaps he had grasped at every flaw to discourage his grandson.

"When Lucien announced plans to marry Cecilia, I strictly forbade it. I told him of her reckless flings while he was at sea, but he didn't believe me. Cecilia convinced Lucien that she was pure and loyal. Since he had courted her like a respectable gentleman, he had no way of knowing about her indiscretions.

"If the marriage had taken place, I don't know how she planned to convince him of her innocence. Knowing how deceptive she was, I suspect she would have concocted a way to fool him.''

Micaela frowned. She didn't approve of such scheming, especially after she had become the victim of it so often over the past few weeks.

"When Cecilia learned that I refused to accept her, she confronted me with threats. She vowed to turn Lucien against me if I didn't bless the marriage. It was then that I discovered how spiteful and hateful she could be. Cecilia possessed a duel

personality. Ah, the language that flooded from her lips would
have sizzled the ears off a priest!''

''Did she succeed in causing this dissension that exists
between you?'' Micaela questioned.

Adrian nodded grimly. ''Cecilia went straight to Lucien,
claiming that I tried to buy her off. She told my grandson that
I claimed she wasn't good enough for him, simply because her
family couldn't match the Saffires' prosperity. I had said nothing of the kind,'' Adrian said emphatically. ''It was her duplicity
that I disliked. In Lucien's presence she was all adoring smiles
and gushing devotion. I swear, I've never met anyone who
could change personalities as quickly and convincingly as that
female did.''

Although there might have been three versions to every tale,
Adrian was so intense in the telling that Micaela was convinced
he spoke the truth. Apparently, Lucien had sided with Cecilia
and refused to heed his grandfather's warning.

Micaela stared intently at Adrian. ''Do you believe Lucien
loved Cecilia, despite her failings?''

Adrian sighed audibly as he pondered the question. ''I believe
that because of the tragedy that had befallen us, Lucien wanted
to fall in love. He was too proud and stubborn to admit he was
wrong about Cecilia. Even Vance had heard the rumors and
tried to persuade him to retract the proposal. But Cecilia never
allowed Lucien to see the manipulative, deceitful side of her
nature. She turned on her tears and smiles to suit her purpose.
She treated Lucien like royalty, catering to his every wish, and
he misinterpreted her manipulation as devotion.

''I firmly believe that a man is never so easily deceived as
when he doesn't care if he is,'' Adrian said. ''Lucien was
looking for stability in his world turned upside down, and he
didn't want to believe that Cecilia had more use for his pouch
of coins than for his heart.''

''But if Lucien felt so strongly about the match, why didn't
he simply defy you?'' Micaela asked, puzzled. ''He was of
legal age to marry, wasn't he?''

Adrian's gaze dropped to the knotted fists on his lap. His
very posture, the tautness of his body, were outward indications

of his inner turmoil. He suddenly looked older than his years, much more vulnerable.

"During our last confrontation, I told Cecilia that I was not turning control of the fortune over to Lucien, except in the form of a modest living allowance from trust accounts. Cecilia stormed out the door of the plantation, gushing crocodile tears, shrieking about how she would get even with me, one way or another." He paused, inhaled a fortifying breath and stared bleakly at Micaela. "And then Cecilia . . . killed herself."

The words fell like stones in the silence.

Micaela cringed at the tragic ending of the tale. Now she understood why Adrian and Lucien were at such great odds. By taking her own life, Cecilia had proved to both men that what she felt for Lucien was strong, so strong that she chose not to live at all if she was forced to live without her love. Cecilia had made good her threat to destroy the bond between Adrian and his grandson.

Even in death, Cecilia had won Lucien's everlasting devotion and exacted her revenge against Adrian. Cecilia had placed such insurmountable obstacles between Adrian and Lucien that five years had yet to dissolve them.

"Lucien was so overwrought with grief and resentment that he accused *me* of killing her," Adrian burst out. "He found her mangled body at the base of the stone cliff overlooking the river. Lucien actually accused me of *pushing* her to her death to be rid of her!"

After a long, strained moment, Adrian lifted his head, as if emerging from a living nightmare. "I tried everything to rebuild the bridge that separated us, but Lucien refused to speak to me. He began renovations on his schooner, making it his home, shutting me completely out of his life. I begged and pleaded in messages delivered by Hiram and Vance, but Lucien ignored them all.

"I was so desperate to communicate that I even resorted to threats, hoping for nothing more than a continuation of the arguments, anything to break the maddening silence. I wanted to see Lucien happily married, but he set out to ruin his reputation and drag mine through the mud with his. And before you came along, lass, I spent a week interviewing women, hoping to find someone worthy enough to be his wife. Someone whose strength of character and strong will could match him stride for stride.''

''You should have confided in me, Adrian, as one friend to another.''

''Just as you have confided your past to me?'' he countered.

Micaela shrugged. ''I have no intention of dragging you or anyone else into my problems. Mine are better left alone and forgotten.''

''I'm sorry, Micaela,'' Adrian said again. ''In my desperation, I've become as guilty of manipulation as Cecilia. I wanted you and Lucien to have a proper courtship and a true marriage, but if it cannot be, then I will see that you lack for nothing. Despite my scheming, I am exceptionally fond of you.''

Micaela couldn't help herself. No matter what Adrian had done, she couldn't find it in her heart to hold a grudge against him. His purpose had been sincere and noble, even if his methods left much to be desired. He had been thinking with his heart, trying to bring his unruly grandson to heel and make amends. Adrian had taken Micaela in when she had nowhere to go. He had offered her the kind of affection and protection her own supposed father had denied her. He respected her intellect and capability, while most men treated women like witless imbeciles who couldn't entertain a single thought without losing track of it in the cobwebs of their seldom-used minds.

''Please don't leave me, lass,'' Adrian beseeched. ''You have made my life bearable again. I won't dictate to you, as I tried to do to my own grandson, for that has been another of my many mistakes. You'll have all the freedom to live as you please, I promise you that.''

''And you have become my haven.'' Her forgiving smile dazzled like the midday sun, and Adrian beamed in response. ''We will both put the past where it belongs and make the most of our lives. You and I will make the best of this arrangement, agreed?''

''Agreed.'' Adrian opened his arms and clutched Micaela to him in an affectionate hug. ''And now, young lady, I think we should pack for our journey to Saffire Plantation. If you can put that place in the same efficient working order as you have the townhouse, I'll be most appreciative. I have neglected the plantation the past few years, but I'm going to give you free rein to restore it and make it prosper again. I suspect you can make it run as efficiently as Lucien once did.''

Micaela liked the sound of that challenge. Perhaps Arnaud would never know that she was competent and respected for her abilities, but *she* knew. That was all that mattered now. There had been a time when she felt a compelling need to prove herself worthy and competent, having spent her life trying to gain Arnaud's attention, win his affection. But no more.

And furthermore, Micaela had never been one to back away from a challenge . . . except when it came to winning her new husband's love, she amended. That was an impossible feat. Lucien immortalized a woman who was long gone, and no one could take Cecilia's place in his heart. And beginning now, Micaela wasn't going to spare Lucien another thought. She vowed not to let the images of their wedding night soften her resolve toward him. Though it shamed her to think how wildly she had responded in his arms, she refused to let herself be seduced by him again. She was going to make the most of this bargain and enjoy the freedom Adrian offered her.

Eager to meet the challenging task Adrian offered her, Micaela bounded up the steps to pack her belongings. She couldn't wait to put her ideas into action at the plantation. The old patriarch was giving her free rein—something Arnaud would never have done. Life was going to be good for a change, Micaela told herself optimistically. With Adrian, she could prove herself worthy and productive, and she wasn't going to ask or expect more than that.

"Where the hell have you been?" Vance muttered. He slapped the ledger into Lucien's hand, then shoved him into the center of the circle of merchants who were yammering all at once.

Ignoring Vance's curt question, Lucien held up his hand to

demand silence. "Gentleman, we will have the cargo sorted and sold in a few minutes, if you will cease squabbling among yourselves, I assure you that no one will be short-changed. If you will be so good as to pull your wagons to the warehouse, your freight will be loaded for delivery as quickly as possible."

The crowd dispersed within seconds, and Vance's shoulders sagged in relief. "I've been catching flack for more than hour. You know how I hate to negotiate with those greedy merchants. You have a knack for this sort of thing, and I would appreciate it if you wouldn't leave me in charge again."

He stared at Lucien good and hard. "Now where the hell have you been? At the townhouse begging forgiveness for last night's fiasco, I hope. I didn't approve of that ugly affair, in case you failed to notice."

How could Lucien not have noticed the condemning glares and snide remarks Vance interjected into the ceremony.

"You'll be relieved to know that my bride has been returned to my grandfather's safekeeping," Lucien said before he pivoted toward the warehouse. "Adrian was shocked by the unexpected twist I put in his plans, but he got his way and so did I. The compromise was the best bargain we could make."

"And what of Micaela?" Vance fired the question at Lucien's departing back. "You and Adrian made her a victim in all this. How does she feel, or did you even bother to ask?"

"She has unlimited wealth and considerable independence," Lucien tossed over his shoulder without breaking stride. "And since Micaela is a survivor she'll manage quite well—because of, or in spite of me, I suspect."

"Damn it, Lucien, how can you shrug off your new bride?" Vance grumbled. "You treated that poor girl horribly, and I regret my part in that crazy shenanigan. I must have had a momentary lapse of sanity to agree to officiate at that farce of a wedding."

Lucien wheeled around so quickly that Vance, who followed as closely as a shadow, plowed into him. "I did what I had to do," Lucien defended himself. "If you're hounded by guilt, then you can apologize to my bride when you see her. That will be exactly two weeks from now, because you are cordially

invited to attend our wedding reception. If you feel the need
to present yourself as Micaela's knight in shining armor, then
by all means feel free to do so.''

"Thank you for the invitation, but I plan on being ill two
weeks from now," Vance said with a snide smirk.

"Then you can also plan a speedy recovery," Lucien parried
just as sarcastically.

"I will definitely apologize to Micaela, but I will not get
caught up in another power struggle between you and Adrian.
Unless of course, you and Adrian decide to march off the
customary twenty paces and blow each other to kingdom
come.''

"What a brilliant idea," Lucien said with mock enthusiasm.
"Then the fortune will fall to Micaela, and you can marry her.
Now wouldn't that be convenient for the man who seems eager
to become her devoted champion.''

"If the deadly duel takes place, then maybe I will," Vance
shot back. "And maybe *I* should have married her. For certain,
I would have treated her with the respect she deserves. You
have been so busy being spiteful and bitter that you've failed
to notice how utterly charming Micaela is.

"I found that out quickly enough while Hiram and I were
strolling around the gardens with her. She makes the rest of
female aristocracy look like empty-headed twits. Too bad
you're too stubborn to realize how fortunate you are.''

"My God, you sound as if you have fallen head over heels
for her," Lucien said, stunned by the jealous bite that nipped
at his heels.

"What would you care if I had?" Vance snapped. "You're
too busy gloating to notice the worth of the prize. And let me
tell you, Lucien, you don't deserve Micaela. She's too damned
good for you.''

"Maybe I don't deserve her, but I've got her, even if I don't
want her," he burst out in stubborn pride.

"Good, that probably makes you even. If last night's protests
were anything to go by, I don't think she wants you, either!"

Lucien swallowed the biting rejoinder that leaped to his

tongue. Wheeling around, he strode into the warehouse, cursing
Vance's brutal honesty—and his own nagging conscience.

Lucien hated to admit Vance was right. He had treated
Micaela discourteously, forcing her into marriage and then into
his bed. The thought of resorting to tying her to the bedposts
made him grimace in regret. Lord, Micaela would never forgive
him for that, even if he had treated her with tenderness and
patience when he lured her into his arms.

The morning after their night of rapture had been awkward,
to say the very least. Micaela had refused to speak or glance
in his direction. She hadn't allowed him near her until he
encircled her in his arms and kissed her farewell on Adrian's
front porch.

Yet, despite what had come before, and after, their wedding
night, they had created a magical space out of time. They had
ignited a blazing passion in each other. There was no denying
it.

Some marriages didn't have physical attraction going for
them, Lucien reminded himself. He could name a dozen friends
and acquaintances who took wives from their social class, then
merely tolerated the presence of the mothers of their children.
Indeed, those same men saved their passion for their mistresses.

For better or worse, Lucien and Micaela were legally married,
and Lucien had outfoxed the old fox. Now the newlyweds could
get on with their separate lives and play the charade of wedded
bliss at the reception. After that, it might be another five years—
maybe even ten!—before Lucien visited the townhouse or plantation.

Micaela threw herself into renovating the plantation, with
tireless enthusiasm. Just as she had consulted the servants at the
townhouse, requesting suggestions, she met with the plantation
staff. Her sincere concern for the servants and her desire to
make their tasks as pleasurable and manageable as possible
won her the same instant respect she had received in Charles
Town.

Within ten days, the mansion had been scrubbed and dusted

from top to bottom, and the staff never missed their well-earned breaks for rest and refreshment. Micaela labored right alongside the servants, teaching them French and Spanish folk songs to sing while they worked.

When Micaela announced her intentions to whitewash the fences and outbuildings, in order to give the run-down plantation a much-needed facial, the staff volunteered to help. When the job became dull and tedious, Micaela instigated paint-brush battles that resembled dueling sword fights. Squeals of amusement and laughter erupted during the challenges that left opponents smeared with paint rather than blood.

Now and again, war broke out in the ranks, and servants wielding brushes like rapiers entered gay free-for-alls that ended in uproarious laughter.

Chuckling in disbelief, Adrian watched the goings-on from the gallery which overlooked the fence that lined the entrance to the plantation. It still amazed him that this lively female had won the affection and respect of his servants so quickly. They absolutely adored her.

The ongoing paint-brush fights were another example of Micaela's playful methods of turning work into amusement. She taught the staff to find pleasure, no matter what they were doing.

A water fight had broken out the previous day while Micaela and three young male slaves had been mopping the gallery. Before they were through slinging mops and water at each other, a dozen servants arrived to join in the antics. Lo and behold, everyone was singing a merry tune while they mopped every floor in the mansion.

Saffire Plantation had come to life right before Adrian's eyes. The polished walnut banisters and oak floors shined. White paint gleamed in the sunlight, and flocks of sheep grazed the lawn—under the watchful eyes of servants who refused to let the livestock make a meal of the flowers and shrubs instead of clipping off the grass.

The day Adrian announced their departure to attend three consecutive parties in Charles Town, Micaela had rattled off a list of tasks she had hoped to accomplish over the following few days. During her absence, the servants—like the shoemaker's elves—surprised her by completing the chores before she returned.

These days, the servants were more eager to please Micaela than the master himself. But Adrian didn't mind one whit. He delighted in watching this hurricane of a female whiz around as if she had a magical wand in hand.

Deservedly, Micaela had earned the title of mistress of the house. She met every challenge with astounding success. Nowadays, Adrian couldn't wait to rise each morning, anxious to see what task Micaela and her cleaning brigade would undertake. She cajoled the servants into enjoying their work, and she always took time to voice a kind word and compliment for a job well done. She showed such sincere interest in the servants that they broke into smiles at the mere sight of her.

To Adrian's further delight, the parties they attended in Charles Town had been a smashing success. Just as he predicted, men lined up to share Micaela's company. Not only was she an excellent conversationalist, but she was a good listener.

After Adrian let it be known that Micaela needed youthful companionship while her husband was away, a stream of men arrived to vie for her attention. Adrian noted Micaela was not as leery of men as she had once been. She graciously tolerated the troop of admirers who were attracted to her.

And what was most amazing of all, Adrian thought with a wry smile, was the bouquets of flowers that arrived every other day at the plantation. Interesting, wasn't it, that Lucien—for all his stubbornness—had sent flowers to his bride during his absence. The boy's conscience must be working overtime—as well it should—thought Adrian. Why, if one didn't know better, one would think Lucien didn't want his wife to forget about him after all.

"Adrian?"

He glanced down from the gallery to see Micaela standing on the lawn, covered with a coat of paint. She never batted an eyelash at looking like the hired help in her white-washed breeches and speckled shirt.

"Yes, my dear?"

"Do I have permission to spread a coat of paint on the overseer's cottage?" She smiled up at Adrian, her paint-splattered hand shielding the sunlight from her eyes. "Barnaby said I wasn't to touch his precious cottage, for fear I would whitewash his windows. But now that all the outbuildings are shining with fresh paint, the cottage sticks out like a sore thumb."

Adrian stared across the grounds to survey the cottage. Micaela spoke the truth. Barnaby Harpster's cottage looked misplaced in this white wonderland surrounded by clipped grass.

Barnaby was the only person within two square miles who resented Micaela's authority and her presence. There had been a conflict of strong personalities from day one, and Barnaby refused to concede to the efficient lass. Adrian supposed Barnaby saw Micaela as a threat to his position as overseer. Micaela had gotten more done in ten days than Barnaby had accomplished in years. The man's pride was obviously smarting. But fact was fact. The cabin definitely needed paint, even if Barnaby blustered and complained about it. After all, that cottage did belong to Adrian. He would decide if and when to paint it.

"You are quite right, lass," Adrian agreed. "Tell Barnaby that I insist on paint. Just do him the courtesy of sparing his windows, in case another paint-brush battle breaks out in the ranks."

Smiling mischievously, Micaela presented him with a saucy salute, then spun around to trot back to join the paint brigade. Adrian couldn't recall seeing anyone with so much bounce in her step—except for Lucien in his younger days.

Before the loss of his parents, and Cecilia's death, Lucien had been lighthearted and carefree. Then bitterness and cynicism spoiled his temperament. It was a shame Lucien refused to let Micaela's infectious spirit affect him. . . .

Adrian's thoughts trailed off when he saw Barnaby storm around the corner of his cottage to confront the paint brigade. Spinning around, Adrian scurried toward the steps. There was enough friction between the overseer and Micaela without inviting more trouble. Adrian decided it would be best if he issued the order rather than Micaela. Barnaby had stalked into the

mansion four times already, complaining that Micaela was
pushy and domineering and that she was interfering with his
authority over the field hands. Further resentment on Barnaby's
part would only lead to conflict.

Panting for breath, Adrian stepped between Barnaby and
Micaela. Barnaby was in the process of biting Micaela's head
off while she courageously stood her ground, refusing to be
intimidated by the man's bulky size.

With an expansive wave of his arms, Adrian decreed the
cabin would be painted and Barnaby would accept the decision,
like it or not, which he obviously didn't.

Muttering and growling like a cranky bear, Barnaby lumbered off, but not without flinging Micaela a mutinous glower.
While the paint brigade attacked the cottage from four directions
at once, Adrian returned to the house to partake of refreshments
with the staff who had called a mid-morning halt to their chores.

Ah, there was never a dull moment around here, Adrian
noted. He plunked down at the kitchen table to rub elbows with
his servants. He reached for a freshly baked tart, and thanked
the Lord above for the young woman who had put meaning
and renewed pleasure in his life.

Nine

In mute amazement, Lucien reined his steed to a halt and stared down the hill at Saffire Plantation. The neglected estate resembled a show place! My lord, he thought, Adrian must have hired an army of workers to renovate the plantation to its former elegance. Although the gardens were still overrun by a jungle of weeds, the white fences and outbuildings gave the place a neat, clean appearance.

Obviously, Adrian intended to impress the guests he had invited to the wedding reception. The old man must have worn himself out in his effort to prepare for this party.

Swinging down from his mount, Lucien strode up the marble steps. No one appeared at the door to greet him, so he let himself inside. He frowned in puzzlement when he heard laughter echoing behind the kitchen door. Lucien went to investigate.

Lucien halted in his tracks when he saw his grandfather sitting amid the servants, spinning yarns of the early years in the colony. The servants, with tarts and drinks in hand, listened to the old man with rapt attention. At least they *had* been listening, until Lucien breezed in to stare at the informal gathering in stupefied astonishment.

"Lucien? I wasn't expecting you for at least two more days."

Adrian hoisted himself from his chair and turned to greet him. "Your voyage must have been devoid of delays."

Before Lucien could turn to follow his grandfather into the hall, one of the servants scuttled up to place a tart in one hand and a cup of apple toddy in the other.

"Good to have you back, sir." the butler said with a smile. "The staff sends their warmest greetings and we wish to compliment you on your lovely wife. We adore her."

Lucien glanced from his refreshments to the butler's departing back, then focused on Adrian. "What was that all about?"

"The refreshments?" Adrian questioned in mock innocence. "I expect the servants thought you would enjoy food and drink after your journey."

"That isn't what I meant and you damned well know it," Lucien grunted before biting into the apple-filled tart. "Since when do you mingle with the help, and since when do they congregate in the kitchen for between-meal appetizers?"

"All this came to pass after your bride arrived." Adrian informed him. "I put Micaela in complete charge of the plantation. She attacked this run-down estate with energetic enthusiasm, and she scheduled breaks from daily chores as incentive for the servants. You can see for yourself that her methods met with resounding success. These mid-morning and mid-afternoon breaks for snacks and socializing have improved the staff's efficiency and morale. Micaela has only to look as if she wants something done and servants trample all over themselves to volunteer to help."

Adrian smiled smugly as he stepped outside to inhale a breath of air. "I doubt you have acquired the same enthusiastic cooperation on your ships. You should ask Micaela for suggestions on how to increase your crew's efficiency and inject them with high spirits."

The barb stuck like a porcupine quill. "I haven't heard any complaints from my men," Lucien said, offended.

"Of course, you haven't. Crews and servants grumble among themselves, but they seldom voice their grievances to the management for fear of being discharged. In order to know their true feelings you have to mingle with them, ask their opinions, as Micaela does. Have you tried that practice?''

''No.'' Lucien was sorry to admit that he hadn't. He'd spent the past few years trying to cut himself off from the rest of the world, too lost in his own misery to see beyond his private pain.

''Perhaps you should try Micaela's policy,'' Adrian advised as he sank down on a chair to admire the view.

Lucien was aggravated that Adrian raved about Micaela-the-miracle-worker and didn't mention the fact that this was Lucien's first formal visit to the plantation in five years. Clearly, the old man had become exceptionally fond of Micaela. In Adrian's eyes, she could do no wrong.

''Just where is my miracle-working bride who lifts the flagging spirits of all mankind?'' Lucien asked sarcastically. ''Does God's sister take a day off on the Sabbath, or is she too busy recreating the world according to her specifications to rest?''

Adrian's dark eyes narrowed disapprovingly behind his spectacles. ''You needn't be sacrilegious and sarcastic, all in the same breath, Lucien. Your wife is an absolute marvel, so why don't you simply accept that. Everybody else has.''

Lucien opened his mouth to fling another snide remark, but Adrian plowed on before Lucien would wedge in a word. ''Micaela deputized herself as commander of the paint brigade. The last time I saw her, she was attacking Barnaby's cottage with a paint brush. But I don't advise that you go near her right now. She might paint a more cheerful expression on your face, and I know how you delight in being sour these days.''

Lucien, swallowed the last bite of his tart, downed the apple toddy and pivoted toward the steps. ''I'll take my chances with Her Royal Majesty in her kingdom of the Painted Realm.''

''You do that,'' Adrian snickered as Lucien swaggered away. ''Just don't venture too close to Her Highness. She might whitewash your black scowl.''

Lucien muttered an oath that he was thankful Adrian didn't ask him to repeat.

''Oh, by the way,'' Adrian called after him. ''The flowers you sent to Micaela were a nice touch. I must say I was a bit surprised by the gesture. Made me wonder why you were extending such a courtesy to a woman you couldn't wait to drop back on my doorstep. Just why did you send the flowers?''

Lucien ignored his grandfather's goading. Hell, he didn't know why he'd made arrangements to keep the flowers coming to Micaela. He just had. Maybe he had been trying to pave the way for this encounter. Or perhaps he hadn't wanted his new wife to forget him, because putting her out of mind while she was out of sight hadn't turned out to be as easy as he had hoped.

The servants had been mumbling and grumbling among themselves since Barnaby threw his ridiculous tantrum about painting his cottage. Although Micaela appreciated the servants' loyalty to her, she couldn't allow the staff to criticize Barnaby's rude behavior to her. She didn't want to cause friction between the servants and Barnaby. The ongoing conflict was strictly between her and Barnaby, and she didn't want to taint his association with everyone else. Micaela decided it was time for a distraction, something to take the servants' minds off the unpleasant confrontation.

When a groom-turned-painter muttered about Barnaby's disrespectful remarks to her, Micaela wheeled around with paint brush in hand. "Disrespectful, Chaney?" she said, grinning impishly. "Now *this* is disrespectful!" She made two quick swipes with the brush, spreading paint on both his ruddy cheeks.

A playful battle broke out within seconds, and Barnaby Harpster was forgotten. Micaela lurched around to retaliate against the other groom who had whacked her on the shoulder with his paint brush. She turned so abruptly that her elbow bumped the bucket that sat on the step ladder. The pail bounced on the ground, catapulting paint into the air.

Chaney, who was standing directly in the path of flying paint, dived to the ground in the nick of time.

The innocent victim who rounded the corner of the cottage was unaware that paint was flying at him—until it hit him right in the face.

White paint splattered all over Lucien Saffire. Squawking in surprise, he stumbled back, trying to wipe paint from his eyes. He tripped over the rock border of the flower bed. In an effort to regain his balance, he flapped his arms—both of which were covered with paint. He went down in an awkward sprawl, his hand sliding down Barnaby's window, smearing paint on the pane.

Micaela tried not to laugh at the amusing spectacle, but Lucien looked so ridiculous she couldn't help herself. She laughed alone. The servants stood frozen to their spots, fearing repercussions. Micaela strode forward with cloth in hand, still snickering. Instead of handing Lucien the cloth to wipe his face, she stepped over him to clean the paint from the window pane. She had no intention of giving Barnaby another reason to grouse at her. As for Lucien, she rather thought he deserved a slap of paint in the face after he had used her as his pawn and then abandoned her like unwanted baggage.

After Micaela had removed the last speck of paint from the glass she offered the cloth to Lucien. "I think you'll find one dry spot on the corner of the cloth," she said, lips twitching with ill-disguised amusement. "You should have come dressed in more practical garments if you planned to help with the chores."

With as much dignity as the situation allowed—which wasn't much—Lucien wiped the paint from his eyes and mouth and rolled to his feet. He turned his stormy gaze on Micaela who didn't look the least bit repentant. Then he glared at the servants who stood rooted to their spots.

"Who threw the paint?" he demanded in a quiet hiss.

"I did," Micaela said without hesitation. "I didn't actually throw it. I accidentally knocked it off the ladder. You were just in the wrong place at the wrong time." As if her explanation made everything all right, she extended her paint brush to Lucien and smiled brightly. "Would you like to try your hand at renovation?"

Lucien carefully reached out to grab her wrist, avoiding the dripping brush. "No, I would like a word with you, in private."

He propelled Micaela toward the creek, but she twisted away

to toss a reassuring smile to the servants. Chaney, her self-appointed champion, came rushing forward to block Lucien's path.

"You aren't gonna punish her, are you?" he asked anxiously. "If you are, I'll take her punishment. It was really my fault. I was grumbling about Barnaby's nasty attitude toward Micaela. She was only trying to tease me back into good humor by instigating a paint battle."

"Micaela?" One whitewashed eyebrow flattened to a disapproving angle. "Her name is *Lady Saffire* to you, Chaney."

"Now see here, Lucien—" Micaela objected.

He flung up a painted palm to silence his wife, then focused again on Chaney. "Since you have appointed yourself Lady Saffire's *white* knight, let me assure you that I mean her no bodily harm."

Lucien managed a civil smile, wondering why he was so damned irritated with the man who was prepared to die for Micaela. "Now, Chaney, I would appreciate it if you would take charge of the paint brigade. I haven't seen my wife for more than a week. Surely you understand my desire to be alone with her."

Lucien rather thought this all too well-built, and too-good-looking swain understood that desire exceptionally well—judging by the longing glances Chaney sent Micaela's way. Chaney had been a devoted indentured servant the past six years, but he was also all man. Lucien diagnosed the emotion which triggered Chaney's chivalry as a severe case of infatuation.

Damn, leave this woman alone for almost a fortnight and she has men following at her heels, Lucien thought irritably. How many other servants were harboring secret fantasies about Micaela? More than Lucien cared to count, no doubt.

Chaney bowed respectfully—to Micaela, Lucien was quick to note. Then he retrieved Micaela's brush—or was it the good fairy's magic wand? The famed sword Excaliber? Whatever symbolic power that damned paint brush held, Chaney grabbed hold of it and left, none too soon to suit Lucien.

"May your battle be victorious, Sir Chaney, Knight of the Painted Realm," Lucien flung at the retreating groom.

"Later, I will apologize to Chaney on your behalf," Micaela muttered as he shepherded her toward the creek. "You're behaving like a boorish clod. We were only amusing ourselves while we worked. I see no crime in that."

"Chaney is a servant here, or at least he was when I left. Just because you have elevated him to the position of knight doesn't mean I have to tolerate such nonsense. And may I remind you that you are not one of the servants. And you are definitely not Chaney's responsibility," he added pointedly. "If you persist in behaving in such an outlandish manner in his presence, he'll think you are inviting certain intimacies. You might find yourself flat on your back in a pile of hay, Your Majesty. And I'll throw out your knight on his shiny . . . armor!"

Micaela wriggled loose, then glowered at the towering mass of velvet and white paint. "Chaney is more of a gentleman than you can ever hope to be, despite your lordly title," she snapped. "*He* is entertaining and amusing."

"What the hell has that got to do with anything? What Chaney *is,* is a man, and he is falling in love with you, in case you've splattered so much paint in your eyes that you haven't noticed. If you encourage him in the least you'll have his male juices percolating like a tea pot. Is that what you want?"

Micaela was taken aback by the comment, and the question. Surely not. Lucien had misread the situation. Micaela had treated Chaney like her older brother Henri—or at least the way she liked to treat Henri during those few-and-far-between times when Arnaud permitted her to associate with him. Arnaud was cautious never to let brother and sister spend much time together, probably because he thought Micaela would corrupt Henri.

After coming full circle in her thoughts, Micaela glanced at Lucien who had squatted down to cleanse his face in the stream. Her irritation mounted. How dare he try to make something lurid of a blossoming friendship between her and Chaney! And anyway, it was none of Lucien's business what she did—or with whom. Those were the terms of his bargain. He was the

one who laid down the rules, and he could damned well live
by them!

Micaela would have bet her right arm that her rakish husband
had done far more than entertain lusty thoughts while he was
sailing between West Indian ports. She knew he made a habit
of taking women to his bed. Everyone Micaela had met at the
parties in Charles Town had made mention of the fact that
Lucien enjoyed a reputation with the ladies. Micaela had tolerated the embarrassing remarks, but she was ready to take out
her grievances on their true source.

Consequences be damned, Micaela decided as she stared
down at Lucien's hunkered form. She placed her foot on his
back and gave him a forceful shove. His startled squawk erupted
a second before he landed facedown in the water. Bubbles and
ripples undulated in all directions as he floundered to upright
himself.

Micaela smiled in satisfaction. There, served him right. She
felt ten times better after relieving her frustration on this infuriating man who occupied her thoughts far more than she preferred. She hadn't wanted to think about him at all the past ten
days, but she had. She was reminded of him each time another
colorful bouquet of flowers arrived, and she wondered why he
bothered since he obviously had so little respect and use for
her.

Lucien could not believe this misfit's audacity in shoving
him into the creek. Muttering, he slogged ashore. On second
thought, he shouldn't be surprised by her retaliation. This was,
after all, the same sassy, free-spirited imp who eluded him
on his ship and wrestled for freedom during their wedding
ceremony. Lucien reminded himself that he wasn't dealing with
a normal, docile female. Adrian had allowed Micaela to run
wild, doing and saying whatever she pleased, in whatever manner she chose. Why, in a month, she would be impossible
to control—and Adrian wasn't even trying. The old buzzard
encouraged her uninhibited behavior.

Counting to ten—twice—Lucien strode toward Micaela who
looked anything but apologetic. *Defiant* better described her
expression and her stance. Though her shoddy breeches and

shirt were slopped with paint, her delicate features splattered with white freckles, she had a militant look about her. Her glorious mane of curly blond hair was wrapped in a splotched handkerchief and her green eyes sparkled with hostility. Lucien knew what she was thinking when she darted a glance toward the cottage. He could see her thinking it. If he laid a hand on her, she would scream bloody murder and the servants would rush down here to rescue her. Lucien had the unmistakable feeling that if he raised a hand to her, the servants would descend like a swarm of hornets. They were her loyal friends, even if her enemy turned out to be Squire Lucien Saffire himself.

"Feeling better now, squirt?" Lucien inquired.

"Yes, thank you very much for asking," she said smartly. "And thank you for sending the flowers."

"It was nothing."

"I know. That's why I hesitated in bothering to thank you for them."

Lucien blessed her with a roguish grin as he moved a step closer. "Kiss me hello, my dear wife. I've missed you."

Missed her? Ha! He would've missed a festered boil more. Lucien had been as eager to shove her onto Adrian's stoop as she had been to return there.

And Micaela wanted no more of this man's kisses, either. His embraces left her weak-kneed and vulnerable. She might have been the pawn played to counter Adrian's scheme, but she would never become Lucien's devoted whore. Lucien had women aplenty in every port of call. He didn't want—or need— her.

Although Micaela had suffered from a few foolish romantic fantasies that fateful night of her wedding, she wasn't going to make that mistake again. She knew she couldn't leave a lasting impression on a man like Lucien. A woman would need a chisel to carve her initials in that chunk of rock he called his heart. And anyway, she didn't care to win Lucien's affection, because it didn't matter. *He* didn't matter to her.

The only reason Lucien intruded into her thoughts—she tried to convince herself—was because he'd been her first experiment with passion. Since then, Micaela had been enjoying the company of other men for the specific reason of forgetting this ruggedly handsome libertine. After dealing with Lucien, no other man seemed much of a threat to her. She had lost her innocence, and her modesty, to Lucien Saffire. No other man could take more than that from her.

"If you'll excuse me, sir, I have tasks to tend to before lunch," she said as she spun on her heels. "If it's a kiss you want, kiss yonder frog."

"The name is Lucien, not sir," he muttered.

She half turned, raking him up and down from the lofty heights of disdain. "Your name could be Lucifer and it wouldn't surprise me. But whoever you are, I am offering only civil respect. I ask no more than your distant respect and I will accept nothing less. If and when you start behaving in an acceptable manner, then you will have my courtesy and consideration. Until then, I suggest you give a wide berth to me."

When Micaela sailed off, Lucien grabbed the soggy moss that clung to his shoulder and slung it to the ground. Damn that woman. She treated the servants like royalty and treated him like a lowly peasant. Why should he pay her the slightest courtesy when she went out of her way to infuriate him?

And why, Lucien asked himself, had he gone out of his way to annoy her? He knew perfectly well she preferred shooting him to kissing him. He had requested her kiss, as if it were her duty, knowing it would ruffle her feathers ... because his feathers had gotten ruffled when that damned, noble-hearted Chaney came rushing to her rescue.

Well, it was time to stop being childish by picking fights with Micaela, Lucien told himself. He would put a better foot forward at lunch, he decided. On that positive thought, Lucien sloshed toward the house, detouring long enough to retrieve his luggage from his horse. To his dismay, Adrian met him at the door and stood there grinning in devilish amusement.

Adrian stared at the slime on Lucien's jacket, then glanced at the water puddles at his feet and the paint on his chest. "The reunion with your bride obviously went well," he smirked in wicked glee.

Lucien grunted in response as he sidestepped around Adrian and strode up the staircase.

Adrian was relentless. "Next time try removing your clothes before taking to the water to wash off the paint stains."

"Enough!" Lucien pivoted on the landing of the stairs, staring down from the throne of steps. "Have the servants send up a bath. That is, of course, if Her Majesty will allow the servants to tend the menial task between their mid-morning break and the noon hour."

Still sniggering, Adrian went to fetch a servant. Although Lucien had married Micaela in a whirlwind—bypassing all the proper protocol of courtship—he was having to deal with Micaela's ill-feelings toward him.

Whether Lucien realized it or not—which he didn't yet— he faced a tremendous challenge in progressing backward through this marriage of his. Lucien's male pride wouldn't permit him to become the laughingstock at his own plantation. Very soon, Adrian predicted, Lucien would feel obliged to take his feisty, strong-willed wife in hand and save face. In so doing, what Lucien *refused* to let happen might just happen. That stubborn rake might accidentally fall in love with his wife, and vice versa. Adrian would like nothing better. Then the bitterness of the past could be put behind them at last and Lucien could learn to enjoy life again.

When Lucien returned to the dining hall—scrubbed and immaculately dressed—he found his grandfather seated alone at the table. The minute Lucien strode into the room, Adrian picked up the bell that sat by his hand. The bell, Adrian informed his grandson, was also Micaela's idea. She saw no sense in servants hovering around, waiting to serve, unless the family was seated and ready to dine. According to Her Majesty, servants had better things to do—like eating their own meals.

When two plates of steaming food arrived, Lucien glanced curiously at Adrian. "Aren't we waiting for Her Highness to join us? Or is a staggered noon hour another of her bright ideas?"

Adrian took a sip of pumpkin flip and then shook his head, causing the powdered wig to ripple around him. "Micaela planned a picnic under the magnolia trees for the servants. She saw no reason to bathe and change for lunch when she intended to undertake the battle of the weeds in the gardens and orchard this afternoon." Adrian grinned wryly at his disgruntled grandson. "Micaela, of course, sends her apologies for ignoring you at lunch."

"I'll bet she does," Lucien said, and scowled.

After swallowing down his meal like a python, Lucien took a shortcut through the kitchen and strode out the back door. Sure enough, Micaela was sitting cross-legged with her plate in her lap, eating and chatting with the servants. Apparently, being reunited with her husband ranked somewhere behind socializing with the legion of servants who doted over her.

That rankled Lucien, for this sassy misfit had been all he could think about during his voyage. Of course, he would've cut out his tongue long before he admitted any such thing to her, or to Vance who had been giving Lucien hell about this hasty marriage.

Lucien frowned when Micaela set her plate aside and ambled toward one of the recently painted outbuildings. Curious, Lucien circled through the trees to investigate.

Micaela drew herself up in front of the oversize man whom she'd seen lurking in the shadows. She was sorry to say that Barnaby Harpster's physical appearance was as offensive as his personality. His head thrust forward, making him look as if he were ever-ready to bite someone's head off—whether he actually meant to or not. His chin, and the upper portion of his forehead, receded, making his long nose appear more pointed than it was. His eyes were deep-set and his turned-down mouth gave him a sour expression.

Despite her dislike for the overseer, Micaela wanted to set aside their conflicts and call a truce. "Barnaby, I want no ill feelings between us," she insisted. "I know you think I'm trying to undermine your authority, but that isn't true. I only want to see this stately plantation restored to its grandeur, and the servants have offered to help.''

"No, you don't," Barnaby sneered, his bushy brows rippling on his forehead like woolly caterpillars. "You're trying to make me look bad in front of Adrian and the servants. I never heard of a woman managing a plantation before, unless there were no menfolk around to do it. It isn't natural.''

This same insulting attitude had dragged Micaela into many a heated debate with Arnaud. She had to caution herself to hold her temper and employ diplomacy—which she'd neglected to do when dealing with her supposed father. "There is nothing wrong with a woman taking an active interest in business,'' she assured Barnaby.

His narrowed hazel eyes roved over her in a most disrespectful manner. "Women were put on earth to pleasure a man and to take his orders. Obviously your husband hasn't been around enough to teach you your place. Maybe what you need is a real man to show you how to enjoy your place—on your back beneath him.''

The crude remark sprang the trap on Micaela's temper. She had tried to be considerate of Barnaby's feelings, but his revolting attitude made it impossible. And worse, he was undressing her with his eyes, making her skin crawl with repulsion.

To Micaela's surprise, Barnaby snaked out his brawny arm like a hook and snatched her to him. When his head came toward hers, intent on ravishing her lips, Micaela twisted her face away and raised her knee. The blow to the private parts of his anatomy sent his breath gushing out in a furious growl. When he reared back to backhand Micaela across the cheek, Lucien's ominous voice rolled like thunder.

"If you lay one hand on my wife, you will deal with me!''

It was the first time Micaela was relieved to see Lucien. His intimidating presence spared her from a brain-scrambling blow—not to mention what would've happened shortly thereafter. Lucien had one saving grace, she decided. Although he disliked her, he felt a certain responsibility to see that she didn't come to harm. He probably intended to reserve that privilege for himself, she tacked on cynically.

Reluctantly, Barnaby loosed his grasp on Micaela and stepped away, but his smoldering gaze remained fixed on her. Sneering, he lurched around and lumbered off.

Micaela rearranged the garment Barnaby had twisted around her. "Thank you."

"You're welcome." He stepped closer, without intruding into the space she preferred to keep between them. "I know you consider yourself indestructible, but please exercise caution when dealing with that man. I may not be around to intervene the next time you clash. And don't forget that male pride can be a fragile thing. You're infringing on Barnaby's private territory—or at least it has been his undisputed territory for five years."

"You should consider replacing Barnaby. He is unnecessarily cruel to the field hands. I intend to make their plight my next crusade."

Lucien rolled his eyes skyward. This crusading wife of his was doomed to butt heads with Barnaby Harpster again. Lucien shuddered to think what would happen if he wasn't around to restrain her—or Barnaby.

"I'll speak to Barnaby on behalf of the slaves," he offered. "But I want your promise that you'll stay away from him."

"Agreed. But I'm planning to hold classes for all the slaves," she informed him. "They have been neglected and I want to teach them to read and write. They also deserve the same rest periods and refreshments the household and stable servants enjoy. And it seems to me—"

"Whoa! Slow down, woman," Lucien interrupted. "Rome wasn't built in a day."

"This is not Rome," she pointed out. "The needed changes won't come if I don't set them in motion immediately."

"Once you've won your crusade here, what do you plan to do? Take on the world. Madam Attila?"

Micaela tossed him a taunting mile. "No, my next scheduled attack will be on you." There. Let him chew on that unsettling possibility and see how he liked it. Maybe it would provoke him to avoid her while he was in residence. Micaela hoped so.

Seeing him triggered thoughts of intimate moments that she was trying exceptionally hard to forget.

Lucien smiled roguishly at her, his blue eyes twinkling. "There is no need of battle when you can melt me with just one kiss. You're simply too much the coward to attempt the feat."

Her chin elevated to a proud angle. "I may be many things, none of which you approve, but I'm not a coward. Neither am I a fool. You used your potent powers of seduction on me once, but never again."

"They were that potent?" Lucien grinned and waggled his eyebrows.

"Yes—no!"

Micaela backed away when he reached for her, but he gently drew her body against the full length of his. To bolt and run would have proved her to be the coward he claimed. Lucien had cleverly entrapped her into permitting his embrace—not by force, but by using her own hastily-spoken declaration. Stubborn pride put her in the circle of his sinewy arms, and it was that same damnable pride that kept her there to save face.

Lucien tilted his dark head just so, smiling in challenge, drawing her nearer, until his sensuous lips were a scant few inches from hers. "If you're such a brave soul, then why don't you kiss me, wife? Have I shown myself to be as brutal as Barnaby?"

"No." She gulped hard and tried to inhale a breath, but the air was thick with his alluring male scent.

"Did we not conclude that the only torture we experienced on our wedding night was the most exquisite kind imaginable?" he murmured, his warm breath caressing her flushed cheek.

"I suppose we did," Micaela bleated, her voice two octaves higher than normal.

Oh, how she resented the phenomenal power this man held over her. He made her feel wobbly and defenseless. He made her feminine body betray her.

"Do you refuse to exchange these last ten days of unrestricted freedom for a simple kiss, Caela?" he whispered huskily. "Aren't you as curious as I to retest our reactions to each other? I'm wondering if you can still make me burn with that same white-hot flame you ignited on our wedding night. I haven't forgotten even one delicious moment of it.''

Pulse pounding, she waited, expecting him to kiss her, but he didn't. Obviously, he possessed more patience than she did. Oh, the hell with it, she thought. What harm could come from one quick kiss? It was broad daylight, after all. Servants were buzzing around like a swarm of mosquitoes. And true, she wondered if this rascal could still stir her passion after that first eye-opening encounter. She was no longer a naive innocent, she reminded herself. Now, she would be immune to Lucien. She would kiss his sensuous lips right off him and she would walk away feeling nothing but smug victory.

Micaela slipped her arms around his neck and pushed up on tiptoe. She could be as much the rake as he was if she felt like it, she told herself. Her lips settled upon his . . . and she cursed her foolish conceit. It was impossible to remain unaffected when she could taste, touch and breathe this muscled giant. Suddenly she was transported back to that night when she had taken her first drink from passion's cup and found herself intoxicated on the taste of this man. Those same warm tingles of excitement rippled down her spine and coiled in the core of her being. Her heart leaped and her breath came in ragged spurts. When Lucien's hands glided down her ribs to press her hips familiarly to his, Micaela felt herself melting, burning, wanting him in the most desperate way. *Mon Dieu,* his kiss was as potent as ever—maybe even more so!

Blast it, this wasn't supposed to be happening. Forbidden memories were bursting to flame. Micaela didn't know where her mind went after that. She couldn't think past Lucien's delicious kisses and bold caresses. He made her body glow with unfulfilled pleasure, made her want more than just the tantalizing touch of his hands and lips. . . .

When Lucien released her and stepped back a pace, Micaela's legs buckled. If he hadn't reached out to steady her, she would have collapsed at his feet. Even worse, this ornery rake knew to what extent his kiss disturbed her.

"Forgive me, Caela," he said, staring specifically at her

wobbly knees, then at her flushed cheeks. "I asked only for a kiss. We'll finish what we started tonight . . . when we're alone . . . in our bed."

"No, we won't. I kept my part of our bargain," she replied, her voice not as steady as she would've preferred.

The only satisfaction Micaela enjoyed, before Lucien turned and walked away, was noting the bulge in his trim-fitting breeches. He may have schooled his voice and expression, but he was as aroused as she was. But it didn't matter who had aroused whom, she reminded herself. The point was that Lucien wasn't going to come trotting back to the plantation and hop into her bed after he had caroused with women in every tropical port. Maybe she wasn't as immune to him as she would like to be, but she was not going willingly to his bed. She would exhaust herself with work, that's what she'd do. Her traitorous body would be too fatigued, too numb to respond to his devastating touch.

Smiling at her own cleverness, Micaela ambled back to the servants. She would leave no weed unplucked in her tiring efforts. She hoped she would be snoring in Lucien's ear the instant her head hit the pillow. That should put a sizable dent in his male pride. Then he'd go away and leave her alone for good.

Lucien didn't want her, not really. She had his name, but she would never have his heart. It was tied to a living memory of another woman. Micaela couldn't let herself become too attached, because Lucien had the power to hurt her as no man could. She would *not* let herself care too much. And that, Micaela decided, was the end of that!

Ten

"The woman is an energetic marvel," Adrian observed while he stood at the bay window beside Lucien.

Micaela was pulling weeds like a vicious warrior engaging in hand-to-hand combat. She was setting such a swift pace that the weed brigade couldn't keep up with her.

"I tell you, Lucien, there is no task above or beneath her. She is eager to do anything and everything, as if she'd been deprived of the opportunity all her life. Although I promised not to pry into her past, I often wonder what kind of existence she led before she came here."

Lucien glanced solemnly at his grandfather. "Since I won't always be around to keep an eye on Micaela, I want you to exert control over her," he requested. "She has *too* much zest, and she'll wear herself out completely if you let her."

Two gray brows elevated in mock offense. "You want me to *interfere* in Micaela's life? *You?* The man who has spent five years punishing me for exerting control over *your* life, because of what I thought best?"

Lucien gnashed his teeth, noting his grandfather's gloating amusement. For the first time, Lucien could see Adrian's side of the issue that kept them at odds. It was humbling to find

himself guilty of that domineering characteristic he had so
fiercely objected to.

"I'm sorry, m'boy, but I've already meddled too much in
other people's lives. I learned from my mistakes, and I won't
repeat them. Micaela is your wife, and your responsibility. It
is my place simply to enjoy her."

"But damn it, I won't always be here to watch over her,"
Lucien muttered. "She has already clashed with Barnaby
severely. She shows no signs of letting up on the man, either."

Adrian ambled over to retrieve his glass of pumpkin flip
from the tilt-top table that sat beside his favorite chair in his
study. "If you are concerned about her welfare, then make
arrangements to be here more often or take her with you when
you go to sea," he suggested. "I'm too old to match Micaela's
fast pace. The stress would kill me." He turned to look over
his shoulder at Lucien. "Or is that what you prefer?"

Lucien was stunned to realize that he and Adrian were engaging in discussion without jumping down each other's throats.
Micaela's presence had brought them toward a peaceful coexistence they hadn't enjoyed in years. She had become the glue
that held them together. And despite the bitterness of the past,
Lucien did not wish ill of this ornery old buzzard. He cared
about Adrian—in an exasperating sort of way.

"What I want," Lucien elaborated, "is to see Micaela living
less dangerously, and at a more reasonable pace, but not at the
expense of your health. There seem to be two measures of time
in this world—God's and Micaela's. Her inner time clock beats
a mite too fast for her own good."

"You are criticizing her because she does more living in the
course of a week than most people can manage in a month?
That is the policy you have followed for years, I might point
out." Adrian chuckled, then sipped his drink. "Micaela has
youthful enthusiasm on her side. Now that I've adopted the
live-and-let-live philosophy, I'm through preaching to others.
I've suffered the consequences of sticking my nose in places
it doesn't belong, and I've vowed not to do it again."

Scowling, Lucien turned to the bay window. Micaela's pace
had escalated another notch. She was yanking up weeds with

both fists, leaving a pile behind her on the sidewalk. Lucien suspected this fanatic attack on the garden had everything to do with the comment he'd made earlier that afternoon. Unless he was mistaken—and he doubted he was—Micaela intended to wear herself out so she would be excused from her wifely duties.

Micaela was purposely defying him, refusing to succumb to the sultry sparks they ignited in each other. Hell's fire, they were man and wife. It was no crime to physically satisfy each other. One night with Micaela hadn't been enough to satisfy him, despite all his stern lectures on forgetting her the minute she was out of sight. Curse it, what kind of mystical hold did that green-eyed spitfire have on him anyway? And why was he so entranced by every move she made? He couldn't seem to get enough of her, even when she defied him at every turn.

Lucien pried himself away from the window. It was time he exerted control over his wife. In purposeful strides, he marched out the door and headed toward the garden. He hadn't rushed through his duties on the wharf, left half of them in Vance's lap, and rode hell-for-leather, just to watch Micaela pull weeds with a vengeance. He wanted to spend time with her. And by damned he would, whether she liked it or not—which she obviously didn't. Wooing his wife had become a challenge Lucien could not turn his back on.

Micaela didn't realize Lucien was standing behind her until he cleared his throat pointedly. She glanced over her shoulder to see polished black boots amid her pile of weeds. Lifting her gaze, she expected to meet Lucien's disapproving frown. Instead, he greeted her with a smile.

Outstretching his hand, he hoisted Micaela to her feet, then turned to Chaney. "You're in command of the weed patrol while my wife and I take a ride around the grounds to inspect the fields."

Micaela pried her arm from his grasp, intent on avoiding his touch—no matter how casual. The fact was that it affected her, and she was better off if she didn't let him touch her at all. "I don't know how to ride, Lucien. I was never allowed to learn."

"You don't ride?" He stared at her in feigned astonishment. "It must be the only thing you don't know how to do. But never fear, we'll alleviate the problem immediately."

"But—"

"Come along, love. I'll have you riding in no time at all. I'm sure you'll love that."

It was true that Micaela had always resented her father's refusal to let her mount a horse, but she wasn't sure she wanted Lucien to be the one to instruct her. And why this sudden desire to spend time with her? she wondered suspiciously. She didn't think he liked her all that much, and she had her heart set on keeping her distance from him!

"I can't go riding dressed like this," she protested as he ushered her alongside him. "I'm filthy. I'll offend the horse."

"Your horse won't care how you look," he said, annoyed that she was more concerned about what a horse might think than her own husband. That pretty much signified where he rated, didn't it? "A horse has a distinct aroma of its own, so there is no need to fret about offending it."

While Lucien saddled two horses, Micaela cleansed herself as best she could with the bar of soap and pail of water that sat outside the barn. When Lucien set her atop the roan mare, she took up the reins and steered the animal down the tree-lined path that led to the rice and indigo fields. The mare took off in a trot, jostling Micaela's bones from their sockets.

"Stand up in the stirrups," Lucien instructed, moving his bay gelding alongside her. "No, don't hold the reins up by your shoulder. You're forcing the mare to jerk her head to an unnatural angle. She can't guard her step if she's staring at the sky."

Micaela did as she was told.

"Now, press your knees into her flanks to hold your position. Guide the mare with the pressure of her ribs. The horse will behave herself once you assure her that you're in control and that you won't tolerate her mischief."

Micaela glanced sideways at the man who sat so easily and confidently in the saddle. "Are we discussing me or the horse?"

Lucien smiled wryly. "If the theory applies to both of you, then . . . the theory applies to both of you."

She eyed him warily. "What do you want from me, Lucien?"

"I want the pleasure of your company, and to teach you to ride."

"I'm sorry, but I don't trust your motives." She sent him another wary glance before concentrating on her riding skills. "I have found myself in tangles of ulterior motives once too often in the past few weeks."

"But despite everything, we are man and wife," Lucien pointed out. "If we are to project an image of compatibility during the reception Adrian is planning we need to become better acquainted, don't you agree?"

Micaela flung her nose in the air. "I had intended to call upon my acting ability to see me through the reception."

"Are you always this stubborn?" Lucien inquired.

"Usually I'm worse," she smarted off. "You caught me on one of my good days."

Lucien reached out to rein her steed to a halt and then stared her squarely in the eye. "Why are you trying so hard to hate me?" he asked. "This morning you demanded my courtesy and respect, which I am trying to give." A roguish grin curved the corners of his mouth upward. "Could it be that you like me more than you prefer? Does the thought disturb you, Caela?"

"You do not disturb me," she burst out, operating on the theory that the louder the proclamation, the easier it was to believe.

"Then prove it," he challenged before releasing the reins and nudging his steed into a gallop.

And just how was she supposed to do that? Befuddled, Micaela watched Lucien and his powerful steed move like a centaur, gobbling up the ground in graceful strides. What did that rapscallion want from her that he hadn't already taken? He had stolen her innocence—well, not exactly stolen, she reminded herself. She had actively participated, much as it shamed her to admit it. He had deprived her of her freedom of choice. Now he was after her heart—just to say he had it, she predicted. Well, he wasn't going to steal her heart, no matter how charming he tried to be.

Emulating Lucien's riding skills, Micaela urged her mare into a canter. Something very peculiar happened while she was racing the wind, feeling slightly out of control and yet exhilarated by the muscled strength beneath her. A wild rush of excitement buzzed through her as she matched the mare's rhythmic strides.

Ah, riding was like flying, she realized. This was yet another taste of freedom Arnaud refused to let her enjoy. Micaela leaned down, pressing her cheek against the mare's neck, giving the animal its head. With the nudge of her heels, Micaela sent the mare into her fastest gait, passing Lucien as if he were standing still. The pounding of hooves beneath her, the whispering wind in her ears, transported Micaela into a world she never realized existed. She relished each wild, thrilling moment . . . until the mare swerved around the bend of the road and Micaela soared off in the opposite direction.

Panicky fear quickly replaced the sensation of flight. Shrieking, Micaela soared across the underbrush and crash-landed in the creek.

For a moment she lay facedown in the stream, evaluating the condition of her body. Although she felt like a quivering tuning fork, she was pretty certain nothing had been broken or severed.

Behind her, she heard the thrashing in the bushes and Lucien's alarmed voice. "Caela, are you all right?"

Rolling over in the shallow channel, she flashed him a grin. "Of course, I'm all right. I was only trying my hand at spectacular dismounts."

When Lucien saw Micaela soar off like a wingless bird, he expected to find her in a broken pile—just as he'd found Cecilia. . . .

"Damn it, woman, had I known you had such suicidal tendencies, I would have—" Lucien cursed the tormenting thought, the reckless remark provoked by unpleasant memories.

Almost at once, Micaela knew what had provoked his angry

outburst. Lucien wasn't angry with her. He was making tormenting comparisons to another time and place. Micaela had unintentionally scared the pants off him. The incident must have triggered thoughts of his long lost love.

"Do you despise me so much that you would take your own life to avoid this marriage?" Lucien muttered. "I had to endure the torment of a woman who refused to live without a marriage. Now I'm dealing with a female who loathes being married to me. God in heaven, what did I do to deserve this?"

Micaela was on her feet in nothing flat. She had never seen the vulnerable side of Lucien's personality. He had always been in perfect control, exposing only the superficial emotions he allowed the rest of the world to see. Although Micaela had never lost a loved one, she imagined it was a painful, traumatic experience. Her heart went out to Lucien. She blamed herself for provoking that private anguish simmering just beneath the surface.

Her hand settled on his rigid chest, but even her compassionate touch didn't rouse him. He was lost to haunting memories. How many times had Lucien agonized over the tragic incident, wondering what he might have said or done to prevent calamity? His reaction to Micaela's near brush with catastrophe made her realize how deeply Lucien had loved Cecilia. She also realized she would never be able to take the woman's place, even if she tried.

"Lucien?" she murmured, brushing her hand over his chest. "Truly, I'm all right. And I'm not like her, either," she felt compelled to tell him. "Though we have our differences, I have no intention of ending it all because of this marriage. I realize I can't compete with your precious memories of Cecilia, but I'm not used to being loved, or even wanted, so don't think—"

Lucien clutched her to him, cutting her off in midsentence. Although he despised this overwhelming feeling of vulnerability, maddening fear still buffeted him. He felt uncomfortable letting Micaela see the cracks in his veneer of self-control, but holding her seemed as vital as breathing.

The instant Micaela had catapulted through the bushes, an

awful feeling of terror had twisted in Lucien's gut. Returning
to the plantation, wandering among the bittersweet memories of
those months with Cecilia had been bad enough. But watching
Micaela swan dive was more than he could stand. Lucien needed
to hold her, to go on holding her, until the unnerving sensations
that linked the present to his tormented past went away.

His lips slanted over hers, forcing everything but the feel of
her luscious body and honeyed mouth from his mind. In less
than a heartbeat, passion burned through him like a fiery river.
He couldn't get enough of her fast enough to satisfy himself.
His hands and lips moved of their own accord, rediscovering
every delectable inch of her body. He resented the garments
that separated them, longed to remove those hampering clothes
so he could feel her flesh to flesh and heart to heart.

Micaela was startled by Lucien's impatience and her own
wild response to him. She seemed as eager to recapture their
moments of splendor as he. It occurred to her, as he laid her
down on the pallet of discarded clothes, that she had been
pulling anxiously at his garments, eager to touch him. She knew
he was making love to a memory, that it wasn't her face that
swam before his passion-drugged eyes. Lucien was still a captive of bygone days. He was reaching out to a broken dream,
to unfulfilled love.

Micaela was a substitute for the woman Lucien really wanted,
but she closed her mind to everything except the delicious
sensations caused by his pulse-disturbing caresses. Her feminine body fed on his skillful touch. She craved the erotic sensations that had once consumed her. She returned each caress
with bold inventiveness, knowing she would scorn herself for
her impulsiveness when reality returned. But not now.

Ah, what a cruel master fate was! Micaela knew she was
ten kinds of fool for surrendering to a man who had eyes for
only one woman. She was going to get her heart broken, but
still she cast caution to the wind.

Lucien's seductive magic enthralled her. When his tongue
flicked at the throbbing crests of her breasts Micaela evaporated
like a cloud of steam. When his hands glided over her ribs and
swirled over her belly to caress her hips, a sigh of pleasure

tumbled from her lips. When his lithe body half covered hers, teasing and tempting her with promises of intimacies to come, she felt herself arching shamelessly toward him.

Lucien wasn't sure how it had happened, but wanting Micaela had suddenly become a tangible thing, a mindless addiction. Pulsating need hammered at him. But seeking his own satisfaction wasn't enough when it came to Micaela. It was as if her pleasure released his intense satisfaction.

His hand drifted across the silky flesh of her thighs, nudging her legs father apart to grant himself access to the liquid heat of desire he had summoned from her. His thumb and fingertips caressed her secret warmth, and he felt her body convulsing around him, welcoming him, leaving him burning on the hottest, sweetest flame.

He stroked her until his name tumbled from her lips. She was whispering to him with each ragged breath. He felt her body weep for him, calling out to him in one coiling contraction after another. And yet, he wanted more from her. He wanted her to be on fire for him, to know the same hungry desperation that was burning through him.

When Micaela could endure no more of the wild sweet torment of his kisses and caresses, she cupped his face in her hands and drew his lips back to her. It was vain and foolish, she knew, but feeling the way she did about him, she ached to exorcise the ghost who stood between them.

"Look at me, Lucien," she implored him. "Who do you see?"

"I see an angel sent straight from heaven," he rasped before his lips descended to drink the sweet nectar of her kiss. "Love me . . . I need you. . . ."

When he came to her, his body shaking with need, Micaela couldn't deny him. She stared into those glistening silver-blue eyes and suddenly nothing mattered except holding him, cherishing him, sharing his windswept passion.

It was a wild joining that soothed hungry souls. Lucien drove urgently into her and she matched each penetrating thrust, clinging to him so fiercely that she swore she had left her mark on the whipcord muscles of his back. No matter what conflicts arose between them, this obsessive desire wasn't to be denied. Each time he touched her, she viewed another wild dimension of desire. . . .

Spasms of passion bombarded Micaela. The world spun crazily around her. It was as if the universe had swallowed her alive. She trembled beneath the onslaught of sensations that tore at her sanity, her heart and soul.

Only when Lucien groaned deep in his throat, and clutched her frantically to him, did Micaela find sweet release. When his body shuddered on hers, she experienced a sublime sense of satisfaction. And long after the waves of contentment flooded through her, she was still adrift in a hypnotic sea of wishful fantasy.

Minutes later—or was it hours? Micaela found it impossible to measure time when she was sailing in Lucien's arms—later, at any rate, she saw the mist of passion part and felt reality intrude. She had allowed her compassion for Lucien's past to dictate her responses. She had permitted herself to become the embodiment of his gone-but-not-forgotten love. Lucien had confirmed her worst fear when she asked him who he saw when he looked at her. An angel from heaven, he'd said. Cecilia, no doubt.

No matter how hard Micaela tried to rationalize, she knew she was only a substitute. Lucien would wind up hurting her, as he was hurting. She had broken her promise to herself, and she had no one to blame for this unplanned tryst but herself. She had gone to him to console him, but that wasn't where it stopped.

The tears clouding Micaela's eyes slashed at Lucien like a knife. In his frantic desperation, he must have unintentionally hurt Micaela. Although she was no longer a virgin, she was still innocent and ill-prepared for the intensity of a man in the throes of ardent passion. Damn it, he should have been more patient and caring, he chastised himself.

"I'm sorry," Lucien murmured. "Did I hurt you, Caela?" Lord, he had promised never to hurt her again after that first night, and now he'd taken her in a heated rush.

Hurt her? Ah yes, he'd hurt her more than he would ever

know. Somehow or other, he had melted her heart and broken through her defenses. Learning that this handsome rake wasn't as invincible as he would have her believe had touched her. Micaela was more than a little afraid that this helpless physical attraction had inspired deeper feelings—forbidden feelings that would invite heartache. She'd come to enjoy testing Lucien's temper, curious to see how much he'd allow her to get away with before he called her to task. She delighted in matching wits with him. She loved the way he made love to her, even when she knew he saw someone else when he looked at her. Already, she was in too deep, she realized. She was floundering in quicksand.

When Lucien eased away, Micaela scooped up her clothes and hurried off to track down her mare. Lucien watched her scurry off, feeling as if he were chasing the wind when he pursued her. Since the first time he'd seen those green eyes twinkling at him in challenging mischief, she'd been infuriatingly elusive. Even now, after he'd married her, she was still a mystery to him, an equation he couldn't figure out, that proverbial itch he couldn't quite reach to scratch.

Rolling to his feet, Lucien scooped up his clothes and dressed. In years past, he had been the first to walk away from intimate encounters. Now, he was the one left behind. Imagine that! He had been content to linger, but Micaela was up and gone. Confounded female, he grumbled. He was always one step behind Micaela, never quite catching up.

"Lucien, I can't find the mare anywhere," she called in frustration.

He ambled up from the creek, smiling wryly. "The mare must be like her mistress," he said. "She's always running off before you can catch up with her."

Micaela tilted her head to a defensive angle, then stared at the air over Lucien's head. "I suppose she thinks that once she's served her purpose, there's no need to tarry."

"Caela . . ." His voice was soft but it hummed with disapproval.

"Well, it's so," she insisted. "Although you refuse to speak of Cecilia, I know all about her. Adrian told me. I know what she meant to you, and I know that every time you look at me, or any other woman, you see *her*."

There. She'd said it flat-out. It was time Lucien faced that fact, and high time Micaela accepted it.

There was a long pause—too long—before Lucien murmured. "That isn't true." When she turned to walk away, he grasped her arm. "That is not true."

He was trying to deceive her with that sincere-sounding tone, but he wasn't fooling Micaela for a minute. "You're going to have one impossible time convincing me of that," she told him. "When a man spends five years eating his heart out for a woman—"

"I do not wish to have this conversation," he bit off.

"That implies the subject is too painful to discuss."

"It implies nothing of the kind!"

"Then what does it imply?" she prodded, even when she knew Lucien's temper was near its flashpoint. The signs were all there—the flicker in his eyes, the muscle ticking on his clamped jaw, the rigidity of his stance.

"You can climb on behind me," he insisted as he spun away to untether his horse.

"I'd rather walk, thank you—"

She yelped when Lucien trotted past, hooked his arm around her, and hauled her up behind him.

"You are a most impossible man, Lucien Saffire," she muttered at the back of his head.

"You would know all about impossible, being an authority on it," he shot back.

Neither of them uttered a word during the ride to the mansion. When Micaela glanced sideways she saw Barnaby sloshing through the rice field toward the young slave she had recruited the previous day to help with the painting. To her outrage, she heard Barnaby bellow at Abraham who had fallen to his knees, apparently bitten by a snake while he was planting seedlings in the waterlogged field. When Barnaby backhanded the boy for refusing to obey the order to stand up, Micaela tried to bound from the saddle to intervene.

"No." Lucien clamped hold of her before she dismounted.

"But that vicious brute—"

"Now isn't the time," he told her. "I'll speak to Barnaby after I take you to the house. If I dress him down in front of the field hands, it will only cause more trouble. And you, my dear lady, have crossed the man too often already."

Difficult though it was, Micaela stayed put. This was the third time she had seen Barnaby strike out in bad temper. She had come close to feeling the sting of his hand herself. And when she clashed with him again—and that was inevitable— she would remember to duck when she saw that ugly sneer curling his lips and his bulky arm coiling to strike.

Micaela had every intention of marching down to the slave quarters this evening to check on Abraham. She also intended to upgrade the living conditions of the field workers, even if she had to confront Barnaby a dozen times. He treated the slaves abominably and it was going to stop! If he didn't change his cruel ways, she would pester Adrian until Barnaby was dismissed. In fact, Micaela would assume his job herself until a replacement could be found. That man definitely had to go!

While Lucien and Adrian were playing a game of piquet with Vance Cavendish, who had arrived in time for supper, Micaela strode toward the row of slave cabins. With a pouch of medical supplies draped over her shoulder, she sought out Abraham, who lived in a small cottage with his parents and younger sister.

Pure rage boiled inside Micaela when she realized what pitiful condition the lad was in. The fourteen-year-old Abraham was sprawled on a cot, a wound festering on his ankle and an unsightly bruise on his cheek. Damn that Barnaby! He must have forced the injured boy to keep working in the field, despite Lucien's order to send the boy to the house. Barnaby had no sense of compassion or decency whatsoever, she fumed.

Micaela sank down beside Abraham and immediately went to work on the wound. She cleansed the infected area and applied a poultice. Before she could bandage his ankle, elephantine footsteps resounded on the wooden stoop.

"Lights off," Barnaby growled. A snarl puckered his homely features when he saw Micaela playing nursemaid to the slave boy. "I warned you about this, woman. That boy is my responsibility, not yours."

Micaela secured the bandage, offered the feverish lad a reassuring smile, and then rounded on the heartless overseer. When she remembered what Lucien had said about challenging Barnaby's authority in front of the slaves, she snatched up her pouch and motioned for Barnaby to follow her outside.

"I will not tolerate abuse on this plantation," she told the oversized brute. "Abraham was injured and you mistreated him, refused to give him first aid, refused to send him home when Lucien told you to do so!"

"That brat sassed me," Barnaby sneered. "It has become an increasingly bad habit among the slaves since you showed up to incite one riot after another."

"Abraham was only trying to explain what happened to him, but you not only refused to listen, you didn't even care," she hissed furiously. "And if you think I'm trying to instigate a rebellion against you right now, you haven't seen anything yet! You'll find yourself receiving the kind of punishment you inflect on these servants. I'll see to it!"

Hazel eyes flashed in the lanternlight that streamed from the cabin window. Micaela stepped back cautiously, knowing Barnaby was coiling to strike. His first reaction was to backhand whoever irritated him.

"Are you threatening me, bitch?" he snarled nastily.

"I'm giving you fair warning," she clarified. "Perhaps Adrian doesn't realize what a tyrant you are, but I'm well aware. I also know who's at fault for neglecting this plantation. If you spent as much time working as you do abusing servants, this run-down estate wouldn't require so much of my attention."

"And if you would confine yourself to your ivory tower, Your Highness, I could do the job I'm paid to do. It's clear to me that you don't spend enough time on your back, doing the things a woman was born to do," he added.

"Of all the—oh!" Micaela was so furious she was seeing red.

"You're like that bitch Lucien planned to marry," Barnaby smirked. "She was all haughty airs and prissy gestures. The only difference was that she liked to spread herself beneath a man. You aren't woman enough to please anybody."

The remarks caught Micaela off guard. She was so shocked she forgot her outrage. She wondered if Barnaby was the man Adrian had hired to keep surveillance on Cecilia. Barnaby certainly seemed knowledgeable about Cecilia—either from firsthand experience or rumor.

Micaela decided to end this unpleasant conversation before it turned into a knock-down-drag-out. "Abraham will not be working in the field until his wound heals," she told Barnaby in no uncertain terms.

"Are you planning on taking his place?" Barnaby jeered disrespectfully.

"No, I expect *you* to do it," she flung right back at him.

Micaela veered around the human blockade and strode off. Barnaby Harpster definitely had to go. Micaela was certain the field workers' efficiency and morale would improve one hundred percent when that vicious overseer was replaced. . . .

Micaela shrieked when she rounded the chicken house to find herself captured in bulky arms. Barnaby had darted between the slave cabins, taking a shortcut to intercept her. The man was utterly mad! Did he think she would be so humiliated by his attack that she would keep silent? If he did, he was doomed to disappointment. No matter what he did to her, she would see him put behind bars and left to rot!

Barnaby clamped his hand over her mouth and dragged her toward the clump of pines. When he shoved her to the ground and sprawled on top of her, Micaela discovered the difference between brute force and Lucien's seductive persuasion. Grimy hands groped at her, and Micaela bit and thrashed and squirmed to escape the mauling.

"Now we'll find out if you're as good in the hay as you are at tongue-lashings," he taunted as he clawed at the bodice of her gown. "If you breathe one word about this to anyone, I'll make sure you regret it . . . ouch!"

Micaela bit savagely at his hand. When Barnaby instinctively recoiled, she screamed at the top of her lungs. Although Barnaby pinned her hands over her head, she writhed sideways, knocking him off balance. When he tried to cover her mouth with his hand again, she bit another chunk out of his stubby fingers. Barnaby reared back, his eyes flashing with fury. Micaela hurled herself aside before he struck her on the cheek.

Again, she burst loose with a bloodcurdling scream. Barnaby swore ripely and jerked her gown over her face, muffling her protest as he wedged his knee between her clamped legs. Micaela dug her heels into the grass and scooted backward, knowing she was prolonging the inevitable, but she was determined to make this a full-scale battle to the bitter end!

Eleven

Lucien's card game was instantly forgotten when he heard Micaela's distant shriek. He hit the floor running, zigzagging through the hall and racing out the back door. The second terrifying scream went through him like a sizzling lightning bolt. Lucien growled in furious outrage when he saw the silhouettes spotlighted by moonlight. Without breaking stride, Lucien charged straight at Barnaby. His uplifted boot caught Barnaby squarely in the chin. Grunting in pain, Barnaby toppled to the ground. Hissing and cursing, Lucien pounced. He pounded the brutal overseer with one powerful blow after another.

Barnaby's face was covered with blood, and he could do nothing but fend off the relentless attack, but Lucien didn't back off. He rained a dozen more blows on the beast who dared to attack Micaela. Lucien reared back to deliver another brain-scrambling punch, but Vance Cavendish rushed up from his blindside to grab Lucien's arm.

"You'll kill him," Vance said, holding Lucien at bay.

"That's the whole idea," Lucien snarled. "Let go, damn it!"

Vance didn't let go. He yanked Lucien back, forcing him

off balance. Barnaby rolled to his belly like the snake he was, then levered onto his hands and knees.

"If you ever go near my wife again, I'll see you roasting in hell," Lucien hissed as Barnaby staggered to his feet and plunged into the underbrush to escape.

Chest heaving, Lucien shook himself from Vance's grasp and hurried over to assist Micaela to her feet. While she pulled her gown back into decency, Lucien clutched her protectively against him.

The tears Micaela had tried to hold in check came streaming down her cheeks. She buried her head against Lucien's chest, her body quaking in the aftermath of the frightening assault.

"Go find him, Vance. You're the one who let him get away," Lucien growled. "And take some of the grooms with you. I want that bastard punished to the very limit of the law for what he did."

Nodding grimly, Vance strode off to gather a posse.

"What in the hell were you doing out here alone?" Lucien muttered at Micaela.

"I was checking on Abraham," she said between sobbing gulps. "Barnaby threatened me, then he—"

Lucien swept her into his arms and carried her to the house. "This is the last straw. You are never going out alone at night— ever. You flirt with disaster so often that it makes me crazy. Damn it, Micaela. Must I lose you, too? Is this the torment you've designed to punish me for forcing you into this marriage?"

Just listen to the man! He was scolding *her,* as if this incident was her fault. Damnation, he sounded like her father, blaming her for every single thing that happened. Micaela had stood up for what she believed, and Barnaby tried to abuse her into submission. She was *not* in the wrong, that vicious beast was!

The instant Lucien burst through the front door with Micaela cradled in his arms, Adrian clutched his chest. His wrinkled face turned as white as flour. "Is she all right? What happened?"

Lucien was so intent on his destination that he didn't bother with explanations. He wanted Micaela settled comfortably in bed, so he could examine her for injuries.

Shoving the door open with his shoulder, he made a beeline toward the bed. Since Micaela's gown had already suffered irreparable damage, Lucien ripped it down the middle in his haste to get her situated so he could check for cuts and bruises.

"Are you mad?" Micaela gasped, staring at the shredded gown. "I have yet to repay Adrian for that dress, and now you've—"

"You are not paying for even one pair of pantaloons," Lucien said sharply. "You're my wife and I can afford to buy your clothes and discard the ones that aren't fit to wear again— like this one." He tossed the torn garment aside, as if touching the fabric Barnaby had put his filthy hands on repulsed him. "I never want to see this garment again, *ever.*"

Despite Micaela's protests, he peeled off her torn chemise, flipped back the bedspread and tucked her between the sheets.

"Lord Almighty," Micaela muttered, trying to cover herself from his probing gaze. "I've had enough rough handling for one night. Just go way and leave me alone!"

"I'm not leaving until I'm sure you weren't seriously injured," Lucien said as his hands skimmed over her flesh. He cursed when he spied the claw marks on her shoulders and chest, the bruises and scrapes on her thighs.

What the hell had gotten into Barnaby? he wondered. True, Micaela could test a man's temper to the limits, but common decency should have restrained the overseer from abusing this dainty female.

When Lucien was assured that Micaela hadn't suffered serious injury, he drew the sheet up to her chin and dropped a kiss to her puffy lip. "Don't put me through that kind of torment again," he whispered against her cheek. "Don't you know that when you're hurt, I'm the one who bleeds?"

Micaela blinked, astonished. Why, if she didn't know better, she might think Lucien actually cared about her. But she did know better, didn't she? Lucien would have been concerned about anyone who suffered from a traumatic experience. He, after all, knew the torment of calamity, had lived with it for five years.

"That surprises you?" Lucien said perceptively.

"Yes, it does. I was under the impression that you tolerated me because I'm you're wife, for better or worse. Worse, as this marriage happens to be. And truly, I haven't tried very hard to make you like me."

One of the things Lucien adored about this feisty female, besides her sassy humor and quick wit, was her honesty. She was better at opening up to others than he was. But then, Micaela had too much vivacious spirit to contain it. She was also more vocal and demonstrative than Lucien. He had spent years burying emotion. But his emotions were running high after the incident Micaela suffered. It was becoming increasingly evident that when Micaela was in danger, Lucien sweated blood.

"Caela, I ask a favor," he said as he traced her elegant features with his forefinger. "From now on, until after the reception, could we possibly call a truce and set our differences aside?"

She smiled, her eyes regaining that shiny luster that the frightening episode with Barnaby had tarnished. "Is this truce scheduled to last until the stroke of midnight on Saturday? You know what a fanatic I am about being organized, right down to the last minute."

Lucien marveled at her resilience. She'd taken a nose-dive off her horse this morning and barely escaped a mauling tonight. And still she rallied to crack jokes. Amazing.

"Let's keep the truce going until half past the witching hour," Lucien suggested, smiling in response to her infectious grin. "Some of our long-winded guests might not retire at the exact stroke of midnight."

"And what are the terms of this truce?" she wanted to know.

"No fighting, no power struggles, and no wandering around alone at night to avoid each other," Lucien specified.

Micaela chewed on her bottom lip, pondering the stipulations. "You realize you're asking a lot." She peeked impishly at him through thick lashes. "I'm short on patience and I'm a bit argumentative by nature. I also have a rebellious streak and obsessive need for independence. And to be honest, I never considered myself good marriage material to begin with. If you had gotten to know me better before you spoke your vows, you could have avoided this situation entirely."

Lucien drew back in feigned astonishment. "Not marry you, madam? And allow you to get your greedy hands on my rightful fortune? Why, I would go to any extreme to secure my inheritance so I can languish in the lap of luxury until the end of my days. I couldn't do anything *but* marry you!"

His teasing remark made her wonder just why he'd gone to such drastic measures to marry her. She knew Lucien wasn't desperate for money. He had made his own fortune in shipping. Obviously, his only motivation was to outfox Adrian, just to prove he could if he wanted to.

"You married me to throw a wrench in Adrian's scheme. It seems you did make your point with him," she said thoughtfully.

"You have to admit the old buzzard asked for it," Lucien contended. "But he appears to have learned his lesson. I can only hope you have learned yours. No more traipsing around alone at night."

Micaela stared into his ruggedly handsome face for a long moment. "Lucien, what do you really want from me?" she asked, point-blank.

He clasped her scraped hand in his and brushed his lips over her knuckles. "I want half a chance to make a fresh start. What began all wrong might end up right. I don't want to be your enemy, Caela."

"And I don't really hate you, if that's what you've been thinking," she murmured, marveling at the tender emotion inspired by his affectionate display.

Lucien rose to his feet and grinned at the saucy female whose tangled blond mane looked as if it had been styled in a cyclone. Odd, he hadn't smiled so much in years, he realized. No doubt, his face was going to crack wide open if he spent too much time in Micaela's entertaining company.

"Perhaps what I want isn't for you *not* to hate me, Caela, but for you to actually like me," he murmured, lips twitching. "A marriage in which both parties are in *like* would be a step in the right direction, don't you think?"

Micaela rolled to her side and braced her disheveled head on her hand. "Is that all you want, Lucien? For me to like you?"

"Are you prepared to offer more?" he questioned her question.

"I—" Micaela clamped her mouth shut and averted her gaze. Yes, she could offer Lucien more if he could see her for herself, not as the substitute for the woman he'd lost. But every time she found herself in a scrape, Lucien made comparisons to other tormenting moments in his life. He still hadn't separated the past from the present, and Micaela refused to be a substitute for the woman he really wanted. If she let herself fall in love with him she could get her heart broken.

"I'm very tired," she murmured belatedly. "I think I should rest."

"Yes, I think you should, too," was all Lucien said before he doused the lantern and quietly left the room.

Saffire Plantation took a decisive turn for the better after Barnaby Harpster disappeared, despite the posse's attempt to track him down. Lucien and Adrian appointed Chaney as overseer, and he was fair and compassionate to the slaves under his supervision. The fact that both men had consulted Micaela before making their decision filled her with a sense of pride and satisfaction. Compared to life under Arnaud Rouchard's iron rule, Micaela's new home was paradise. Lucien and Adrian treated her as an equal, while Arnaud had treated her like a second-class citizen whose opinions and needs counted for nothing.

Lucien took Micaela riding twice a day, allowing her to practice the skills he taught her. He even involved her in the conversations he had with Adrian and Vance. She was encouraged to ask questions and express her opinions on political issues concerning the colonies and their growing difficulties with England, many of which resembled the problems the French had with the Spanish in New Orleans. Lucien made her a part of his circle of family and friends, rather than excluding her the way Arnaud had.

Since Lucien called a truce, he had maintained a polite and respectful distance from Micaela. True, he had done nothing to warrant her complaint, but he no longer flashed those rakish smiles or tossed seductive suggestions at her. He conducted himself like a perfect gentleman—and for some reason, Micaela had liked him better when she hadn't thought she liked him at all. She was beginning to realize there was just so much dignified respect and courteous distance a woman wanted between herself and the man who drew her attention and affection.

Lucien decreed that she needed to recover from her two near brushes with calamity, and he had been conspicuously absent from her bed. He insisted that his presence might trigger terrifying memories of her ordeal with Barnaby.

The foolish man, didn't he realize she had discovered the difference between his tender lovemaking and brutal ravishment? Lucien was treating her like a delicate flower—and she resented it.

Micaela intended to discuss the subject with Lucien the night of the elaborate reception Adrian had planned. The house hummed with last minute activity and guests arrived ahead of schedule, forcing Micaela to postpone her conversation with Lucien. Later, before the truce ended, she would approach him, she promised herself as she hurried upstairs to dress.

While Micaela arranged her hair and fluffed the lace that adorned the neck, sleeves and hem of the gold satin gown Adrian had purchased for this occasion, she reminded herself that she was about to be put on display for the crême de la crême of Charles Town and nearby plantations. A week earlier, she had entertained spiteful thoughts of getting even with Lucien for forcing her into this wedding, but he had been so charming and respectful the past three days that she felt guilty about embarrassing him in front of his peers.

Micaela frowned when a suspicious thought occurred to her. Perhaps that was exactly how Lucien wanted her to feel. Maybe that was what this truce was all about. He was treating her with kindness in order to bring her under his thumb.

"Micaela? Are you ready to make your appearance?" Adrian called from outside the door.

"Coming, Adrian." Micaela appraised her reflection in the mirror, then tugged at the plunging neckline that was a mite too revealing for her modest tastes. But Adrian had ordered the gown specifically for tonight and she felt obliged to wear it.

Inhaling a deep breath—which was almost too much for the form-fitting gown—Micaela drew herself up to dignified stature, pasted on a smile, and mentally prepared herself to meet the gentry who filled the mansion to overflowing.

Lucien leaned casually against the banister, wedged shoulder to shoulder with the crowd that milled in the foyer like a pen of cattle. Nothing, Lucien reminded himself, drew a mob of socialites like an aristocratic wedding or a lynching. For the past half hour he had listened to this cluster of friends and acquaintances rave on—and on—about his beguiling wife whom they'd met at balls and dinner parties the previous week.

Some of these cocky rogues behaved as if they were as familiarly acquainted with Micaela as Lucien was. That annoyed him, especially when several men indicated that Lucien's notorious reputation must have been an embarrassment to his new wife. Lucien wondered how Micaela had reacted to the gossips who filled her ears with tales of his wild shenanigans. Had she decided to prove herself as much the rake as her new husband by carousing at other social gatherings?

Lucien had been given the third degree about how, where and when he'd met this dazzling beauty he'd married. Everyone was eager to believe he had deflowered Micaela and forced her into wedlock. That was not the kind of gossip Lucien wanted spread around town. Micaela had enough to deal with. She didn't need to tolerate gossip about finding herself with child and forced to marry Lucien.

Since Micaela had not been born and raised in the Carolina colony, Lucien let it be known that he met his ladylove during one of his voyages. There he courted her—very properly, of course—and then asked for her hand. Lord, if the gossipmongers learned that she had stowed away on his ship and duped him a dozen times while she charaded as a waif, they would have a field day.

"Sweet mercy, that is one of the loveliest creatures I've ever seen," Bradford Clodfelter breathed in awe.

Lucien glanced over at the wide-eyed dandy who stood beside him. Then he lifted his gaze to see Micaela and Adrian poised like reigning royalty. All activity and conversation died into silence. All eyes—most especially the masculine ones, damn it—devoured the bewitching female whose smile radiated like the golden gown that advertised and emphasized every alluring curve and swell to its best advantage. The garment alerted every man with eyes in his head as to what he was missing. Damn, Lucien felt *his* knees wobble in reaction to that trim-fitting gown and that sparkling smile. Truly, Micaela possessed a unique inner spirit, and it gave her an effervescent aura that turned heads and captivated eyes.

Lucien's appreciative gaze drifted from the shiny halo of hair that framed her delicate features to. . . . He winced in dismay when his attention landed on the plunging neckline that exposed more creamy flesh than Lucien preferred. His eyes narrowed to thin blue slits as he glanced right and left, watching male mouths water. That gown definitely displayed too much cleavage, Lucien decided. Never in his life had he complained about that—until it was Micaela who drew such rapt attention.

Lucien scowled when he noticed that Vance, who was supposed to be his oldest and dearest friend, looked as if he were entertaining the kind of masculine fantasies that deserved a slap on the cheek.

"Ladies and gentleman," Adrian announced with all the pomp and pageantry he believed this grand occasion deserved. "May I present my lovely granddaughter, Micaela Saffire."

Lucien, and everyone else, noted that Adrian hadn't said granddaughter-in-law. The omission was a subtle declaration that Adrian was so fond of this beguiling lady that he accepted her as if she were blood kin. She bore Adrian's stamp of approval and, Lucien noted sourly, if masculine eyes could leave prints the way hands could, Micaela's bodice would have been well fondled before she even descended the steps!

Double damnation, Lucien muttered under his breath. He felt the insane urge to storm up the steps and drape a shawl over Micaela's shoulders. He wasn't sure how much more of this lusty ogling he could tolerate from this male crowd.

I'm jealous, Lucien realized with a start. *And possessive to boot,* came a needling voice. *Looks like you got exactly what you deserve, Saffire. You may have claimed this bewitching bride, but there are plenty of men here who would prefer that you didn't keep her.*

Lucien couldn't recall feeling quite so strongly about anything in a long time. And if anyone in the crowd dared to touch Micaela too familiarly on the dance floor, Lucien would punch him right in the damned nose.

Micaela tossed a smile to everyone she greeted as she descended the steps. She knew Adrian was anxious for her to make a good impression. This was his night, she realized. He was formally announcing that his grandson—infamous rakehell and libertine—had finally settled down. That was important to Adrian. He wanted the name of Saffire restored to a place of respect.

Her thoughts trailed off when she saw Lucien at the foot of the steps. His squinted eyes and pinched expression indicated he wasn't entertaining nice thoughts. Good Lord, had she done something to annoy him already? The man who had been the epitome of charm and politeness the past few days now resembled a grizzly bear in a gold brocade waistcoat, black velvet jacket and matching breeches. Although his expression was a might sour, Micaela couldn't help but admire his striking appearance.

She reminded herself of the nights on board the schooner when she lingered in the shadows, silently admiring this dashing raven-haired captain who stood at the bridge, with the midnight moon spotlighting him. His powerfully-built physique and confident poise had drawn her eyes and her thoughts.

Though there were a dozen handsome men in attendance tonight, Lucien stood out in the crowd. His towering height, broad shoulders, and spellbinding blue eyes drew attention. He was receiving coveted glances from other women, and Micaela wondered how many of these gaily-adorned females knew Lucien as well as his wife did.

The thought stabbed Micaela's pride. Hurriedly, she reminded herself that this marriage wasn't about fidelity and devotion. Lucien asked only that she like him. He hadn't asked for her love and loyalty, nor had he promised her anything except freedom and financial security. If she knew what was good for her, she would remember that—tonight, and every other night—especially while Lucien was out from underfoot. Which, she reminded herself, he planned to be—a lot.

"Please welcome my granddaughter into your hearts, as I have," Adrian murmured as he bowed to Micaela.

Amid the round of applause—into which Lucien hadn't joined, Micaela noted—Adrian formally presented her to each guest. Micaela had her hand kissed so many times in the following few minutes that her fingers looked as if they'd been soaking in water. Carolinians, Micaela decided, were hand-kissers, while the Spaniards who once ruled Louisiana preferred to peck both cheeks. Micaela preferred the former to the latter. The French had always been huggers—except for Arnaud—and she had never been exceedingly fond of that, either.

"My lady, you dazzle like the sun," Bradford Clodfelter gushed while he bowed and slobbered over her hand.

"How kind of you to say so," Micaela said politely.

Micaela had met Bradford twice while attending the balls with Adrian in Charles Town. Bradford had been the picture of fawning gallantry and had followed her around like a puppy. Micaela found Bradford mildly amusing—usually at his own conceited expense. His exaggerated manners and foppish ways brought smiles to her lips. She considered him harmless, but there were times when she wondered if he didn't have a hidden agenda.

He had made it a point to inform her that he, Lucien and Vance had sailed to England to study at Oxford. He admitted he enjoyed competition with his hometown classmates in every endeavor. Micaela wondered if Bradford was still competing with Lucien, wondered if she had become the object of competition.

There were those in this world who obsessively wanted what someone else had, if only to pride themselves in having acquired it. Bradford, she suspected, was one of those highly competitive individuals who took satisfaction in stealing what others thought they had secured—right out from under their noses.

"Come dance with me," Bradford insisted, drawing Micaela away from the cluster of fawning admirers.

Micaela looked across the congested crowd, wondering what had become of Lucien. He had vanished from sight. Obviously, he planned to put in an appearance to carry off the illusion. He would dance with her a time or two, then hand her to other arms so he could dance with the eager females who had been eyeing him with blatant interest.

Micaela reminded herself that Lucien had agreed to this reception to appease his grandfather. The more she thought about it, the more she suspected her first hunch was correct. Lucien had become excessively courteous and kind before the reception, because he wanted to ensure that she didn't embarrass him. This gala affair was a mirage designed to keep her in line while Lucien went through the motions of a proper, devoted bridegroom.

The thought hurt more than Micaela cared to admit. She had wanted Lucien to like her—really like her—despite their differences. But from all indications, this truce was meant only to get Lucien through this reception, part of the compromise Adrian had forced him to endure.

"How many glasses of spiked cider and sangaree do you plan to ingest before this evening is out?" Vance questioned, as he watched Lucien down the sixth consecutive drink while he lounged in the tufted chair in the study.

"Am I supposed to be counting?" Lucien polished off the cider and reached for another sangaree.

"You are supposed to be dancing with your bride," Vance

reminded him. "She has been in every other man's arms tonight, except yours."

"Including yours, I'm sure," Lucien parried, squinting through heavily-lidded eyes at his handsome friend.

"Of course, mine. It's common protocol to pay respects to the bride on the dance floor. Micaela dances divinely, by the way. You ought to go see for yourself."

When Lucien clasped another drink in hand and stared at the mantel, Vance frowned. "What the devil is wrong with you tonight?"

"Nothing."

"Knowing you as I do, I'd say you were sitting here sulking."

"I'm sitting here *drinking*," Lucien corrected. "Is there a law against that?"

Vance swiped a glass of claret from the servant's tray before the man strode off, then he parked himself in the silk damask chair across from Lucien. He stared at Lucien for a long, pensive moment, then blinked like an owl adjusting to bright light. "My God, I do believe you're jealous," he said. "That's what this drinking routine is all about."

"I most certainly am not," Lucien said with a scoffing snort.

Vance threw back his head and laughed heartily. "You are, too. That bewitching wife of yours is standing in the limelight, right smack dab where you're accustomed to standing. That really gets your goat, doesn't it? In that gold satin gown, Micaela looks—"

"Half dressed," Lucien cut in sourly. He glared at Vance. "And don't tell me you didn't notice. You were devouring her as enthusiastically as the rest of those lusty ogres."

"And you're possessive, too." Vance chuckled in gleeful amusement. "Well, if that doesn't beat all. You connived to marry that rare jewel of a woman in a flaming rush, just to prove your point to Adrian. Lo and behold, you fell in love with her."

Lucien glowered poison darts at his outspoken friend. "Clam up. You're making me sick with your wild conjectures. Love wasn't part of this bargain and you damned well know it."

"It's all those drinks, combined with lovesick jealousy, that

soured your stomach," Vance diagnosed, grinning wickedly.
"I've heard it said that a man can conceal everything from the
world, save two—when he's drunk and when he's in love. I
think you're suffering from both."

"And *I* think you're a philosophical bag of wind," Lucien
muttered.

"All you wanted was to even the score with Adrian," Vance
went on—and on. "But Adrian still defeated you, didn't he?
You have a wife you can barely control on your good days.
You're sitting here brooding because she doesn't share the
same intense affection that has sneaked up on your blind side.
A man should expect to find a few sour grapes in the fruit bowl
of love. And by damned, Lucien, you deserve this."

Lucien slammed his glass down on the end table, slopping
sangaree on his sleeve. "What I do not deserve," he growled
through clenched teeth, "is your harassment. When this farce
of a reception is over, I'm going back to the sea and Micaela
will do exactly as she pleases. That is of no concern to me.
What I feel for this wife I'm shackled to—because of Adrian's
conniving—is a responsibility to keep her in the manner
befitting the mistress of Saffire Plantation. I have kept my
obligation by portraying the respectable husband and I will
continue this charade until half past the midnight hour—"

The movement in the hall caught Lucien's attention. He
glanced over Vance's blond head to see Micaela hovering in
the doorway. The expression of hurt and betrayal on her face
indicated she had been standing there, listening to every unkind,
defensive word Lucien had said—words Lucien wouldn't have
uttered at all if Vance hadn't been taunting him unmercifully.

Noting the direction of Lucien's bloodshot gaze, Vance swiveled in his wing-backed chair to see Micaela swish around in
a flurry of satin and vanish from view. "Shall I summon Dr.
Thorley?" Vance inquired, amber eyes glistening devilishly.
"Lucky for you that the physician is in attendance tonight.
You'll need a doctor to surgically remove both your feet from
your big mouth." He raised his glass in mocking toast, then
took a sip. "You've just ensured that your pretty wife never
expects more from you than the material wealth you've pro-

vided. Congratulations, Lucien, I've never seen anyone make an ass of himself more superbly than you."

Cursing under his breath, Lucien bounded to his feet—a mite wobbly though they were. "This is your fault, Vance," he growled accusingly.

"My fault?" Vance echoed. "You're the one who was shooting his mouth off, not I."

"You provoked me into saying things Micaela didn't need to hear. She and I agreed to a truce and, thanks to you. I'll probably face a rebellion before the night is out. If this reception ends in disaster, I'll hold you personally accountable."

Undaunted, Vance rose to follow in Lucien's wake. "If you would have admitted the truth to me, and to yourself, this wouldn't have happened, Lucien. Your stubborn pride put you in hot water to begin with, and it's what is keeping you there. Go tell Micaela how you feel about her."

"Go to hell, Vance."

"I'd rather not," Vance said with a snicker. "It would be much too crowded with you down there with me."

With Vance cackling behind him, Lucien stormed out the door. Damn it, if he didn't make amends immediately, this truce would blow up in his face. And damn it to hell, why hadn't he ignored Vance's razzing rather than denying and defying it? He'd made matters a hundred times worse. That wounded look on Micaela's face was killing Lucien by inches. Even the whiskey he had poured down his throat couldn't numb him to this bone-deep feeling of regret. He had hell to pay and he knew it.

Twelve

"Micaela, come dance with me. Every man at this party has held you, and I've gone without you as long as I can stand."

Micaela's back stiffened like a flagpole when the thick baritone voice, and the scent of whiskey, settled over her. After overhearing Lucien's biting remarks to Vance, she had rushed back to the ballroom, aching for any kind of distraction that would ease the hurt of hearing her suspicions confirmed. The past few days had been a charade designed to keep her in line so she wouldn't humiliate her husband at this damned party.

Her heart twisted in her chest. She knew Lucien was still playing games with her, even now. His request to dance was cleverly broadcast to the crowd. Everybody else might have been convinced that he was fond of her, but she knew differently.

Well, just wait until they were on the dance floor, she silently fumed. He would know exactly what she thought of him, of his deceit, and his superficial attention to husbandly obligations!

Pirouetting like a graceful ballerina, Micaela plastered a cheery smile on her face—all for appearance sake, which seemed to be so crucial to this husband of hers. When he curled his arm around her waist to lead her onto the dance floor,

Micaela discreetly jabbed her elbow in his belly. When Lucien pulled her into his arms, she purposely trounced on his toes, then took satisfaction in watching him swallow a howl of pain. Each time he glided across the floor she pinched his arm, then ground her heel into his boot—all in perfectly synchronized rhythm with the music.

"Micaela, I'm sorry," Lucien murmured, then dodged the discreetly uplifted knee aimed at the most vulnerable part of his anatomy. "I—"

"I don't want to be your obligation," Micaela interrupted, her bitter words contrasting the dazzling smile she displayed for the crowd's benefit. "I don't want anything from you, especially not this charade. When you leave here tomorrow, I never want to see you again."

"Your wish is granted," Lucien replied, sporting the same radiant smile she offered the guests. "Anything else?"

"Yes, you can go straight to hell, Lucien."

"I've been there."

Yes, she supposed he had, loving Cecilia and losing her the way he had. Dealing with her anger was nothing compared to the torment of losing the woman he loved. After all, Micaela was nothing but a part of this charade that would be played until half past midnight.

"To Lucien and Micaela!" Adrian boomed over the orchestral music. "May their marriage be a long and happy one!"

When Lucien halted in the middle of the floor to give his bride the customary kiss, Micaela bit down on his lip. She knew she was being spitefully childish, but he'd hurt her—badly. The affection she'd come to feel for him had given him the power to hurt her. No man, she vowed, would ever hold that advantage over her again.

When the music faded, Micaela backed from his arms. "Don't you dare come near me again," she hissed for his ears only. "I'll hate you till the day I die."

Micaela spun toward the terrace door. She was angry, hurt and fed up with pretense. Gripping the railing, she stared up at the stars that winked mockingly at her. Willfully, Micaela blinked back her tears. Curse that man to hell, she raged silently.

He couldn't know how it hurt to be considered an obligation and responsibility maintained for appearance sake.

Arnaud had reluctantly raised his brother's child as his own. He resented her presence, just as Lucien did. Oh, how she'd hoped Lucien would be different from Arnaud, but he was just the same . . . *just the same!*

"Micaela?"

She froze when that quiet voice wafted toward her. "Kindly leave, unless you want more of the same treatment you received on the dance floor," she managed to say without spitting the words at Lucien.

Lucien wasn't sure who infuriated him most—Micaela, Vance or himself. The damaging conversation in the study, and the subsequent battle on the dance floor, put Lucien in the foulest of moods. He wanted to shrug aside the past half hour, but emotions were nagging at him—dozens of them. He didn't know how to explain, where to begin apologizing—not that Micaela would believe or accept an apology. She was too furious to listen, but he felt compelled to try.

"What you heard was bruised pride and whiskey talking," he tried to explain.

Micaela abandoned all ladylike conduct and swung over the railing of the terrace. "There is nothing you can say to smooth over the truth," she hissed between her tears. "I still plan to hate you until I die," she sputtered before she scurried through the shrubs to disappear from sight.

Lucien muttered under his breath as he followed Micaela's unconventional path through the bushes. He didn't have the slightest idea what he was going to say when he caught up with that female cyclone, but he couldn't let it end like this.

Maybe he should simply make his apologies for behaving like an ass—as Vance had so candidly pointed out—then bid Micaela goodbye. It would probably be for the best. He and Micaela had fulfilled their obligations to pacify Adrian. Now all that remained was to accept this marriage for what it was and go their separate ways. The peaceful co-existence he and Micaela had shared for the past few days had ended like a cannon blast erupting a temporary truce between two opposing armies.

Damn it, Lucien cursed as he tried to track Micaela down—without success. Nothing he did, when it pertained to his fiery, high spirited bride, ever came out right. Lucien was beginning to think he carried a curse when it came to women.

Swiping at the tears, Micaela scurried into the stables. She intended to climb on the mare and recapture the exhilarating feelings she had experienced while Lucien taught her to ride. She longed to feel the powerful steed beneath her, carrying her away from the torment of knowing she had come to care so much for a man who was still in love with a memory, a man who patronized her to produce the kind of behavior he wanted from her. Damn him to the nethermost regions of hell!

And damn all men everywhere while she was at it, Micaela decided. If Adrian hadn't schemed to lure her in as bait to entrap Lucien, she wouldn't be in this impossible tangle. And if Vance hadn't buckled to Lucien's crazed demands, she wouldn't have been forced into a wedding ceremony. She had fled New Orleans, craving personal independence, wanting the chance to exercise her freedom of choice. And still she hadn't been allowed to live her life without the influence and manipulation of men!

"Chaney?" Micaela whispered as she inched inside the darkened room at the rear of the stables. It was then that she remembered Chaney had moved into Barnaby Harpster's cottage after he had taken the position of overseer.

Since the other grooms were in the kitchen, socializing with the household staff, Micaela bridled the mare herself, then led the bareback steed a good distance from the house before climbing the split-rail fence to ease onto the mare's back.

The mare adjusted to the billowing skirt that flapped around her while Micaela set a swift pace along the moonlit path. She was familiar with this route, for it was the same one Lucien took when he accompanied her on their morning and evening rides. Micaela had learned to flow with the motion of the steed, and she took the bend of the road without launching into the underbrush as she had that first day on horseback.

Although Micaela's ride granted her time to regain her shattered composure, her stomach was still tied in aching knots. Overhearing Lucien's comments to Vance was like pouring salt on a festering wound. Micaela had already tolerated several hours of snide remarks from women who had bent her ear with tales of Lucien's notorious reputation. One spiteful twit— Jessica Landberg was her name—had claimed that anyone with any sense knew that Lucien had never gotten over Cecilia, even if he had decided to take a wife.

And speaking of sense, Micaela decided Jessica didn't have an oversupply of it herself. She was short on brains and long on tongue. Jessica claimed to have been one of Cecilia's closest friends. The prissy red-haired chit had rattled nonstop for a half hour about what a beauty Cecilia had been, how Lucien had doted on her, how madly in love the couple had been before tragedy struck. Then to make matters worse, Micaela had heard Lucien confirm her suspicions that he considered his wife an obligation and nothing more.

Inhaling a deep cleansing breath, Micaela pulled the winded steed to a halt and dismounted to amble along the tree-lined path. The mare jerked up her head and snorted as she followed Micaela, who felt the need to walk off some of her frustration. Micaela paused to survey her surroundings. Whatever sound had caught the mare's attention seemed to have vanished, because the steed plodded methodically alongside her.

Lost to troubled thoughts, Micaela walked along the road until she reached the stone cliff that overlooked the river that glistened like mercury in the moonlight. Clumps of pines and cedars skirted the bluff—except for the furthermost peak that towered over a wild tumble of rocks and boulders that spilled down to the riverbank.

Adrian had told Micaela that a log cabin once sat upon this looming bluff. During those first years when hostile Indians terrorized white settlements, this peak had been a lookout point. . . .

The rustle of pine limbs brought the mare's head up again,

and she nickered uneasily. An eerie tingle trickled down Micaela's backbone. Instinct warned her that someone—or something—was lurking in the shadows.

Lucien, she suspected. He had probably decided to follow her so they could have it out in private. Well, that was dandy fine with Micaela. She couldn't completely speak her mind when surrounded by a crowd of guests. Now she could shout her irritation at Lucien to high heaven.

Micaela wheeled around to lambaste Lucien with several greeting insults, but she strangled on her breath when the voluminous form of another man lumbered toward her. Sensing impending doom, Micaela retreated an involuntary step. Her eyes widened in terror when she saw it was Barnaby Harpster who stalked toward her.

His taunting sneer rolled past her, echoing around the stone peak, coming at her from all directions. "I've waited four long days to make you pay, wench," he said as he came closer. "And believe me, you are going to pay dearly for costing me my job. . . ."

Growing more concerned by the minute, Lucien circled to the front door of the mansion to request Vance's assistance.

"What's wrong?" Vance questioned, coming immediately to his feet to follow in Lucien's wake.

"I can't find Micaela anywhere."

He stepped outside in time to hear the thunder of hooves in the distance. Sickening dread seeped through him when he recognized the roan mare Micaela had taken as her mount. The steed raced into the barn, reins trailing on the ground.

In fiend-ridden haste, Lucien and Vance dashed to the stables to saddle their horses. With Vance at his heels, Lucien galloped off in the direction from which the lathered mare had come.

God, how he wished he could turn back the hands of time to that moment when he'd blurted out those stupid, defensive remarks. He'd tried to salvage his bruised pride while battling unprecedented feelings of possessive jealousy—and too much whiskey. The combination proved disastrous. He had unintentionally hurt Micaela with his cruel denials and left her racing off to parts unknown.

Lucien exhausted his repertoire of curses—ones directed solely toward himself. But the oaths lost their zing, and he had to invent a few new ones as he rode hell-for-leather. Lucien was feeling sufficiently guilty and repentant by the time he reined his steed to a halt at the bend of the road. Frantic, he thrashed through the underbrush to reach the creek, but Micaela was nowhere to be found.

In a single bound, Lucien was back in the saddle, racing along the path that skirted the river. When he saw the stone bluff that incited his nightmares, icy fear froze in his chest. No, Lucien tried to reassure himself. Disaster wouldn't dare strike twice in the same place, would it? History hadn't repeated itself, had it?

It had been five years since Lucien had approached this lonely cliff, asking what he might have done to prevent the terrible tragedy. The urge to reverse direction very nearly overwhelmed him. He didn't want to stand on that crumbling rock bluff and peer down the cascade of boulders, for fear of seeing what he didn't want to see.

"Vance?" Lucien's voice crackled as he dismounted, his gaze glued to the rocky precipice.

"Don't start leaping to conclusions," Vance said as he hurried up beside Lucien. "Micaela probably just climbed off her horse to take a walk and the mare did what all horses do when left to their own devices. The horse followed its nose instead of its tail, heading for the stables and the grain trough. I'm sure Micaela is fine—furious but fine."

Lucien wished he could be certain of that, but he couldn't. He was stung by foreboding, by a premonition that all was not well. Gritting his teeth, he strode to the edge of the bluff, swamped by so many haunting memories that he had to force himself to go where his faltering footsteps were reluctant to take him.

In that horrifying moment, when Lucien looked down to see not one but two mangled bodies sprawled on the wind-scoured boulders, he swore the pulse of his very existence shriveled like a dead blossom. The cavity that once held his heart echoed with an empty silence nothing could fill. The tormenting sight below him brought such numbness of mind, body and spirit that Lucien staggered to stay on his feet.

"Oh, my God, what have I done!"

A roar of immeasurable anguish resounded along the bluff. Every tortuous emotion Lucien had held in check came flooding out like a bursting dam. The haunting sound echoed down the river, taking every ounce of Lucien's self-control with it. He shook his fists at the heavens, and cursed the cruel twist of fate that left Micaela sprawled on the stone boulders, just as Cecilia had been five years earlier.

Lucien's stark terror turned to frantic desperation. Hands trembling, he yanked off his jacket and shirt, then tied his waistcoat to his other garments to form the beginning of an improvised rope.

"Sweet mercy," Vance gasped as he stood beside Lucien, staring down the cliff in shocked disbelief.

"Give me your shirt and jacket," Lucien hurriedly ordered Vance.

Dazed, Vance tried to comply, but he couldn't move quickly enough to suit Lucien who was already jerking at his sleeves. With undo haste they designed a rope that Lucien secured to the saddle. Easing himself over the rocky ledge, Lucien inched down the face of the cliff. Vance came shortly thereafter, using small footholds in the stones to steady himself.

Once they had negotiated the ten-foot drop, Lucien tied the free end of the rope to the jagged peak of a boulder, ensuring his horse didn't wander away while he made the next leg of his downward climb.

After several strenuous maneuvers over and around slanted boulders, Lucien came upon Barnaby Harpster sprawled on the slab of stone. The man looked as if he had been staked out by a war party of hostile Indians, except that no ropes bound him. Barnaby's sightless stare seemed to be directed at the moon.

"He's dead," Vance pronounced grimly.

Lucien stared down at Micaela's lifeless body, which was wedged between two perpendicular boulders. Her arm hung limply over the stones, and her head drooped against her chest. It took all the strength of will Lucien possessed to make that final descent toward Micaela. He had taken this route once before, when he lost the woman who was to become his wife. Now he was retracing the same agonizing path to retrieve the woman who was his wife.

And not by her own choice, Lucien thought dismally. His attempt to outsmart Adrian had brought Micaela to this lowly, painful end. His cruel words had sent her running. And as was so often the case, bad luck struck when one was being careless and reckless.

Micaela had left herself vulnerable to a man who was out for revenge. But somehow Micaela had managed to take Barnaby Harpster with her when she fell. Even in death, Barnaby hadn't claimed victory over this daring beauty. Micaela had defied him to the end. . . .

Lucien's hand hovered inches above Micaela's dangling arm. He was afraid to touch her. For if he found no pulse, all hope that she survived would wither and die right here on this spot. Inhaling a shaky breath, Lucien made himself reach down to curl his arm between Micaela's body and the boulders.

With Vance's assistance, Lucien lifted her free. When her head rolled against his bare chest, Lucien felt the moist streak of blood that smeared her cheek. When he felt her lifeblood spilling out of her—and onto him—everything inside him crumbled like pillars of sand.

Vance clutched at Micaela's wrist while Lucien levered her into his arms. "I think she's still alive," he burst out. "Her pulse is weak, but—"

"But will she even survive until we get her to the top of the cliff?" Lucien questioned in torment. He brushed his hand over the back of her head to reveal the bloody wound to Vance.

Vance said no more. He simply turned away to climb to the ledge so Lucien could lift Micaela up to him.

When Lucien reached the ledge just below the peak of the cliff, he sent Vance up the wall via the makeshift rope. The climb, with Micaela draped over his shoulder, had been agonizing. Lucien panted for breath as he tied the rope around Micaela's waist, then waited for Vance to back up the horse.

When they finally had Micaela on solid ground, Lucien sent Vance ahead to inform Dr. Thorley that his patient would be arriving shortly.

Lucien kept his gelding at a walk and cradled Micaela against him. His lips grazed her forehead, wishing that silly fairy tale about the prince rousing a lovely princess from death-like sleep really could come true. Although Lucien doubted Micaela heard him, he yammered to her every step of the way home. He held firm to the belief that Micaela wouldn't be so impolite as to die in the middle of a conversation. She was known to take her leave directly after having the last word, but never while someone was still talking. Therefore, Lucien talked nonstop, refusing to let Micaela slip away from him, praying that his words would soak through the dark silence and provide her with the will to fight for her life.

"Don't believe a word I said, Caela," Lucien murmured against her wan cheek. "Vance was badgering me unmercifully. You know how ornery he can be, don't you?"

Although Micaela didn't answer Lucien kept right on talking.

"If you want the truth, I'd been in a sour mood since I saw you poised at the head of the steps, looking like an angel in a cloud of gold. You were drawing a damned sight more attention in that revealing gown than I preferred.

"Where did you get that dress anyway? And why didn't you sew a tippet into that plunging neckline? Do you think I enjoy watching men gawk at you? Well, I don't. And you should have heard Bradford Clodfelter carry on about you while he frothed at the mouth! He can be such a nuisance with his overactive sense of competition. Since our college days at Oxford, he's wanted whatever Vance and I had. Of course, I can understand Bradford's fascination for you, but. . . ."

Lucien leaned down to ensure that Micaela was still breathing. Thankfully, her faint breath whispered against the hair on his chest. Good. She was still with him and they were halfway home.

"I know it wasn't part of our bargain for me to be jealous

of all your fawning admirers,'' Lucien continued. ''That's why I cloistered myself in the study before I lost what was left of my temper and socked one of those dandies for drooling all over you. The fact is that I've developed a . . . certain attachment to you. And the God's truth is that I requested this truce so I could change your low opinion of me, not manipulate you. It's not what you thought at all, wary cynic that you've become.''

Lucien nodded, as if Micaela had flung a rejoinder at him. ''I know, I'm as much the cynic as you are, but hell, at least I was trying to smooth the wrinkles out of this marriage of ours. You must have wanted that, too, because you had been meeting me halfway . . . until that cursed conversation I had with Vance.''

Again Lucien paused to consider what Micaela would have said in response. ''All right, so you didn't really want me all that much, not that I can blame you. You were cooperating for Adrian's sake, I suspect. He has pampered and spoiled you, and he was anxious for you to be accepted by his peers. He expected you would be the one who could undo the damage I've done to the Saffire reputation the past few years. And, Caela, though I know you have every right to hate me, I—''

The image of Micaela standing in the middle of the ballroom, smiling pretentiously while she voiced her disgust, sprang to mind, tormenting Lucien to no end. God, how he wished he could retract every unkind word he'd uttered that sent Micaela dashing off into the night, and into calamity!

''That is all behind us now,'' Lucien insisted as he brushed his lips over her forehead. ''I swear to you that when you have recovered, we are going to make a fresh start. I promise that I will never hurt you again—''

''Lucien?''

Vance's quiet voice jostled Lucien from his tormented rambling. He found himself sitting in front of the mansion, surrounded by concerned guests.

''Dr. Thorley is waiting to examine Micaela. Hand her to me,'' Vance requested.

When Lucien just sat there clutching Micaela to him like a frightened child clinging to the only security he had left in his shattered world, Vance smiled compassionately. "I'll be as careful with her as you have been. Trust me, Lucien."

Staring at Micaela, as if he feared he'd never see her again, Lucien leaned out to drape her limp body in Vance's uplifted arms. "Talk to her, Vance. Keep talking to her," he said urgently.

The anguish in Lucien's eyes, the tormented expression on his bronzed features, put a lump in Vance's throat. If it were possible for Lucien to look worse than he had that tragic night five years past, he had indeed exceeded himself. Vance knew that losing Cecilia had devastated Lucien, but no words adequately described the expression on his face now. The poor man was suffering a dozen kinds of hell, and Vance's heart went out to his friend.

Vance was halfway through the vestibule, murmuring to his lifeless companion when Lucien overtook him. Although Lucien allowed Vance to carry Micaela up the flight of steps, he clutched her hand and continued speaking, as if she were hanging on his every word.

She was hanging on all right, Vance thought bleakly. Hanging on by one fragile thread in that chasm between life and death.

The instant Vance laid Micaela on the bed Dr. Thorley shooed everyone out of the room, even Lucien, who planted himself solidly by the door and refused to budge from the spot—until the physician ordered Vance and the nearby servants to bodily remove him.

Lucien walked down the hall like a victim of a trance. When Vance guided him into the study, he quickly poured two glasses of brandy. The glass in Lucien's hand shattered into a zillion pieces when he hurled it across the room. Vance cringed when Lucien's tormented bellow ricocheted off the walls like the howling voices of the eternal damned.

"Do you know what her last words were to me?" Lucien said in an agonized whisper.

"No," Vance murmured. "What did she say?"

"I'll hate you till the day I die. . . ." Lucien's voice broke and his head dropped like an anchor plunging into a bottomless sea. Tears swam in his eyes as he sank into his chair to stare blindly at the wall. "I'll hate you till the day I die . . ."

Lucien knew he was just beginning what already seemed like the longest night of his life. Guilt and regret rode him like a brutal horseman lashing out with a biting whip. Fear beat in rhythm with his aching heart. He didn't want to lose that green-eyed misfit who made the plight of others her crusade. He didn't want her going to her grave loathing him—didn't want her to go at all! The world would never seem right if Micaela wasn't out there in it somewhere.

Lucien prayed for God to forgive him for hurting Micaela, because he knew she wouldn't, knew he couldn't blame her if she didn't. He had destroyed something pure and vibrant and sweet, and he cursed himself all the way to hell and back for it. And just when Lucien had begun to believe there was more to life than existence, he was tormentingly reminded that he was all too familiar with the bitterness, grief and heartbreaking regret this world had to offer. . . .

Thirteen

Activity at Saffire Plantation came to a screeching halt after news of Micaela's tragedy spread like wildfire. Servants and slaves who depended on Micaela's lively spirit for inspiration and guidance moved mechanically through their duties. Laughter and animated conversation no longer filled the halls.

Shortly after Micaela was examined by Dr. Thorley, Adrian collapsed. The physician found he had two patients on his hands. Lucien was beside himself with concern and regret. The thought of losing all the family he had left was almost more than he could bear.

Lucien fully understood the anguish Adrian had endured over the past five years. Without family, Lucien realized, there was no link to the past or the future. Lucien forgave the old man for all his threats and scheming to reunite the family. Lucien experienced the same desperation to make everything right, to end the anger and regret and make peace.

Lucien looked up anxiously when Dr. Thorley came downstairs. The physician shook his head gloomily, murmuring that only time would determine if Micaela would survive. As for Adrian, the combination of shock and old age had gotten the best of him. Dr. Thorley insisted that Adrian was a tough old bird and should be back on his feet within a few days. It seemed the patriarch was more concerned about Micaela than himself, and the need to tend to the lass was all the inspiration required for him to recover.

Although Micaela had not regained consciousness, Lucien refused to leave her side. She lay there in a death-like trance that tore Lucien's heart in two. Tormented, he sat beside her for two days—and nights. It haunted him beyond words to see this vivacious female, who put a spark in so many lives, lying there motionless, hovering at death's doorstep. Her thick lashes lay against her pale cheeks like delicate butterflies. A bandage surrounded Micaela's head like a turban, and other bandages covered the gashes on her arms and legs. She looked so frail and defenseless that Lucien could barely stand it.

"Lucien?"

Vance's hushed voice filtered through Lucien's tormented thoughts. Lucien glanced at Vance with red-streaked eyes that testified to his lack of sleep, the extent of his concern.

"What do you want me to do about the schooners?" Vance asked. "We are to set sail for Savannah tomorrow."

"You take command," Lucien requested, his attention straying back to Micaela. "Have Louis Beecham take command of my ship and follow in your schooner's wake. The other two vessels are bound for England with cargo. Check the warehouse and the ledgers to ensure that all the goods that are being shipped to London are on board."

"Is that all?"

"No." Lucien peered bleakly at Vance. "You can pray for all you're worth while you're at it."

"I have been," Vance murmured before he eased the door shut behind him.

Lucien stared at the window, noting the thick gray clouds that blanketed the plantation. "Do you see that, squirt?" he questioned Micaela. "You've taken the sun away from the day. How long do you intend to lie here while the rest of us drift like rudderless ships? You might show a little consideration for those of us who feed on your strength of character and spirit—"

His voice dried up when he noticed the faint flutter of lashes. His hand curled around her fingertips, giving them an encouraging squeeze. "Come back to me, fairy princess. Your kingdom of devoted servants awaits you. We need you to put the sunshine back in our lives."

It was a silly whim, he knew, but he couldn't resist dropping a kiss to her dewy-soft lips. To Lucien's delighted relief, her tangled lashes swept up to reveal dull green eyes that stared in his general direction. Lucien wanted to shout his joy to high heaven!

"Lord, squirt, it's good to have you back. Don't go away. I'll be right back." Lucien shot across the room to alert the physician and announce to all the world that Micaela had finally regained consciousness. Even Vance, who was on his way out the door, switched direction and took the steps two at a time to greet Micaela.

Micaela licked her bone-dry lips and peered at the blurry faces that hovered above her. She stared at each face, then glanced around the room. "Where am I?"

When Dr. Thorley eased down on one side of bed to examine her Lucien sank down on the other. "You're in your room at the plantation," he informed her.

She swallowed uneasily, trying to remain perfectly still while the physician stuck his face into hers to check the dilation of her pupils. "Next question," Micaela continued. "*Who* am I?"

The blurry faces stared at her in shock and the crowd of onlookers gasped collectively. Micaela tried to ease into a more comfortable position, but she felt like a limp jellyfish. She had no energy, and she was unnerved by this room full of people she had never seen before. Her head throbbed something fierce and her mouth was as dry as dust. She was sure she could drink an ocean of water and still not quench her thirst.

"May I have a drink, Mister. . . ?" She directed the questioned to the ruggedly good-looking man with piercing blue eyes and several days growth of beard on his jaw.

"Mister Saffire. Lucien Saffire." He frowned in concern as

his hand folded around hers. "I'm your husband, Micaela. Don't you remember me?"

"I'm Micaela?" she bleated. "And you're my . . . *what!*" Squinting, she reappraised the muscularly-built man who sat beside her. "How can we possibly be married? I don't even know you!"

When Micaela tried to prop herself up to get a closer look at the man who claimed to be her husband, Dr. Thorley gently pressed her head back to the pillow.

"Just relax, my dear. You are recovering from a serious accident in which you received a sharp blow to the skull, a dozen bruises and several nasty scrapes. We will fetch you a glass of water, but you must promise to lie still until we get back."

Micaela frowned when the entourage followed the doctor and Lucien out the door. "How many people does it take to fetch a glass of water?"

Lucien half turned to smile gently at her. "We'll be right back, sweetheart, with all the water you can possibly drink."

Dr. Thorley closed the door, then turned toward the anxious crowd that filled the hall. "Micaela appears to be suffering from amnesia. Considering the fall she took, it could have been caused by the blow she suffered. But we cannot rule out the possibility of emotional trauma. Only Micaela knows what happened before she and Barnaby Harpster ended up on those boulders below the cliff."

"How long before her memory returns?" Lucien questioned.

Dr. Thorley's shoulder lifted in a noncommittal shrug. "It could be a few days, a few weeks, or—" He sighed audibly. "Or the damage could be permanent. Micaela may never recall who she is or what happened. In cases like this, where physical impairment and emotional trauma are both concerned, it's impossible to give a definite prognosis.

"Familiar faces and familiar surroundings may prompt partial memory. But I'm most hesitant to take her back to that cliff until she is in good health and feels comfortable with all of you. You must be patient and understanding with her," he coached. "It will be frustrating and confusing for Micaela to have to accept everything you tell her as fact, when she cannot recall who she is or where she was until this exact moment in time.''

"Yoo-hoo! Is anyone there? Where did everybody go? If someone would kindly fetch me some water I will be eternally grateful!''

Bodies collided with one another in haste to do Micaela's bidding. Lucien wheeled back toward the room. Despite the doctor's order, Micaela had propped herself up against the headboard to inspect the bandages on her arms.

Lucien smiled to himself. Perhaps Micaela couldn't remember who she was, but that same willful spirit that drove her in the past was hard at work. She had never—Lucien reminded himself—been able to take orders worth a damn.

Smiling in amusement, Lucien stood just inside the study, watching Micaela tiptoe through the abandoned hallway. She was trying to slip outside without alerting the houseful of guardian angels who had been smothering her for the past week. Lucien couldn't honestly say he was surprised to see Micaela sneaking down the steps like a criminal making a getaway. Since she had regained consciousness she had been begging to part company with that ''confounded mattress''—as she referred to it.

Lucien had carried Micaela down to the porch twice the past week so she could enjoy the fresh morning air, but he had adhered to the doctor's orders of limited physical activity, though Micaela insisted—on numerous occasions—that she was perfectly all right. According to her, cabin fever was the worst affliction she had to contend with.

"Going somewhere, squirt?'' Lucien stepped from the shadows the moment Micaela grabbed the door knob.

Micaela stopped dead in her tracks when she heard the rich baritone voice behind her. Although Lucien claimed to be her husband, and everybody she asked confirmed it, Micaela couldn't remember marrying this strikingly handsome rake. True, she found him magnetically appealing and utterly charming, but he was still a stranger in an overwhelming world of unfamiliar faces.

"I really do need some more fresh air," she insisted, daring Lucien to deny her the privilege.

"Very well, my love, if that is your wish, then it will be granted. But you must agree to share my company. I don't want you wandering around and getting lost."

Lucien was making it impossible not to like him. Of all the individuals who had appointed themselves as her nursemaids, Lucien was the only one who granted her the slightest freedom. Why she felt this innate need for freedom she didn't know, but she sorely resented not having the choice to do what she pleased, when she wanted to do it.

"Let me fetch a cloak for you," Lucien insisted. He stepped around the corner to grab a wool cloak off the hook. "There's a chill in the air. I don't want you to catch the grippe. You'd be confined to bed again, and I know how you detest that 'confounded mattress.'"

Micaela grinned when Lucien wrapped the cloak around her shoulders. The feel of his arms lightly caressing her was oddly comforting—like a distant memory that touched the corner of her fuzzy mind before flitting away. "I suppose you think I'm a frightful shrew for complaining about being confined to quarters." She stared curiously at Lucien. "Was I always a mite rebellious or is it the amnesia and confinement that prompts this compulsive need for freedom?"

Lucien reached around Micaela to open the door. His lips grazed her cheek momentarily. "You've always been strapped with the kind of feisty spirit that won't quit, and a fierce desire for independence," he said with a smile. "I have had my hands full trying to control you in this marriage of ours. You have constantly gone off half-cocked, though you know perfectly well that I worry about your safety and welfare."

"How long have we been married?" Micaela asked as she stepped outside to inhale a breath of crisp autumn air.

"A month," Lucien reported.

Micaela glanced up at him. "Were we happy?"

Lucien stared down into that bewitching face so alive with

curiosity and felt his heart twist in his chest. What he and Micaela had been, he reminded himself, was very much at odds. But if she didn't remember, he wasn't about to tell her. This was his chance to make a new beginning, a better beginning. He had vowed to do just that if Micaela survived her terrifying ordeal. And considering what she'd been through, she deserved to enjoy contentment, security and considerably less emotional turmoil while she recuperated.

"Yes, my dear, we were extremely happy." Lucien spoke the lie without batting an eyelash. Maybe he couldn't change the past, but he could mold their future. And by damned, he would compensate for the hurt and frustration he'd caused her.

When Lucien strode off to hitch up the carriage, Micaela admired the masculine grace with which he moved, the intriguing way his jacket rippled over the muscled contours of his back. Now, why wouldn't she have been happy with this appealing man? she asked herself reasonably. What was there about Lucien Saffire *not* to like? He was amusing and considerate and he seemed devoted to her. She must have loved him dearly, she decided. Lucien said himself that she was a bit independent and belligerent, but he didn't seem to mind. And if she had *not* loved him with every beat of her heart, she certainly wouldn't have consented to marry him, now would she? Micaela couldn't be sure, but she didn't think that sounded like something she would do.

When Lucien returned, Micaela was surveying the stately mansion, the immaculate gardens and freshly-painted outbuildings. "Who is responsible for keeping this estate in such grand condition? It truly is lovely, isn't it?"

Lucien chuckled as he scooped Micaela into his arms and seated her in the carriage. "You may congratulate yourself, madam. It was you who organized the paint and weed brigades that gave this estate a much-needed facial."

"Me?" Micaela blinked, stunned.

"You," he confirmed as he climbed up beside her. "I reminded you that you were the mistress of the plantation, not one of the servants. But holding true to form, you took paint brush in hand like a general raising his sword to call the troops

to battle. You attacked every last building and picket fence. . . .
What's wrong, Micaela?''

A flash of memory raced across her mind like a shadow. For
a brief instant, she glimpsed a dark, snarling face. Before she
could identify the image and attach it to a specific incident
from the past, the vision vanished.

"Nothing." Frowning, she squirmed on the seat. "I thought
I remembered someone—or something—but it escaped me as
quickly as it came. And curse it, Lucien, I can't tell you how
frustrating it is to rely on everyone else's word about who I
am and what has happened! I don't know any of you very well,
and I know myself even less !''

Lucien gathered her in his arms to give her a comforting
squeeze. A feeling of contented familiarity flooded through her
when she caught a whiff of his masculine scent.

"Have patience, love," he whispered before he dropped a
featherlight kiss to her lips. "Time will fill in the gaps. Now,
what would you like to do on your first official outing? Tour
the rice and indigo fields? Take a stroll through the meadow?
Try your hand at archery?''

Micaela stared up at him. "I am adept with a bow and
arrow?''

"No, madam, I haven't had the chance to teach you yet, but
I plan to. It isn't too strenuous, and it will offer you an excuse
to go outside.''

Micaela straightened on the carriage seat, her chin tilting to
that determined angle Lucien well remembered, even if she
didn't. "I prefer that you take me to the place where I had
my accident. I want my life back, Lucien. If the scenery and
surroundings prompt even one memory, then I've taken one
step in the right direction.''

Chastising himself for offering to take Micaela anywhere
she wanted to go, Lucien popped the reins, sending the horse
down the dirt path. Since the accident, he had been unable to
deny Micaela anything. He had made a pact with himself that
he would compensate for the hurt and torment he'd caused
Micaela. Perhaps she would eventually remember more than
he preferred, perhaps this peaceful coexistence would be lost

forever, but he owed her, damn it. If not for his cruel words, Micaela would never have flitted off alone to encounter the vengeful man who tried to dispose of her.

Micaela wracked her brain, trying to conjure up fragments of misplaced memories. When Lucien reached the horseshoe bend beside the stream, Micaela grasped his sleeve, urging him to stop. For a split-second, she felt the sensations of flying. Something familiar in her surroundings must have triggered that odd feeling.

"You took a nose-dive off your horse and into the creek during your first riding lesson." Lucien prompted. He cupped her chin in his hand, directing her pensive gaze to him. Ever so gently, his lips whispered over hers. "After I dashed through the bushes, afraid you'd broken every bone in this lovely body of yours, we made wild sweet love on the creek bank. Do you remember, Caela?" he murmured. "It's a day I will never forget."

A hot blush stained her cheeks, and she withdrew into her own space. Thus far, Lucien hadn't pressed her for his husbandly rights. He had taken up residence in the sitting room beside the boudoir. Although she knew she was being unfair to him, the thought of intimacy unsettled her. She simply wasn't ready to take that step with this husband who still seemed like a stranger.

Micaela cleared her throat and stared straight ahead. "Yes, well, I'm sure it was very ... um ... pleasurable, loving you as I did—do," she corrected awkwardly.

Lucien chortled softly, watching her face blossom with color. She was a constant source of amusement to him. She was like a wide-eyed child discovering a new world, and half pretending awareness of a life that escaped her memory. Now that the trouble and conflicts between them were forgotten, Lucien was learning just how satisfying life could be. He had been given a second chance to find happiness.

"What are you laughing at, Lucien?" she asked, puzzled.

"That our lovemaking was very ... um ... pleasurable," he couldn't resist teasing. "If there is one thing you could remember, I wish it would be that *pleasurable* is all too modest a description for what we shared.''

Micaela blushed profusely, then darted a sideways glance at Lucien. ''Let's get on this with, shall we? No one is more eager to remember the past than I.''

Lucien wished with all his heart that he could pick and choose what Micaela remembered. He would have her recall each wondrous moment of passion, each instant of laughter. He wanted to protect Micaela from the tormenting incident that transformed a night of frustration and conflict into a living hell for her.

When Lucien pulled the buggy to a halt beside the wind-swept cliff, Micaela sensed this was their destination. Her gaze drifted from the skirting of trees to the stone precipice that overlooked the river. Before Lucien could hop down to lift her from the carriage she stepped to the ground. With the brisk wind billowing in her cloak, she approached the cliff, drawn by an emotion she couldn't name.

For several seconds she hovered on the ledge, demanding the past to open like the deep chasm before her and reveal itself to her. Inching close to the edge, Micaela stared down at the jagged boulders that were strewn against the face of the bluff. When her foot slipped on the crumbling pebbles, memory flashed in her mind like an explosion. A horrified scream raced through her mind and she remembered falling into the vast expanse of nothingness. In desperation, Micaela lurched around. Lucien stood a few feet away, and she latched onto him like a drowning cat clenching its claws in driftwood. She hung onto him for dear life, waiting for the pocket of memory to stop replaying itself.

Lucien hugged Micaela close, feeling her body trembling against his. It was a dozen kinds of hell to stand on this bluff, lost to his own agonizing nightmares. He remembered that awful night well enough for both of them. If she could forget the terror she must have experienced here, he would spare her that—and so much more.

The same snarling face that had leaped to mind when Micaela peered at the overseer's cottage a half hour earlier materialized.

The frightening vision shook her to the roots of her soul, for reasons unknown to her. Trying to recapture the situation surrounding the haunting memory was like grasping a fistful of fog. It was all there in confused tangles, just beyond her comprehension, swirling like shadows. Micaela couldn't bring the hazy thoughts into the light to analyze the sensations that ricocheted through her.

"It doesn't matter now," Lucien murmured as he framed her face in his shaky hands. "Can't we leave the past behind us where it belongs?" His thumbs glided over her cheeks, rerouting the shiny tears that spilled from her eyes. "All that concerns me is that you are alive and well and back in my arms."

When his sensuous lips slanted over hers, sending the whirling haze back into the darkness, Micaela gave herself up to a different set of sensations. Lucien kissed her with an explosive familiarity that suggested he was accustomed to kissing her—and very passionately—and that she was accustomed to liking it. By instinct or habit—she wasn't sure which—Micaela responded. She marveled at Lucien's phenomenal ability to chase those frightening specters away, leaving a flame of desire flickering in the cold, empty core of her being. Ah, she must have loved him deeply, unconditionally, if he could stir her so quickly.

It was a long, breathless moment before Lucien found the will to drag himself away from delicious temptation. When he did, he fell straight into the misty depths of her eyes. She was looking up at him so trustingly, so adoringly that his heart gave an enormous lurch.

"Caela, I—" He paused abruptly, then smiled down at her. "I think we should go back to the house."

Micaela was still reeling from the giddy effects of his kiss. She was warming to the idea of being hopelessly in love with this caring, attentive husband of hers. Her arms glided up the padded muscles of his chest, then she looped her hands around his neck. Smiling, she pulled his head back to her parted lips.

"I think I'd like to have the privacy to practice what I've forgotten."

His thick brows jackknifed in response to her suggestive comment, to the scintillating way her body brushed against his. Lord! What a saucy seductress she was when she wasn't so busy hating him. "Madam, you have my permission to practice as long and as often as you like. You're the one who has to decide when you are ready—" he grinned roguishly, "to . . . um . . . you know." Reluctant though he was to withdraw from his amazingly responsive bride, he grabbed her hand and led her to the carriage. "We better get back to the house before you catch a chill, love."

"Your concern is very touching, Lucien," she murmured. "I adore and respect you all the more for it. I also appreciate the fact that you grant me choices."

After Lucien placed her on the carriage seat, Micaela glanced back at the jutting cliff. "What do you think happened here that night? I asked Adrian, but the color drained from his face when I posed the question. I was afraid to press him for fear he would collapse. When I tried to quiz the servants, they couldn't back out of my bedroom fast enough to avoid me. You are the only one I can depend on to be honest with me."

Honest? Lucien winced as if he'd sat down on a scorpion. He had been anything but honest with Micaela. He told her only what he wanted her to remember, refusing to upset her during her recovery. Yet, her trust and confidence in him demanded that he divulge part of what she wanted to know.

"You had gone riding alone, but I don't know why you stopped here. There was a man—" Lucien stopped short when Micaela stared alarmingly at him. "He must have followed you."

"But why?" she asked urgently.

"He meant to do you harm, because the two of you had clashed several times the past week. Before I could have him jailed for attacking you, he went into hiding. I can only guess that he tried to retaliate by pushing you over the cliff. Somehow, you must have managed to hang onto him, because he was found lying on the boulders near you."

"What was this man's name?" Micaela whispered, staring into the distance.

"Barnaby Harpster."

She nodded bleakly. "I keep seeing a scowling face in the blurry shadows of memory. No wonder the vision gives me goose bumps. In a way, I'm thankful I don't remember what happened. Perhaps there is a cowardly part of me that continues to block out the horror of the incident."

Micaela curled her hand around Lucien's elbow and cuddled up beside him. "Your strength and comforting presence makes this easier," she confided. "I'm very fortunate to have you, Lucien. When I chose to wed you, I chose well."

Lucien didn't speak, he simply held her to him as he drove home. Guilt and shame at his own dishonesty were eating him alive. He would probably be sentenced to hell for lying to her, for spinning this artificial cocoon of blissful security around her. But damn it, he had to spare her from the hurt of the truth of *why* she had dashed out into the night.

When Lucien pulled the carriage to a halt in front of the mansion, a horde of humanity spilled from every doorway. All eyes, Lucien noted, were on Micaela, as if searching for more bruises and injuries.

"Is she all right?" Adrian demanded frantically. "What happened?"

Lucien grinned in amusement as he watched all the anxious gazes fixed on Micaela. He couldn't remember receiving so much attention or concern when he returned to the plantation— and he'd lived here most of his life! It was evident that Micaela had made such a lasting impression on Adrian and the servants that if she went missing for more than ten minutes the whole plantation went into an alarmed uproar.

"Micaela is fine," Lucien announced to the world at large. The world breathed a collective sigh of relief, he noticed. "She was feeling smothered and confined, and she requested some fresh air and change of scenery. I saw that she had it."

"Well, you should've bloody well told somebody," Adrian grumbled, shooting Lucien a reproachful glare. "When Micaela wasn't to be found in her room, or anywhere in the house, chaos broke loose.''

"I'm sorry," Micaela apologized as she tried to climb down from the buggy.

A flock of grooms rushed forward to assist her. It was Chaney, Lucien noted, who led the flock to scoop her up, then gently set her to her feet. While the servants buzzed around her, offering to fetch food, drink—or anything else she might possibly want—Lucien hopped down to face his frowning grandfather.

"A little consideration would've been nice," Adrian grumped. "Are you trying to drive me into another collapse? I know you've spent five years resenting me, but you don't have to kill me!"

Lucien wrapped a supporting arm around Adrian and escorted him up the steps. "Did I tell you, Grandfather, how much I appreciate your finding me such a suitable wife, since I didn't have the time to find her myself?"

Adrian missed a step and his jaw sagged against his chest. "You are *thanking* me for finding Micaela?"

Lucien nodded his raven head. "And I'm sorry if I've distressed you. But Micaela was at the end of her patience, tired of the smothering attention she's been receiving," Lucien explained. "She was sneaking out the front door when I spotted her. I didn't stop to think what turmoil her absence would cause. I should have notified you before we left."

"I'm terribly fond of that lass," Adrian declared. "If I didn't care so much, I wouldn't be so upset. Having found that new spark that gives my life meaning, I don't want to lose her."

"Neither do I, Grandfather, neither do I," Lucien murmured as he followed Micaela up the steps.

Adrian's eyes gleamed in satisfaction. The young scamp was hooked. Bullheaded though Lucien was, he might not yet realize what emotion was wrapping around his heart. Maybe Lucien wasn't head over heels yet, but Adrian didn't think that rapscallion had far to fall.

A sentimental mist clouded Adrian's eyes as he watched Lucien hurry to catch up with Micaela. Adrian removed his spectacles and dabbed his eyes with his kerchief. Although he'd lost his beloved Elizabeth a decade earlier, the memories of their years together never faded from his thoughts. He wanted Lucien to inherit that same legacy of love and devotion, to experience what Adrian and Elizabeth had shared while they labored to turn their small farm into a prosperous plantation. Ah yes, there had been struggle, strife, and occasional disagreements, but love had always sustained them.

Perhaps that was why Adrian had become so fond of Micaela. She possessed that same irrepressible spirit Elizabeth had, and she had matched her husband stride for stride. Adrian and Elizabeth had done a century of living in their forty-one years of marriage. Lucien could enjoy the same happiness, if only he would open his cautious heart to Micaela. She could heal Lucien's wounds of agony and despair. She was the one who had brought Adrian and Lucien back together.

Although Adrian wasn't at all certain that Lucien's insistence on keeping the past from Micaela was the right approach, he didn't intervene—not this time, not again. Adrian vowed to let Lucien handle his dealings with his wife. Damned tricky situation, in Adrian's estimation. He hoped and prayed that Lucien would find the right time to explain the conflicts of the past in such a manner that it wouldn't incite Micaela's hostility.

Adrian ambled into the parlor to rest his weary bones after the frantic search. He was damned glad he wasn't in Lucien's shoes. Finding the right way to tell Micaela the truth about this marriage was going to be anything but easy!

Fourteen

With firm resolve, Micaela stared at the door that separated her room from Lucien's. For two weeks, she had spent her days and evenings in Lucien's charming company, getting to know him, coming to love him—as she must have before amnesia stripped away memory. Tonight, she decided, she would become Lucien's wife in every sense of the word.

Smoothing her nightgown into place, Micaela opened the door. Anticipation thrummed through her as she stared across the moonlit room to see Lucien's silhouette on the bed. She mentally prepared herself to share the intimacy she had forgotten, *wanting* to share that intimacy again. . . .

Lucien choked on his breath when the door that joined his makeshift bedroom to Micaela's boudoir inched open. A shaft of lanternlight streamed into his darkened room. Micaela hovered by the door, like an angel in a flowing white gown that was sheer enough to leave Lucien's imagination running rampant. Her golden hair lay over one bare shoulder in a loose braid. A trace of a smile curved her lips as she all but floated across the room to hover beside Lucien's bed.

Lucien hardly dared to move, for fear of sending this lovely apparition into flight. For more than six weeks, Lucien had chased after this bewitching beauty, but she always seemed just out of his reach. Tonight she had come to him, but he knew she would never have come at all if she remembered why she had run away that fateful night a fortnight ago.

Since that night, Lucien had done his best to create a protected, secure world for Micaela. He had catered to her whims, accompanying her on every outing, never pressing her, keeping the distance she needed while she got to know this forgotten husband of hers. Lucien had lain awake for nights on end, wanting her like hell burning. But he had waited, hoping Micaela would come to him. Now that she finally had, he could scarcely believe it.

When Micaela reached up to unfasten the shoulder clasp of the shimmering gown Lucien swallowed air. His gaze riveted on Micaela in erotic fascination as the fabric glided over her luscious curves, revealing every inch of feminine perfection. Lucien swore his heart had turned to melted butter and dripped down the ladder of his ribs when Micaela eased gracefully down beside him.

There was no need for words between them. Her willing migration from her room to his said all that needed to be said. She was ready to experience the intimacy she didn't remember.

When her delicate fingers trailed over his lips, Lucien's masculine body pulsated with long-denied hunger. As the golden light from the adjoining room spilled over her shapely figure, caressing her as he ached to do, Lucien forced himself to lie still. He had waited two weeks for this night, and he would be damned if he frightened Micaela away by knuckling under to lusty impatience.

When Micaela eased beneath the sheet and snuggled up to him, Lucien was sure he'd died and gone to heaven. He'd never dreamed the sight of Micaela coming willingly to him could stir so many emotions.

"Lucien?" Her quiet voice drifted across his sensitive flesh like the skipping summer wind. "Show me the way it was between us."

He levered up on an elbow to stare down at her. He was afraid to touch her, for fear the strength of his resolve would crumble and he would frighten her away. He knew it had been difficult for Micaela to bridge the space between them when he was still like a stranger to her. The bond between them was fragile. Even if self-denial drove him mad, he could wait another week until he was sure this was truly what she wanted.

"Are you certain, Caela?" he whispered huskily.

"If I weren't certain, would I be here now?" Soft laughter tripped from her lips. "You are the one who seems reluctant." She paused momentarily, then lifted questioning eyes to him. Her smile faded into the shadows. "Or is the truth that I've never really pleased you and that you've been too kind and considerate since my accident to admit it?"

"Madam, the only thing about you that did *not* please me in the past was that you didn't please me often enough. If I had my way, you would never be out of my bed for too long a time."

"I married a lecher?" she inquired, her eyes twinkling impishly.

"No," Lucien said, his dark head moving steadily toward hers. "You married a very willing lover who has kept his distance from you for about as long as he can stand. I've missed making love with you, Caela. I've missed the spark of magic that leaps between us when I take you in my arms."

When his lips touched hers, Micaela surrendered to the onrush of fiery pleasure spilling through her. A sense of right and belonging consumed her when his muscular body moved suggestively against hers.

What she didn't know for certain she must have known—subconsciously—all along, she decided. This man was her soul mate. Her love for him transcended the obstacles of hazy shadows that stood between her and the memories of her past. If she knew nothing else about all the yesterdays that escaped her, she knew she belonged with this blue-eyed rake whose engaging smile eased her troubled soul and filled her heart with indescribable pleasure.

Micaela sighed when Lucien's warm kisses misted over her

eyelids and fluttered over her cheek. Her heart flip-flopped in her chest when his lips skimmed her shoulder to explore the swells of her breasts. She felt a coil of fire radiating through her, felt her entire body burst into flames when his masterful caresses splayed over her belly and wandered arousingly lower.

When his hand drifted between her thighs, and she felt the gentle pressure of his fingertip dipping into the moist heat he had called from her, Micaela struggled to breathe. When he slipped two fingers inside her, the gliding penetration of his intimate caress sent her over the edge. She could feel herself shivering around him, weeping for him in the most intimate ways. When his hand moved again, another onslaught of splintering pleasure bombarded her.

In that erotic moment, Micaela became the pulsating shell that housed the most phenomenal kind of sensations. Each kiss, each penetrating caress intensified profound needs that left her shaking, left her wanting him beyond bearing.

"Was it always like this?" Micaela gasped as she clutched desperately at him.

"Always," he assured her. "Magical . . ."

Micaela pressed Lucien to his back, and he went down without resistance. She wanted to reacquaint herself with her husband, to know him by touch as well as by heart. She wanted him to experience the same wild pleasures that engulfed her when he caressed her so skillfully.

With loving hands and questing lips, she investigated each lean plane and muscled contour of his body. She created new memories to replace the blank slate of time past. She discovered each place Lucien liked to be touched. She teased him into breathless arousal, and then began all over again, memorizing him with hands and lips.

Lucien swore he was the one suffering amnesia when Micaela laid her hands upon him. Her lips and fingertips were everywhere at once, satisfying and tormenting him. She fed the fires of passion and triggered every sensual impulse, until he was hanging onto his self-control by one flimsy thread.

When her hand enfolded him and her lips feathered over the velvet length of him, a fiery burst of need vibrated through him. Her lips whispered over the satin shaft of his manhood, making him throb and ache and groan in sweet torment. Her fingertips glided up and down the length of him as she took him into her mouth and tenderly suckled. Her flicking tongue teased him until his body clenched with barely restrained need.

Lucien shuddered, gritted his teeth, and battled the exquisite sensations that converged in a bolt of inexpressible pleasure. When she kissed him so intimately, holding the very essence of him so gently in her hand, the silvery evidence of need escaped his control.

When she brought the sultry taste of him to his lips, poignant awareness pooled in the core of his being. His willpower—which obviously wasn't as strong as he once believed it to be—faltered. This skillful seductress was absorbing him, inch by inch, pore by pore, sensation by sensation—until ardent need consumed him body and mind.

"Dear God!" Lucien hissed through his teeth. "I'm not sure I can survive if you keep doing what you're doing."

"I love touching you," she whispered against his aching flesh.

Groaning in nearly unbearable need, Lucien hooked his arm around her waist and drew her beneath him. Gentle patience bowed down to trembling urgency. He needed her now, or he would explode in untold torment! She had already become the very air he breathed, the source of every wild sensation sizzling through him. Only when they were flesh to flesh and soul to soul would he be satisfied.

Micaela gasped when he lifted her hips to his, moving her body in hypnotic rhythm—teasing her, preparing her to accept his masculine invasion. And when his powerful body uncoiled upon her, and he became the living flame inside her, she surrendered all she had to give to him. When she would have held him to her, marveling at the infinitesimal pleasure of their joining, he withdrew to brace himself on his forearms. She peered up at Lucien, lost in the depths of his intense blue eyes.

"If you cannot remember what the paradise of our passion was like, then promise me that you won't forget this night—the way we are now. Because this is my heaven and you're the angel in my arms. Love me, Caela. Make this memory burn away all measures of time.''

When he came back to her, she welcomed each penetrating thrust, matched his ardor. She clung to him as if he were the other half of her lost soul, riding the cresting waves that tumbled and rose and then tumbled again. She followed him into the whirlpool of rapturous sensations, whispering his name with a sense of awe and wonderment.

Much later, when the tide of turbulent passion ebbed, Micaela stroked his back and hips, then brushed a kiss to the throbbing pulse beat at the base of his neck. "I've been told who I am," she whispered, stirring provocatively beneath him. "But I'm not certain where I've been. Wherever it was, I would like to go there again, with you."

One black brow arched in surprise. "You mean right now?" he said.

"When a woman has no past, she tends to draw heavily upon the present . . . and her immediate future," she said with an elfin grin.

"Lord-a-mercy, I can barely find the strength to move, much less repeat a performance that depleted every last ounce of energy I possess. It seems there are several things you've forgotten about men, my demanding wife."

"What things?"

"For one thing, a man needs time to recover from over-whelmingly passionate lovemaking," he told her in ragged breaths.

"I thought you said that you were a most accommodating lover who couldn't be satisfied often enough." Her hand swirled over his hips, then drifted between them, caressing him, arousing him.

When she moved provocatively beneath him, Lucien felt the wild familiar flame burning anew. How could she tease him back to hungry arousal in less than a minute? he wondered with an incredulous shake of his head. One moment he swore he didn't have the energy to move and the next moment he was on fire for her.

"Now what were you saying, Lucien?" she purred playfully.

He smiled down at his seductively mischievous wife. "Forget what I said, love. You just proved me wrong."

"No," she murmured as she framed his face to bring his lips down to her kiss. "It is love that works this potent magic. And I do love you, Lucien. I wouldn't be here with you now if I didn't."

Her softly uttered confession shook the foundations of his soul. Lucien gathered her in his arms and made love to her as if there were no yesterday or tomorrow—only this one bright, shining moment to end all moments.

If and when Micaela recalled that it had been her hatred for him that drove her out into the night, and into the arms of disaster, Lucien would still cherish this night. And when she realized that he had built castles in the air, enshrouding her with misconceptions about their marriage, he would loose her love and her trust. Sooner or later Lucien had to find a way to tell Micaela the truth . . . but not now. He wanted to make the most of her newfound love for him, to enjoy the happiness he'd found with her.

Even as the tumultuous winds of passion swept him up and carried him away, Lucien knew that as much as Micaela thought she loved him now, she would despise him tenfold for deceiving her. Ah, he wished Micaela could never remember what he wanted to forget. Hearing Micaela whisper her love for him was his heaven . . . and hell in one. . . .

Hell might have been lurking on the horizon—and Lucien didn't fool himself into thinking it wasn't—but he enjoyed heaven while it lasted. After the night Micaela stepped over the threshold into his room and professed her love, the walls of her self-reserve came tumbling down. The halls of Saffire Plantation rang with the sound of Micaela's laughter. Lucien watched this breathtaking butterfly spread her wings and fly. She was like a child again, evolving through the phases of her life that she'd forgotten.

He inwardly cringed when he imagined losing the loving camaraderie they now shared. They awoke in each other's arms to spend their days together—whether it was fishing, riding, teaching her archery or attending parties in Charles Town. They had become inseparable, and Lucien had cautioned everyone at the plantation not to discuss the past, to let Micaela thrive in the happiness she had found.

Lucien was very careful never to leave Micaela stranded at parties with vicious gossipmongers who could destroy this peaceful harmony. He was protective and possessive of his bride, causing a new kind of rumor to spread through the socially elite of the colony. Word around the social circles was that Lucien had fallen so hopelessly in love with Micaela that he couldn't tear himself away from her, refused to let other men share so much as a dance with her.

There were times when Lucien saw Micaela withdrawing into herself, as if scenery, scent or some fleeting thought jostled pieces of forgotten memory. He held his breath, hoping that whatever triggered a pocket of hidden memory wouldn't cause dissension between them.

When Lucien received word that Vance had returned from the West Indies, with the schooners laden down with cargo, Lucien bundled Micaela into the coach and took her with him to the wharf. The instant Micaela saw the magnificent ship, with its luxurious Great Cabin, a spark of memory flashed. While Lucien helped unload the cargo, Micaela ambled around the splendid cabin, sensing that she had been here before. But she couldn't track down the memory that niggled at her.

It was exasperating to have fragments of memory torment her momentarily, then evaporate without answering her questions. One second she was on the verge of grasping a link to her past—and poof! The vision retreated into nothingness.

These past weeks Micaela had been visited by vague reminders of the life she must have known. She kept seeing images of a child bounding through the halls of a spacious home much like Saffire Plantation, glimpsing nameless figures. She was pretty certain those flashbacks came from her childhood. It was as if she were retracing her own footsteps, closing the gap to her past. . . .

When the cabin door swung open, Micaela lurched around to

see a vaguely familiar face in the doorway. And then suddenly, a sliver of memory slashed through her mind. She recalled seeing this same blond-haired man standing before her, reading from a book. Micaela didn't have time to pursue the puzzling thought, because the instant she blinked the vision vanished. Blast it. These fuzzy images and split-second sensations were driving her crazy!

Vance Cavendish strode forward to hug her in greeting. "God, I'm glad to see you looking so well, Micaela." He dropped a kiss to her cheek, then gave her another affectionate squeeze. "You gave us all a terrible scare."

Lucien had told Micaela of the role this handsome blond-haired captain had played in rescuing her that fateful night. She recognized him from this description, and she smiled gratefully. "I never had the chance to thank you, Vance. I'm forever indebted to you."

"So, you are beginning to remember the past?" Vance asked.

Micaela glanced around the spacious cabin. "Thus far, I remember very little, only bits and pieces that I can't place in chronological order. But this cabin strikes a chord of memory for some reason. I saw the image of you standing here just a moment ago. You were facing me with a book in hand, and then I lost the train of thought."

Vance shifted uneasily from one foot to the other. "You and Lucien were married here. I performed the ceremony."

Micaela didn't understand why Vance seemed reluctant to divulge that information, but she smiled reassuringly at him. "Then I must thank you for that, too. I only regret that I can't remember what must have been the happiest day of my life."

"The happiest—" Vance choked, recovered, and faked a smile.

What the hell had Lucien told his oblivious bride about their wedding day, Vance wondered. Whatever it was, it was obviously a gross misrepresentation of the truth. What was that rascal trying to do? Change the course of history to suit his preference?

"Um . . . yes," he said belatedly. "It was a most memorable occasion for all of us."

"Now that you're back, maybe you can help me sort out the pieces of memory from my life and put them in proper perspective."

Vance peered at the enchanting beauty who was dressed in pink satin, unsure what he was getting himself into.

"Adrian told me that he and I met at the pier, but he knows very little about my past." Luminous green eyes, surrounded by a fan of long, thick lashes, focused inquisitively on Vance. "Do you have any idea where I came from? You can't imagine how perplexing it is to have your life begin three months from yesterday!"

"You came from New Orleans. Didn't Lucien tell you that?"

Curse that rascal, Vance thought. What game was the man playing with this poor woman? Just wait until Vance got Lucien alone. Vance had a few choice, precise comments to make about the omission of facts!

"New Orleans." Micaela frowned ponderously. Again, visions of a young girl climbing through a gigantic live oak skittered across her mind. Ah-ha. She had one definite link with her past!

Impulsively, she flung her arms around Vance's neck and planted a grateful kiss on his cheek. Remembering herself, she stepped back, then tossed him a grin. "Sorry about that. I didn't mean to embarrass you. Lucien says I have always been a mite impulsive and rambunctious."

Vance chuckled heartily. "My dear lady, you haven't offended me in the least. I'm ready and willing to accept any hug or kiss you send my way."

Micaela eyed him consideringly. "So . . . you must be the notorious ladies' man I've heard the women whispering about at parties, when they didn't think I was listening."

"No, that would be—"

Vance clamped his jaw shut so fast that he bit his tongue. Lucien was the one with the infamous reputation. True, Vance had developed a bit of a reputation himself, but it didn't hold a candle to the gossip Lucien had inspired while he was purposely aggravating his grandfather. But Vance suspected that was one tale dear, darling Lucien had neglected to tell his amnesiac wife. That sneaky scamp!

"It must have been some other rake," Vance finished belatedly. "It wasn't I, I assure you."

Offering his arm, Vance ushered Micaela to the door. "There is another place on board this ship that might spark your memory. I'll show it to you."

Micaela went along eagerly. Vance knew she was desperate to piece her life together, and he was annoyed with Lucien for conveniently omitting what he didn't want Micaela to know about their whirlwind wedding.

The crazy fool, Vance fumed, as he escorted Micaela into the hold. Didn't Lucien realize he was making matters ten times worse by not being honest and forthright with Micaela? If she began to remember her past—which she was gradually beginning to do—Lucien would earn her loathing resentment. The man was sailing on a collision course with disaster!

Vance couldn't fathom what Lucien thought he could gain by creating this illusion, but it was damned well going to stop if Vance had anything to say about it, which he sure as hell intended to! This lovely lass wasn't going to go on living a lie, then wake up one day to discover she had been purposely deceived. Vance had reluctantly officiated Micaela's marriage, but he wasn't going to be a party to this kind of deception.

Starting this very minute, Vance was going to dedicate his time to prompting Micaela's memory, to giving her back her forgotten life—as much as he knew about it, that is. He was sorry to say that it wasn't much.

As for Lucien, Vance thought sourly, he could go to the devil for turning his marriage into a cunning illusion! That rascal ought to be shot, and Vance would like to be first in line to do it!

Concern etched Lucien's brow when he returned to the Great Cabin to find it empty. He wheeled around to go locate Micaela, but Vance barged in, nearly colliding with Lucien.

"Have you seen Caela?" Lucien asked anxiously.

"Indeed I have. And I must say she looks as enchanting as ever. I put Timothy Toggle and Jeremy Ives in charge of reacquainting her with the schooner while I have a private word with you."

"Is there a problem?" Lucien questioned as he turned to pour two glasses of brandy.

"I request that you take the north-bound cargo to Boston. I've been at sea for two months without much shore leave, while you were taking care of Micaela. Now that she has recovered, you can captain your schooner and leave me in Charles Town for a needed break."

Lucien handed Vance the glass and scrutinized him for a long moment. "Are you volunteering to keep a watchful eye on my wife during my absence? I can't leave her with Adrian. He's too old to keep up with the fast pace she sets."

"I'd be happy to assume the task," Vance assured him, sporting the kind of smile that made Lucien frown warily.

"Make sure you focus your amorous attention on some other woman besides my wife," Lucien said pointedly.

"I'm your best friend. I'm not trying to steal your wife."

"Best friends have been known to do such things on occasion."

"Believe me, I have your best interest—and Micaela's—at heart," Vance declared. "And mine, too, of course. As much as I love sailing the high seas, I also enjoy socializing occasionally. Knowing that you love the sea, above all else, I thought this might give you the excuse to sail again."

Of late, Lucien had been too preoccupied with Micaela to miss a single voyage. But he had dumped the shipping business in Vance's lap, and it was time to reassume his duties. "I'll take the next leg of the voyage to Boston, but I have a few words of caution about Micaela," he murmured before sipping his drink. "We are enjoying peaceful harmony, and I intend to preserve it. Don't distress her with talk of the past."

So Vance was right on the mark. Lucien had created a tidy little charade, utilizing Micaela's amnesia to keep her in line and elicit the behavior of a dutiful, doting wife. That devil!

Before this was over, Lucien was going to get exactly what he deserved for his connivance. If Lucien wanted to earn Micaela's love, respect and devotion, then he was going to do it the right way! Allowing Micaela to think her wedding was the grandest day of her life was deceitful. This marriage hadn't been made in heaven, it had been arranged by two feuding men. And damn it, it was Micaela's life Lucien was messing with!

"You do understand what I'm saying, don't you, Vance?" Lucien asked, with a somber stare.

"I understand." Oh yes, Vance understood all too well.

"Then I can count on you to care for Micaela while I'm gone, to ensure that she is protected and happy," Lucien persisted. "I mean it, Vance. I want nothing to disturb the progress we've made together. What she doesn't know about the past she doesn't need to know."

That was a matter of opinion—Lucien's, obviously. "Just why are you keeping her in the dark?" Vance prodded.

Lucien glanced at the far wall, avoiding Vance's probing stare. "It was your taunting questions and my spiteful answers at the reception that brought this disaster down on Micaela. After the horror she endured, I decided to leave the past where it belongs—all of it—for as long as possible."

"So this secrecy is prompted by feelings of pity, regret and guilt, is that it?" Vance snorted. "Somehow I suspect there is more to it than that."

Lucien wasn't a man who felt comfortable discussing his innermost thoughts and feelings. He had learned long ago to keep his own counsel. Now was no exception. What was between him and Micaela was personal and private, and the more interference, the more difficult the problems. "Let's just say that it's best for all concerned to let Micaela begin her life from this point in time."

"How very convenient for you," Vance said, and smirked. "I suspect you want to forget how much she despised you. Damn, Lucien, I didn't realize you were such a coward."

"I'm not a coward," Lucien snapped. "I'm only trying to preserve the peace."

"You're avoiding the inevitable, and you damned well know it. You better reconsider what you're doing or you'll spend the rest of your life regretting it. Micaela is beginning to remember fragments of her past. If you don't tell her the truth soon, this entire charade is going to blow up in your face.''

Lucien stared long and hard at his friend. ''I know that nothing lasts forever. I've decided to take each day as it comes, to reap whatever pleasure can be found.''

''Ah yes, hang onto that philosophy,'' Vance said flippantly. ''Just prepare yourself for the day this house of cards comes crashing down. When Micaela remembers what you have obliterated, when she realizes you erased the past for your own purpose, you'll never be able to make the steep climb from your fall from grace. In this game of deceit, Lucien, be very careful that you do not deceive yourself.''

Lucien glanced up when he heard the swish of satin skirts and bubbling laughter. His attention shifted to Micaela's smiling face. Lucien swore the sun had just risen in his cabin when she burst into the room. She scurried toward him, flinging her arms around his neck, giving him an affectionate kiss. When her gaze darted to the bed, and then back to him, Lucien smiled at the seductive gleam in her eyes.

''Vance, if you'll excuse us,'' Lucien murmured, never taking his eyes off Micaela's sultry smile.

Vance shot him a reproachful glance, then exited. Lucien meanwhile discarded the previous conversation and concentrated on Micaela. Perhaps Vance didn't understand this need not to tamper with paradise, but Lucien did. He was happier than he'd been in years. He was also compensating for the hurt Micaela had suffered. What was the crime in that? he asked himself.

''I've investigated every nook and cranny on this magnificent schooner,'' she informed him as she loosed the buttons on his cream-colored shirt. ''All except the captain's bed. . . .''

Lucien clutched the wandering hand that was bound for intimate places. ''There's a full crew on deck, madam. I'm due to meet with the merchants at the warehouse—''

''Then you're destined to be several minutes late, Captain. Your skillful services are needed elsewhere,'' she told him saucily.

When she peeled way his shirt to spread a row of steamy kisses across the expanse of his chest, Lucien put his obligations on hold. Since he was taking the schooner to Boston, he would be deprived of the wondrous pleasures of Micaela's unconditional love. He had to make the most of every precious moment . . . for as long as it lasted.

When Lucien scooped her up and carried her to bed, Micaela lifted parted lips to him. Lucien bent to kiss her—and slammed his shin against the bedpost. When he lurched off balance, Micaela clanked her head against the wall.

"Are you all right?" Lucien asked in concern.

"Don't look so worried, love," she whispered. "I'm fine . . . or rather I will be very soon."

Like a man entranced, Lucien came to her, desperate to create another wild, sweet memory to carry with him to Boston. He made love to Micaela with a passion that burned away time— and the torment of knowing he was living on deceitful lies. Maybe he had rewritten the past, but it seemed worth the weeks of happiness they had shared. This kind of heaven was worth the hell that awaited, Lucien told himself before he forgot everything he ever knew and set sail on a sea of rapture. . . .

Fifteen

"Do you know how very much I love you," Micaela whispered in the aftermath of soul-shattering passion. "I can't imagine how empty my life must have been before there was you."

His lips feathered over her kiss-swollen mouth, claiming one last honeyed taste before he withdrew.

When Lucien didn't return her confession, Micaela frowned. Silently, she watched him gather his clothes and dress to keep his appointment with the merchants. She had intended to tell Lucien that he was going to become a father, but she had wanted to hear his profession of love before she gave him the news.

As loving and passionate as Lucien was, he had never spoken the words she longed to hear. Had he said them before and she simply couldn't remember? Or was it that he chose to express his feelings in deeds rather than words?

Lucien did love her . . . didn't he? He had spent all his days with her since the accident. They had laughed and teased and made love. When he ventured to town, he returned with gifts for her. He had purchased an emerald and diamond necklace with gems big enough to choke a horse. Three days later he'd shown up with a wedding ring to replace the oversize gold band she had been wearing. Why, the jewels in the new ring would have blinded a sightless beggar! Weren't those gifts an expression of his affection? . . . Or were they compensation for the feelings he didn't possess? Were the gifts given out of pity for her injury and loss of memory? It made Micaela wonder.

"I've got to leave, Micaela," Lucien said as he stuffed his feet in his boots. "I've tarried too long already. Vance wants a few days of shore leave and I consented to take the ship to Boston."

Micaela surveyed Lucien's broad back, watching the finely-tuned muscles flex and relax as he rose to shrug on his jacket. It disturbed her that Lucien hadn't asked her to accompany him on the voyage, but she refused to invite herself along. Maybe she had become too demanding of his time. She knew he had been actively engaged in shipping before her accident. He had remained ashore until she recovered, but he had obligations to attend. She had too much pride to become the albatross around his neck.

Lucien probably needed some time to himself, she diagnosed. She could also use some time alone. And while he was away, perhaps he would realize how much he loved her.

"How long will you be gone?" She stopped herself when she reflexively lifted her hand to touch him.

"A week, maybe more."

"I'm sure I can find something to occupy my time," she said lightly.

"Just make sure *things* occupy you, not *people*— ones of the male persuasion to be specific. I would hate to find myself replaced, madam."

"Thanks to you, I've discovered that I have a voracious appetite," she teased. "A week is a long time, Lucien."

"Then read a book, but don't go looking for trouble, squirt. I'm not one of those liberal husbands who shares his wife with other men."

"Are you one of those husbands with a roving eye?" she wanted to know. "I've overheard gossip at social gatherings, and I've learned that there are certain aristocrats hereabout who keep mistresses for their pleasure."

Lucien leaned down to brace his arms on either side of her bare shoulders. "And how could I possibly be one of them when my lovely wife's voracious appetite depletes all my energy, hum?"

Micaela flashed him an elfin smile. "Just checking."

"There is no one but you, Caela," he whispered, then kissed her lightly. "I hope you'll remember that while I'm gone."

"But Lucien, do you really i—" She clamped down on the impulsive question before it sprang off her tongue. She wasn't going to pry a confession of love from him. It had to come freely. "When are you leaving for Boston?" she asked instead.

"At dawn." He pushed upright, then spun toward the door. "Since you so thoroughly distracted me, I'll be dealing with those impatient merchants until long past dark. If you want to return to the townhouse, Vance will accompany you."

When Lucien opened the door to leave, Micaela peered curiously at him. "One more thing."

He half turned, smiling. "Yes?"

"Why do you call me squirt?"

He didn't reply, merely turned and walked away. "Later, love," he murmured before he closed the door behind him.

Micaela rose from bed to gather her strewn garments. A flash of memory raced across her mind when she glanced at the wooden bedposts. What a peculiar thought! For a second, she swore she remembered being strapped to this very bed like a prisoner. *Mon Dieu*, her mind must be playing strange tricks on her. . . .

Mon Dieu? Micaela blinked, bewildered. She spoke French? Well, of course she spoke French. Vance said she hailed from New Orleans. Frowning, Micaela glanced at random objects in the cabin, discovering that she could not only identify them in English and French, but also in Latin and Spanish. Where had she learned to speak so many languages? And why did she have the odd feeling she had once been tied to this bed?

Micaela massaged her aching temples, wondering if the slight blow to her skull, when Lucien tripped while holding her, had shaken loose a few pockets of hidden memory, sending them tumbling helter-skelter through her mind. Ah, she would give

most anything to know what her life had been like before she
married Lucien. He kept assuring her that nothing from the
past mattered, but he wasn't the one who couldn't remember
his childhood. He didn't understand how tormenting it was to
live without memories.

Why wouldn't he want her to remember her past? she asked
herself. Was there something he preferred to forget? Or something he preferred *her* to forget?

Micaela discarded the disturbing thought and wiggled into
her gown. Perhaps she wouldn't be suspicious if she was certain
Lucien loved her as deeply as she loved him. Had *she* done
something to test *his* love, and he refused to speak of it? Had
she—? *Mon Dieu!* Had she entered into an affair with another
man while he was at sea? Is that why he had given her specific
instructions to stay away from men while he was gone?

Micaela made a mental note to interrogate Vance during
Lucien's absence. He seemed to know a few things about her
past, though he seemed reluctant to disclose them. . . .

Micaela half collapsed when a shocking thought buffeted
her. Had she been involved in an affair with Vance? Did this
child belong to another man? *Vance* perhaps? Had she injured
the babe during her fall?

Troubled and confused, Micaela scurried down the companionway to return to the buggy waiting on the wharf. She was
going back to the townhouse alone to wrack her befuddled
brain. And if she didn't come up with satisfactory answers, she
was going to give Vance the third degree, even if he was the
man she'd been unfaithful with. If this child didn't belong to
her husband, the awful truth could destroy the happiness she
had discovered with Lucien.

Had she been with child before her accident? Was this unborn
babe at risk? The frightening thought sent her befuddled senses
reeling. But no matter how upsetting the truth turned out to be,
Micaela vowed to reclaim her past—somehow or another!

Lucien stepped down from the carriage to the wharf as the
sun made its glowing appearance on the horizon. He pivoted

to stare into the flawless face that peered down at him. Since he'd returned home the previous night, Micaela had been distant and withdrawn. He'd been forced to repeat himself a half dozen times throughout the evening. This spirited beauty, who had freely offered her affection and attention the past few weeks, hadn't come near him since they'd made love in the Great Cabin yesterday afternoon. Lucien didn't know what was wrong, but he sensed something was.

"Micaela, are you upset because I didn't invite you to Boston? If you are, then you have my invitation to make the voyage with me."

"No, I'll stay here." She pulled her cloak more tightly around her to ward off the cool sea breeze. "I've come to depend on you too much. I realize that now. You have business to conduct, and young Abraham reminded me the other night that I promised to teach him, and the other children, to read and write." Her gaze locked with his, then flitted away. "I have been smothering you, but I didn't intend to make a nuisance of myself. In fact—"

"A nuisance?" Lucien interrupted. "Good lord, woman, where did you get that ridiculous notion?"

"I think we need time to ourselves. We need to readjust after my accident," she said, staring out to sea.

"I like things just the way they are." Lucien reached up to touch her just once more before he weighed anchor. "I'll miss you, squirt."

"Will you truly? I thought you might be anxious to be rid of me since I've been clinging to you like Spanish moss."

Hell and damnation, what had he done to give her that impression? Micaela was changing, right before his very eyes, and the thought of losing the closeness, the contentment they shared was agonizing.

When Micaela blew him a kiss and drove off, Lucien stared after her for an apprehensive moment. He had the inescapable feeling his life was about to take another of its abrupt turns— undoubtedly for the worst. The faith and trust Micaela had placed in him seemed to be eroding by the minute. Why, she

could barely meet his gaze. What emotion was lingering in
those luminous green eyes that he couldn't quite decipher?

Lucien felt as if he were standing on sinking sand, expecting
the earth to open and swallow him alive. And later, while he
stood on the quarter-deck, watching the spires of St. Michael's
Cathedral disappear on the horizon, he kept wondering just
how short the walk was going to be from heaven to the open
jaws of hell.

Micaela manufactured a smile before venturing down the
receiving line at Dr. Thorley's grand ball in Charles Town.
When the physician inquired about her health, Micaela assured
him that she had recovered from her bruises and scrapes. Physically, she was in tip-top condition. Emotionally, however, she
was at the height of exasperation.

Over the past few days, visions of a young girl wandering
around a vaguely familiar plantation appeared at irregular intervals. Several faces kept popping to mind at unexpected
moments. Were those the faces of her family? No one seemed
to know about her family or her early years. It made Micaela
wonder how she had come to be in Charles Town.

"Would you care to dance, Micaela?" Vance invited, ush-
ering her away from the receiving line.

Micaela glanced up at the striking blond man who had offered
to escort her to the party in Lucien's stead. Thus far, Micaela
had not been able to work up the nerve to ask Vance if they
had been conducting intimate affairs behind Lucien's back.
Why else would Vance know so much about her if they hadn't
been having an affair, she reasoned.

"Vance, may I ask you something personal," Micaela murmured as she moved with the rhythm of the music.

"Fire away."

Micaela inhaled a courageous breath and blurted out the
burning question. "Did you and I have an affair?"

Vance trounced on her toe and tripped over his own feet.
Bug-eyed, he gaped at her when he'd recovered his balance.

"What?" he howled, unintentionally drawing the attention of nearby dancers.

"I said . . ., did you and I—"

"I heard you, for God's sake. Don't repeat it in this ballroom full of rabbit ears," he muttered as he guided her toward a vacant corner. "Gossip is going to be flying if you don't guard your tongue."

"Well, did we or didn't we?" She wanted to know that very second.

"No, would you like to?" he asked with a rakish grin.

Micaela flung him a withering glance. "No, I would not. I just need to know if we did sometime in the recent past. And if I didn't have one with you, did I have one with someone else?" She glanced apprehensively around the ballroom, wondering if there were other men she had been seeing behind Lucien's back. "If I didn't have an affair, then why did Lucien give me such a strange look when I playfully teased him about finding someone else to amuse me while he was in Boston?"

Vance opened his mouth to reply, but Micaela rattled off the other troubling questions that had been hounding her in rapid succession. "I don't understand why no one knows how and where I spent my childhood. Do I have family in New Orleans? Are these blurred visions the memories of my younger days? And what names belong to the faces that creep to mind at unexpected moments?

"Vance, tell me everything you know—good or bad, it doesn't matter," she implored him. "Please don't hold anything back. I've got to know who I was and what I am. Frustration is driving me crazy!"

Sympathy got the better of Vance. He could see the torment in her expression, a torment Lucien refused to dissolve. That rascal! Didn't he realize he was being cruel to Micaela by hiding the truth? Curiosity was hounding her half to death.

Scooping up two glasses of punch, Vance gestured for Micaela to follow him onto the gallery so they could speak privately. After he handed her a glass he ordered her to drink all of it. Then he shoved the second glass at her.

"*Mon Dieu*, that bad?" she asked apprehensively.

"You'll have to be the judge of that," he said, pushing the glass to her lips. "Once you have taken the edge off your frazzled nerves, I'll tell you what I know."

Formulating his thoughts, Vance tried to decide where and how to begin. God, no wonder Lucien had such difficulty spitting out the truth. No matter where Vance considered taking up the tale, there were awkward obstacles in his path. Nervously, he paced the gallery, conjuring up and then discarding a half dozen where-to-begins.

"Sweet mercy," Micaela choked out. "Did I have affairs with every man at this party? What kind of woman am I, for heaven sake!"

"Will you forget about the affairs," he muttered.

"Plural?" Micaela groaned miserably. "So there was more than one? With more than one man?"

Vance lurched around, flinging his arms in an expansive gesture. "There were no affairs, Micaela. None. You have been a credit to your wedding vows, though you threw a ring-tailed tantrum when you were forced to speak them."

Micaela blinked, startled. "I didn't want to marry Lucien? Why not? I love him."

Good God, this was going to be difficult—if not impossible. Vance chose to avoid that question by receding through time. "Lucien and I met you when you garbed yourself like a waif and stowed away on the schooner. We docked in New Orleans to sell our cargo, and you sneaked aboard during the revolt in which the French ousted the Spanish officials from their garrison on the Mississippi River. While I was in the Indies last week, I learned that Don Antonio de Ulloa, and his Superior Council, sailed to Cuba to await orders from King Charles III. Another Spanish Commissioner and his aides have arrived to retake control of Louisiana."

Vance paused, hoping he had stirred a dormant memory, but Micaela just stared blankly at him. "Do you recall any of this, Micaela? Do you have the faintest idea why you fled from New Orleans? Were you part of the rebellion? Could your family have been involved? Or were you on such friendly terms with the Superior Council that your connection with them forced you to flee in fear of your safety?"

Micaela flung up her hands to halt the barrage of questions. "I remember nothing of a rebellion. And I can't say if my family might have been involved. You could threaten to torture me within an inch of my life and I'm not certain I could remember why I fled New Orleans. The only way to reclaim my past is to return to the city. Perhaps someone there will recognize me and point me in the right direction."

"An excellent idea," Vance agreed.

"Will you take me to New Orleans?"

"Well, perhaps . . . um . . . we should delegate that task to Lucien," he stammered.

"But he won't be back for more than a week. I plan to leave tomorrow."

"Tomorrow?" Vance crowed.

"Tomorrow," she confirmed. "Your ship has been repaired and is in port, is it not? Since I control half of Adrian's estate . . ." Micaela frowned, bemused. "How the devil do I know that?"

Vance could tell random thoughts were filtering through her head, alongside those fleeting visions she mentioned. Her mind was becoming fertile ground, and she was prepared to produce even more memories, given the right stimulation and environment. The time had come to give Micaela back her life. Vance felt obliged to help her piece the puzzle back together—starting at the moment when she fled New Orleans. For certain, Lucien wasn't in any hurry to do it.

Of course, Lucien would probably kill him, Vance predicted. But Lucien had made the error in judgment, and it was time to right the wrong. Micaela was desperate for facts, and Vance sympathized with her. He knew it had to be tormenting to live in a world that began a few months ago. Merciful heavens, the poor girl might have passed her birthday and no one would ever know it!

"Very well, Micaela, I'll take you to New Orleans. We'll sail at dawn . . . if I can round up my crew."

Micaela bounded excitedly into his arms, showering him

with kisses. Her timing was absolutely awful. Two old dowagers—who made a career of gossiping—ventured onto the gallery to find Vance and Micaela in a clinch. Vance could see the wicked delight in Beatrice—the Busybody—Huxley's eyes before she whirled around to scuttle inside with her tale of scandal. Micaela thought she'd had an affair with Vance, and Beatrice would confirm it by yapping to everyone she knew. Now Micaela wouldn't know whether to believe him or the rumors.

"I hope you know what you just did, imp," Vance said, stepping back a respectable distance. "Charles Town socialites are, at this moment, linking us together. When we make an early departure to gather our belongings for the voyage to Louisiana, the gossipmongers—commandeered by Beatrice Huxley—will claim we've sneaked off for a secluded tryst."

Micaela shrugged off his concern. "I was told that the truth needs no defense or explanation. People always believe what they choose to believe. If we live in goodness and truth, we have nothing to hide and nothing to fear—"

Vance grinned when Micaela stared at him, shocked by the quote that rolled so easily off her tongue. "You don't happen to remember who told you that, do you?"

"I don't have the foggiest notion," she said, shoulders sagging.

"It sounds like something a nun might say. Perhaps you were schooled at a convent. That would explain your ability to read and write better than most women who have been deprived of formal education."

"The convent!" Micaela yelped when a fragment of memory speared through her mind. "The Ursuline Convent! The Gray Sisters and the Padre! That's it, Vance. They will know where I belong."

Vance found himself the recipient of another exuberant hug. The two dowagers—who had returned with a passel of snoops, peeked around the corner the instant Micaela launched herself at him.

"Oh, for heaven's sake," Micaela grumbled when she spied

the ratlike eyes peering at her. "Can't a woman give a man a hug around here without you making something lewd of it?"

Micaela clutched Vance's hand and towed him toward the gaggle of gossips. With wicked delight, she dragged the prune-faced Beatrice Huxley into Vance's arms. He accommodated by giving the snippy harridan a playful squeeze and a peck on the cheek. The outrageous prank drew dozens of shocked gasps, but Micaela was too thrilled with the sparks of memory to concern herself with the meddling old women who had nothing better to do than spy on people.

When the old hens, their fine feathers ruffled, waddled off, Vance snickered in amusement. "Now here is the spunky female I remember. Lucien is going to be in for one helluva surprise when he returns from Boston. You might very well be back to your old feisty self, and he is going to have his hands full with you."

"We had best pay our respects to Dr. Thorley," Micaela insisted, towing Vance along behind her. "It might take some time to convince Adrian that I need to retrace my footsteps through the past."

Micaela made note of the whispers and glances that accompanied her through the ballroom and into the foyer. Rumors were indeed going to be flying when she and Vance made their early departure. She could almost hear the gossip now: Micaela simply cannot remember from one moment to the next who her husband is. Or is it convenient amnesia, do you think? And poor Lucien, he is being cuckolded.

Well, she would sit Lucien down and explain everything to him when he returned from Boston and she returned from New Orleans, Micaela promised herself. He would probably be pleased that she had reclaimed her past. Then she could tell him that he was to become a father without fearing that she'd had an affair with another man. By then, Micaela would hopefully have her memory in proper working order, and there would be no frustrating lapses to ruin her marriage.

* * *

Hiram Puckett ambled into the parlor where Adrian was sitting with his morning glass of mint julep. ''Sir, Dowager Huxley is standing on the stoop, demanding to speak with you.''

Now what did that old bat want? As if Adrian couldn't guess. For years, that shriveled up bag of bones, with her viper's tongue and gutter mind, had hounded him to death. Adrian had purposely kept his distance, even though Beatrice invited him here and there and showed up everywhere he went.

When Adrian had shunned the widow's attention, she had turned exceptionally vicious by spreading rumors about the Saffires—Lucien in particular. Since Lucien had been out to destroy his reputation to spite Adrian, Beatrice had a field day reporting on that scamp's wild activities.

No doubt, the old bag had dug up more dirt to fling in Adrian's face. With a sigh of resignation, he set aside his glass to venture onto the stoop. With a polite—but nowhere near friendly—nod, he greeted the dowager who was obviously taking her wagging tongue for its customary morning walk.

''Good morning, Beatrice.''

The wrinkled-faced harridan didn't bother with a greeting. She dived headlong into her brew of gossip. ''I just thought you would like to know that Lucien's bride threw herself at Vance Cavendish last night at Dr. Thorley's party. Vance didn't throw her back, either. He was as eager as she was.'' She smiled, displaying the missing tooth at the corner of her pinched mouth. ''We caught them in the clinch twice. It seems Lucien is getting a taste of his own medicine, after years of chasing skirts—married and single alike.'' She leaned closer, still smiling in fiendish delight. ''And this morning, while Millie Grove was taking her stroll past the wharf, she saw Vance and Micaela boarding the schooner together. They have run off, embarking on one long, shameless tryst on the high seas.''

Adrian gnashed his teeth and resisted the urge to wrap his fingers around Beatrice's throat. ''Well, do tell! One of your dear friends, who shall remain nameless, was here earlier to inform me that you were also seen embracing Vance, because you have such a penchant for younger men." There, let the old fuss-budget stick that in her craw and choke on it.

Beatrice's beady eyes bulged and her jowls sagged. "Why, that is absurd!"

"That's what *I* said," Adrian replied, straight-faced. "But the bearer of the scandalous gossip claimed you had been chasing younger men for years. My anonymous informant said the reason Micaela was sticking close to Vance was to protect him from you."

"That is ridiculous!" Beatrice howled. "Who would dare concoct such a vicious pack of lies?"

"One of your friends *would* and *did,*" he informed her. "But no need to fret, Beatrice, I quickly came to your defense. I told that nasty-minded gossipmonger that you had been chasing after *me* for years and that if you couldn't catch an old man like *me,* there was no way you could keep pace with a handsome young rake like Vance Cavendish."

Beatrice recoiled as if she'd been slapped, gasping and sputtering in indignation.

"I know you want to thank me for setting the record straight." Adrian beamed at the dowager who was still emitting spasms of hisses. "And you are quite welcome. Now, if you will excuse me, my breakfast is getting cold. Have a nice day, Beatrice."

Before she could find her tongue, Adrian closed the door and pivoted to find Hiram tucked beside the office door, his thick shoulders shaking with silent amusement.

"I do believe you rendered the old bag speechless, sir. I'm glad I was on hand to witness the historic event."

"Come join me in a glass of mint julep, and we'll celebrate the occasion," Adrian invited. "Micaela forewarned me last night that I could expect to hear gossip, so I was prepared for the old biddy."

Sinking down in the Windsor chair, Hiram poured fresh drinks. "I must confess that it does leave room for speculation when a man's best friend, and that same man's lovely wife, sail off together the morning after they were seen hugging on the gallery at a party. But I suppose it will be worth the gossip if this voyage to New Orleans strikes chords in Micaela's memory. She is simply too inquisitive to leave her missing past alone.''

Hiram paused with his glass poised inches from his lips and peered apprehensively at Adrian. ''You don't think there is something to the rumor that Micaela and Vance are interested in each other, do you? She is a captivating young woman, after all, and Vance seems immensely fond of her.''

''I think,'' Adrian said, easing back in his chair to sip his drink, ''that Lucien will have only himself to blame if he loses his wife to his best friend. He is going to wish he'd told Micaela what he knew about her past and the circumstances surrounding their marriage before now. If and when she regains her memory, Lucien is going to have hell—and then some—to pay.''

''You're enjoying this aren't you?'' Hiram asked.

''Indeed. Every twisting, tangling moment of it! Lucien reminds me of a hooked fish battling the line. He has been so busy trying to outsmart and control that lively lass he married that he has forgotten his resentment toward me. He and I have grown closer because of Micaela.''

''I expect your grandson will be hopping mad when he returns to learn Micaela sailed off with Vance,'' Hiram predicted.

''Mmm, yes, I expect so,'' Adrian agreed, grinning wickedly. ''But he can't blame me for being unable to restrain Micaela when she set her mind to pursuing her past. Lucien was the fool who opted not to tell what he knew, and he ordered the rest of us to keep the silence. I'd say it serves him right.''

''Do you think the day will come when Lucien and Micaela can live in true, peaceful harmony?'' Hiram asked.

Adrian barked a laugh and very nearly spilled his drink down the front of his brocade waistcoat. ''Harmony? Those two stubbornly independent individuals? Not hardly! Don't you see, Hiram. That's the beauty in this. Those two enjoy doing battle. I do believe they thrive on it, and on each other.''

Hiram blinked, confused. ''You mean to say you never expect them to fall in love and settle into a peaceful existence? I thought you said they were perfect for each other.''

''Oh, they are, they are. Micaela is just the kind of woman

Lucien needs, and he is just what she needs—whether or not either of them will realize it until after the sparks start flying around here again. Then Lucien will have to come to terms with his wife, once and for all.''

''Unless Vance takes his role as Micaela's guardian a mite too seriously,'' Hiram mused aloud. ''Who knows what might happen when those two are alone together on the voyage.''

The comment wiped the wry smile off Adrian's lips and caused his graying brows to furrow. ''There is that,'' he admitted reluctantly.

''It's a long way to New Orleans—and back.''

''Damn, whose bright idea was it to give that lass permission to leave here?'' Adrian grumbled.

''Yours,'' Hiram reminded him.

Adrian sipped his drink, wondering if he had been hasty in granting permission for this adventure. A spirited young beauty like Micaela might be one temptation Vance might not be able to overcome. Lucien certainly hadn't been able to resist Micaela, now had he? And the young scamp had tried in the beginning. Who was to say Vance Cavendish would bother to try at all?

Sixteen

With supreme concentration Micaela studied the shoreline lined with swamps and deltas where the Mississippi River flowed into the gulf. She tried to remember the landscape, tried to attach a floating piece of memory to it.

"Apprehensive, Micaela?" Vance questioned.

Micaela glanced over her shoulder and smiled. "I'm *anxious*," she clarified.

"Before long you can begin your search." Vance lifted his hand to smooth the silky tendrils that danced in the sunlight like threads of spun silver and gold. "We'll dock in two hours."

"Vance, don't look at me like that," Micaela teased, green eyes twinkling. "I thought you were my friend."

"I am that, my dear lady." He chuckled, then braced his arms on the railing. "But I'm also a healthy, normal man. I find it disconcerting that you seem oblivious to the effect you have on men."

"And I am a reasonably normal woman, I think," she replied. "I have no need to tell you that I find you charming and attractive. Surely that is evident. But I am also very married. Now kindly focus your attention on the reason for this cruise and stop looking at me as if I'm one of your paramours, you rake!'' she added with a teasing smile.

Vance burst into chuckles. "That is one of the things I adore about you. You believe in plain-spoken confrontations, rather than beating around proverbial bushes." He smiled hopefully at her. "You don't happen to have a twin sister, do you?"

"I haven't a clue whether I do or don't," she replied.

Although Micaela had tried to maintain a respectable distance the past few days, Vance curled his arm around her and gave her an affectionate squeeze. More and more, she'd come to realize that Vance was taking her feelings for him too seriously. As much as she respected Vance, delighted in his entertaining company, he didn't stir her the way Lucien did, didn't fill her with the same sense of right and belonging. She had discovered the best way to deal with Vance's growing attachment was to tease him into behaving himself.

"Stop toying with me, you hopeless libertine," she chided when he hugged her close, mashing her nose against his broad chest.

"I'm not toying with you," he assured her, his tone suddenly serious. "You'll have to learn to live with the fact that I care about you, even if I'm limited to offering friendship."

Micaela leaned back in the circle of his arms to study him pensively. "Are you quite certain we never had an affair?"

"Believe me, if we had, I'd remember, even if you cannot."

Since Vance was waggling his blond brows and grinning roguishly—and not for the first time since this voyage began—Micaela decided to call his bluff. It was time to determine if Vance was as devoted to Lucien as she thought he was.

Micaela looped her arms around his shoulders and drew his head toward hers. And sure enough, despite his provocative remarks and come-hither glances, Vance went absolutely still, obviously paralyzed by his conscience and his sense of propriety.

Micaela arched a brow in mocking amusement as she traced the curve of his full lips with her forefinger. "Something wrong, my dear Romeo?"

Sighing, Vance backed off. "No wonder Lucien has such a difficult time handling you. You have a most exasperating way of making a man battle his own worst enemy—himself. You make a man cling to his disgustingly noble ideals.''

Micaela playfully patted his cheek. "There, there, Vance. I was only reminding you of how well you know yourself. You are simply too honorable to betray a friend's trust, and I consider you a trusted friend. Now that we have that settled and out of the way, I intend to return to the cabin to make myself presentable for my homecoming.''

Vance's frustrated gaze followed Micaela until she disappeared into the companionway.

Micaela scurried across the gangplank, eager to begin the search for her missing past. During her voyage from Charles Town, she had been visited by various and sundry of flashbacks. There were times when she could almost grasp a complete thought before it whirled back into the fuzzy haze. Of one thing Micaela was certain. She had spent considerable time with the Gray Sisters of Ursuline Convent. That was a start, and it gave her hope of finding further links to her past.

"Slow down," Vance requested, snagging Micaela's arm before she got lost in the crowd milling around the wharf. "I know you're overly anxious, but let's not run over everyone in our path while dashing from one place to another, shall we?"

Although Micaela was hopping up and down with excitement, she forced herself to keep Vance's swaggering pace. He pulled her to a halt to study the Spanish men-of-war that lined the harbor.

"Now what?" she questioned impatiently.

"The Spanish are definitely back in control here. That doesn't bode well for the French," Vance mused aloud.

Although Micaela was eager to be on her way, Vance steered her carefully through the throng of sailors and keelboatmen. "One never knows from one week to the next how well received American merchant ships will be in this Louisiana port. Lucien made arrangements with the Spanish powers before the rebellion, but since Don Antonio de Ulloa was replaced, it might be a good idea to know which way the wind blows around here. Since you

aren't sure where you belong, I don't want to attract trouble when
I don't know which way it might be coming from."

Clutching Micaela's arm, Vance ushered her toward the nearest
pub to pick up the latest scuttlebutt from the locals. He paused
in front of the door, unsure what to do with Micaela. Smoke-
filled grogshops were no place for a lady, but neither was the
bustling wharf that teemed with rowdy sailors, beggars and
thieves. Finally, Vance decided on the lesser of two evils and
positioned Micaela directly beside the door.

"Don't you dare move," he ordered, shaking a lean finger in her
face. "I'll be inside only as long as it takes to gather information. If
anyone bothers you, or even looks at you wrong, start screaming
your head off and I'll be back lickety-split."

Micaela nodded reluctantly and backed up against the rough-
hewn wall to keep a posted lookout for trouble. "Be quick about
your fact-finding mission, Vance. I'm short on patience."

"Really? I hadn't noticed," he chuckled as he opened the door
to the dimly-lit tavern.

Gradually, Vance's eyes adjusted to the smoke-filled darkness.
There were at least two dozen men throwing down mugs of
ale, boasting about their favorite subject—women. Vance was
thankful he hadn't exposed Micaela to the crude remarks flying
around the grogshop. She would have been highly offended.
Knowing her, she probably would have lit into this raft of men,
just as she had done when Beatrice Huxley, and her gaggle of
gossips, had tried to make trouble at Dr. Thorley's party.

Bracing himself against the sticky bar that hadn't been cleaned
in weeks, Vance ordered a drink and posed his question to the
chubby-faced bartender whose bald head shone like the moon in
the lanternlight. "When did the Spanish arrive?"

The rotund proprietor snorted in disgust. "His highness Don
Alejandro O'Reilly, a bloody damned Irish mercenary in the
Iberian service, docked a week ago with twenty-six-hundred sea-
soned soldiers. The whole town came down to the levees to watch
O'Reilly strut across the dock."

"Damnation. His Hispanic Majesty must have crashed his fist
down on all of Louisiana in a fit of black temper after the rebellion," Vance speculated.

The proprietor nodded grimly. "A second French rebellion would have been suicidal. The illustrious military general marched his men to the Place d'Armes, hauled down the French flag, and hoisted up the Spanish flag. O'Reilly took over the garrison at Tchoupitoulas Gate and abolished every French regulation. The Spanish laws are back in effect, and O'Reilly has tightened the regulations so that no one in New Orleans doubts who the mighty ruler is."

Lord, things were worse than Vance imagined. If he and Lucien hoped to trade in New Orleans again, they might have to deal with a new set of officers on the Superior Council—ones who might not be as eager to accept bribes, as Carlos Morales had done. Vance wondered if Morales was a part of this new regime. He supposed only time would determine that.

"O'Reilly swore there would be no reprisals against the French rebels who ousted Ulloa," the proprietor went on to say as he refilled Vance's mug. "But without warning, his high and mighty majesty went on attack. He arrested the members of the rebellion and imprisoned them."

The bald-headed barkeeper leaned close, his gaze darting cautiously around him, before imparting the next piece of information. "Joseph Villeré and five other known leaders of the rebellion were brutally executed. Six more rebels have been dragged to jail. Madam Villeré learned that her husband had been taken aboard one of the frigates, and she went to plead for Joseph's life. In answer to her tearful pleas, the Spaniards tossed her a bloody shirt that had been torn to shreds by dagger blades."

Vance grimaced at the gruesome news. Had he known so much trouble was brewing in the city, he would never have consented to bring Micaela here.

"Of course, Bloody O'Reilly, as he's come to be known, insisted that Villeré flew into a fit of rage about his captivity and dropped dead of a heart attack." The proprietor smirked sarcastically. "Villeré dropped dead from an attack all right— from a *knife* attack. You Americans would be well advised to tread lightly around O'Reilly. He is ruthless and deadly and devious—"

A piercing feminine scream reverberated around the tavern,

sending Vance into immediate action. He shoved bodies out of his way to barrel through the door. Elbowing his way through the cluster of sailors who had gathered outside, Vance watched in stunned disbelief as Micaela—kicking and screaming—was dragged away by a half dozen uniformed Spanish officers.

Outraged, Vance stormed toward the dragoons. He came to an abrupt halt when he realized that none other than Carlos Morales was in command of the troops.

"What the devil is going on here?" Vance demanded.

Swords glided from their sheaths to hold him at bay.

Carlos pivoted, then nodded a greeting. "Ah, *Capitan* Cavendish, I didn't realize you and *Capitan* Saffire had returned to our fair city."

Vance hadn't realized Morales had returned to the fair city, either, so that made them even. But discovering that Morales had taken Micaela captive made Vance just plain furious.

"Where are you taking this poor woman?"

Carlos's eyes flashed as he half turned to glare at Micaela. "You need not concern yourself with the wench," he gritted out. "She was part of the conspiracy that sent us fleeing for our lives. She, like the other members of the French revolt, will be properly punished for treason."

"What?" Vance gaped at Micaela in disbelief. She stared back at him in baffled astonishment.

With a flick of his wrist, Carlos sent his men marching off with their captive in tow. "If you and *Capitan* Saffire wish to make certain arrangements, I will meet you at the Place d'Armes after dark," he murmured confidentially. "Although O'Reilly has restricted American trade, and subjected your cargo to excessively high tariffs, I believe we can strike a bargain that he doesn't have to know about."

When Carlos sauntered off, flaunting his lofty position like a peacock in full feathers, Vance cursed the air blue. The accusation that led to Micaela's arrest knocked the wind out of his sails. There was no telling what Carlos and Bloody O'Reilly would do to that girl!

The expression on Micaela's face assured Vance that she didn't recall taking part in the rebellion. He wondered if the shock of meeting a vicious man from her past, and facing imprisonment, would cure her amnesia in one helluva hurry. Most likely, he imagined. Micaela had learned more than she probably wanted to know about her past.

Damnation, Vance thought, unsure what to do next. He wished the hell he had stayed home where he belonged. This voyage to reclaim Micaela's past had quickly evolved into a nightmare!

Lucien stepped ashore in Charles Town, anxious to return to the townhouse to check on Micaela. Finding Bradford Clodfelter poised in front of him, smiling smugly, had Lucien muttering impatiently.

"Well, well, look who is back in town." Bradford chuckled as he flicked an imaginary piece of lint from his lacy sleeve. "Have you heard the latest news that is chasing itself back and forth across the highest social circles?"

Now how could that be possible? Lucien wondered. He'd spent several days in Boston, so he couldn't possibly know what gossip was drifting around town. For the most part, Lucien shrugged off Bradford and paid him little mind. But the man had become increasingly annoying since he began spouting remarks about Micaela's activities at the parties they had mutually attended shortly after the wedding. Lucien wondered what exaggerated tale Bradford felt inclined to tell before he took himself off to pester someone else. Offensive pestering was his true calling in life.

"It seems, Lucien, old friend—"

Lucien bristled immediately. He didn't consider himself *old* or a *friend* of Bradford's.

"—that you have been cuckolded." Bradford smiled wickedly. "Isn't it ironic that a man you blindly trust has become your worst enemy?"

Lucien's jaw clenched, and he itched to curl his fingers around Bradford's scrawny neck. This latest bit of gossip sounded worse than Lucien anticipated.

"Micaela and Vance were seen wrapped in each other's arms, not once but twice, at Dr. Thorley's party last week. Not only did they arrive together, and smile longingly at one another while they danced, but they sneaked onto the terrace to embrace in the moonlight before departing noticeably early—together.'' Bradford grinned in spiteful glee, then added, ''The very next morning they sailed off on one of the ships from your fleet. They were New Orleans bound, as I heard it told.''

Without a word, Lucien veered around Bradford to rent a carriage. Dealing with Bradford, who had been at his obnoxious best, put Lucien in the worst of all possible moods. When Lucien burst into the townhouse a half hour later his temperament hadn't improved.

Adrian glanced up from the game of chess he and Hiram were playing to state the obvious. ''Lucien, you're home.''

''I wish I could say the same for my wife!'' Lucien burst out in black temper.

''The nasty gossip must have greeted you at the wharf,'' Adrian speculated.

''Indeed it did, in the form of Bradford Clodfelter, fastest mouth east of the Appalachians,'' Lucien said, and scowled. ''He took fiendish delight in conveying the news that my unfaithful wife and my disloyal friend cruised off together. Damn it, Adrian!'' His words ricocheted around the parlor and echoed through the hall. ''Why didn't you stop them?''

''And how was I supposed to stop them? Was I to throw myself at Micaela and tackle her before she whizzed out the door? Should I have snatched up a pistol and shot Vance down before he stepped off the stoop?''

''You could have forbidden them from leaving!'' Lucien boomed.

''*Forbid* them?'' Adrian cast Lucien a withering glance. ''I marvel at your lapse of memory. The last time I forbade someone from doing something I didn't think was best, disaster struck. I told you that I've been cured of interfering in other people's lives.''

Lucien wanted to hit something—preferably Vance Cavendish. Unfortunately, the imbecile was sailing the seas with his wife. Hell fire and damnation!

Before Lucien recovered from being furious, an insistent rap rattled the door hinges. While he stood there glowering at his grandfather, Hiram rose from his chair to answer the door. To Lucien's further frustration, Roddy Blankenship, the helmsman from Vance's schooner, skulked inside. The sailor nervously kneaded his cap in his fists, purposely avoiding Lucien's homicidal glare. The fact that Roddy had arrived in Vance's stead didn't bode well. Lucien felt impending doom drop on his shoulders like an anvil.

"Well?" Lucien bugled impatiently. "Spit out what you came to say."

Roddy blanched at the harsh tone, swallowed uneasily, then fidgeted from one soggy boot to the other. "I have a message from Captain Cavendish," he squeaked.

"Fine. What the hell is it?"

Roddy tugged nervously at his collar, as if it were a noose. "Captain Cavendish requests that you sail to New Orleans immediately."

"And for what reason does your captain think I'm needed?" Lucien snapped.

With visible reluctance, Roddy met Lucien's stormy glare. "Because, sir, your wife has been imprisoned for her part in the revolution against the Spanish regime."

"WHAT!" Lucien howled.

"Captain Cavendish asks that you come quickly," he rushed on. "Your wife has already been in prison for four days. It will take at least that long for the return trip, given favorable winds."

Lucien glanced over at Adrian whose skin had turned the color of eggshells. "Hiram, fetch my grandfather a drink of brandy. This is no time for Adrian to collapse." While Hiram scuttled off, Lucien knelt in front of Adrian who was viciously fanning himself with his kerchief and gasping for breath. "I need you and Hiram to deal with the merchants whose cargo I delivered from Boston. If I have to waylay, it will cost me the entire day. Can you do that for me, Grandfather?"

The urgent request snapped Adrian out of his shocked state. He nodded determinedly and sat up a little straighter in his chair. "Leave those fussy merchants to me," he panted. "You can set sail immediately on Vance's ship."

Lucien bounded up to leave, motioning for Roddy to follow him. "Roddy, you can brief me on our way to the dock. When we arrive, have your crew board my schooner to help unload cargo. As soon as the task is complete, I want you to load west-bound cargo. I'll have Louis Beecham bring my ship to New Orleans as soon as she is reloaded."

"If you're planning on bargaining your cargo for your wife's freedom, I wouldn't get my hopes up, sir," Roddy advised as he raced alongside to match Lucien's long, hurried strides. "The new Spanish regime is ten times worse than the old one. Even though Captain Cavendish has been trying to make arrangements with Carlos Morales, who is still serving on the Superior Council, the new commissioner—ooofff!"

Lucien stopped so abruptly that Roddy slammed into him.

"Carlos Morales?" Lucien parroted.

Months ago, Micaela had told Lucien that Morales was the man she was contracted to marry. That was sure to complicate a touchy situation. Obviously Carlos had more than one ax to grind with his ex-fiancée. Damnation, when that high-spirited wife of his leaped into a cauldron of trouble, why did the pot always have to be at a rolling boil?

"Captain Cavendish tried to appeal to Carlos's sense of decency and compassion, but the cocky Spaniard refuses to release Micaela. Carlos eagerly took the bribe so we can trade cargo without paying the tariffs, but he hasn't budged an inch on the matter of your wife, sir."

"Christ," Lucien muttered, quickening his step. He shuddered to think what the resentful ex-fiancé had in mind for Micaela. Lucien wondered if she even remembered being pledged to marry that greedy scoundrel. She might not even realize why she was being subjected to his wrath.

If wishing could have made it so, Lucien would have sprouted wings and flown to New Orleans. Knowing how unscrupulous Carlos Morales could be in business dealings, he suspected the man would be far worse in dealing with women. If he had to lock horns with Carlos, he might find himself behind bars— spoiling any chance of rescuing Micaela [and trading in the bus-tling port.] How much had Vance told Carlos? Lucien wondered.

He hoped Vance had the presence of mind to keep his trap shut as much as possible.

Aside from these troubles awaiting Lucien in Louisiana, he might have to contend with an irate wife. He wondered if the shock of finding herself arrested might jolt Micaela's memory. She'd be in one fine fit of temper about being held captive, and another fine fit of temper if she realized Lucien had withheld information from her. She had trusted him to tell her all he knew about her past, and he had purposely deleted what he didn't want her to remember. If he managed to bargain for her freedom from her resentful ex-fiancé, Lucien didn't expect to receive one word of thanks, because his wife would be back to hating him with a passion.

Here comes that short walk from heaven to hell, Lucien thought as he helped carry the cargo ashore.

By the time Roddy explained the circumstances surrounding the hostile takeover in New Orleans by Bloody O'Reilly, Lucien was sick at heart. He had dreaded the day he had to tell Micaela the whole truth, but never in his worst nightmare did he dream he would be doing it while she was locked in jail for treason— held captive by a spiteful ex-fiancé who wielded the kind of power that could send heads rolling. Lucien cringed when he wondered how Carlos would take the news that Micaela had not only fled from him but had married Lucien. Those complications were sure to add fuel to the already blazing fire. All hell was probably going to break lose in New Orleans. Micaela would be in the thick of it, and Lucien didn't have the slightest idea how he was going to alleviate the situation!

In the inky darkness of her prison cell, Micaela tossed fitfully on her cot. Specters rose in her dreams like a gray haze swirling on a moonless night. Muffled sounds and echoing voices whirled through the corridors of her mind, entrapping her in a nightmare that collided with reality.

Gradually, the fog evaporated, transporting Micaela back to that fateful night when the chronicles of her past had been wiped from her memory. The horrible incident rose like a curtain on a stage, playing itself out in terrifying intensity.

Each unnerving emotion, thought and experience that assailed her that disastrous night on the bluff bombarded Micaela. She wasn't sure she wanted to revisit the vision that spiraled from its hidden pocket of memory. But she saw herself poised on the cliff and relived the events of the catastrophic night as if it were happening for the first time. . . .

Micaela flinched in panic when she saw the scowling face of the man who stalked toward her. She backed up as far as the stone ledge would allow, finding nowhere to run from the snarling man who approached. Lips curled, Barnaby Harpster lifted the makeshift club that was clenched in his right hand. His left hand was knotted in a tight fist, indicating the violent menace that roiled inside him. Sputtering foul curses, Barnaby hurled the tree branch at Micaela's mare, sending the horse thundering away.

Venomous laughter rumbled in Barnaby's thick chest as he blocked every escape route, save a daring leap over the cliff into infinity. "That's where they found her body, too, did you know that, wench?"

Micaela clenched her trembling hands in the fabric of her gown and braved a glance over the towering bluff. Was Barnaby hinting that history was about to repeat itself? Her mind reeled, trying desperately to recall everything Adrian had told her about the night five years ago when Cecilia had died, trying to remember the previous remarks Barnaby had made about Cecilia.

What was it Barnaby had said about the woman? Micaela struggled to think while panic tried to engulf her. A prissy bitch with haughty airs who enjoyed a variety of lovers—or something to that effect—Barnaby had said.

Micaela stared at the stocky brute who grinned at her in satanic amusement. Was Barnaby the man who spied on Cecilia? Or was he one of the men who bedded her . . . or raped her? Micaela decided that was nearer the truth. Barnaby was more than capable of brutish maulings. She had firsthand knowledge of his abuse.

Frantic, Micaela's mind raced, as she tried to figure out how

*to extricate herself from this deadly situation. When Barnaby took
an ominous step toward her, she burst out with the first thought
that found its way to her tongue.*

"Were you in love with Cecilia, too, Barnaby?"

*The question took Barnaby by surprise. He halted, then snorted
derisively. "Love that scheming bitch? I should say not! All
Cecilia wanted was for me to help her change Adrian's opinion
of her so she could secure her marriage to Lucien's fortune. She
wanted his money and the Saffire name."*

*Micaela stalled for time, praying help would come—and
doubting it would. "Are you the man Adrian hired to follow
Cecilia? Did you witness her indiscretions?"*

"What does it matter to you?" Barnaby snapped.

*"It is my husband's lost love we are discussing," she reminded
him. "I'm curious to know what happened to her."*

*"I didn't follow that bitch to tattle on her. Chaney did. When
Chaney told Adrian about her secret lovers, Cecilia came to me,
trying to convince me to side with her to refute Chaney's story."*

*"What did Cecilia want from you?" Micaela asked as she
discreetly calculated the distance to the nearest bush where she
could hide from this brute. If only she could keep him talking
and catch him off guard, she might have a chance to elude him.*

*"She wanted me to tell Adrian that Chaney was madly in love
with her and that he'd concocted the whole sordid tale to ensure
Cecilia didn't marry Lucien," Barnaby muttered in explanation.
"She wanted it to look as if Chaney's possessive jealousy provoked
him to speak against her."*

*"Was Chaney truly jealous?" Micaela glanced hither and yon,
poised for the moment when she could dart away.*

"Maybe, maybe not."

*Damn, the man wasn't cooperating. She wanted him to offer
lengthy explanations, not clipped phrases. "What about you, Barnaby? Were you jealous of Lucien, too? Did you want Cecilia
for yourself?"*

*Micaela sorely wished she hadn't posed that particular ques-
tion. Barnaby snarled mutinously. Micaela wanted to back away
from that frightful expression that puckered his homely features,
but she was too close to the ledge to retreat another step.*

"I wanted her, young fool that I was," he muttered, as if he resented the admission. "She met me here that night, promising me the pleasure of her ripe body, but when I reached for her, she backed away. She teased me with that shapely body of hers by unbuttoning her bodice. Then she ordered me to go to Adrian and repeat the tale she had invented. But I wanted her first, to make sure I got what she offered. When I grabbed hold of her, she bit me!"

Micaela didn't need to hear any more. She knew how Barnaby reacted—the way he instinctively reacted whenever provoked. His first impulse was a backhanded blow across the cheek.

"You struck her, didn't you, Barnaby?" Micaela dared to ask. "Cecilia didn't leap to her death at all, did she?"

For once, Micaela truly and surely wished she'd kept her mouth closed. The question put a sardonic glow in his eyes and a murderous curl on his lips.

"She got what she deserved and so will you," he jeered, stalking imminently closer.

Stark, blood-pumping fear riveted Micaela as she tried to duck under Barnaby's outstretched arms. But she couldn't bolt away before he caught hold of the back of her gown and spun her around to face him. Micaela shrieked when he hooked his arm around her neck and shoved her toward the crumbling edge. Frantic, she gouged him with her elbow and kicked his shins, but nothing deterred him.

"Because of you, bitch, I lost my job and my home," he breathed down her neck. "Because of you I've been living like hunted prey in the underbrush. Now you're going to pay for all the trouble you've caused me. . . ."

Barnaby's meaty hands clamped around her throat. Micaela's feet slid on the loose pebbles when she tried to squirm from his grasp. Her legs dropped out from under her, and Barnaby's forward momentum left him off balance. His raging bellow mingled with Micaela's shrill cry as they toppled over the bluff in a wild somersault.

Barnaby's massive body cushioned Micaela's head when they collided with the first boulder. She felt a dull groan rumble in Barnaby's chest while he crushed her against him. His arms *suddenly fell away, leaving him sprawled—half on, half off the gigantic slab of stone.*

Micaela had nothing to shield her or cushion her fall as she cartwheeled further down the slope. She screamed in terror when she saw another jagged boulder flying at her. She flung up an arm to protect her face, but nothing prevented her from plowing into the boulder. Her outflung arm offered no protection against the brain-scrambling blow that sent shards of unbearable pain shooting through her skull.

Darkness swallowed Micaela so quickly that she didn't have time to battle the looming vulture of unconsciousness. Pain sent her to drown in the kind of silence nothing could penetrate. . . .

A howling wail burst from Micaela's lips when she landed with a thud on the floor of her cell. Her body was drenched with perspiration, and her breath came in ragged spurts. Pulling shaky legs beneath her, she climbed back onto the cot and balled her shaky hands in her lap. She stared at the dingy walls of her cell and shuddered uncontrollably, trying to compose herself after reliving the terrifying incident on the cliff.

A string of forgotten memories paraded through her mind, bringing thoughts of the past into sharp focus. After months of racking her befuddled brain, Micaela began to remember things she wished she could forget all over again.

It must have been the jolting shock of her arrest, the outrage of being subjected to cruel captivity, that activated her memory, she diagnosed. That, and the passage of time which healed her head wound. But whatever was responsible for curing her amnesia, Micaela was steadily regaining her memory, tormentingly aware that she had been living one deceitful, calculated lie after another.

It came back to her with vivid clarity. She remembered her conversation with Arnaud, recalled the smug Spaniard who recognized her on the street and arrested her for treason. Carlos Morales . . .

Micaela cringed when she remembered how Carlos had attacked her the night of the Spanish ball. She was supposed to marry that disgusting vermin, because Arnaud had signed her life away after telling her that she wasn't his child. *That* was why Micaela had fled New Orleans.

Suddenly, Micaela remembered everything about her hellish existence at Rouchard Plantation, recalled everything that happened up to the point when she was imprisoned. But nothing compared to the horrendous sense of hurt and betrayal she experienced when she realized the man she loved to the very depths of her soul was the exact same man who had claimed he wanted nothing to do with her. *That* was what had sent her riding off into the night to find Barnaby Harpster waiting to shove her off the cliff.

Lucien had used her amnesia to his own advantage, creating a devious charade to elicit her devotion to him. Micaela, oblivious to her past, had trusted him explicitly, depended on him, adored him. Curse that manipulative scoundrel's black heart! He had made her a willing substitute for the woman he'd lost, playing out the life he had designed for himself and Cecilia!

Micaela wasn't allowed the luxury of dealing with every emotional blow and heartbreaking incident that had befallen her. She was deprived of the healing power of time. Her tormenting past came crashing down like a rockslide, pelting her with so many fierce, intense emotions that she didn't know which one to deal with first. *Mon Dieu*, the impact of bitter memory was enough to leave her bawling. But she would be damned if she cried for Lucien Saffire! He wasn't worth the tears or the wasted emotion.

And by God, she thought furiously, she never wanted to see that cruel, deceptive rake again for the rest of her life! He had played his last charade with her!

Seventeen

The sound of footfalls echoing in the musty corridor between the cells in the dungeon jostled Micaela from her tormented musings. She glanced up to see two burly guards halt in front of her cell.

"Get up, señorita."

When the barred door whined open, one of the guards lumbered inside to clutch Micaela's arm. She found herself shepherded down the corridor, bookended by the two furry-faced Spaniards. She was trooped past the cells that housed French rebels she now remembered seeing the night Don Antonio de Ulloa and his council were ousted from New Orleans.

"Where are you taking me?" Micaela wanted to know, pretty certain she was about to come face-to-face with a firing squad.

No answer. She presumed the guards were reluctant to give her the grim news.

Micaela was marched outside and led past the row of cabins that lined the military parade grounds at the garrison. When the guards paused to rap on one of the cottage doors, Micaela found herself standing face-to-face with Carlos Morales. Her punishment was probably going to be worse than a firing squad, she decided. When Morales finished doing his worst she was going to wish she were dead.

Carlos latched onto her arm and towed her inside. He ordered the guards to remain outside his cabin, then turned to appraise the smudges on Micaela's face, the mass of tangled hair that cascaded down her shoulders.

"After rotting in jail for several days, I thought perhaps you would be in a better frame of mind to consider my bargain," he said, grinning devilishly.

Micaela regarded the cocky Spaniard with wary consternation. "What sort of bargain?"

Carlos smiled again, his black eyes twinkling like obsidian in his pitted face. "I have the power to take your life, or spare it if you agree to my terms."

Micaela could just imagine what this lusty ogre's terms were. Although her temper flared in offended dignity, she swallowed the condemning words that flocked to her tongue. She needed an opportunity to escape. Having dealt with a manipulative rogue like Lucien Saffire, Micaela was well schooled in designing charades. If Lucien could pretend to be her doting husband, while he pined away for another woman, then she could create a similar kind of illusion for Carlos.

"And what am I expected to do to avoid the executioner?" she inquired, as if she didn't know.

"You will become my mistress, a willing one," he added emphatically.

Men! She distinctly remembered why she hated them—one and all. They schemed and connived to get what they wanted from women. Carlos was about to take lessons in manipulation, she vowed fiercely. Micaela had been trained by the very best!

"You want me in your bed, as I am?" She glanced down at the soiled gown that looked the worse for wear after days of captivity. "I have been locked away and denied the simplest necessities, and I doubt you would find the thought of touching me appealing."

Carlos gestured toward the bedroom. "I have considered that, *querida*. I've made arrangements so you can refresh yourself."

Micaela glanced over her shoulder to see the inviting brass

tub that awaited her, the fresh set of clothes that lay temptingly on the bed. When Carlos gestured toward the candlelit table and covered trays of food, Micaela realized this sly Spaniard had starved her in order to cow her into agreeing to anything he asked in exchange for a meal and a bath.

"Very well, Carlos, you have offered me a bargain I cannot refuse."

He beamed in triumph. She rather thought he would—the bastard.

"Your bath awaits," he declared, doubling over at the waist in an exaggerated bow.

Micaela pivoted on her heels and strode into the bedroom. When she closed the door behind her, she cursed the fact that there was no lock to hold unwanted intruders at bay. But then, she expected no less from Carlos. He was a man, after all. She knew how exceptionally good men were at plotting to ensure that women did their bidding.

Bitter outrage stabbed at her soul when Lucien's ruggedly handsome face rose before her. She had made a complete fool of herself where that cunning blackguard was concerned. First she had believed what Lucien wanted her to believe about their not-so-perfect marriage. Then she had professed to love him, had become hopelessly devoted to him. She had been hurt when he didn't return her heartfelt confession, and now she remembered why he'd never said those three little words. His heart was tied to the memory of another woman who had deceived him, though he was unaware of Cecilia's treachery. All Micaela had ever been to Lucien was an obligation, a responsibility, a pawn used to outfox Adrian. Oh yes, Micaela remembered the entire affair from its sour beginning to its bitter end.

Her resentful thoughts trailed off when she sank into the long-awaited bath. She had no time to brood over Lucien's deception. She needed to concentrate on escaping from Carlos. One glance at the window indicated Carlos had taken the precautionary measure of locking the panes together from the outside. If Micaela tried to use the window as her avenue of escape, she would have to shatter the glass. She might as well

light a fuse to a cannon. The racket would alert Carlos and
send the guards running after her.

Mentally plotting her strategy, Micaela scrubbed away the
filth. She sincerely hoped Carlos was lounging in his chair,
biding his time by sipping Madeira wine. The more wine the
better, she decided. When the time came to deal with Carlos, she
hoped his mental and physical capabilities would be impaired by
drink.

On that encouraging thought, Micaela settled back against
the rim of the tub for a nice, *long* bath, giving Carlos plenty
of time to drink his fill—on an empty stomach.

Four days and seven hours of frustrated apprehension had
eaten away at Lucien while he sailed to New Orleans. His
temper was at a rolling boil by the time he stalked across the
gangplank to see Vance Cavendish standing on the pier. Lucien
held Vance personally accountable for every ounce of painful
emotion spurting through Lucien's veins.

"God, am I glad you're here," Vance declared as Lucien
closed the distance between them in clipped strides.

Lucien greeted his *supposed* friend with a doubled fist in
the jaw. The unexpected blow sent Vance staggering back. The
second punch left him spread-eagle on the dock.

"You idiotic fool!" Lucien hissed between clenched teeth
as he loomed ominously over Vance. "I trusted you to keep
an eye on my wife, and I return home to hear the gossip
launched by a thousand wagging tongues. If that isn't enough
to infuriate me, you sailed off on a voyage that landed Micaela
in jail for treason. Damn you, Vance. I called you friend. With
that kind of devotion I hardly need enemies."

Stars were still revolving around Vance's head, disorienting
him, when Lucien snaked out a hand to haul him to his feet.
"Where is she?" Lucien gritted out. "How much did you tell
Carlos?"

Vance massaged his aching jaw and took a few tentative
steps on his noodly legs. Drawing Lucien farther away from
the crew who had witnessed Lucien's raging display of temper,

Vance explained. "Micaela has been locked in the prison behind Tchoupitoulas Gate for over a week. Carlos has permitted no visitors, so I'm not certain of Micaela's condition. Nor do I know if she remembers any of her past. She was beginning to recall certain scraps of facts, but the last time I saw her, she still suffered from amnesia.

"As for Carlos, I told him nothing about our connection to Micaela or your marriage. He thinks I was only a curious bystander who tried to intervene when she was apprehended on the street. And," Vance added, rubbing his throbbing jaw, "if you ever hit me again, I'm going to come up fighting with both fists. If I didn't think I deserved two hard punches I would have retaliated."

Lucien let out the breath he'd been holding for what seemed a week. "I'm sorry I took my frustration out on you, but damn it, things are even worse than you know. Carlos Morales is the man Micaela was fleeing from when she stowed away on my schooner. Her father contracted her into marriage to forge an alliance between himself and the Spanish government. You're fortunate that you didn't make the blundering mistake of telling Carlos that Micaela has a husband."

Vance stared at him, owl-eyed. "Damn, then Carlos has two reasons for venting his rage on Micaela—her participation in the revolt and a broken engagement."

"I'm sure one reason would have sufficed," Lucien grumbled sourly.

When Lucien wheeled around and stalked down the wharf, Vance fell into step behind him. "I've made contact with Carlos thrice this week. He's been more than willing to discuss bribes for importing American cargo, but when I mention Micaela he changes the subject faster than a cricket hopping from one spot to another. I don't have a clue what that bastard has in mind for Micaela."

Lucien didn't, either, and that worried the hell out of him. From personal experience, Lucien knew Carlos enjoyed bargaining and double-dealing. The Spaniard's foremost concern was for himself. He craved wealth and lorded his position in the Spanish regime over one and all.

His mind racing, Lucien hailed a carriage. His destination was the Spanish garrison. He didn't have the slightest idea what in the hell he was going to say to Carlos, provided he was allowed to speak to the son of a bitch. But when he arrived, he was relieved that the guard recognized Vance, because of his frequent visits. At least Vance had done something right this week, Lucien thought to himself.

Once they gained entrance, Vance directed Lucien's attention to the dimly-lit cabin where two guards, the size of gorillas, leaned casually against the door. Lucien frowned, wondering why Carlos felt the need to have guard dragons posted outside his cottage. When Lucien strode up to the door, the sentinels snapped to attention and blocked his path.

"Is Carlos under house arrest?" Lucien questioned. "Vance and I are acquaintances of his. I just arrived in town and would like a word with him. It shouldn't take but a few minutes."

The two woolly-faced guards glanced at one another, then stepped back apace. Lucien rapped on the door, waiting impatiently for Carlos to respond. A few moments later, the elaborately-adorned Spaniard appeared, a wine glass clasped in his hand and his eyes streaked with red. Lucien didn't await an invitation, he barged in as if he owned the place.

A quick glance around the parlor indicated Carlos was planning to entertain someone of the female persuasion. There were two place settings on the candlelit table and Carlos, decked out in his military finery, was clearly prepared to impress the lady in question.

"I'm afraid you've come at a bad time, *amigos,*" Carlos slurred out.

"I just arrived this evening, and I was anxious to see if you had been reinstated in the new regime. By the way, I was sorry to hear about that unfortunate revolt last fall," Lucien added in what he hoped sounded like a sympathetic tone.

Lucien's assessing gaze swung to the oak bureau to see the half empty bottle of wine. Lucien would dearly like to know what Carlos was celebrating. And it damned well better not be Micaela's recent death!

When the bedroom door swung open, Lucien strangled on

an oath. There stood his missing wife, decked out in a Spanish-style, off-the-shoulder gown that displayed her voluptuous figure to its finest advantage. Lucien silently fumed as he gazed roved over her. He had been worrying himself sick about her, thinking she was mildewing in that stinking dungeon. But from every indication, she had bargained her body to Carlos to escape confinement.

The instant Lucien's gaze locked with Micaela's, he saw the flash of hatred in her eyes. She had regained her memory—all of it, he realized. She knew he had deceived her, and now she was offering herself to Carlos to spite him, to gain that precious freedom she'd always wanted. Lucien wanted to wring her lovely neck as badly as he suspected she wanted to wring his!

In the looming silence, Vance stepped forward, placing himself between Micaela and Lucien. "It is good to see you again, mademoiselle," he murmured, flashing her a discreet warning glance. "I don't know if you remember me or not, but I was on the street the day you were arrested. I've been concerned about your welfare." He half turned to toss Carlos a semblance of a smile. "I'm relieved to know that it was all a terrible mistake, Carlos. This must be your way of compensating for bringing false charges against this lovely young lady."

Carlos shifted awkwardly from one polished black boot to the other, obviously caught off guard by Vance's remarks. "*Si*, there was a mistake, as I have just recently discovered. I had hoped to make amends to the señorita by inviting her to dinner."

The thought of Micaela spreading herself beneath this Spanish peacock made Lucien's blood boil. Though she had spent time in prison, she was ensuring she'd seen the last of that dismal cell. She had chosen Carlos's bed instead. Damn her!

Since Vance—bless him—had cleverly designed a role for her to play, Micaela eagerly accepted it. She could see that Carlos was too far into his cups to think rationally. She had stalled so long in the tub that he had definitely overindulged. Good, that would make her escape easier.

As for Lucien's unexpected arrival, Micaela could barely abide the sight of him. Bitter resentment curdled her stomach like an indigestible meal. If he'd been honest with her, if he'd told her what he knew about her past, she would never have returned to New Orleans until she knew it was safe. This was all his fault, damn his conniving hide.

And furthermore, she silently fumed, she didn't give a damn what Lucien thought was going on here. She didn't care what he thought of her, because she couldn't have thought *less* of him if she tried. If she managed to gain her freedom from Carlos, she was declaring independence from that raven-haired devil she had married, too! She would not ever let him come near her again. She would divorce him, or at the very least lead a separate life as far away from Lucien as she could get.

If Adrian tried to intervene, she would not listen to his pleas. She was keeping her distance from Lucien Saffire and he would never know that she carried his child, just as he had deprived her of the knowledge about her past.

"Would you gentleman care to join us?" Micaela invited, ignoring the stunned expression on Carlos's face. "I don't believe we have been formally introduced, monsieur." She directed the comment to Vance—her only salvation, her trusted friend.

Vance dropped into a gallant bow. "Vance Cavendish at your service. And this is Lucien Saffire."

Lucien didn't come near her—didn't dare. She flashed him a glare that consigned him to a much hotter climate than prevailed in steamy Louisiana. She noted that he returned her glower with equal, burning intensity.

"It's a pleasure to meet you," was all he said.

Wasn't it just! Micaela silently fumed. She couldn't believe Lucien had the audacity to show his face here. He must not have suspected that she had recovered from amnesia, hadn't realized she would recognize a slimy, devious snake when she saw one.

"Carlos has been more than apologetic for mistakenly linking me to the rebellion," Micaela said as she swanned across the room. "I'm sure he has prepared a feast large enough to feed the four of us. If you'll sit down, I'll serve us."

Vance took his cue and plunked into a chair. Carlos wobbled over to retrieve the wine and took his place at the table. Lucien parked himself across from the vacant chair intended for Micaela, wondering if he could stomach the sight of his wife sitting across from him without spoiling his appetite. He wanted to chew on *her* for agreeing to this tryst with Carlos!

Pasting on a civil smile, Lucien poured himself a drink and then leaned over to refill Carlos's glass. "Now that the Spaniards have regained control of New Orleans, I was hoping we could make arrangements to sell American imports, just as before. I'm sure Vance has mentioned the matter during my absence."

Carlos nodded groggily, then sipped his wine. "I'm still willing to negotiate, as usual," he mumbled. "Now that O'Reilly has tightened regulations, there will be a few more . . . er . . . expenses and precautions for me to consider, of course."

Micaela knew exactly what Carlos was trying not to say in her presence. She knew of his double-dealings. She also knew Vance and Lucien were trying to retain their ties to this swindling Spaniard. That was what this pretense was all about, she imagined. If Lucien demanded her release, because she was his wife, Carlos wouldn't take kindly to having a wrench thrown in his plans of seduction and revenge. Considering Carlos's position in the Superior Council, he could toss all three of them in prison—never to be seen or heard from again. Damn it, this was a ticklish situation, she realized.

She suspected Vance and Lucien were sitting there, conjuring up and discarding a half dozen ways to avoid trouble that could affect their business ventures. It looked as if it would be up to her to instigate a plan of action—not that she had any intention of sitting around waiting for Lucien to come up with one. She'd had enough of his schemes to last two lifetimes—the one in reality and the illusion he had designed for her!

"More wine, gentlemen?" Portraying the cordial hostess, Micaela ambled over to fetch another bottle of wine. "The meal was absolutely delicious, Carlos. After living on prison rations, this was indeed a welcomed feast.''

Micaela returned to the table with wine bottle in hand, lingering at Carlos's side. With malice a forethought, she clutched the neck of the bottle and clanked it against Carlos's skull. The Spaniard slid down in his chair, slamming his chin on the edge of the table, then collapsed on the floor in an unconscious heap.

Two pair of disbelieving eyes zeroed in on Micaela. "Well, I couldn't sit here all night waiting for you two to analyze the situation to death and arrive at a solution,'' she defended herself. "Perhaps you're reluctant to cross swords with Carlos, but I'm certainly not.''

She thrust the bottle at Vance, flagrantly ignoring Lucien. "If Carlos rouses before I return, kindly hit him again.''

"I realize hasty decisions and immediate action are your forte, but if it isn't too much to ask,'' Lucien muttered caustically, while he stared at the Spaniard who was sprawled on the floor like a misplaced doormat, "would you mind letting us in on this ingenious scheme you've devised. I hope you remember there are two guards posted outside the door. They are armed to the eyeballs, if you hadn't noticed.''

Micaela was in no mood for Lucien's sarcasm, and she returned it in the mean spirit it was given. "I'm well aware of the guards. Who do you think marched me over here to listen to Carlos's lurid proposition? Carlos let me wallow in filth and starved me for a week so I would become desperate enough to accept his disgusting bargain.'' She flashed him a glare blazing with fire and brimstone. "But as you can see, I've gotten exceptionally good at dealing with conniving men.''

"Touché, madam,'' Lucien said with a slight inclination of his head. "Now, what the devil are you planning? I would hate to bungle your scheme, because if it fails, and I won't be surprised if it does, your lovely neck will be stretched out longer than a giraffe's.''

Micaela set her resentment aside, assuring herself that she would have time to vent her fury on him later. "When I toss the night stand through the back window, the two Goliaths at the front door will rush around the cottage to see what the racket is all about.''

''No doubt, they will,'' Lucien smirked. ''That's what guards get paid to do, after all.''

''After you send up a shout for assistance, I plan to saunter out the front door and disappear into the crowd that will be spilling from Spanish headquarters. Since the wall surrounding this garrison is only four foot tall, I'll have no trouble scaling it in the breeches I plan to be wearing.''

She glanced quickly at Vance. ''Did you leave the carriage by the front gate?'' When he nodded affirmatively, Micaela smiled. ''Good, then if you will do me the courtesy of giving me a ride back to the wharf, I'll be most grateful. I'll meet you down the road where the guards can't spot me.''

Before Lucien could open his mouth to question what in the hell Micaela thought she was going to do if she *were* spotted, she darted into the bedroom. A few minutes later, he heard the night stand crash through the window. Micaela came through the bedroom door, dressed in Carlos's spare military uniform. Her gown had been rolled up and tucked inside the jacket, leaving the impression of a pot belly. A hat sat low on her forehead, concealing her long blond hair.

While Micaela dashed toward the front door, Lucien and Vance hurried into the bedroom to send out a call of alarm.

''She's going to get caught, sure as hell,'' Vance grumbled as he stared through the broken glass.

''And knowing that, we'll have plenty of time to figure out how to extricate her from the next tangle she'll inevitably find herself in,'' Lucien said to the back of Vance's head.

''The woman has escaped!'' Vance trumpeted at the two guards who rushed around the corner of the house. ''I think she went that way!''

Tearing off in the direction Vance indicated, the guards gave chase into the shadows. Lucien wheeled toward the parlor to drag Carlos back into his chair and shake him awake.

''Carlos?'' Lucien slapped him across the cheek a couple of times to rouse him. It was a task he thoroughly enjoyed.

Groaning miserably, Carlos pried open one bloodshot eye.
"What happened?" he bleated.

"The young lady you falsely accused of treason must have
decided to have her revenge," Lucien explained. "After she
clobbered you with the wine bottle, she crashed through the
window before Vance and I could latch onto her. The guards
are searching for her now."

"That crafty little witch!" Carlos muttered drunkenly.
"That's the second time she's escaped my bed. I'll—" His
voice trailed off and his eyes rolled back in his head.

"You better lie down," Vance insisted. "You don't look
well. Lucien and I will see if we can track down the lady while
you rest."

Nodding dazedly, Carlos allowed himself to be put to bed.
"Someday, somehow, I'm going to get even with that wench,"
he slurred out, then sagged into a mindless stupor.

Lucien and Vance lingered by the door to monitor the progress of the search. The commotion at Carlos's quarters had
drawn considerable attention at the garrison. Uniformed soldiers were darting off in all directions to capture the escapee.

When Lucien spun around and strode back into the bedroom
where Carlos was snoring up a storm, Vance frowned. "What
are you doing? We're supposed to be making our way to the
gate to reach the carriage."

"I'm just making one last check on Carlos," Lucien said
with a nonchalant shrug.

When Lucien and Vance stepped outside the cottage, Lucien
veered left instead of right. "Now where are you off to?"
Vance asked, bemused.

"I have an errand to attend," Lucien said evasively. "I'll
meet you outside the gate in a few minutes."

When Lucien reappeared a few minutes later, Vance was
waiting in the carriage. "Well, that was simple enough," Vance
murmured as Lucien sank down on the seat beside him.

"Micaela isn't out of the woods yet," Lucien warned. "She
could still end up with a noose around her neck."

"Did you have a better plan in mind?" Vance asked mockingly.

"No," Lucien mumbled, then scowled. "I can't say that I did."

"Neither did I."

Lucien hated to give Micaela credit, but she had cleverly resolved the problem without implicating him or Vance. She had granted them the chance to ship cargo into New Orleans without spoiling their relations with the Spanish. But her consideration had been totally unnecessary. Lucien had no intention of dealing with Carlos after the conniving scoundrel imprisoned and starved Micaela, scheming to get her into his bed. In fact, Lucien had already made the arrangements to set his plan in motion so he could even the score with Carlos Morales—once and for all.

Clutching the reins, Lucien drove down the road. A mile later Micaela appeared from a clump of vine-covered trees beside the road. She had donned the seductive gown Carlos had given her in payment for the night of pleasure he never got to enjoy.

Micaela climbed into the carriage, ignoring Lucien as if he were no more than a pesky gnat, and seated herself beside Vance. In silence they moved down the streets of the French Quarter to reach the wharf. Without warning, Micaela leaned over to rip the reins from Lucien's hands and jerk the horse to a halt.

"What the hell—?" Lucien crowed.

Micaela bounded from the coach and dashed toward the dark-haired gentleman who shrank away from her as if he'd seen a ghost.

"Mikki?" Henri Rouchard croaked, staggering to keep his feet. "I thought you were dead."

Micaela blinked, stunned. "Dead? Why would you think that?"

Henri recovered from shock and hugged his sister close. *"Mon Dieu,* it's a relief to know you survived. Papa told me you had been caught up in the attack on the Spanish garrison last fall. He said he'd searched the entire city, but that you must have been a victim of foul play and wound up floating down the river. Where the blazes have you been all these months?"

Micaela told Henri about the revolt and her reason for escaping to Charles Town in hopes of avoiding the marriage Arnaud had arranged for her.

"How did you survive without funds?" Henri questioned in concern.

"She married well in Charles Town," Lucien interjected from behind Micaela.

"I had not intended to impart that information to my brother," she hissed in his ear. "It isn't something I'm proud of."

Ignoring Micaela's snide comment, Lucien curled his arm around her waist. He appraised the lanky, elegantly-dressed Henri Rouchard, who looked to be twenty-three or somewhere thereabouts. "Aren't you going to introduce us, love?"

Reluctantly, Lucien noted, Micaela did as requested. After a quick round of how-do-you-dos, Lucien glanced apprehensively in the direction they had come. "Micaela, if you would like to continue this reunion with your brother, perhaps he could join us on board ship." He directed her attention toward the Spanish patrol that had appeared beneath the street light a block away.

"Will you come, Henri?" she asked anxiously.

"Of course," Henri said, tossing Lucien a wink and a grin. "I would like to become better acquainted with the brave soul who has undertaken the dubious task of exerting control over my rambunctious sister."

Hurriedly, Lucien escorted Micaela to the carriage and tucked her beside him. After giving Henri directions to the schooner, Lucien sent the steed into a trot. He didn't slow the pace until he reached the schooner's berth.

Seeing his private schooner sitting beside her sister ship assured Lucien that his crew had opened full sail to arrive in time to provide reinforcements—should extra manpower be needed to free Micaela. Lucien volunteered to wait above deck for Henri, while Micaela scurried out of sight to avoid the Spanish patrols.

Lucien watched her duck into the Great Cabin, feeling a sense of loss. The castle he'd built in the air, the clouds of protective security he'd spun around Micaela while she suffered from amnesia, had evaporated into thin air. He knew the confrontation was coming and he dreaded it.

Staring up at the midnight moon, Lucien counted each and every step on the rocky road that led from heaven to hell. Very soon, he predicted, he was going to pay penance for deceiving Micaela while she recovered from her injuries. On the whole, Lucien decided, this was going to be one of the worst nights of his life. He was going to lose something that had become very precious and dear to him. The sad part was that he knew that he deserved Micaela's hatred and disdain. He had waited too damned long to tell her the truth. His mistake, he mused. Since he'd been the one to make it, he was going to have to learn to live with it.

Eighteen

Micaela paced from wall to wall like a caged tiger, remembering every unpleasant incident that had occurred in this Great Cabin. Every time she thought about how Lucien had purposely withheld the truth about their stormy marriage she muttered another insult to his name. He had betrayed her trust and she would never forgive him for that! And if she hadn't been so anxious to be reunited with Henri she would be—at this very moment—reading Lucien Saffire every paragraph in the riot act.

Oh, how Lucien must have delighted in watching her fawn over him like a lovesick fool. Well, he would never see her behave so idiotically again. She would treat him with the disrespect he deserved.

When the door swung open, Micaela willfully set aside her spiteful musings. Henri strode into the cabin, chatting with Lucien who was playing the charming host. While Vance poured a round of drinks, Micaela gestured for her brother to make himself comfortable in Lucien's favorite chair.

"You seem to have married exceptionally well," Henri said, glancing appreciatively around the resplendent cabin. "I've never seen such luxurious quarters on board a ship. This reminds me of a floating palace.''

"I have tried to ensure that my wife travels in style and comfort when she accompanies me," Lucien commented.

Micaela flung him a withering glance, but kept her mouth shut. If the truth be known, Lucien would probably just as soon stuff Micaela in the hull and forget she existed. After all, she was no more than a responsibility he felt obliged to support because they were legally bound together.

"Mikki, I'm afraid I have some distressing news," Henri murmured. "After you were given up for dead, Mother packed up and left for St. Louis. Papa has been in a towering rage ever since, and refuses to have your name, or Mother's, mentioned in his presence. I cannot imagine what possessed Mother to abandon Papa after all these years. She didn't state her reasons in the note she left at my house in the French Quarter."

Micaela knew why Marguerite wanted to escape human bondage. She had been browbeaten into submission for long enough. Micaela sincerely hoped her mother found happiness after going through the mundane paces of life for years on end.

While Micaela and Henri discussed family matters, Lucien lounged against the wall, sipping his brandy. From the gist of the conversation he realized Micaela's father had treated her like an outcast, separating her from her brother as much as possible. Although Lucien had never met Arnaud, he disliked the man—sight unseen. How any man could close his heart to a vibrant woman like Micaela was inconceivable. It was certainly Arnaud's loss that he had rejected his daughter.

When Henri rose to leave, Lucien noticed the sentimental mist clouding Micaela's eyes. "I hope you can visit us often in Charles Town," Lucien invited. "I know Micaela will be anxious to see you whenever she has the chance."

Micaela glanced warily at Lucien. Now what game was that scamp playing? Did he think to soothe her irritation by generously offering Henri a standing invitation? Well, it wouldn't work. She wasn't going to forget how Lucien had misled her and betrayed her trust. Perhaps Henri was impressed by Lucien's suave, charming facade, but she wasn't. She knew Lucien better!

If Lucien thought for one minute that she was going to ignore the past and overlook his ploy to mold her into a doting wife, then he was kidding himself. She still wanted a divorce. She was not spending the rest of her life with this impossible man, even if he was the father of her child. Marguerite had tolerated Arnaud for years, but Micaela refused to suffer the same submissive fate. Life was entirely too short to spend it in misery.

After Henri bid her adieu, Micaela waited out of sight, then made a beeline for Vance's ship. That was where she had left her belongings when she traveled to New Orleans, and that was where she intended to reside during the voyage to Charles Town. She was not going to stay in Lucien's cabin, not if he planned to be in it. Spacious though the cabin was, it wasn't big enough for the both of them. The continent wasn't big enough for the both of them!

When Lucien strode across the gangplank of Vance's ship, Vance smiled wryly. "I just saw your wife storm past," he reported. "I think you're headed for a helluva battle, Lucien. Shall I fetch a chair and whip before you march off to beard the lioness in her den?"

Lucien's gaze riveted on Vance. "No, what I prefer is that you answer a question—simply and honestly."

Vance lifted a blond brow. "What question is that?"

"Did the gossips in Charles Town actually see you and Micaela wrapped in each other's arms, twice?" Lucien asked, point-blank.

Vance shifted uneasily. Lucien was quick to note Vance was hesitant to meet his probing gaze. "Well? Was it fact or vicious rumor?" Lucien demanded.

"It was fact, but—"

"I see," Lucien cut in, his voice as cold as the arctic wind. Reluctantly, he asked the question that had been tormenting him for days on end. "Are you in love with her?"

"Oh, for God's sake, Lucien—"

"Very well, if you don't wish to reply to that question, then perhaps you'll respond to this one," Lucien continued in a harsh growl. "Have you slept with my wife?"

Vance gasped, affronted. "Damn it, Lucien. We are best friends!"

"I didn't ask you how good of friends we are," Lucien said between his teeth. "I asked you if you slept with Micaela during your voyage to New Orleans."

"No," Vance snapped back.

"But you would have liked to," Lucien accused, growing madder by the second.

"Yes," Vance all but shouted.

Lucien stared Vance squarely in the eye. "I will ask you again, Vance," he said softly—too softly. "Are you in love with Micaela?"

"Yes, damn it. There, I've said it, so I hope you're satisfied," Vance grumbled resentfully. "But it makes no difference how I feel. Micaela is still your wife. I respect the bounds of matrimony, even if you have stretched it to its limits with your damned charades."

"And if I consent to grant Micaela the divorce I expect she wants, what then, Vance?"

"Then you are the biggest fool on the planet," Vance said with a snort. "Excuse me for being so blunt, but if you let Micaela go, then you will be making the greatest mistake of your life. And if I'd known you intended to keep the incidents surrounding your wedding a secret from her while she was recovering from her injuries, I would have told her the day I left for sea. How could you have been so stupid?"

"Because I—" Lucien bit down on his tongue and stared at the distant lights of the city.

"Because why?" Vance pressed relentlessly. "Because you enjoyed playing your devious games with her? Because you enjoyed taking her to bed, as if she had become another of your conquests? Did you want to mold her into a doting wife? Did you want her to become as fawning as Cecilia?"

"Shut up," Lucien hissed. "You don't know what the hell you're talking about."

"Don't I? I wonder," Vance said dubiously. "I've found myself growing attached to that green-eyed beauty, torn between desire and my loyalty to a lifelong friend. But damn it, man, I'm not sure you deserve my consideration, not after the way you deceived Micaela. And to this day, I can think of not one good reason why you would have done such a thing, except to bring that wild-hearted female under your thumb, just so you could say it could be done!"

"Are you quite finished?" Lucien snapped, blue eyes blazing like bonfires.

"No, not quite." Vance inhaled deeply, his chest inflating like a bagpipe. "You talked me into officiating at that ridiculous wedding ceremony. I kept my mouth shut while you took Micaela to your bed that night, knowing that was the last place she wanted to be. I have stood aside, watching you botch up what could have been a good marriage. And while I am being perfectly honest, you may as well know that if Micaela demands a divorce, and you consent to it, I will definitely court her— properly. And you, my foolish friend, can go straight to the devil! . . . And now I am quite finished!"

When Vance spun on his heels and stalked off, Lucien stared after him. He knew he deserved every word of that blistering tirade, because he hadn't dealt fairly and honestly with Micaela. Learning that she hadn't enjoyed a pleasant childhood and knowing she was enduring an even more unpleasant marriage left him wondering if perhaps he should grant Micaela the freedom she had long been denied. Because of him, Micaela had been manipulated into marriage, and then ruthlessly attacked by a man who wanted lethal revenge. Because Lucien had withheld information, Micaela had returned to New Orleans, unaware of her past, and found herself imprisoned and bribed by her ex-fiancé. If Lucien had told her what he knew, she might not have returned to Louisiana.

Now it was time to compensate for the torment she'd suffered—indirectly and directly—because of him. Drawing himself up, Lucien strode off to confront Micaela in Vance's private cabin. His day of reckoning had arrived. For once, he was going to be noble and decent and do what was best for Micaela. He owed her.

Micaela glanced up when she heard the quiet rap at the door. Hurriedly, she fastened the ties on the front of her nightgown, then padded barefoot across the room. She smiled in greeting when she opened the door to find Vance poised before her.

"May I come in?"

"This is your room. I only borrowed it for the voyage," she reminded him, stepping aside.

Vance caught her by the waist, drawing her close to give her an affectionate hug. "I worried myself sick about you all week," he murmured as his lips grazed her forehead. "I tried to visit you in jail, bringing along extra rations of food and blankets to make your sojourn in hell as comfortable as possible. But that bastard refused to let anyone near you."

Micaela reached up to smooth away Vance's concerned frown. Of all the men she had dealt with in her lifetime, Vance had been the only man she felt she could trust. He was nothing like Lucien, thank God!

"I survived my ordeal, and I think the solitude was a blessing in disguise. I had plenty of time to sort out the confusing memories and put them back in proper perspective."

"Micaela, I'm sorry," Vance said with genuine regret. "I'm sorry about everything that has happened. If I could turn back the hands of time, I assure you I would have done things differently. You wouldn't have been forced into marriage and I would never have left you floundering to unlock the secrets of your forgotten past. And I certainly wouldn't have brought you to New Orleans if I'd known calamity awaited you. You deserve better than you have received. . . ."

Before Micaela realized Vance's intent, his lips slanted over hers in a tender kiss. In the past, Vance had limited himself to hasty pecks on the cheek and playful hugs. But this was different. And if Micaela hadn't been so furious with Lucien, she would have reminded Vance that he was overstepping the bounds of friendship with this kind of kiss. Instead, she wrapped her arms around Vance's neck and kissed him back. If the gossips in Charles Town were having a field day with the excited hugs she'd bestowed on Vance at Dr. Thorley's party, they'd have a heyday with this news. Micaela didn't give a damn if the gossip spread from port to port!

Lucien halted in the open doorway, watching his best friend kiss the breath out of Micaela—while she kissed him back. He felt as if he'd received a staggering blow to the midsection, robbing him of breath. Lucien wondered if Vance had lied about the nature of his relationship with Micaela. A man certainly had cause for doubt when he saw his wife—in her revealing nightgown—and his best friend plastered so closely together that a gnat would have trouble finding enough air to breathe!

Rage bubbled inside Lucien and it was all he could do to prevent shoving Micaela and Vance apart. Somehow, he managed to make his presence known without broadcasting his irritation to every sailor on the ship.

"If the two of you can tear yourselves apart for a few minutes, I would like to speak to Micaela alone," Lucien said through gritted teeth.

Vance spun to face Lucien's icy glare. Without apologizing for taking liberties, Vance veered around Lucien, then paused by the door to glance at Micaela.

"If you need me, I'll be on the quarter-deck."

Micaela nodded mutely before glancing in Lucien's direction. Damn, the man appeared so self-contained and unruffled that Micaela swore his emotions had been sealed in a canning jar. His casual demeanor assured her that she meant absolutely nothing to him. They were right back where they started the night of their wedding reception. It was as if the happiness they had enjoyed for the past few months never existed. Those days when she fancied herself in love with Lucien were no more than a whimsical dream. *This,* she reminded herself, was reality.

"I'm never going to forgive you for what you did," Micaela burst out, anxious to get this over with.

"I don't expect you to forgive me."

"Good, because you don't deserve forgiveness or consideration," she hissed.

"I'm not asking for either one, Micaela," he said quietly.

"Then why are you here?" Micaela was totally baffled by his refusal to ply her with lame excuses or engage in verbal battle. Honestly, Lucien seemed so distant and remote that she didn't know how to deal with him. His voice was so empty of emotion that they might as well have been discussing the weather. He didn't even have the decency to attempt to apologize for deceiving her. Didn't he care anything at all about her? Obviously not, judging by his complaisant attitude, his lack of emotion.

"The only reason I'm here is to find out what you want and where we go from here," he told her.

"What *I* want? Since when has that been of the slightest concern to you?"

Lucien gave a wide berth to Micaela as he moved to pour himself a drink, hoping to ease the knot of frustration he was valiantly trying to control. Before he could down the brandy, Micaela sped over to snatch the glass from his hand. She consumed the drink in one gulp, choked on the fiery taste, wheezed, then stuck out the glass, demanding more. Lucien noted that the second drink went down easier. He almost broke into a smile when Micaela demanded that he fill her glass a third and fourth time. She seemed to be trying as hard as he was to drown the simmering frustration and get through this ordeal.

This, Lucien decided, was the best method of settling divorce proceedings. When both parties were besotted, maybe they wouldn't give a flying fig about much of anything. They could discuss arrangements like two impartial strangers.

While Micaela was doing hand-to-glass combat, Lucien grabbed another glass and filled it level full. After chugging the drink, he reached for the bottle, only to find Micaela holding the flask up to him.

"Allow me," she offered in a mocking parody of politeness.

After Lucien threw down another drink, he refilled Micaela's glass. In exaggerated formality, they refilled each other's glasses until the bottle ran dry. Lucien pivoted unsteadily to retrieve another from Vance's liquor cabinet.

It was impossible for him to measure time while he and Micaela were going through whiskey as if there were no tomorrow. But certainly, Lucien was capable of winning this drinking contest. He'd had lots of practice in pubs and grogshops in ports around the globe. While he maintained a reasonable sense of balance, Micaela wobbled each time the ship swayed with the incoming surf.

"I think you should sit down," Lucien advised.

"Don't tell me what to do," she slurred before collapsing on the floor, missing the chair by a mile.

Chuckling, Lucien sank down Indian-style beside his inebriated wife and offered her another drink—which she readily accepted.

"My, this whi*th*key does leave a body experiencing the most baffling sensa*th*ions," she babbled. "My nose is numb. Is that normal?"

When she stared at him through glassy eyes, Lucien nodded and grinned. Or at least he thought he grinned. His facial muscles felt as if they were sliding down his cheeks like melted butter.

"Before we get too soused to think, we had better discuss the matter at hand," Lucien prompted.

"What matter?" Micaela peered blankly at him.

"I believe our marriage is in question here." Lucien swallowed a gulp of brandy. "You realize, of course, that divorce will cause considerable scandal in our social circle. It is far more acceptable to merely murder one's husband than to divorce him."

"Don't plant any ideas in my head," she warned sluggishly.

"You no longer find me capable of fulfilling your needs, is that it?" he asked after a moment.

Micaela stared at him as if he'd just ask the stupidest question anybody had ever asked. "You satisfied me exceptionally well and you know it," she said honestly. "You just didn't love me while you were making love to me. I suspect the same holds true for all the somebody elses you've bedded while you were flitting around from one port to another, before and during our marriage.''

"So you assume I've been unfaithful," Lucien concluded.

"And devious, manipulative and . . ." Micaela sighed heavily. "I could name dozens more adjectives, but I'm having trouble thinking straight."

Lucien stared at Micaela as she struggled to bring the glass to her lips—and missed her target. Whiskey dribbled down her chin and chest, causing the gauzy fabric of her alluring gown to cling to the full swells of her breasts. There were several questions Lucien wanted answered before Micaela was too far gone to respond. The liquor was working like a truth serum, but if Lucien waited much longer Micaela wouldn't be able to remember the questions, much less offer answers.

Setting his glass aside, he framed her flushed face in his hands, demanding her attention—what there was left to give. "I want you to tell me what happened the night you fled from the wedding reception. The night Barnaby stalked you—''

Micaela recoiled. "I'd rather not."

Lucien was persistent. He had been tormented beyond measure, wondering what had happened that night. "Did Barnaby try to rape you? Did he try to push you over the edge when you resisted?''

Tears welled up in her eyes. Micaela was suffering a torment that Lucien couldn't comprehend—one she was reluctant to explain. If she offered Lucien details, it would shatter his idealistic illusion of the woman he'd immortalized for five years. No matter how bitter Micaela was about Lucien's deceptions, she wasn't so cruel as to tell him that Cecilia had been unfaithful and had plotted to become his wife only because she was anxious to get her hands on Lucien's money.

"Tell me all of it, Caela," he demanded. "I want to know everything."

"I can't tell you what you want to know!" she railed. "Please don't ask. You won't like what you hear."

The careless comment caused Lucien to frown, bemused. "What secrets are you keeping from me?"

"Just grant me the divorce and let it be over," she said on

a sob. "You don't want me. You never wanted me, only *her*. And she wasn't—" Micaela wiped the squiggles of tears away, cursing under her breath for letting her tongue outdistance her pickled brain.

"She wasn't what?" Lucien hooked his arm around her waist, drawing her onto his lap. "Barnaby knew something and he told you about Cecilia, is that it?"

Micaela cautioned herself to answer only the questions that revealed nothing of Cecilia's scheming and betrayal. She would take the secret to her grave. But if it eased Lucien's mind to know Cecilia hadn't leaped to her death, then Micaela would reveal that much to him.

"Barnaby was there the night you cannot forget," she slurred out. "He and Cecilia argued. Barnaby backhanded her and she stumbled and fell over the edge. Chaney had told—"

Micaela buried her head against his chest, praying for deliverance from her runaway tongue. Her thoughts were whirring around her mind and tumbling off her lips in rapid succession. She couldn't trust herself to speak, for fear she would convey what she vowed never to tell.

"I won't tell you any more. Just leave me be," Micaela insisted.

The feel of her ripe body draped over his lap, her breasts brushing enticingly against his chest, sent Lucien's thoughts veering off in the wrong direction. As desperately as he wanted to know the details of that fateful night and understand Barnaby's link to Cecilia's death, the need to hold Micaela overrode the torments of his past. If this was to be the last night he spent with her, then he wanted a sweet memory to cherish in the empty years to come.

The sparks that leaped between him and Micaela, even while they were at odds, had always been too strong to deny. Even though Micaela despised him—and with justifiable reason— he still cared about her, still wanted her. His need for her wasn't contingent on whether she wanted him in return. He simply couldn't control what he felt when he touched her, held her.

Micaela was the one woman who twisted his insides into hot, aching knots. If he let her go, as she demanded, then he would have only the memory of those days when Micaela had loved him, when she'd smiled up at him in amusement and affection, unaware of their troubled past. Just one night, Lucien thought as he inhaled the soft feminine scent that clogged his senses. If she would love him just once more, if only for the night, he wouldn't make selfish demands on her when she negotiated for her freedom.

When Lucien's warm, moist lips drifted over that sensitive spot beneath Micaela's ear—the one only he knew existed—she felt tingles of desire flickering through her body. The sensations reminded her of those wondrous moments when she foolishly gave her heart away—freely, trustingly, unconditionally—only to discover she was living an illusion.

"Lucien, don't," she murmured, her breathing altered by masterful caresses that glided over the sensitive flesh of her thighs. "You're taking unfair advantage when you know I've had too much to drink."

Lucien had had a tad too much to drink himself, that was part of the problem. Masculine pride—and something else he chose not to name—had a fierce and mighty hold on him. He knew he had to let Micaela go, because that was what she wanted, because he owed her that and much more, but he wanted this night, the memory waiting to be created. For this space out of time, he ached to recapture the splendorous pleasure he had discovered when Micaela had been in love with him.

A soft moan tripped from Micaela's lips when Lucien pressed her to her back and spread a row of sizzling kisses down her throat. The heated closeness caused hungry sensations to weaken her mind and body. Micaela lifted her gaze to see Lucien poised so close that she could feel every lean contour, inhale the masculine scent that had been imprinted on her senses.

"Why can't you touch me without starting these uncontrollable fires?" she rasped. "It hurts too much to burn alive when I know the man I want loves another—"

His mouth came down on hers as he clutched her body to his, summoning a response Micaela couldn't restrain—not when whiskey had stripped away all inhibition. Fighting the fiery needs ignited by his kisses and caresses was a hopeless battle. If there was one thing that could be said about this handsome, raven-haired rake, it was that he knew how to touch a woman and make her respond in wild abandon.

Micaela had never been able to resist walking into the flames Lucien left blazing around her, not even on their wedding night when she'd feared the torture of a man's touch. Lucien could make her forget everything except the phenomenal needs that intensified until she ached to return the delicious pleasure of his touch.

Ah, if only he could have loved her the way she wanted to love him. She would have been content in their marriage, raising this child in mutual love—something she had been deprived of in childhood. But Lucien had always loved Micaela with his body, never his heart. He had given his love to a woman who didn't deserve his loyal affection. He worshipped Cecilia and made himself a living monument to her memory. Oh, why couldn't Micaela be the one to share his life, his dreams?

The wishful thought swirled away as gentle hands and lips skied over her body. Micaela arched shamelessly toward his caresses. The warm suction of his mouth suckling her nipples unleashed such ardent need that she surrendered to the ungovernable desire he called from her.

The raspy sound of his name on her lips was like a hypnotic incantation. Lucien wanted Micaela so much he ached. He couldn't get enough of the feel of her luscious body beneath his seeking hands and hungry lips. He wanted to taste all of her, to touch her in every intimate way imaginable.

His lips and fingertips feathered over her belly, savoring the scent and taste of her silky flesh. He wedged her legs apart with a gentle nudge of his elbow and glided down her body, longing to love her in ways he had never loved another woman. At the initial touch of his fingertips he felt the secret essence of her feminine body contracting in response. His flicking tongue drew a quiet moan, a quiver of pleasure. He moved her hips until her quavering body was gliding toward his lips on its own accord, and he caressed her until she opened to him like a delicate flower unfolding its petals to the warmth of the sun. He touched her until the sweet pulsations of her desire vibrated through him, arousing him as he aroused her.

Over and over again, he drew her to the edge, holding her suspended in breathless desire. He called forth every secret response, until each sensuous movement, each intimate touch left her sweet body weeping for him.

Lucien vowed to etch this one memory of their intimate lovemaking on her mind for all eternity. He didn't want either of them to forget how potent their passion was, how sweet and wild their surrender.

He shifted Micaela's trembling body until he could settle between her thighs. "Caela, look at me," he whispered. "I want you to remember this night and what we have together. I want you to remember who I am."

And please don't let it be Vance she sees when she looks at me, Lucien thought to himself.

Her tangled lashes swept up to meet his burning gaze. Her hand slid down his chest in a sweeping caress. "So many foolish games between us," she murmured. "Do you think I don't know who you are? Though you're making love to me, you're the man who looks at me and sees someone else." A rueful smiled quivered on her lips as she lifted her hand to trace his chiseled features. "Ah, Lucien, don't you realize I would know you just as well if I were deaf and blind? I've always known you by mere presence alone. Even when I could remember nothing else, I knew you the moment you took me in your arms. Those feelings and sensations surpassed all bounds. Though I doubt you can understand, I once loved you with my body, heart and soul."

His sensuous lips claimed hers in a tormentingly tender kiss. "Then show me how you used to love me, Caela, just once before you go. Teach me to see beyond sight, so I can find you wherever you are."

Micaela accepted the challenge to make him love her the way she had loved him all those months when he'd become her life, her very existence. Her hands skimmed over the washboarded muscles of his belly, the hard columns of his thighs and hips.

He wanted to know what it was like to love someone with every part of his being, did he? Then she would show him the depths of this ill-fated love that burned inside her.

Her hands and lips glided over Lucien's body, finding and caressing each sensitive point, discovering a few new ones along the way. When her fingertips skimmed the throbbing length of his manhood, Lucien forgot why he needed to breathe. He seemed to be sustained by the pleasure of her touch, the gentleness of her caress. She teased him, she satisfied him, she aroused him to the extreme. She tormented him with pleasure until he was no more than a flaming coil of unfulfilled desire burning for her, because of her.

The warm suction of her mouth dragged a rough gasp of need from his throat. Lucien nearly choked for breath when she grasped his hand and drew it across his belly to his thigh. Her fingertips entwined with his as she enfolded him. Lucien sizzled with heightened awareness of his own raging need.

Her lips coasted over his curled fingertips, gliding over the satiny hardness of his arousal. He could feel her flicking tongue encircling him, driving him wild with insatiable hunger. Her whispered breath flowed over his skin until the evidence of his barely restrained desire spilled forth in helpless response.

"Caela . . . no," he groaned as her lips closed around his pulsating flesh. Despite his attempt to restrain the restless urges of his body, he arched toward her intimate kiss. "You're killing me. . . ."

She smiled against him, nipped playfully until he groaned in tormented pleasure. "But you like dying at my hands, don't you, Lucien?" When he didn't respond immediately, she drew him into her mouth and stroked him with her tongue.

"Yes," he breathed huskily. "Yes. . . ."

Micaela granted him only a few seconds to regain his control before her fingertips glided over the aching length of him. Once again she brought him to the brink, forcing him to reestablish the limits of his self-control, challenging him to endure the pleasure, even after he swore he could tolerate no more.

"Please . . ." Lucien inhaled a shuddering breath and squeezed his eyes shut, trying to contain the need that hammered relentlessly at him. "No more." He was coming unwound, fighting the burgeoning pleasure that cost him every smidgen of willpower. "No more, Caela—"

His voice evaporated when she flicked out her tongue one last time to taste his need for her. Lucien felt his defenses falter, felt his body rumbling like a volcano. He was going to burst with the pleasure of her touch if she didn't give him time to regain control.

Her questing lips and sweeping hands retraced their erotic paths, transforming flesh to molten lava. She moved again, her honeyed mouth poised above his, her luscious body brushing temptingly against his.

It was as if this passionate angel were hovering over him—so close, so maddeningly far away. She teased him, stoked every fire she had previously ignited—until he was burning alive with his need for her.

"Look at me, Lucien," she demanded, tossing his own words back at him. "Who do you see?" *And please, Lord, don't let it be Cecilia! Not this time, please not this one last time we spend together!*

"I don't have to see you to know who and where you are," he said hoarsely. "I would know you anywhere, Caela, even in the darkness of a thousand moonless nights. I could hear your voice echoing in impenetrable silence. I could reach out and know you would always be there. . . ."

When he came to her in urgent desperation, Micaela surrendered all to him, knowing he now understood what had been so difficult for her to explain. He knew how she felt when she had loved him beyond reason. Even if he never made love to her again, she knew he'd become an essential part of her that time and distance couldn't erase. The taproot of emotion ran too deep. She could never love another man when the memory of Lucien was emblazoned on her soul.

He alone had made her vulnerable to afflictions of the heart. She would never forgive him for that—for making her love him despite everything. She had fallen in love with what *might have been,* just as Lucien had loved what *could never be* with Cecilia. And at long last, Micaela understood the kind of torment Lucien had suffered when he lost Cecilia. She knew the anguish of impossible dreams and unrequited love.

When fervent desire consumed her, Micaela gave herself up to the flood of sensations channeling through Lucien's masculine body and rippling through hers. She met each urgent thrust, feeling the flames leap higher and higher, until the fiery holocaust of ecstasy consumed her. She clung to Lucien while the world spun crazily around her. Inexpressible pleasure exploded, devastating her. She clung to Lucien, hearing his muffled groan, feeling the shuddering impulses of his body blending into hers. She wanted to whisper her love for him one last time, but mindless passion—and a tad too much whiskey—sent her swirling into the dark blur of sated silence. . . .

Nineteen

A long while later, Lucien found the strength and will to raise his head. Good Lord! He and Micaela were sprawled on the rug, half under the table. He and Micaela had been so caught up in the storm of passion that they never even made it to the bed. The soft mattress had been only a few steps away, but it might as well have been a thousand miles. Lucien had been so overcome by need that he hadn't cared where he was when passion swallowed him alive. He could have been stretched out on spikes and he doubted if he would have noticed.

"Micaela?" He braced himself on his forearms and stared down into the angelic face that was bathed in flickering lantern-light. Lucien smiled tenderly at the sight of Micaela lost to peaceful sleep.

He should have expected this, he supposed. Micaela had imbibed enough whiskey to set two sturdy men afloat. Lord, the hangover she was going to have when she roused! Lucien predicted she would be begging for mercy and finding none forthcoming. He ought to know, he'd drunk himself half blind, and completely out of his mind, in those wild days when he'd set out to ruin his reputation and infuriate his grandfather.

Lucien eased away, though why he bothered to be quiet

about it he didn't know. He wouldn't have disturbed Micaela if he'd dropped an anchor on the floor beside her. He padded across the room to turn back the quilt, then scooped Micaela in his arms and tucked her between the sheets.

Donning his clothes, Lucien circled to the foot of the bed to stare at the sleeping beauty whose golden hair spilled around her like glowing sunshine. He smiled to himself, remembering the incredible passion they had shared—tonight and every other night they'd been in each other's arms. Despite the friction between them, there was definitely something that drew them together and held them like magnets.

Lost in thought, Lucien eased the door shut behind him and ambled down the companionway. He and Micaela had resolved nothing about their future. She had demanded a divorce, but she had asked for nothing in the way of financial compensation. She wouldn't, of course. She was far too independent to consider relying on anyone but herself.

No matter what Micaela chose to do with the rest of her life, Lucien promised to give her the freedom of choice that she had waited her whole life to enjoy. That, he suspected, would be the most cherished gift he could give her.

The fact that Micaela refused to answer his questions about that horrible night on the cliff frustrated Lucien. She knew something, something she refused to divulge. But she had hinted at things that left Lucien wondering—

"Lucien?" Vance's voice wafted across the abandoned deck. "I want to apologize."

"For what?" Lucien stared straight ahead, watching the midnight moon cast its silvery rays on the river.

"You know perfectly well *for what*," Vance grumbled.

"For lusting after my wife or raking me over coals? In either case, I understand, and I deserved it."

Vance drew himself up in front of Lucien, staring him squarely in the eye. "I want you to know that nothing happened during the voyage to New Orleans. I'll see that Micaela, and her belongings, are transferred onto your ship before we set sail for Charles Town."

"I believe she would prefer to stay on your schooner for the return voyage," Lucien informed him.

When Lucien turned to leave, Vance clutched his arm. "One more thing. Roddy Blankenship returned from town a few minutes ago. He brought the most interesting piece of information. After the fiasco at the Spanish garrison this evening, Carlos Morales was called on the carpet by General O'Reilly himself. According to reports, someone exposed Morales as a swindler who offered and accepted bribes on foreign cargo. When Carlos was taken into custody and searched, English coins were found in his pocket. Morales also stands accused of imprisoning a young woman because she rejected his marriage proposal. They say he tried to coerce her into his bed in exchange for dropping the trumped up charges against her."

"How interesting," Lucien commented.

"Isn't it though," Vance chuckled. "I wonder who put the bug in O'Reilly's ear?"

"I cannot imagine."

"No? I wondered why you went back to check on Morales while he was snoring in his bed. You stashed coins in his pocket, didn't you? Then you dropped by headquarters to register complaints with O'Reilly before you met me outside the front gate."

Lucien shrugged nonchalantly.

"You also might be interested to know that Carlos Morales has been dismissed from the Superior Council and thrown into the dungeon. My guess is that he'll be spending the best years of his life under lock and key." Vance studied Lucien for a long moment. "Why did you do it? You know you've severed all chances of selling cargo in this port without paying these ridiculously high tariffs."

"I wanted Morales to pay for what he did to Micaela. I would rather lose the Louisiana market than deal with that conniving bastard. If I hadn't exposed him, I suspected he would have betrayed us eventually. Better that *he* gets caught rather than *us*, don't you agree?"

"I have no wish to endure the hell Micaela suffered in prison," Vance said with a shudder of repulsion.

"With this new Spanish regime in control, smugglers will have a field day providing the city with products that cannot be obtained from Spain. Let the freebooters take the dangerous chances. Besides, I have no desire to return here when I leave only unpleasant memories behind. There are other ports that continue to welcome our trade."

Lucien hopped onto the gangplank, then glanced back at Vance. "Take good care of her, my friend," he murmured before he strode to his own ship.

Micaela groaned miserably as she squirmed in bed. She was positive she'd died sometime during the night and no one had bothered to inform her. Her head pounded, as if miniature carpenters were driving spikes into her skull. Her stomach rolled like angry waves, and the world spun furiously when she opened her eyes.

When the bed felt as if it had dipped beneath her, Micaela threw her head over the side of the mattress, just in case. She tried to sit up, but it took entirely too much effort.

Micaela made a pact with herself, there and then. She was never going to touch another glass of whiskey as long as she lived—which, judging by the way she felt, wouldn't be much longer.

Finally, she managed to rise to her feet and stagger across the room, bracing herself on one stick of furniture and then another. Moaning sickly, she plunged her face into the basin of water. The floor tilted sideways, and Micaela had to anchor herself to the commode before she toppled off balance. Submerging her head in water hadn't eased her nausea—she hadn't thought it would—but she felt better momentarily. The relief was so short-lived that Micaela wobbled back to the bed and collapsed with a groan.

It was then that she realized she had been tramping around the cabin stark naked. Before she could puzzle out why and when she had stripped down to her skin, the world turned a fuzzy shade of black. She slipped back into the blessed darkness, begging for relief from her misery.

* * *

Hours later—years maybe—Micaela roused again. It seemed that the week she'd spent in prison, the emotional turmoil of regaining her memory, and the hellish hangover had combined to zap her strength. Propping herself upon a shaky elbow, she clawed the tangle of hair from her face and glanced around the dark room, trying to remember where she was. Had she drunk so much that she'd lost her memory again? The previous night was a blur. No, that wasn't entirely correct, she realized. She remembered encountering Carlos and being reunited with her brother.

Micaela slumped back on the pillow to fight her way through the jungle of images that cluttered her mind. She remembered that Lucien had arrived after Henri left. She had started drinking to take the edge off her frustration, then Lucien had pumped her for information about the night she'd fallen from the cliff.

Micaela strained her throbbing brain, but she couldn't recall exactly how much she'd told Lucien about Cecilia. Micaela frowned apprehensively. Had she blurted out the truth about Lucien's unfaithful love? Surely she hadn't been that careless and cruel . . . had she?

Panicky, Micaela groped around the dark room to retrieve one of Vance's shirts and a pair of breeches from his sea chest. If she had told Lucien the demoralizing truth, she had to apologize immediately, even if she had to take a lifeboat and row between the two sailing schooners to do it! She wasn't going to spend this voyage stewing over what she had said to Lucien. She had to know if she'd shattered his dreams of a lost love who had deviously betrayed him!

Micaela burst from the cabin and heard the wind howling overhead. She suddenly realized that it wasn't only her hangover that caused her to be dizzy and nauseous. A tropical storm had descended on the schooner to aggravate Micaela's self-inflicted illness. And worse, she couldn't row to Lucien's ship to apologize for revealing too much about the woman he had loved.

A frothy wave crested over the schooner, sending torrents

of water flooding down the steps. Micaela clutched the railing
to save herself from cartwheeling down the slick steps. She
struggled onto the main deck in time to see a heavy squall
splashing against the bulwark.

Micaela groaned in dismay. The merchant ships were riding
the brisk winds and being sucked into the eye of the storm.
They were leagues away from New Orleans, being bombarded
by raging gales that were obviously dragging them from the
customary shipping lanes.

The moment Micaela reached the quarterdeck, the ship
dipped into a deep trough and slid sideways, forcing Micaela
to anchor herself against the railing before she was washed
overboard. Lightning speared through the low-hanging black
clouds like bony fingers. Amid the drumroll of thunder, Micaela
heard Vance screaming orders to the crew. Sailors scurried off
to trim the sails that snapped and popped in the brisk wind.

Lightning crackled, illuminating the twilight. A gigantic
wave rolled toward them from port bow. Micaela steadied
herself against the rail while mariners dived to grab supporting
beams and tackles to prevent being washed away. Micaela
swore she heard a collective intake of breath before the spray
of water avalanched over her and the hapless crew.

The instant before Micaela swore her lungs would burst, the
water receded. She managed to catch her breath and mop the
hair from her eyes, but another blast of wind threatened to take
her feet out from under her.

Blinking the salt water from her eyes, Micaela stared at
the ship sailing ahead of them. She could see Lucien's crew
scampering around the deck, tending their duties. Lanterns
swung crazily on their hooks, making the eerie shadows in the
distance dance like ghoulish specters on the rain-slickened deck
of Lucien's ship.

Micaela searched the lead ship for a glimpse of Lucien. She
noticed him standing at the bridge, his feet askance, his arms
braced against the wheel, fighting to keep the schooner on
course.

High above the deck of Lucien's ship, a lone sailor scrabbled
over the spar of the foremast to untangle the torn sail that

flapped like laundry on a clothesline. Micaela shuddered at the thought of being perched on that slippery beam, maneuvering around heavy blocks and tackles that swayed in the wind.

When lightning shot through the clouds like silver spears, the sailor on the spar stumbled and yelped. Flying cables from the ripped sail slammed against his shoulder. Micaela swallowed her breath when the sailor became entangled in the ropes and toppled off balance. His bloodcurdling scream brought every head around on both ships. Everyone waited in dreadful apprehension, expecting the seaman to plunge to his death.

When Lucien's ship rose a quick ten feet on the cresting wave, then nose-dived into the deep trough, the helpless mariner slid from his precarious perch. He was left dangling upside down, his leg entangled in the ropes, waiting for the angry breaker of the sea to pour over him. The force of the wave flung him against the beam like a rag doll, and his horrified scream sent chills down Micaela's spine.

Her heart rose to her throat when she saw Louis Beecham rush to the helm to take Lucien's place as Lucien charged off to rescue the defenseless sailor. He leaped into the air to grasp the yardarm, then pulled himself onto the slippery beam. Employing the standing riggings that secured the whipping sails, Lucien inched toward the entangled sailor who hung over the bow.

Thunder rumbled and lightning flashed, spotlighting Lucien who was maneuvering higher on the mast like a daring acrobat. When another blast of cold wind sent the schooner careening, Lucien halted long enough to cut one of the ropes loose with his dagger, then lashed it around his waist to steady himself.

"Damn that daredevil," Vance scowled as he stalked up beside Micaela. "He could hang himself in his attempt to save John Garver." He cupped his hands around his mouth and yelled a warning to Lucien. "Watch your step! Another monster wave is approaching from port bow!"

Frantic, Micaela scurried toward the bow to get a better view. Lucien lunged from one spar to another. Each time he made progress toward the dangling sailor, he untied one rope and reached for another to make his perilous trek.

Micaela swore her heart ceased beating when Lucien untied his supporting rope and reached out to grasp the yardarm that secured the jib. He was dangling from the swinging spar, his attention fixed on the rope that was tangled around Garver's leg like a deadly python. As the beam swerved in the wind, Lucien hooked his leg over the dangling riggings and released his grasp on the yardarm.

"Damn it, Lucien!" Vance bellowed in apprehensive frustration.

For an agonizing moment, Lucien was left clawing air before he clutched both arms around the swaying tackles. If he hadn't been as agile as a cat, he would have been swinging upside down like the man he was trying to rescue! Micaela wanted to shake him until his teeth rattled for scaring ten years off her life.

In helpless exasperation she watched Lucien untangle his leg from the riggings, then inch forward like a caterpillar to reach the unfortunate sailor. When the fading light of dusk gleamed upon the approaching wave, Micaela screamed in horror. The twenty foot monster rolled forward, threatening to swallow Lucien—and the schooner—alive. Lucien was about to take the brunt of the frothy wave head-on, with no more than the dangling rope to anchor him.

Micaela swore all hell had broken loose when a lightning bolt speared down from the ominous sky. St. Elmo's fire glowed on the metal tip of the foremast. Sparks danced on the tackles directly above Lucien and John Garver's heads. The blinding light flashed, thunder boomed, and the timbers groaned.

In horror, Micaela clung to Vance, her nails digging into the rigid muscles of his arm. Flailing sails, swinging tackles and whipping ropes collapsed with the wooden beam that had been lightning-struck. The scent of charred wood hung heavily in the wind as spars and riggings crashed toward the deck below. Louis Beecham instinctively hurled himself away from the falling debris. The wheel spun furiously, sending the damaged schooner reeling out of control. The ship darted into the deep trench below the oncoming wave, taking the monstrous wall of water broadside.

Although Micaela wasn't a seasoned sailor, she knew what could happen when a ship wasn't skillfully guided into an oncoming wave. Lucien's schooner sat at a precarious angle, teetering in the trough below the avalanche of water. Screams of terror rose above the ship the instant before the destructive tidal wave buffeted the deck. Sailors were flung helter-skelter. The bow of the ship—where Lucien and John Garver dangled like bait on a hook—plunged into the sea.

Micaela shrieked Lucien's name as she impulsively dashed forward. Vance dragged her back, bracing her between himself and the rail as the wave rolled toward them.

"We can't reach him yet," he yelled above the thunderclap. "If you don't hold on for dear life, you'll be washed overboard!"

Micaela dragged in an enormous breath and sent a hasty prayer winging heavenward, asking that Lucien be spared. Vance held her steady when another onrush of frothy brine spilled over their schooner.

After what seemed a century of anguish, Micaela clawed the tangled hair from her eyes and stared anxiously into the distance. When lightning flashed, she could see the waterlogged crew of Lucien's ship scrambling toward the lifeboats. The bow of the damaged vessel tipped upward, and Micaela screamed in unholy torment. Lucien's ship had taken on so much water that waves sloshed down the companionway. Those who couldn't clamber into the dinghies to escape the sinking ship had dived overboard, attempting to swim toward Vance's ship.

Wild with fear, Micaela flung herself from Vance's arms, determined to secure a lifeboat so she could rescue Lucien.

"Micaela, for God's sake!" Vance roared as he rushed after her.

Micaela scrambled toward the men who were lowering lifeboats to rescue Lucien's crew. She could hear Vance cursing as he lowered the ropes to send the skiffs splashing into the sea beside the schooner. When she shinnied down the rope to seat herself in the boat, Vance muttered again.

"Lucien is tangled in the riggings," she choked out, groping for the oars. "If we don't save him he's going to drown."

While Vance eased down into the skiff beside her, Micaela peered grimly at the half submerged schooner, watching the bubbles and brine dance on the deck. Silver foam rumbled over the rail as the ship spun like a runaway carousel. Cries for assistance went up around the two ships as Micaela and Vance rowed toward the doomed schooner. The wind wailed and the sky opened as the darkness of night descended on the storm-tossed sea. Huge raindrops splattered against Micaela's tear-stained cheeks as she watched the lanterns on Lucien's ship sizzle and smoke beneath the sheet of rain.

Micaela couldn't see the broken mast and tangled ropes that dangled from the bow. Wild with panic, she rowed toward the spot where Lucien had gone down, hearing the schooner gurgle like a drowning swimmer. When she and Vance navigated toward the bow one small ray of hope flickered in Micaela's heart. There, floating on the choppy water, thrashing to untangle the riggings that entrapped them, were Lucien and John Garver.

"Lucien!" Micaela called out, working the oars like a wind-mill.

With a dagger clamped in his teeth, Lucien jerked up his head and twisted around. A raft of curses exploded from his lips when he saw the oncoming wave rising up from the sea like a demon from the deep.

"Vance, turn back. Get Micaela to safety!" Lucien let go of his grip on the broken mast to gesture toward the swelling mountain of water.

"Dear God!" Vance wheezed when he followed Lucien's gaze.

Wild-eyed, Micaela watched Lucien frantically clawing at the twisted ropes that ensnared Garver. There were only a few precious seconds separating Lucien from disaster—separating all four of them from disaster, Micaela amended with a terrified yelp.

She stopped breathing when she saw the bloodstains on Lucien's sleeve. She knew he had been struck by the flying tackles when the mast collapsed. When she saw him scrambling to free Garver instead of himself in those last few seconds, sickening horror twisted her stomach into knots.

And then the frothy wave rose up like a dragon from hell, sucking the lifeboat into the deep trough. Micaela swore she heard a death rattle seconds before the suffocating wave crashed down on the lifeboat, capsizing it. She was hurtled into the water and towed beneath the surface. Her head spun, her life flashed before her eyes as she was swallowed up by inky darkness.

The force of the water sent her tumbling and floundering, unsure which direction was up. An unidentified object collided with her hip. She wasn't certain if it was the capsized lifeboat or one of the barrels that had washed off the deck of the ship. Blindly, she reached out to dig in her nails before the object skittered from her reach.

The powerful undertow sent her careening, and her lungs burned like fire while she held her breath. But Micaela refused to surrender to the cold, enveloping darkness. She had to save Lucien! He needed her help!

The vision of Lucien's hair plastered against his scratched face, his shirt soaked with blood, his leg tangled in ropes, flooded Micaela's mind. She had to fight her way back to the surface. Lucien was lashed to a sinking ship—the ship he'd called home for the past five years. Everything he held dear had been inside that luxurious Great Cabin that was now submerged in water. Lucien was about to lose his priceless possessions and his life! She had to get to him—somehow!

After a hellish eternity, the sea chest to which Micaela found herself clinging for dear life bobbed to the surface. Sputtering and wheezing, she flung her leg over the trunk and then sprawled upon it. Rain pounded against her back and thunder bellowed in the black of night. Salt water stung her eyes, and Micaela let go with one arm to wipe her face.

For a moment she couldn't determine where she was. All she could see was another snarling wave rolling toward her. Grasping her floating sea chest, Micaela laid her cheek against the slick wood and waited for the wave to lift her and send her plunging into the churning sea. The instant she was riding the top of the crest, she raised her head and scanned the sea. What she saw put a scream on her lips and tore her heart asunder.

Lucien's ship, the gracious lady of the sea that once sailed in royal elegance, had gone to her watery grave. The broken mast—to which Lucien and Garver had been lashed—was no longer visible.

Micaela burst into tears, uncaring if the approaching squall flung her sideways and sent her nose-diving into the swirling depths. She now knew how Lucien felt the day he found Cecilia's body flung against the boulders below the cliff. Anguish—the likes she had never known—stabbed through her chest.

Lucien was gone. He had died trying to save the defenseless sailor. And very soon, Micaela would be standing on the shores of the Great Beyond, gazing at the horizons of eternity.

Another soul-shattering sob broke from her throat as she was tossed and spun around by the crashing wave. She wondered if Lucien had gone to his grave knowing that Cecilia had not been faithful to him. Micaela assumed she had unintentionally shattered his dream the previous night, giving away too much while she was under the influence of whiskey.

God forgive her! She had stood there in a fit of temper, demanding a divorce, cursing Lucien for deceiving her. She had refused to tell him that she carried his child. She had refused to tell him that she still loved him—would always love him, even when she knew he loved the memory of another woman. And if she had blurted out too much about Cecilia, she was going to curse herself forever for shattering Lucien's long-held love for a woman who didn't deserve his devotion!

At least Micaela had one sweet memory to carry with her as she drifted on the blackened sea, she consoled herself. For one glorious moment in time, she and Lucien had soared in unrivaled passion. They had been one heart beating for another, joined in body and soul. The conflicts between them had bowed down to a desire that nothing could diminish or restrain.

While the waves swamped and buffeted her, Micaela heard Lucien's voice calling out to her, just as it had the previous night while they were drifting in splendor. All she had to do was close her eyes and she could feel his reassuring presence beside her. The words he had whispered to her before he became the living flame inside her echoed through her tortured soul. *I don't have to see you to know where you are. I would know you anywhere, even in the darkness of a thousand moonless nights. I could hear you, even in impenetrable silence. I can reach out to touch you no matter where you are . . .*

When another monstrous wall of water rose up, Micaela took a deep, fortifying breath. She reached out to the image of sparkling blue eyes, raven hair, and a roguish smile that had always tugged at her heart. Even the cold water that avalanched over her couldn't douse the flame of Lucien's memory. She reached out to him through the watery darkness, knowing he would be there, knowing her love for him would transcend all boundaries . . . even death. . . .

"Micaela!" Vance's tormented voice rolled across the frothy sea and died in the wailing wind. But he refused to give up hope. Over and over, he called Micaela's name, clinging to the capsized skiff that had become his salvation.

"Captain Cavendish!"

Vance swiveled his head around to see Timothy Toggle and Jeremy Ives holding their lantern and paddling their lifeboat toward him. They had taken the precaution of tying a rope to the schooner to prevent suffering the same disaster that had befallen Vance and Micaela.

"Just hold on, captain," Timothy yelled. "We're coming for you."

"Micaela? Have you seen her?" Vance croaked as he struggled to keep his head above water.

Neither sailor responded. They maneuvered the dinghy into position and stretched out their oars to Vance. Once he pulled himself into the skiff, Jeremy navigated around the capsized lifeboat, pried it upright with his paddle, and secured it with a rope. Grimly, the sailors rowed toward the surviving schooner that dipped and dived in the rolling waves.

"Has anyone seen Micaela?" Vance demanded the instant he climbed on deck.

Dozens of bleak faces glowed in the lanternlight. Heartsick,

Vance snatched up a lantern and held it over one railing and then another, searching all sides of the schooner. He called Micaela's name until he was hoarse, praying for a glimpse of her, but darkness and pounding rain played hell with visibility.

"Captain." Timothy clamped a beefy hand on Vance's wrist, detaining him from his futile search. "They're gone, sir. All of them—Captain Saffire, Garver, Micaela, and two other sailors. You did everything you could to save them, but—"

"I'm not leaving this area until I know for certain," Vance snapped.

Timothy thrust his bulky body squarely in Vance's path. "None of us want to accept the worst," he said gravely. "But you know they don't have much of a chance of survival in this storm. You saw Captain Saffire go down in the waves, tied to the mast, and Micaela—" His head dropped, and he stared at his soggy feet. "She's only a woman, captain, without the strength of the men we pulled from the sea. If any of them survived, the winds and currents could have swept them anywhere. We've lost them, and there is nothing we can do to change that."

Vance's stomach twisted in an aching knot. Damn it, what a fool he had been to let Micaela climb into the rowboat and paddle off to save Lucien. Her daring heroics had gotten her killed. . . . Vance stifled the negative thought. And Lucien. . . . His heart gave another painful lurch, remembering that Lucien had asked Vance to take good care of Micaela. God, he had failed Lucien and Micaela. . . .

"Captain, we've got an overloaded schooner," Jeremy Ives reminded Vance. "Some of the men need medical attention. We've got to get the ones in the worst condition bedded down for the night. We have to place the plight of the *living* before the plight of the *lost.*"

Vance knew Jeremy spoke the truth, but it was killing him, bit by excruciating bit, to accept dismal reality. Vance had lost his lifelong friend and the vivacious beauty who had touched his heart. Dear God in heaven! The thought of carrying the devastating news to Adrian nearly tore out Vance's soul. The

Saffire legacy had been wiped out in the course of one stormy night. Lucien had been lost at sea, just like his parents.

Adrian had buried both his sons—one in infancy and the other in the prime of life. The old man had lost his beloved wife, his daughter-in-law, and now Lucien. After a five-year feud, Adrian and Lucien had been reunited for only a few months before they were torn apart forever. Adrian had outlived them all . . . and the news would probably kill him.

"Captain, the men need you," Timothy insisted as he steered Vance toward the helm. "The schooner has suffered considerable damage and the decks are in chaos."

Resigned to his responsibility, Vance took command of his battered ship. And all the while, he listened, praying he would hear signals of distress rising from the sea, hoping he could find the lost. But there was nothing besides the sound of lapping waves, rolling thunder, the creak of timber, and the lonely whispers of specters floating in the shadows of the night. . . .

Twenty

Micaela awoke to find herself clamped to the floating sea chest, drifting aimlessly in the ocean. She was amazed by her own fierce instincts of survival, when she no longer cared what became of her. Why didn't she simply loose her grasp on the trunk and sink into the black depths and end it all? What was the sense of living when her heart felt as heavy as an anchor? She had swallowed an ocean of water, and her future was so grim and short-lived that it didn't bear thinking about.

The image of Lucien tangled in the riggings on the broken foremast kept flashing in her mind, squeezing all emotion from her soul. Even now, she could hear his baritone voice shouting the order to go back in the direction she'd come, to save herself. He had known his chance of survival was virtually nonexistent, and his last thought had been of saving her. At least he cared that much—after all they had been through together.

Tears trickled down her cheeks as she laid her head against the sea chest. Lucien was gone, and she hadn't been able to rescue him. How long would it be before her strength ebbed, and she slipped into fiddler's green?

Micaela muffled a sniff and blinked back the tears. She'd been too proud, stubborn and frustrated to admit she loved

Lucien. Now it was too late to tell him. She had only fooled herself into believing she despised him. But Lucien could never have hurt her so deeply if she hadn't loved him so dearly.

Those weeks they had spent together after her terrifying fall from the cliff had been the closest thing to heaven Micaela had ever known. Now she couldn't tell him the truth, couldn't apologize for shattering his idealistic belief in Cecilia. She was dreadfully sorry she had sent him to his grave doubting the only woman he had ever loved.

Micaela squeezed her eyes shut when another wave lifted her and sent her skimming across the sea. Even if she were rescued—and the chance of that happening seemed nonexistent—she would be nothing but a hollow shell filled with empty ache and regret. All she had left of Lucien were bittersweet memories and an unborn child who would never have the chance to live. Oh why did fate have to be so cruel? she wondered as she closed her eyes and waited for the inevitable.

Lucien groaned, then rolled onto his back to watch the inching fingers of dawn creep across the cloudy sky. He hadn't expected to see another sunrise after wallowing in liquid hell. Although he had miraculously escaped disaster, John Garver hadn't been so fortunate. Lucien had slashed the last rope that entangled Garver before the gigantic wave crashed down on them, but ironically, that had not turned out to be a blessing. Garver had been hurled against the bow of the sinking schooner by the force of the water, while Lucien remained lashed to the broken mast.

The fierce wave had dragged Lucien under, snapping the mast and riggings in two. Although Lucien swore he'd drown before the section of the mast floated free of the debris, he had managed to snatch much-needed air before another wave sent him skidding in the trough. He'd had the presence of mind to cut away the remaining ropes from his thighs and fashion a halter to secure himself to the makeshift raft of canvas and timber.

Lucien had seen the distant pinpoints of lights glowing on

the deck of Vance's schooner, but he'd been too far away to be heard over the howling wind. All through the night Lucien had been adrift, pushed southwest by the force of the storm. He wondered how many of his crew had perished, wondered if Micacla. . . .

Lucien grimaced as he absently massaged his injured arm. Micaela, that daring female, had tried to save him—at her own expense. If she had gotten herself killed he was never going to forgive her. Of course, he suspected she preferred to have *him* dead rather than alive. Then she would be free of this marriage. She would have wealth beyond her wildest expectations and the freedom to do anything she pleased while Adrian doted over her.

Micaela had risked everything to save a man who had manipulated and deceived her, a man she planned to divorce. Of course, he thought with a smile, she had always been a determined crusader, even if she was battling lost causes. She was simply too pure of heart, too noble of character to stand aside and watch anyone perish without attempting rescue—even her unwanted husband.

Micaela had pitted herself against Barnaby Harpster to ensure young Abraham received proper medical attention. She considered the plight of every servant and slave at the plantation and townhouse, determined to enrich their lives and bring them enjoyment. She always put the welfare of others above her own. She strived to ensure no one suffered as she had suffered during her childhood, strived to make everyone feel welcome and wanted—as she had not been.

God, Lucien couldn't imagine life without Micaela. He had spent five years lamenting Cecilia's passing, only to realize that she had never been what he thought she was. Micaela hadn't intended to reveal the truth about Cecilia, but Lucien had the unmistakable feeling that Micaela knew what Vance and Adrian had been trying to tell him for years. But all those past torments seemed a dim memory compared to the prospect of losing Micaela.

There had been times the past few months when Lucien had come close to admitting that he was in love with that spirited beauty who had turned his life around. Yet, the guilt of manipulating and deceiving her prevented him from whispering the words he sensed she wanted to hear. Lucien had allowed Micaela to believe she had always cared deeply for him, that she had come willingly into wedlock. He had created a make-believe world of warmth and security and happiness to compensate for the torment she'd suffered at his hands.

To confess to love her, after he had nobly vowed to remember Cecilia until the day he died, had ridden heavily on his conscience. Lucien had indeed placed his first love's memory on an unreachable pedestal, refusing to let anyone or anything disturb that monument. And then along came a free-spirited, vibrant sprite who sent his resolutions spinning in orbit.

It was no longer Cecilia's face—and it hadn't been for a good long while—that he saw when he closed his eyes. It was Micaela's. He could see her leaning negligently against the wall of the quarterdeck, dressed in dowdy breeches, her cap sitting at a jaunty angle, a mischievous smile on her lips. He could see her strapped to his bed, spewing curses and expecting to be tortured because she knew nothing of intimacy. He could see her leading her paint brigade around the plantation, giving the run-down estate new life—just as she gave new life and enthusiasm to the servants.

Lucien remembered the fury in her eyes when she whispered her hatred for him at the wedding reception. He recalled, with agonizing clarity, how he had stood on that cursed bluff, looking down at Micaela's lifeless body, praying she would survive, vowing to do anything within his power to compensate for sending her out to meet disaster. And when Micaela regained consciousness, without a memory, Lucien had built a perfect world for her, giving everything of himself to make her happy.

Yes, he loved her desperately, though he hadn't dared to say the words while he created that fairy-tale world and kept the truth from her. That would have made things ten times worse when she recovered from amnesia. Had he confessed what was in his heart, she would only have doubted his affection all the more after she remembered the truth about their not-so-ideal marriage. If nothing else, Lucien would have wanted Micaela to believe that one undying, undeniable truth.

A coil of grief knotted in Lucien's chest. If Micaela hadn't survived her daring rescue attempt, he wasn't sure he could endure the anguish of knowing she was lost forever. He'd already suffered through five years of hell. God, he couldn't bear to think about going through that again, not when Micaela had taught him the difference between a young man's infatuation and a mature man's deep, abiding love. That acknowledgment had been long in coming, but there it was, Lucien thought. What he felt for Cecilia, right or wrong, was nothing compared to the emotions Micaela stirred inside him.

When sunlight sprinkled through the low-hanging clouds, Lucien saw debris bobbing on the waves. Wooden barrels floated like buoys, spotlighted by shafts of sunbeams. Lucien propped himself upright on his makeshift raft of canvas and splintered timber and stared at the sea chest among the floating debris. Squinting into the sunlight, he fixed his astonished gaze on the sprawled body that lay atop the trunk. A mass of blond hair cascaded into the water.

Micaela? Lucien strangled on his breath. Was it a mirage brought upon by the blinding light, by the tormented thoughts that sloshed through his waterlogged brain?

Ignoring the pain that shot down his left arm, he cupped both hands around his mouth and yelled out Micaela's name. When he received no response from the distant mirage, he tried again—and again.

Micaela smiled groggily as she lay upon her trunk, basking in the welcome rays of sun. She had been awakened from sleep by the sound of Lucien calling to her from the Hereafter. He was there, just as she had known he would be—her ever-constant companion in spirit, if not in flesh.

Groaning, Micaela raised her head and stared at the debris that bobbed around her. Her heart skipped several vital beats when she saw the white canvas and broken beam in the distance . . . and the man perched upon it.

"Lucien?" Micaela bolted up so quickly that she nearly tumbled headfirst into the sea. Her gaze feasted on the dark head and muscular physique of the castaway floating on his improvised raft.

Micaela wasn't sure she should trust her eyes, but rising hope begged her to believe what she thought she saw. Despite stiff, complaining muscles, she thrashed her arms in the water like oars, propelling herself forward.

When Micaela began to paddle toward him, Lucien secured himself with a rope and eased into the water to retrieve a piece of wood that could serve as an oar. Once he'd pulled himself back onto the timber and canvas raft, he fought the oncoming waves to close the distance between him and Micaela.

After several minutes, Lucien had to stop to catch his breath. The wind and current were working against him, and it took all his strength to fight the sea. He had lost blood because of his arm wound, but seeing Micaela floating toward him like an angel skimming the waves provided the incentive he needed to struggle to reach her.

While Micaela paddled with the current, Lucien coiled a piece of rope, prepared to toss her the lifeline when she was within range. His first attempt to hurl the rope to her fell short of the mark. Determined, Lucien towed in the rope and tried again. By that time Micaela had paddled close enough to reach the trailing end of the rope that he cast across the sea.

Easing off the trunk, she grabbed the rope with both hands, waiting for Lucien to tow her to him. In Lucien's eagerness to reach her, he almost didn't see the sleek shadow darting just beneath the surface of the water. His heart slammed against his ribs and then thumped like a bounding jackrabbit when grim realization hit him. His throat closed in terror and his shout of alarm came out in a hoarse croak. Wild-eyed, frantic, Lucien struggled to shout Micaela back to her sea chest. Damnation, if she didn't stop flailing and thrashing in the water she was going to attract more attention than she already had!

"MICAELA! GET BACK ON THE CHEST—NOW!" Lucien roared hoarsely. He made frantic, stabbing gestures with his good arm. "SHARKS!"

Micaela gasped in horror when she looked in the direction Lucien pointed. Slick gray shark fins knifed through the water like a flotilla of battleships converging on her. Frantic, she clawed her way back to the sea chest.

"Caela, remain as quiet as possible," Lucien instructed as he glided his makeshift paddle into the water to ease the raft forward. "Tie the rope to the handle on the trunk so I can pull you toward me."

Casting apprehensive glances at the fins that circled her, Micaela did as she was told. When the lead shark whizzed past her, Micaela swallowed a scream, then folded her legs under her chin. The sea chest twirled and swayed, and it was all Micaela could do to retain her balance. She knew one swish from the tail of that shark—it had to be ten feet long if it was an inch!—would send her into the water to become bait for the entire school of fish.

"Lucien, I want to apologize for every hateful word I've ever said to you," Micaela yammered, determined to bare her soul before she was gobbled alive. "I didn't mean to hurt you when I mentioned Cecilia. I don't recall how much I said, but I had planned to take that secret to my grave. I would have said nothing at all if that confounded whiskey hadn't loosed my tongue and left it wagging from both ends. I—"

"Later, Caela," Lucien said in a hiss. He towed the rope, hand over hand, as fast as he could.

"I'm not sure there will be a later," she squeaked, glancing from him to the sharks.

"Curse it, just keep your voice down," Lucien muttered, all flying fists and tangling rope. "I don't give a damn about the trouble we've had in the past. It's the future that concerns—"

Micaela's alarmed shriek cut him off in midsentence. One of the sharks glided beneath the sea chest, causing the trunk to rock to dangerous angles. If Micaela hadn't sprawled on the trunk, she would have plunged into the sea.

Micaela watched Lucien grit his teeth against the pain in his left arm and tug the trunk toward him. Micaela was ready to breathe a sigh of relief—but another shark surfaced and thudded against her trunk. Her terrified gaze locked with Lucien's as she scrambled to keep her balance.

"Oh God," Lucien wheezed, staring to the southeast.

Micaela swiveled her head around to see a demon from the deep barreling up toward the surface, as if it meant to launch itself into the air to attack her. Micaela screamed silently when she saw the pointed nose, beady black eyes, and razor-sharp teeth rushing toward her.

She was on her feet in nothing flat, balancing on the tottering chest. She sprang over the shark fins that stood between her and the raft, leaping away before the trunk toppled to its side.

Micaela landed with a soft thud and glanced up to see Lucien tearing off his tattered shirt and wrapping it around his improvised paddle. While the sharks circled, he hurled the blood-stained garment as far away from them as possible. The scent of blood attracted the sharks. They sped off to fight over the garment-wrapped timber.

Micaela gulped hard when the lead shark devoured the shirt in one crunching bite. It was all too easy to envision herself dragged into the sea and attacked. The thought left her shivering uncontrollably.

While Micaela battled for composure, Lucien retrieved his knife from his boot and crouched on the edge of the raft. His attention was fixed on the shark that had returned to the raft to search for a tastier morsel. With dagger poised and waiting, Lucien watched the fin glide past the timber where he sat. Snarling, he stabbed the passing shark, letting his blade rip through flesh, leaving a trail of blood in the water.

The other sharks turned on the wounded creature like vicious cannibals. Fascinated, Micaela pulled herself onto the broken spar to watch the circling sharks attack. She had never seen anything move so quickly or strike with such deadly force. Micaela might have sat there for several minutes, absorbing the horror that could have easily befallen her, but Lucien demanded her attention.

"Help me rig this raft to make it more secure," he ordered, tossing her a coil of rope. "Lash the spar to the eyelets of the canvas. We'll make a triangular cot with what is left of this sail.''

While Micaela crawled to the end of the yard to grasp one of the sails floating on the water, Lucien slung his rope around the broken mast and towed it toward the spar. The jib—the triangular sail that once projected over the foremast of his ship—became the body of this reinforced raft that repelled water.

Micaela marveled at Lucien's ingenuity. A few minutes ago, this makeshift raft had been nothing but a tangle of canvas, rigging and timber. Now the floating mass of debris resembled a peculiar-looking, but functional cot stretched between beams and ropes. Their hours and days were undoubtedly numbered, but at least they wouldn't have to scrunch up like cats floating on driftwood.

Micaela's thoughts trailed off when she noticed the bloody gash on Lucien's arm. It looked as if splinters of timber had stabbed into his flesh. Micaela grimaced, imagining how painful it must have been to pull out the spear or spears and leave the wound subjected to salty sea water.

Micaela crawled to Lucien's side of the raft and sank down to rip the hem of her shirt into strips for bandages. Once she had tied the fabric around his arm, she peered into the ruggedly handsome face she'd never expected to see, except in haunting visions.

"Lucien, I want to finish apologizing. Perhaps you thought I was being spiteful, but truly, if I said anything to dispute what you believed about Ceci—''

His forefinger brushed her lips to shush her. "I was the one who demanded to know the whole of it,'' he insisted. "I want to apologize for pressing you on the subject while you were too tipsy to know what you were saying. It wasn't what you *said* that confirmed what Adrian and Vance have been trying to tell me for years, it was what you *didn't want to say*. My grandfather was right about Cecilia, wasn't he?''

Her gaze darted across the sea, avoiding his unblinking stare. Lucien cupped her chin in his hand, forcing her to look at him.

"Cecilia wasn't what she pretended to be, was she?'' he

asked point-blank. "You mentioned Chaney that night. Was
he the man Adrian sent to keep surveillance on Cecilia while
I was at sea? The report was accurate, wasn't it? Just exactly
what did Cecilia do? Try to bribe Barnaby into lying for her?
Did she offer him intimate favors for siding with her against
Adrian and Chaney?"

Micaela inwardly groaned. She had said entirely too much
if Lucien had deduced that Cecilia's loyalty and affection was
a charade. Micaela had obviously destroyed what had been a
precious memory for Lucien. Damn, she and her loose tongue!

"I'm so sorry, Lucien. I was unintentionally cruel. . . ."

The words died on her lips when his mouth slanted over
hers in the slightest whisper of a kiss. When he withdrew, he
smiled into her upturned face. Then he grew serious again.
"I'm beginning to understand Cecilia's motives. I can guess
how and why she met with disaster when she tried to bargain
with Barnaby."

Lucien couldn't keep his hands off Micaela, even while he
talked. Touching her was a luxury he hadn't expected to enjoy
again. His fingers glided through the thick mass of curly blond
hair, and he framed her face, loving the feel of those silky
tendrils sliding over his arms.

"But what I don't understand is why you tried to spare me
from the truth about Cecilia. You had justifiable reason to taunt
me with her deception."

"I couldn't, because I—" Micaela clamped her mouth shut,
refusing to continue.

"Yes?" Lucien prodded, his hand trekking across her sleeve
in a lingering caress.

"I didn't want to be the one who destroyed your memory,"
she said reluctantly. "You loved Cecilia. You spent five years
worshipping her memory. It was cruel of me to shatter the
image that you were satisfied with. I hadn't wanted to hurt you,
but I've done it in spite of my good intentions. I never meant
to tell you a blessed thing, and I'm sorry!"

Lucien couldn't believe the intensity in her voice, in her
eyes. She must care a little if she kept apologizing all over the

place. He was determined to discover the depth of her emotions, even if he had to badger her until she erupted in temper.

"You let me live with the lie because you wanted to spare me the pain of the truth." He stared deeply into her emerald-green eyes. "*Why*, Micaela?"

"I already told you why," she muttered. "That is not the kind of thing a wife wants to tell her husband. Discussing the woman you loved was as painful for me as it was for you."

"Yet, you promoted the lie by keeping silent," he softly accused. "But you were quick to condemn me for refusing to reveal the past to you while we were enjoying those weeks of peaceful harmony in our marriage. Was I supposed to shatter our happiness with the ugly truth? Was I to remind you why you rushed out into the night during our reception, swearing you would hate me until the day you died? Was I to remind you of those things I wanted you to forget, things *I* wanted to forget?"

"That was different," she mumbled, shifting uneasily beside him.

"How so, squirt?"

"You lied for your own selfish purpose of bringing me under thumb," she answered.

Lucien shook his head and smiled in gentle contradiction. "I let you believe in the way we were *after* your painful fall from the cliff. I took something that started out all wrong and tried to make it right. What I did was no different from your attempt to conceal the truth about Cecilia. You preserved the lie because you thought it was to my benefit. I did the same thing because you were weak and vulnerable, and I wanted to do everything possible to make you secure and content."

Again, his index finger traced her enchanting features. He marveled at her natural beauty, her amazing resilience. Micaela truly was something unique and special. Lucien couldn't name another woman who could match her in wit, beauty or spirit. She made all other women seem sadly lacking, and he couldn't imagine himself being satisfied with anyone but Micaela.

"Now, tell me, love, which one of us committed the gravest sin?" he asked her. "*You* for trying to spare me from the betrayal of a woman I thought I loved, the woman I immortalized for five years because guilt and regret haunted me? Or did *I* commit the greater sin by trying to compensate for voicing harsh, thoughtless remarks that sent you barreling off into the night to suffer at Barnaby's sinister hands?

"I nearly cost you your life that night, Micaela. You hovered on death's doorstep for days. I suffered all the torments of the damned, waiting and wondering if you would survive. The night when I plucked you up from those boulders and carried you home, I swore by all that was holy that I would do anything and everything to bring you happiness, to see you smile and hear you laugh. I would have sold my soul for you."

Lucien closed his eyes against the tormenting memory of that awful night. "Can you even imagine the horror I experienced while I climbed down that bluff—the same damned bluff I had climbed down five years earlier? Have you any idea how difficult it was for me to reach out and touch you while you lay there like a limp rag doll—exactly as Cecilia had.

"I had to make myself touch you, knowing every ounce of hope would wither if I had to face the horrible truth that I had lost you forever. I knew if I couldn't find your pulse there would be nothing left of my own heart and soul. I would have no second chance to make things right between us. God, I would rather have fallen through the trap door to hell than face the possibility that you had perished."

Micaela stared at him, noting his anguished expression, the hitch in his voice. She hadn't stopped to consider how her near brush with death had affected him, that he had been down that horrible path before. Her calamity had forced him to relive a nightmare in order to rescue her.

Her heart went out to him, and she impulsively flew into his arms, knocking him off balance, sending them toppling onto the stretched canvas that floated between the spar and mast like a water-filled mattress. While Micaela lay atop Lucien, she dropped a kiss to his lips and nuzzled her forehead against his.

"I've been an insensitive shrew and I'm dreadfully sorry for that, too."

"And I've been an insufferable cad and I'm sorry, too," he murmured.

Micaela propped her arms on his broad chest and gathered her courage. No matter what happened, no matter what the future held, she was going to speak from her heart. The way her luck had been running of late, she might not have another chance, so she had better get at it.

"I love you, Lucien Saffire," she whispered softly and sincerely. "I was too leery to say the words when I knew you loved someone else far more than you could ever love me. But I would rather face your rejection than not be honest with you. I do love you, and I will go on loving you, even if I can never be more than second best to a shattered memory."

Tears clouded her eyes as she traced trembling fingers over his sensuous lips. "I would die for you, do you know that? Living without you for just one night was nearly unbearable. I clung to your memory because it was my only salvation. I wanted to follow you into the depths of the sea, because dying with you would have been the easy path. Living without you would have been worse than burning in the fires of hell."

Lucien framed her face and brought her petal-soft lips to his. "I love you, Caela," he said with all his heart. "I never even knew what love truly was until I met you. Wanting you was never enough. I needed your love and respect, but I didn't know how to go about getting them after I'd made such a mess of our whirlwind wedding. If it had been anyone but that sassy squirt I'd met on my ship, I would have rejected the Saffire legacy and Adrian's scheme. I would have walked away without looking back. I used Adrian's manipulations to my advantage. It was an excuse to have you tied to me forever and always. I was too proud to admit that I wanted you every bit as much then as I do now and—"

"It's all right, Lucien," she interrupted, smiling tremulously. "You don't have to say the words to compensate for what has happened in the past. I don't want a divorce. I am prepared to accept you as you are. Truly, Lucien, you don't have to say what you don't really feel in hopes of sparing my feelings. I've spent my life not being loved. You'd have to say I've adjusted to it.''

Lucien shook his head in amazement. This little elf of a female was fully prepared to believe she couldn't take Cecilia's place in his heart. She believed he'd said what he thought she wanted to hear. Blast it, how was a man to convince this stubborn woman that she was everything he'd ever wanted, all he'd ever need?

Rolling sideways, Lucien tumbled across the canvas, pulling Micaela down beside him. He levered up on his good arm to stare into those thick-lashed eyes that bedazzled and hypnotized. "Micaela, listen to me and listen well, because I intend to be absolutely, positively honest with you. I said I loved you, and I damned well meant it. We have been through hell together and back again. I'm sorry to say we may be stranded out here so long that any rescue attempt will come too late. But there is one thing I want you to know, no matter what. My feelings for you aren't going to go away.''

The reality of his words hit Micaela like a blow to the midsection. Tears blurred her eyes, but she blinked them away, determined to memorize every chiseled feature of his face, every muscular contour of his sinewy body. When she flew off to the Pearly Gates his image would be committed to everlasting memory.

Smiling tenderly, Lucien rerouted the tears that slipped down her cheeks. "It seems to me that because your father shut you out and refused to give you his love that you've come to expect nothing from the men in your life. Perhaps your denial of my affection is your safety mechanism, but you don't need a safety net, Caela, because you are more than my responsibility. You have become my reason for living.''

"Lucien, it doesn't matter—''

"It *does* matter,'' he begged to differ. "I've tried to tell you how I feel in a hundred different ways. I have spelled out *I love you* with all the gentleness and affection I possess each time I've made love to you.''

He insinuated himself between her knees until his masculine body half-covered hers, letting her feel the hungry desire she aroused in him. "Look into my eyes, love," he commanded huskily. "Tell me what you see. Is it not the same hungry fire you have seen since that first night I made love to you, and each time hence? That flame is my very soul reaching out to you, asking you to believe. And if these next few days are all we have left together, then my greatest wish is that you truly believe that all I have ever wanted is you. This is what love feels like to me, Caela. Love me as if there were no yesterday or tomorrow."

His husky words unchained every emotion locked inside her. She flung her arms around his neck and held onto him, giving herself up to the holocaust of passion Lucien ignited. Knowing that Lucien loved her for all the right reasons made her heart swell with so much pleasure that she swore it would burst. And if they were to be castaways until the end of their days, she would feast on Lucien's passion and quench her thirst with his kisses for as long as she was allowed.

But it would have been nice if they could have made a new beginning on earth. She yearned to tell him he was to be a father. But as the hours blended from day to night, Micaela was faced with the fact that their new beginning was going to be in the Everafter. . . .

Twenty-One

Muttering in frustration, Vance Cavendish stared at the dismal clouds and wide expanse of sea through his spyglass. He had been sailing in circles on the damaged schooner, hoping beyond hope for a miracle. But it had been two days since the disastrous storm, and he had found no trace of survivors.

"Captain, we would like to speak with you."

Vance pivoted to see Jeremy Ives, Louis Beecham, Roddy Blankenship and Timothy Toggle staring grimly at him. He knew what they were going to say, even before Jeremy appointed himself spokesman and stepped forward.

"Save your breath, Jeremy," Vance said. "I know we lost several barrels of fresh water in the storm. I also know we are running short of rations to feed our oversized crew." He paused to look at each seasoned mariner with firm resolve. "I am asking you to bear with me until sunset. I want to continue following the debris in hopes. . . ." His voice trailed off as he stared into the gloomy distance. "If we find no signs of survivors by tonight, I will set our course toward home."

"Yes sir," Jeremy murmured. "I'll inform the crew of your plans."

When the sailors turned away, Vance braced his forearms

on the railing and muttered under his breath. God, he dreaded
making the return voyage to Charles Town. If he had to deliver
bad news to Adrian, Vance preferred not to return at all!

For two days and nights the makeshift raft had been adrift.
Micaela and Lucien spent their long hours discussing anything—and everything—that came to mind, sharing inner
thoughts they had revealed to no one else. Well, almost every
secret, Micaela silently amended. She simply couldn't bring
herself to tell Lucien about the unborn child, for fear of distressing him.

Micaela had listened to Lucien recite the chronicles of his
life, beginning from the day he could remember incidents and
impressions. She, in turn, explained what her life had been like
while living under the restrictive reins of a proud, bitter man
who would have preferred that she had never been born.

Micaela talked until she was hoarse, while lying in Lucien's
arms. And then he would share another part of his past with
her, until he was too thirsty to speak. Micaela found herself
wondering if their lives would end after they thumbed through
the annals of their past and reached this point in time. Hope
of survival dimmed with each passing hour.

Mon Dieu, she was so thirsty! And what she wouldn't give
to nibble on some tasty morsel. She had resorted to chewing
her fingernails to appease her hunger and licking her lips to
quench her thirst, but nothing helped. She had even prayed for
more rain, anxious to savor the droplets sent down from heaven.

Sighing, Micaela inched away from Lucien who had dozed
off a few minutes earlier. Raking the tangled hair from her
face, she stared northeast, craving the sight of land as strongly
as she craved food and drink. Micaela wasn't certain how many
more days of starvation she could endure before she fell asleep
and couldn't shake herself awake. She had tried to remain
optimistic, but feelings of doom loomed in the back of her
mind.

When Micaela twisted around on the raft, her eyes popped
in astonishment. She blinked once, twice, then pinched herself

to ensure she wasn't dreaming. When she exploded in a shout of excitement, Lucien shot straight up from the raft.

"Look yonder," Micaela said hoarsely. "Tell me I see what I *think* I see, Lucien."

Lucien crawled across the canvas to sink down on the mast beside Micaela. Lo and behold, there was a schooner sailing toward them. It only took a second to recognize the battered ship from the Saffire fleet. Vance—God bless him—hadn't given up hope of finding them.

For over an hour, Micaela and Lucien watched the vessel grow larger on the horizon, hoping the sailor in the crow's nest had spotted them. When the sailor took off his cap and waved it in an arc, Lucien felt relief and gratitude gushing through him.

Smiling, he curled his arm around Micaela's waist and watched her face light up like a lantern blazing on a long wick. "It's just as I thought, fickle woman. When given a choice between remaining with me until eternity and being rescued by a horde of sailors, you choose the latter." One black brow lifted. "Would you like to retract those whispers of love and claims of eternal devotion now that you'll be returned to civilization?"

"I meant every word I said," she insisted, dropping a kiss to his chapped lips. "There is nothing I wish to retract, but there is something I would like to add. I am anticipating being rescued because I prefer to raise our child on Saffire Plantation."

Lucien nearly fell off the raft. "Our child?" he chirped. "Blast it, Caela, you should have told me! I thought we made a pact that there would be no more secrets between us."

Micaela smoothed away his disapproving frown. "I didn't want you to worry."

"You have been on the verge of starvation for three days," Lucien howled.

"And what would you have done to alleviate the problem, had you known? Reached into the sea, plucked up a fish, and baked it over an open fire?"

"How? When?" Lucien choked out.

Mischief flared in her eyes. "Really, Lucien. I should not have to explain to a worldly man like you just *how* it happened. As for when, I think it must have been that first time following my accident—as you insist on referring to it."

"That does it then," Lucien said with a decisive nod. "The instant we return to Charles Town I will see to it that you have plenty of healthy nourishment and a sedate life-style—"

"If you plan to lock me in a sterilized room and confine me for the duration, I assure you that I will let you do nothing of the kind," Micaela protested. "I suggest you learn to control your overprotective instincts before they cause conflict between us."

"Now, Micaela . . ." His brows flattened over his narrowed blue eyes. "You have endured far too much already. I'm only being sensible."

"You are being unreasonable." She sank back on her derrière and studied him with a wry smile. "I thought you told me that you loved me just the way I am, independent streak and all."

"I did and I do, but—"

"Then don't expect me to lounge around like some delicate female who needs and wants to be coddled and pampered. I have never been treated in such a manner, and I wouldn't know what to do with myself. I intend to remain active and that is that."

"Fine, madam, have it your way," Lucien grumbled. "I promise not to treat you like a helpless invalid if you promise to limit yourself to sensible activities. There will be no horseback riding, no sea voyages, and no strenuous exercise—"

"None whatsoever?" she asked, her green eyes twinkling impishly.

"Well, except for that," Lucien amended, returning her infectious smile.

Lucien wondered if he would ever be able to refuse Micaela any whim. He would probably spoil her completely rotten, truth be known. But he was going to exert some power over her for her own good, and for the safety of their child. One thing was certain though, he was going to see that she was happy and protected and loved. He intended to make sure that she knew the meaning of those words, the depth of his affection for her.

When the lifeboat cut through the water toward them, Lucien stared at his longtime friend with renewed appreciation and respect. Through thick and thin, Vance had always been there for him. He considered himself exceptionally fortunate to have such a true and loyal friend and a wife who had turned out to be everything he could possibly want and need.

"Thank God," Vance murmured as he reached out to assist Micaela into the boat. "You are a sight for sore eyes, woman."

Lucien didn't even mind all that much when Micaela hugged the stuffing out of Vance—and he hugged her back. Life was good again, and Lucien wasn't going to let possessive jealousy get in his way. Hell, he wanted to hug Vance himself, and by damned he did—hugged him as one hugs a long-lost-friend-turned-guardian-angel, who had showed up just in the nick of time.

"Did I ever tell you how much I appreciate having you as my friend?" Lucien said as he clasped Vance to him.

"Even when I spout my opinions until you're muttering at me to cease and desist?" Vance questioned, grinning broadly.

"Even when," Lucien assured him as he sank down beside Micaela, pulling her close.

He stared at Vance over the top of her tangled head. The look that passed between them spoke volumes, but it didn't seem enough to express his gratitude. He owed Vance Cavendish his life. This man had saved Micaela and their unborn child. He had badgered Lucien unmercifully—and deservedly—for his reluctance to admit that Micaela had stolen his heart, long before Lucien realized it himself.

"Someday I'm going to find a way to thank you properly for what you've done," Lucien promised. "You've given me a second chance at life." His gaze fell to Micaela, and he brushed a kiss over her forehead. "Thank you, Vance."

Vance smiled knowingly as he took his seat in the boat. "From the look of things I'd say the time the two of you spent alone was worthwhile. It's nice to have you back, Lucien."

Lucien nodded, for he knew exactly what Vance implied.

For the past five years Lucien had found little purpose in life, allowing bitterness and resentment to color his thoughts and taint his existence. But now Lucien had a priceless treasure that he cherished. He had more than enough reason to laugh, smile, and enjoy life again. That reason was cuddled up beside him. And that was where she would always remain—very near and very dear to his heart.

Wrapped securely in Lucien's encircling arms, Micaela stared across the sun-dappled sea to survey the skyline of Charles Town. The voyage had passed without further mishap. Weeks ago, Micaela had set sail from Carolina in search of her missing past. Now she returned, anticipating a bright future. Lucien had become as attentive and affectionate as he had been when she suffered amnesia. He had proved—and quite effectively—that his love was as enduring as it was intense. He was devoted yet playful, and Micaela had already come to dread the day when Lucien equipped a new ship and set out on voyages to trade in the Indies and colonial ports. Lucien had spoiled her with his constant presence, and she swore she would be unbearably lonely when he returned to sea.

"Why the somber expression, love?" Lucien questioned as he nuzzled against her.

"I miss you already and you aren't even gone."

"Oh? And just where am I going?" he asked with a chuckle.

"Back to your mistress—the sea—as soon as you can make the arrangements to get there, I suspect," she grumbled. "And when our child asks who you are, what shall I tell him to call his father? The wind?"

Lucien smiled wryly. "Is this one of those black moods suffered by mothers-to-be?"

Micaela refused to be amused by his playful expression. But she did have to admit Lucien could be impossibly charming and amusing when he wanted to be—which was a lot of late.

"I don't want to be a demanding wife, but—"

"Good," Lucien cut in strategically. "I loathe bossy shrews who try to drag their husbands around on leashes, just because they are hopelessly devoted. So degrading, you know.'' He shuddered for effect.

Micaela opened her mouth to toss a teasing rejoinder but her thoughts stalled when she saw the familiar coach waiting on the dock. While Vance eased the schooner toward its mooring, four figures congregated around the carriage.

"*Mon Dieu!*" Micaela chirped, staring at the wharf in astonishment.

Lucien squinted into the bright sunlight to survey the two unfamiliar individuals who stood beside Adrian and Hiram Puckett.

Suddenly, Micaela wriggled from Lucien's arms and darted toward the bow to have a closer look. She smiled in pure delight when she was assured that her eyes hadn't deceived her. The moment the schooner eased into its berth, and the gangplank was set in place, Micaela lifted her hampering skirts and bounded away.

"Mikki!" Jean Rouchard greeted her with open arms. He clutched her to him, swinging her in dizzying circles as he hugged her close.

"You see? I told you the lass was in good hands," Adrian harumped.

Since Jean Rouchard didn't release his hold on Micaela, Adrian leaned over to press a kiss to her cheek to welcome her home. "This big lummox came stomping onto my stoop and very nearly beat down the door, demanding to know where you were and what my intentions were toward you. He has the most infuriating habit of acting and speaking before a body can wedge in a word of explanation."

Lucien assessed the tall, muscularly-built frontiersman who wrapped Micaela in a bear hug. Then he focused on the petite woman who was dressed in blue satin and lace. Unless Lucien missed his guess, he was about to meet his in-laws—or some facsimile thereof. The delicate woman, who looked to be in her mid forties, strongly resembled Micaela with her curly blond hair and refined features. The man, who very nearly matched Lucien's size and stature, had one very distinct trait that confirmed his identity. Lively green eyes hinted at lively spirit. There was no question that Micaela had inherited her eyes from Jean Rouchard.

During those endless hours on the raft, Micaela had related her life story to Lucien and described family members. She had spoken affectionately of her uncle—or rather her natural father. This man fit the description. Question was: What was he doing here? And why was Micaela's mother with him?

Two seconds after Lucien posed the question to himself, he stumbled upon a half-forgotten memory. He recalled that Henri Rouchard had said his mother had packed up and left for St. Louis. Marguerite Rouchard had apparently cast off her yoke of guilt-ridden servitude and sought the man who had stolen her heart more than a score of years ago.

Micaela leaned back in Jean's brawny arms, then glanced tearfully at her mother. Marguerite's expression begged silently for forgiveness. There was a time when Micaela hadn't understood why her mother had succumbed to Arnaud's tyrannical domination. Now, loving Lucien the way she did, Micaela knew that she, like Marguerite, would risk and endure most anything to be with the man she loved, if only for a few stolen moments. For Marguerite, the sacrifice had been long-lived. Arnaud had made her suffer for her betrayal.

"I'm so sorry," Marguerite said brokenly as she reached out to squeeze Micaela's hand. "When you disappeared I could no longer live the lie, had no reason to stay to protect you as best I could. We had both suffered enough. And *you* most undeservedly."

Although Adrian and Hiram didn't have a clue what Marguerite meant, Lucien understood perfectly. He thought perhaps Micaela had exaggerated about her unpleasant childhood, but Marguerite confirmed her daughter's testimony. Arnaud Rouchard had made life a penance in hell for his wife and his brother's child. Arnaud had raised Micaela, and refused to let Marguerite leave him, only in order to avoid scandal, to protect his reputation.

"It doesn't matter now," Micaela assured her mother. "I would suffer it all again if it brought me to this point in my life." She wiped the squiggles of tears from her cheeks and pivoted to outstretch her hand to Lucien. "I want you to meet my husband, Lucien Saffire. Lucien, this is my mother and father, Marguerite and Jean Rouchard."

Lucien was torn between resentment toward the man who was partially responsible for Micaela's miserable childhood, and gratitude to the striking frontiersman who had sired such an irresistibly lovely daughter. When Lucien glanced at Marguerite, nodding politely, he imagined how Micaela's mother must have looked years earlier. She was still a fine figure of a woman, and she must have been almost as alluring as Micaela in younger years. Lucien would have loved to know the circumstances surrounding Marguerite's marriage to Arnaud Rouchard. Why had Marguerite married the older brother when it was obvious that it was the younger brother she truly loved?

"There is a chill in the air," Adrian declared, turning back to the carriage. "These old bones of mine are in need of warmth. I suggest we continue this reunion at the house." He cast Micaela a quick glance. "And en route, you can explain this dreadful business about winding up in jail."

"Jail?" Marguerite and Jean echoed in unison.

"It was an unfortunate misunderstanding," Micaela quickly dismissed.

"Well, I should hope so." Adrian snorted disgustedly as he hauled himself onto the carriage seat. When Jean assisted Micaela and Marguerite into the coach, but remained outside, Adrian frowned. "Aren't you coming home with us?"

"I thought perhaps I would take the opportunity to acquaint myself with my son-in-law while he is seeing to the duties of the ship," Jean declared.

"We will be only a few minutes behind you," Lucien promised his grandfather.

Adrian glanced from one muscular man to the other while they continued to size each other up. Since both men seemed determined to speak in private, Adrian nodded agreeably. His new policy of refraining from poking his nose in places it didn't belong was still in effect.

When the coach rolled away, Jean stared Lucien squarely in the eye—the direct approach that Lucien had come to expect from Micaela. Straightforwardness was an inherited trait, Lucien decided.

"I wonder if you know exactly who I am, Lucien."

"I know who you are. I do, however, wonder *how* you came to be *who* you are," Lucien replied, unable to keep the undertone of sarcasm from seeping into his voice.

Jean's head snapped up, his chin tilting in a characteristic manner that was strongly reminiscent of Micaela. This man had marked his daughter well, thought Lucien.

"You can take one look at Marguerite and still ask me such a question?" Jean asked with an offended snort. "Are you blind, boy?"

"I am neither blind, nor a boy," Lucien said tightly. "But I am damned curious to know what kind of man would seduce his brother's wife and let her suffer years of misery. From what Micaela told me about her life in New Orleans, I cannot imagine why she would even speak to you after what you did to her and Marguerite."

"What *I* did?" Jean howled. "It is what my brother did. He was four years my senior. According to staunch French tradition, the eldest son inherits all the family holdings. But that was hardly enough for Arnaud. He knew how I felt about Marguerite long before he married her. He contracted the marriage with Marguerite's father, against her wishes, and definitely against *my* wishes!"

Jean inhaled such a deep breath that he nearly popped the leather lacings on his buckskin shirt. "For your information, boy, my brother has always been greedy and desirous of what everyone else had. He couldn't wait to get his hands on the land holdings Marguerite inherited, as well as the sprawling estate belonging to the Rouchards. Arnaud got everything he wanted, and he kept a watchful eye on Marguerite, as if she were his prisoner, not his wife.

"She tried to leave him several times that first year of marriage, but he always caught up with her and dragged her back, lecturing her extensively on her duties as his wife. It incensed him that she risked scandal and gossip that might besmirch the almighty Rouchard name. And don't think that Arnaud's first-born son was a mutual collaboration," he added bitterly. "If I had known the truth about how Arnaud treated her all those years, I would have called him out, brother or no."

He took a step closer, standing toe-to-toe with Lucien. "It was four tormenting years before I was allowed to see Marguerite. When I did, we both let ourselves settle for one moment that had to last us forever. Marguerite was the only woman I ever wanted, and I refused to accept a substitute. I have been devoted to her in spirit, and body. It was not until Marguerite came to me in St. Louis that I learned the whole truth. She was afraid to tell me that Mikki was my child, because Arnaud threatened her, threatened to dispose of Mikki."

"And now, Squire Saffire," he said with a gruff snort. "I have explained my trials and torments and assured you of my lasting devotion to Marguerite. I demand to know if you plan to be the domineering, spiteful bastard of a husband that my brother was. My daughter has suffered enough, and I will not have her married to a man who treats her the way Arnaud did!"

Lucien was eternally thankful this blustering man didn't know about the forced wedding ceremony, and other unpleasant incidents that had tainted the first few weeks of their marriage. Jean seemed hell-bent on protecting the daughter who had been denied him all these years.

"I have been hearing nasty rumors since I arrived in Charles Town," Jean went on to say. "They involve your sordid reputation with women and Mikki's involvement with a man named Vance Cavendish. I will not have Mikki strapped in wedlock for the sake of appearance. I want to know exactly what the hell is going on and I want to know *now!*"

Jean's voice rose to a roar, and Lucien saw so much of the lively, spirited daughter in this overprotective father that he broke into an amused smile. He supposed he could understand why Marguerite kept her misery to herself, for fear the two Rouchard brothers would wind up in a deadly duel. She loved Jean too much to put him at risk, and so she had suffered in silence, doing her best to protect Micaela from Arnaud's wrath.

Lucien also realized that, since Jean had not been able to claim his child for eighteen years, he had embraced fatherhood with great enthusiasm. It was glaringly apparent that Jean refused to let history repeat itself. He wanted to ensure that Micaela was happily married—or not married at all.

"I married the woman I love," Lucien declared. "And Caela loves me, despite any rumors to the contrary. If you don't believe me then you can ask her."

"Oh, I most certainly intend to do exactly that, while you aren't around to intimidate Mikki into saying what you have coached her to say, the way Arnaud did."

"How did you find us?" Lucien queried, tactfully tiptoeing away from sensitive subjects that set Jean off.

"Mikki wrote to me after she escaped from her unwanted engagement in New Orleans. She told me Arnaud had blurted out the truth of her heritage in a fit of temper and that she had fled to Charles Town where she was taken in by an old man who wanted her to be his companion. Needless to say, I had my doubts about the old man's intentions. I packed up to leave for Carolina as soon as I had made arrangements for my partner to assume control of our fur trading business.

"Marguerite arrived the day before I planned to depart, tearfully informing me that Micaela was presumed dead. I showed her the letter from Mikki to relieve her fears, and she broke down and told me the whole truth about her life with Arnaud."

Lucien could well imagine the outrage and regret Jean suffered when the truth finally came out.

"We decided to make a new life for ourselves and be near our daughter. Since I've been deprived of Mikki's company all these years, we plan to live here. I will manage the fur business by making arrangements to transport from Charles Town while my partner collects the hides and ships them East."

Lucien extended his hand, offering a peace-treaty handshake. "I think we are going to get along just fine, Jean, as long as you don't try to monopolize my wife's attention. You will, of course, be allowed to visit your grandchild anytime you wish."

"My grand—" Jean croaked. "Yours, I hope. God, don't let it happen again." He directed the last remark toward heaven, and the powers that be.

"It is my child," Lucien proudly confirmed. "Though I'm

not sure that I aspire to be as overprotective as you have suddenly become, but I suppose time will tell about that. And before you find yourself thinking Micaela is the perfect child, I think it fair to warn you that your lovely daughter is extremely independent, strong-willed and high strung." He rubbed his chin, as if pondering a serious thought. "Where did she inherit those traits, do you suppose?"

"Mmm . . . yes, I wonder." Jean grinned and his green eyes danced with that all too familiar sparkle. "Mikki always was a rambunctious handful."

"She hasn't changed," Lucien assured him. "There have been countless instances when I've tried to persuade her to proceed at a more cautious and slower pace than she prefers to set, but I've yet to find a way to discourage her from doing what she's determined to do. But you may rest assured that my exasperation with her spirited nature is overruled by my affection for her. I'm afraid I'm going to be guilty of spoiling her rotten."

Jean chuckled delightedly. "If Mikki affirms this devotion you claim to feel, then I approve of this match. I want Mikki to be as happy in her marriage as I will be, if Arnaud allows it to take place. And if he doesn't. . . ." He shrugged a thick shoulder and let his words trail into silence.

"I intend to keep Caela safe and happy," Lucien said with genuine sincerity.

"Of course you will, because I will be looking over your shoulder to ensure that you do." He gave Lucien a fatherly pat on the back. "And now, my boy, perhaps you can direct me to a reputable merchantman who can ship my furs abroad."

Lucien returned the wry grin. "I know a very conscientious shipping firm that can meet your demands. That is, of course, unless you prove to be a difficult client."

"As long as I see a smile on my daughter's face I will be a most agreeable client."

As they ambled away, Lucien remembered the utterly seductive smile that had shaped Micaela's bewitching features during their previous night of lovemaking. Lucien wondered if that was the kind of smile Jean referred to. The man was French, after all.

Vance gathered his belongings from the cramped quarters he had used while Lucien and Micaela camped out in his cabin during the return voyage. He wasn't certain how he would spend his evening, though Lucien had asked him to join the Saffires for dinner. Vance had a yearning for feminine companionship. Not just any female, he amended. He wanted to spend his time with a woman of substance and intelligence, someone like—

Clamping down on the exasperating thought, Vance stuffed his clothes in a satchel and headed toward the steps. He veered around the corner—and rammed head-on into an unidentified body. Vance tripped over a pair of legs that were tangled in yards of black fabric. He braced himself before the floor flew up and hit him.

Vance blinked in disbelief when he realized he had fallen atop a soft, fragrant body. He peered down into a ghastly pale face that was coated with layers of what looked to be stage makeup. Wide brown eyes that radiated youthful sparkle peered at him from behind thick spectacles. Strawberry blond hair fanned out from the hood of the cloak that enshrouded the woman who was years younger than her matronly disguise.

"I'm sorry, sir," Rebecca Montclaire wheezed. "I didn't mean to trip you up." Her hands settled on Vance's chest to re-situate him to a less intimate position on top of her. "If you could remove yourself, I would appreciate it."

Vance levered to his feet, then drew the rumpled hag—if that was what she was pretending to be—up beside him. He smiled in amusement as he took a long assessing look at the charading female.

"Vance Cavendish at your service." His blond brows lifted to a teasing angle. "Is there a masquerade party hereabout?"

Rebecca winced and quickly turned away. Voices echoed on the upper deck. Hurriedly, she fished into the pocket of her cloak to retrieve a leather pouch. Clutching Vance's hand, she laid the pouch in his palm and closed his fist around it. "I'm in dire need of assistance, Mr. Cavendish," she whispered, flinging apprehensive glances over her shoulder. "If you would keep this for me until I return to fetch it, you will be well paid for your trouble."

"Dire need, my lady?" Vance inquired, frowning suspiciously.

"One could say that," she murmured. "Oh yes, one could definitely say that."

Vance stared at the pouch in his hand, then focused on the oval face that was covered with thick makeup. "Are the coins in the pouch stolen?"

Eyes like black diamonds danced with the same kind of mischievousness Vance had seen in Micaela's eyes. "And who, Mr. Cavendish, said there were coins in this pouch?"

With that, Rebecca pulled the hood of her cloak around her face and wheeled away in a flurry of black. She evaporated into the shadows of the companionway as quickly as she appeared.

Thunderstruck by the female whirlwind who had blown in and out of his path, Vance inhaled the compelling feminine scent that lingered in the companionway. Curious, Vance loosened the drawstrings to pour the contents of the bag into his hand. He gasped in astonishment when a most impressive collection of rare gems glistened up at him. Bug-eyed, slack-jawed, he ran his fingers over the jewels, then stared at the empty space the mysterious young woman had occupied moments before.

Sweet merciful heavens. These gigantic stones could have been plucked from a royal crown! Now what man in his right mind would assist a masquerading female who hadn't even bothered to give her name before thrusting the gems at him and dashing away?

Frowning pensively, Vance scooped up his satchel and ambled back to his room to stash the pouch out of sight. He had the inescapable feeling he was about to embark on a much-needed distraction. If anything came of his unusual meeting with that strawberry blonde, who had the darkest, most mysterious eyes he'd ever seen, he vowed never to tangle himself in the same predicaments Lucien had encountered. Lucien had proved to be a shining example of the wrong way to handle a woman—until he came to terms with his love for Micaela, Vance amended.

Wondering where this strange meeting with the young woman disguised as an aging dowager would lead him, Vance ambled up the steps to the main deck.

Twenty-Two

The quiet rap at the bedroom door brought Micaela's head around. Laying her hairbrush aside, she padded barefoot across the room to find her mother standing in the hall.

"Since Jean and Lucien have yet to return, I would like to speak privately."

Micaela stepped aside to allow her mother inside.

"I know you have every cause to detest me, Micaela," Marguerite began, her gaze plunging to the floor. Her hands were clenched in the folds of her gown, indicating the apprehension churning inside her. "But I have to explain—"

"I don't detest you," Micaela interrupted, smiling compassionately. "I admire you."

Marguerite blinked. "Admire me for enduring Arnaud's tyrannical reign or for leaving him when I thought you had perished?"

"Both."

"I don't feel the least bit courageous. I feel like a coward." Marguerite sank down in the chair Micaela had vacated. "It was Jean I wanted to marry, since the moment I laid eyes on him. But my father, like Arnaud, believed marriage should be arranged to benefit both families. I felt trapped and betrayed.

When Jean went west to seek his fortune, something within me died.''

Micaela knew the feeling well. When she believed Lucien had died at sea, she had lost the desire to live.

"After Arnaud forced me to ...'' Marguerite paused to rephrase what she was reluctant to explain. ''After Henri was born, I stayed and endured for the sake of my child. When Jean returned from his extensive travels, it was as if he had brought the sun back with him. He arrived on the day Arnaud had gone to town to gather supplies and stay the night with his—'' She faltered and then continued, ''with his mistress. It was as if I had been granted once chance at happiness. I knew what it was like to live without love, and I ached to grasp even one moment of pleasure. I came back to life again ... until—''

"Until Arnaud returned home,'' Micaela predicted.

Marguerite nodded, head downcast. ''Arnaud saw us strolling from the woods, hand in hand. When Jean left, Arnaud forced me to tell him what we had done.''

Micaela grimaced, knowing what method Arnaud had used to pry out close-held information. In his opinion, a good beating worked wonders.

"From that day forward, Arnaud refused to let me out of sight without a dependable chaperone. When he discovered that I carried Jean's child he flew into a rage, threatening all sorts of horrible deeds if I breathed the truth to Jean, to you or anyone else. He held my unfaithfulness over me for years, waiting until he could contract your wedding for his financial and personal benefit.

"When Arnaud claimed that you had died, I couldn't bear to remain in that house, with him,'' she said, her voice cracking.

"And so you went in search of long lost happiness and found it.'' Micaela knelt to clasp her mother's hands in her own. ''All I want is for you to be content for once in your life, just as I am. I have let go of the past, and so must you. You owe it to yourself, and to Jean, to look ahead to the future.''

Marguerite nodded as tears rolled down her cheeks. ''Then

you love Lucien? Truly? You have not been trapped into a loveless marriage and forced to pretend all is well?''

"Lucien is everything I will ever want," Micaela reassured her mother.

Marguerite smiled affectionately as she brushed her hand over Micaela's head. "You cannot know how I have prayed for it to be so. You endured so much for one so young, Micaela. Arnaud refused to let me intervene, and if I dared to speak in your behalf, he punished me. He tormented me by making me keep my distance from you. But it was always my secret wish that one day you would spread your wings and fly—for both of us.''

When Marguerite opened her arms, Micaela went into them, muffling a sentimental sniff.

"Be happy, Micaela. It has been so long in coming," Marguerite whispered.

"Long in coming for both of us," Micaela murmured.

The voices in the hall pulled mother and daughter apart to blot their tears. Micaela rose, turning toward the sound of a rich baritone voice mingling with Jean's animated, staccato tone. When Jean stepped into the room, Micaela noted the flicker of pride, love and satisfaction sparkling in his eyes as his gaze went automatically to Marguerite. It brought another mist of tears to Micaela's eyes to think how long her parents had been denied their affection for each other.

"Sorry we're late," Jean apologized as he moved toward Marguerite without conscious effort, then curled a possessive arm around her. "Adrian has announced that dinner will be served promptly at eight. I thought perhaps we might freshen up, and allow Mikki and Lucien to do the same after their voyage.''

When Jean and Marguerite exited, Lucien closed the door. For a moment he studied the pensive expression on Micaela's face. He knew without asking that she was speculating on what her life might have been like if Jean had been allowed to marry the woman he loved those long years ago.

"We can do nothing about what might have been," Lucien murmured perceptively. "But we can control what is to come.

Our children will bask in the warmth of our love for each other, and I promise that you will have no cause to be unhappy again—''

Micaela dashed into his arms like a homing pigeon returning to roost, spilling tears on his shirt. "I feel sorry for them," she sobbed. "So many wasted years, so much bitterness and resentment that delayed their happiness."

Lucien cradled her in his arms, resting his chin on the top of her curly blond head. He, too, understood years of wasted resentment and anguish. And knowing that, he vowed to enjoy every day to its fullest. Micaela had turned his life around and made him believe in all that was right and good in the world.

"I'm sorry." Micaela murmured, pushing back as far as Lucien's encircling arms allowed. "I don't know what is the matter with me these days. I swear I have spigots implanted in my eyes."

"Another symptom that plagues mothers-to-be, or so I have heard told," Lucien diagnosed, smiling good-naturedly at the teardrops that soaked his shirt.

"And devoted husband that you've become, you intend to tolerate all my drastic mood swings and odd cravings?" she questioned, smiling at him through her tears.

"Tolerate them?" Lucien looked offended. "Indeed, madam, I plan to enjoy all your moods."

One delicate brow arched as Micaela regarded him with amusement. "My, aren't you the epitome of compassion and understanding all of a sudden. What has put you in such a grand mood?"

"Other than loving you madly, you mean?" he asked.

"Yes, other than that." Micaela chortled, amazed at how quickly Lucien could turn her sentimental tears to bubbling laughter.

"The reason for my cheerful disposition is that Vance will be unable to join us for supper tonight."

Micaela looked at Lucien as if he had rhubarb sprouting from his ears. "Vance's absence is cause for cheer?"

Lucien nodded his raven head and grinned widely. "The reason Vance cannot join us for supper is because he is in jail."

"Jail!" Micaela bleated. She lurched from Lucien's arms on her way to rescue Vance. "We have to—"

Lucien clasped her forearm and towed her back into his arms. "We have to do nothing," he insisted. "I have already been to the magistrate's office to speak to the jailbird. That is why Jean and I were late. A squad of English redcoats took Vance into custody. I went to speak in Vance's defense."

"Into custody for what, in God's name?" she demanded to know.

"For aiding and abetting a thief," Lucien explained, grinning for no reason that Micaela could comprehend—she saw absolutely nothing amusing about Vance's predicament. "I, of course, offered testimony to Vance's sterling character and noble breeding. But some fancy English duke arrived from his fancy English dukedom, spouting about thieves and accomplices. The magistrate has no choice but to keep Vance locked up until the blustering nobleman takes his leave."

"That is preposterous," Micaela spluttered. "Vance is not a thief, and anyone who believes he is capable of a crime is a fool!"

Lucien chuckled. "That would be the duke."

Micaela was thoroughly put out with Lucien for enjoying the telling of this outrageous tale. "Lucien Saffire, what has gotten into you? Vance is your best friend and you are making light of this serious situation. Have you forgotten that we owe him our lives? He refused to give up on us and we are obliged to rescue him."

She paused to study her ornery husband for a long, thoughtful moment. "You aren't, by chance, getting even with Vance for those ridiculous rumors circulating about him and me, are you?"

"I'm not trying to get even with Vance because of any rumors, but your father was ready to box his ears when he recognized the name that had been linked to yours in that nasty gossip. As for myself, I'm getting even with Vance for all the stormy tirades and lectures he has delivered to me since the wedding ceremony," Lucien said, stifling another gurgle of laughter. "I am enjoying the fact that my best friend has stumbled into what seems to be a very intriguing misadventure with a very mysterious female who sneaked below deck on the schooner.''

Micaela's brows knitted in puzzlement.

"According to Vance, a young lady, disguised as an elderly dowager, arrived shortly after you left for the townhouse. Vance literally tripped over her. She stuffed a pouch in his hand, requesting that he keep it until she returned."

"Who is this woman?" Micaela quizzed him.

"She didn't divulge her name, but she left Vance with a pouch of jewels to rival a king's ransom. When Vance came on deck, he was swarmed by redcoats and carted off to jail to be interrogated by this blustering duke of something-or-other."

Micaela's eyes widened in alarm. "And Vance had the jewels on his person?"

"No, he stashed them in his cabin, and he made no mention of the mysterious young woman to the magistrate or the ranting duke."

"Why not?"

Lucien snickered and leaned down to press a kiss to the tip of Micaela's upturned nose. "You are a very bright, perceptive woman. Why do you think Vance kept silent about this fascinating pixie and her purse of priceless gems?"

It finally dawned on Micaela why Lucien was so highly amused by Vance's predicament. Vance was intrigued, just as Lucien admitted he had been when he encountered an elusive waif on his ship. Now it was Vance who had been lured into a madcap adventure. He was *allowing* himself to be swept into it, Micaela speculated.

"Well, I hope Vance knows what the devil he's doing," Micaela worried aloud.

"Oh, he doesn't have a clue," Lucien said with perfect certainty. "That is why he's locked in jail and—" He gathered Micaela close, molding her voluptuous body to his masculine contours. "And that is the same reason why I tore this town apart trying to find that cunning green-eyed squirt who had bewitched me. Vance has found himself intrigued. If he wasn't, he would have handed over the jewels and walked away."

The feel of Lucien's sculpted body brushing suggestively against hers altered her breathing and put a throaty purr in her voice. "Are you sure Vance will be all right?" she questioned as her arms involuntarily glided up his broad chest.

"He'll be all right—eventually," Lucien said, his voice raspy from the side effects of holding the one woman who could make him burn like a human torch. "For all his fussing and cussing, I do believe Vance is tolerating the stint in jail in order to ensure future contact with the mysterious young lady. He is obviously as bedazzled as I was by the naive imp who insisted my Great Cabin was a torture chamber and that I was the resident monster."

Micaela broke into a sheepish smile. "You cannot know how foolish I felt to discover how wrong I'd been."

"And you cannot know how I longed to change your opinion of me that night when I walked into this very room to see the elusive beauty I had spent a week searching for all over creation."

"Did you really turn the town upside down looking for me?" Her luminous green eyes probed intently into his.

"Yes." Lucien nipped at the sensitive point beneath her ear. "I left no stone unturned ... except the one place I never thought to look. And here you were, in my bedroom, wearing next to nothing, tempting me without even trying."

Suddenly, Micaela forgot about Vance's plight and the eight o'clock call to supper. All that interested her were the masterful caresses coursing over her body, the love she felt for this ruggedly handsome rogue with eyes as clear and blue as a summer sky and hair as shiny as a raven's wing.

Once upon a midnight moon, Micaela had stared up at this dynamic, wildly sensual man who stood at the helm, and she had felt the magnetic pull of forbidden desire. Lucien had captivated her then, as he did now. He had come to mean the world to her. . . .

The abrupt pounding on the door rattled the hinges. "Lucien, are you coming to dinner or not?" Adrian called from the hall.

"Not," Lucien replied as his roaming caresses flowed intimately over Micaela's luscious curves and swells.

"Why not?" Adrian demanded. "Is it because I'm serving scalloped oysters and steamed clams, even when I know you hate them? Jean says they are his favorites."

Lucien dropped a kiss to Micaela's lips and nearly drowned in the sultry invitation awaiting him. "We'll be there," he relented, "as soon as I reassure my wife that I'm madly in love with her. So madly in love, in fact, that I plan to turn my duties as captain over to Louis Beecham so I can spend the next century at home with her."

Lucien was sure the admission would cause Adrian to laugh himself into a seizure. The old man's mirth began as a snicker, followed by a giggle that gave way to a burst of triumphant laughter that clamored down the hall. Lucien waited for the inevitable reply, but not with one smidgen of hard feeling.

"I told you so . . ."

When the laughter and footsteps drifted away, Micaela smiled curiously at her husband. "I didn't know you hated scalloped oysters. You never told me."

"I never told you how much I loved you until it was almost too late, either," he whispered as he curled his arm beneath her knees and carried her to bed. "But I'm not making that mistake ever again." He bent his knee upon the bed and tumbled with Micaela onto the velvet spread. His hand glided beneath the layer of petticoats to caress the smooth curve of her hip. "All I want in life is you, Caela—through the laughter and the tears, in spite of and because of every radical mood swing and outburst of temper. I love everything about you. You fill my days to overflowing."

When Lucien's sensuous lips settled possessively over hers, Micaela surrendered wholeheartedly to the wild sweeping pleasure spilling through her. She was thrilled beyond measure to know that Lucien was home to stay, that he would always be just a touch away. And here, within the circle of his arms, was her paradise.

"Ah, Caela, I wish there were enough words to describe how I feel about you," he murmured, his voice rumbling with ardent passion tempered by all-consuming love.

Before rational thought whirled away in the storm of passion

Micaela brewed with her steamy kisses, Lucien sent up a prayer that his best friend would someday discover what it was like to be so deeply in love that his very heartbeat whispered the name of that special woman who owned him—body, heart and soul. To be so captivated was to know unlimited freedom. To love and be loved was to possess riches beyond his wildest expectations.

"I love you, Lucien," Micaela whispered as she undressed him one button at a time, giving dedicated attention to each inch of muscular flesh she exposed.

"I know," he said, his voice humming with amusement and pleasure.

"I marvel at your modesty," she purred, her kisses drifting from one taut male nipple to the other—and then lower. . . .

"I commend your taste in men—" His voice became a gasp and a groan when her bold kisses and caresses stripped the breath from his lungs.

"You, my dear husband, *taste* absolutely delicious," she teased. "Far better than those scalloped oysters Adrian is serving for supper."

Lucien blinked. "You don't like those damned things either?"

"Never did, never will. If I never have to eat scalloped oysters again, I'll be as happy as a clam." Her expression became very serious as she leaned down to feather her lips over his. "I'll be happiest of all if you'll love me forever and ever."

"I do, I will," he murmured softly, sincerely.

"I know." That same elfin smile—the one that had caught and captured Lucien's attention when he encountered the feisty stowaway—blossomed on Micaela's face.

Overwhelming emotion and unquenchable desire consumed Lucien. Tenderly, he expressed his deep, abiding love for Micaela with murmured words and gentle passion. And as long as he lived, Lucien would remember that night on his ship when he had stared down, by the light of the midnight moon, to see that rag-tag little squirt peeking up at him. If Lucien hadn't caught sight of Micaela that night, she might have escaped him, and he would never have known the height of pleasure and the depth of love.

Heaven, Lucien thought, the instant before the inexpressible pleasures of passion deprived him of the ability to think rationally. That's what Micaela was to him—pure, sweet heaven. . . .

Adrian drummed his fingers on the table, then checked his timepiece. It was a quarter past eight. Neither Lucien and Micaela nor Jean and Marguerite had made an appearance for dinner. Those Rouchards were a passionate bunch, Adrian concluded as he sipped his sangaree. He smiled in supreme satisfaction, knowing his quest to find Lucien the perfect wife had turned out precisely as he had hoped. After five lonely years, Adrian had his grandson home to stay and a great grandchild on the way. That, served with scalloped oysters, was the perfect way to top off a perfect day!